UNBOUND

Book three of the Alex Crocker Series

LAUREN GRIMLEY

Visit Lauren Grimley's website: www.laurengrimley.com

Note: This is a work of fiction. All characters, places, businesses, and incidents are from the author's imagination. Any resemblance to actual places, people, or events is purely coincidental. Any trademarks mentioned herein are not authorized by the trademark owners and do not in any way mean the work is sponsored by or associated with the trademark owners. Any trademarks used are specifically in a descriptive capacity.

First Edition, Grimm Sisters Publishing

ISBN: 0692330836
ISBN-13: 9780692330838

DEDICATION

To all the other sassy women whose paths I've been lucky enough to cross and to all the men strong enough to love us.

BOOKS IN THE ALEX CROCKER SERIES BY LAUREN GRIMLEY

Unforeseen

Unveiled

Unbound

Unbridled: A collection of short stories from the Alex Crocker Series

ACKNOWLEDGMENTS

Many thanks to my beta-readers, Stephanie, Heather, and Mom, who gave thoughtful feedback with enthusiasm.

To the ladies of the Over-educated Book Club, thanks for sharing my love of literature, laughter, and wine.

And to all my friends, family, colleagues, and students, who put up with my absent-mindedness when I'm writing, thank you for your constant forgiveness.

CHAPTER 1

It was Christmas. Torie's peers were home opening presents and eating ham dinners, grumbling about having to wear ugly sweaters given to them by some crazy relative. They were in cozy, over-decorated apartments that might not have been luxurious, but at least were safe. Her family didn't celebrate, of course, but she knew all the traditions from attending public school and watching too much TV. Someone else in the coven knew them too, apparently. One of the Vengatti vampires had hung a lone wreath of plastic holly on the door to the rented hall as a lame decoy. Any passing humans would think the crowd gathering in the dingy basement was merely a group of late night holiday revelers. Only those entering would see the sanguine ribbon dripping over the spiked green leaves as an ominous symbol of what was to come.

Her father whispered further instructions as she slid out of the backseat into the frigid air. Torie tuned him out. Not because she was almost a teenager and therefore ignored most of what her parents said, but because she'd heard it all before. Listening again would only increase the dread she felt as she crossed the gravel parking lot to the back entrance.

She watched the other families approach the door with the same trepidation. Nearly all had young with them. They had no choice. No one in any of the families had been excused. Most of the kids were younger than she was, young enough she hoped not to fully understand what they were about to witness. Then again, she remembered being forced to a similar meeting as a little kid. More precisely she remembered the nightmares that had lingered for months. She hadn't understood the reason for the violence she had seen, but she had understood her parents' fear. That, of course, was the Regan's intention.

There were a few kids older than her who hadn't yet matured. But they had already begun training with the coven's warriors. So although they too knew what they were about to see, they had the 'benefit' of having been somewhat desensitized to such brutality. They'd learned to turn off their emotions, at least in the presence of the coven's vicious leaders.

Torie would once again stand alone, the only young in that awkward phase between being old enough to know what was happening, yet too young, too small, and too scared to stop it.

"Stay close to your mother, but not behind her," her father hissed stopping outside before the three of them entered. "If Leonce thinks you're hiding, it'll only increase his suspicion. Charlie's doing this to keep us safe."

"All of us," her mother added. Torie knew it wasn't true. None of the other males who escaped the battle against the Rectinatti had anything to hide except for a lack of loyalty, and it didn't take an act of sympathy from some Seer for the Vengatti Regan to figure that out. Leonce would have worked his way through the lot of them, reading each of their memories before killing or beating them. Charlie stepped forward first to take the blame for the entire group, claiming it was his responsibility as the oldest among them. He believed having a gift the Regan utilized frequently might spare him his life. But even Torie knew there were things worse than dying. Watching someone sacrifice himself to postpone what was inevitable, seeing him suffer excruciating pain to save her for a few more lousy years had to be pretty high on that list.

She nodded, unable to speak. Her father brushed her bangs down over her eyebrows, then squeezed her shoulder.

"I know this is going to be hard, Victoria," he said with a tightness in his voice she had rarely heard before, "but try not to react differently than anyone else."

She nodded again and shoved her hands into her pockets to hide her clenched fists. He had already explained all this at home. Too stoic and Leonce would pounce; he was sure to know Charlie was her godfather. Too emotional and he could call her forward as an example of the pain the males' cowardice had caused. Too guilty and he'd know Charlie and she were hiding something.

She was the vampire version of Goldilocks; everything had to be just right. She had to blend in—or disappear.

CHAPTER 2

Waking up to the sound of distant laughter, Alex was disoriented. She had spent the last four days at her mother's new cottage mourning the loss of her father. There had been lighter moments, laughter even, but it echoed hollow, forced. The laughter that drew Alex down the stairs of the farmhouse, where she had returned earlier that evening, sounded light and easy. She hoped it might also be contagious.

As soon as she entered the basement family room, though, she knew she had been mistaken. Fully awake she could sense with greater intensity the others' emotions. The sharp contrast to her own only exacerbated her sullen mood.

Rocky, Sage, and Ellie all looked back at the door from their spots in front of the mammoth flat screen.

"Hey, there. You back on vampire time, yet?" Rocky asked with a wide grin. In order to be company to her mother, Alex had reverted to sleeping nights. Four days wasn't enough to adjust, only long enough to mess up her system completely. It made for a nice excuse to nap when she first arrived home and was overwhelmed by sensing their many different emotions.

"Ah, sort of. I thought maybe Markus would be down here," she mumbled setting up an easy exit. Sage was, of course, eavesdropping on her thoughts and caught the lie instantly, but the Knower remained silent.

"He's upstairs in the office with Darian. Can't you feel him?"

Rocky asked.

Alex smiled, not at his concern for her and her gift, but at the fact it was so clearly the only concern he had had over the last few days. His arm was draped over Ellie, who was free from her Vengatti captors and even her father—for the meantime—a freedom Rocky now shared thanks to Alex. If his joy wasn't contagious, at least it was soothing.

"Yeah, I can. I guess I was still half-asleep when I started downstairs."

"You're here now. Pull up a seat." Coming from Sage, Alex knew this was as much a dare as an invitation. Whether he was testing her control after having her power dramatically increased just days ago, or testing her mettle by luring her into arm's reach of Ellie, who had been quite vocal about what she'd like to do to Alex after the Seer had manipulated her emotions during her rescue, she couldn't tell. And she wasn't about to find out.

"Maybe some other time." She retreated towards the door.

Rocky nodded and flashed her a grin, but she caught his eyes dart to Sage, no doubt trying to see if his mentor's face would give her away.

She didn't stick around to see. She'd had enough well-meaning looks of pity. She made for the stairs, but stopped at the bottom. She could sense Markus and Darian two stories above her. Unlike her vampire housemates, she couldn't hear what they were saying from such a distance, but as a Seer she could feel their emotions. Both were content. Darian, as Regan of the Rectinatti coven, always had a dozen concerns tugging him in every direction, but these were well-contained tonight, at least as much as could be expected less than a week after the Vengatti ambush of the Creator's Day Ball. He'd be dealing with the aftermath of that near-disaster for weeks, if not months. At the moment, though, it didn't seem to be dominating his emotions. Prancing into his office would change that.

Alex had yet to fully account for her involvement in the battle that took place that night. Darian had given her a reprieve from explaining it all to him so that she could see to her father's returning ceremony and have time to grieve with her mother. Now that she was home, it wouldn't be long before he demanded answers. She was ready for that, ready to face the wrath he'd most certainly feel, ready to defend her actions, which even after days of reflection, she still felt were justified and righteous—a trait the coven supposedly honored above all else. She just wasn't sure she could handle it all on two hours sleep.

Then there was the other reason her foot still hesitated on the bottom stair: Markus's joy at having her home. He tried to restrain it when he arrived at her mother's new cottage, safely situated on the far corner of his parents' property. He maintained a solemn air as he greeted both women whom he knew were still hurting. When he pulled Alex into a tight embrace, though, he couldn't hide the happiness he felt having her close or his eagerness for their fast-approaching mating ceremony.

Three nights. Alex took her foot off the step and made her way through the underground hallway to the barn, which served as a gym and training space. Despite her exhaustion, she felt perhaps physical exertion was what she needed. It was just one of the contradictions raging inside her. She was mourning her father, but simultaneously swinging between anger at him for hiding what he knew for so long and guilt over underestimating his love and courage until it was too late. She was grateful for the increased power her father's parting gift had provided and pleased at her ability, so far, to control it. But there was bitterness towards it, too. It came at an awful cost—not the inconvenience of sensing others' emotions with greater intensity, but her father's life. And maybe her own.

The nights at her mother's when she couldn't sleep, she had sat on the porch swing wrapped in a quilt she'd had on her childhood bed, reading the Seers' histories and unraveling the riddles her ancestors had used to keep the secrets of her kind safe. Though she'd discovered enough new information to keep her head spinning for weeks, she always went back to the prophecy. The night she first discovered it—just four nights ago she reminded herself, because it seemed like an eternity—she had been willing to accept Sage's outlook. The words, in the form of a poem, could be interpreted numerous ways using various contexts. All except the last line, the one that foretold her demise. Alex didn't see how that could be read any other way. If the prophecy held true, ending the conflict with the Vengatti would take her life.

Oddly, the thought of her death wasn't her greatest fear. It pissed her off plenty. She knew the expression 'you can't have your cake and eat it too,' but this seemed a little extreme. And she supposed at some level it did terrify her, too, especially since if her death were to be at the hands of the Vengatti's Regan, Leonce, it was likely to be slow and torturous. But what bothered her most was what she'd leave behind, a mother and a mate who each had already lost most everyone they ever loved.

Markus, in particular, was creating her greatest internal struggle. She was as excited as he to be mated. Finally proving to everyone, including him, that she was truly ready to devote herself to him completely would make her happier than she'd ever been. But to Markus, love and devotion demanded absolute openness and honesty. Her vows would mean nothing to him if he discovered she uttered them while concealing something as critical as the final lines of the prophecy. Not that knowing would change his mind. He had fallen for her before her gift matured, when her chances of surviving the month had been slim. She didn't doubt his love. Just the reverse. It was the intensity of his love that kept her from telling him. She was afraid Markus would keep her from fighting in order to keep her safe. She was afraid she'd have to tell him that her own love for him wasn't enough to keep her home, not when others' lives depended on her. She was afraid of breaking his heart . . . again. But it seemed inevitable. At least if it were broken by her dying, it would be the Vengatti, not her, to blame.

"Will you get your self-righteous head out of your ass and give the male some credit?"

Alex startled. She'd been too lost in her thoughts and the rhythm of her fists pounding the bag to sense Sage's approach. She paused and looked up at him where he stood in the doorway. She said nothing; he was just warming up.

"First of all, Markus has been a member of this coven for a hell of a lot longer than you have, honey. You think too highly of yourself and him if you think he'd sacrifice the rest of us so easily."

She opened her mouth to argue, but Sage plowed on as he crossed the room.

"Secondly, I would have thought you learned your lesson about keeping things from him. He's forgiving, but he's not a saint. He has a breaking point, one you've already come very close to in the not so distant past. You want to risk round two? Things like this have a habit of getting out."

"You mean you have a habit of letting them out."

Sage had slipped on the training mitts. Alex didn't have to be encouraged to pound into them.

"I gave you my word, which for me actually means something." He swung his mitt-covered hand at the side of her head forcing her to duck. "You think Darian's going to make the same promise?"

She landed a hook with a loud smack. "Darian's not going to know."

"That's too bad. Because that line in the prophecy about a unity might have been your saving grace when he sits you down later tonight and asks you to explain why you knocked out him and his males in order to release a dozen Vengatti."

"What's he going to do, kill me? Better him than Leonce. Maybe I ought to auction the honor of offing me on E-bay. At least then my mother will have something to cover the cost of cremation."

"We're back to this?" He was coming at her fast now. Alex was hardly able to complete one punch before the other mitt was swinging at her. "I thought you had agreed to train, to fight." He took another swing. Too slow to duck it, she tried to step out of range. She tripped on a knot in the wooden board beneath her and fell hard on her ass. Sage stood staring down at her. He offered no apology, not even a hand to help her up.

"Clearly, it hasn't helped me much to this point." She rolled slowly to her hands and knees and pushed herself to her feet. Her head was pounding. The ribs she'd bruised the night of the ball burned with every heavy breath.

"You trip once and you're ready to lay yourself at Leonce's feet? You're injured, and you've never been worked hard. When Markus 'trains' you, the two of you spend half the time fighting and the rest of it fucking."

Her jaw dropped.

"Please. If you wanted to keep it a secret, you could have kept it down a little. You need a trainer willing to push you—not be a pushover."

"Markus trained you and half the coven. You think you can do better?"

"Well, I sure as hell wouldn't put up with your bullshit. And if I had you on your back, you wouldn't be moaning with pleasure. But that's a moot point, isn't it, because you'd rather die a lying, cowardly slut at Leonce's hands than face your own mate and Regan and admit you're afraid."

She didn't use her gift. She swung at him with every ounce of her strength and rage. She wanted the satisfaction of hurting him with her own hands. Her first punch landed squarely in his gut. She doubted it hurt much, but it had the desired effect. Stepping back to lessen the blow he had leaned forward just enough so she could smash her left hook into his nose. He gasped in pain before catching himself. Alex smiled knowing the brief display of weakness bothered him far more than the broken nose gushing blood down his mouth and chin.

Sage spit a mouthful of this at her feet before meeting her gaze. "See, plenty of fight left in you. Now how about we work on aiming that aggression, and that surprisingly adept hook, where it belongs— at the Vengatti bastards who've systematically picked off your family one by one." He wore his own grin.

She swore and threw the gloves to the ground. She hated being manipulated, but had to admit Sage was a master. "Well played," she muttered heading to the door leading to the yard.

"Is that a yes?"

"To training with you." She stopped and turned to find him breathing down her neck. "Keep your mouth shut about the rest until I say otherwise," she whispered. Markus and Darian had heard enough of their arguing to rush to the front door where they stood watching.

Sage ground his teeth but nodded. He followed her across the yard to the main house. She felt better when she caught him wiping his face on his sleeve before stepping into the light cast from the porch. Markus and Darian backed into the entranceway to let them enter.

Markus's eyes darted between Sage's bloodied, swelling face and Alex's set jaw. He started to speak, but Darian cut him off.

"Welcome back, Alex. It's so nice to have you home." He smiled at Sage's injury.

"Four days and you've let the place go to the mutts, Darian," she returned with her most charming grin.

"Better a mutt than a bi—"

Markus had Sage's lower jaw in his right hand. "Unless you want a broken jaw to accompany that nose, you won't finish that sentence."

A door slammed above them, and all four heads turned to the top of the stairs. Sarah stood on the landing with her long blond hair falling to her waist, wearing an ivory tunic sweater over dark slim jeans and silver flats. She might have looked angelic if one could have seen past her piercing glare.

"Can we please remember what tonight is, gentlemen . . . and ladies?" she added noticing Alex and correctly linking her to the argument.

Markus relinquished his hold of Sage who feigned his best contrite expression. It was somewhat marred by the blood. Darian knocked the two of them upside the head, as if his intentions had always been to admonish them. He then turned on Alex, as if the whole thing were her fault. She supposed it was, but she was in no mood to apologize, especially to Sage.

"Um, what night is it, exactly?" she asked to deflect the conversation. She knew it wasn't Christmas. For one, vampires didn't celebrate the holiday. And she was pretty sure it had passed a night or two after her father's death. She and her mother had landed on half a dozen holiday movies as they flipped through the television channels looking for a distraction. They gave it up quickly, not in the mood for talking reindeer or overly chipper elves.

Sarah sighed, her expression softening as she gracefully descended the stairs. "You didn't think to tell her why you wanted her home so badly tonight?" she asked Markus whose cheeks flushed a bit as he shrugged. "It's Creator's Day, Alex. Your first as a coven member. Markus felt it was important for you to be home, to celebrate with us. We *all* agreed." Sarah paused to shoot Sage a look. Alex half expected him to respond with some retort, but he held his tongue. Apparently Creator's Day was not a night to argue, at least not with the Regan's mate.

"Dia dhuit, Alex," Sarah said turning back to her.

Alex racked her brain. She really needed to brush up on her Latin if she was going to hang around vamps long-term.

Sage snorted. "It's not Latin. It's Gaelic. The Irish use it as a greeting. It means God be with you. An appropriate response, beyond staring with your mouth gaping, would be 'Dia's Muire dhuit.'"

"It means may God and Mary be with you." Sarah continued when Alex still appeared perplexed. Vampires weren't Catholic. "When our coven moved to Ireland centuries ago, the Elders were struck by the Irish Catholics' reverence of the Virgin Mary and the images used to depict her. They were so similar to the way we envisioned our Creator: maternal yet virginal, strong and courageous. Adopting their greeting was not only safer to keep the secret of our identity, but it also seemed fitting. When we use it now we're wishing the protection and blessings of the Creator to the person we're saying it to."

"Oh. Well, um, thanks," Alex stammered. Markus chuckled and whispered the response again in her ear. She tried it. "Dia's Muire dhuit." The words felt odd in her mouth, but it was obviously close enough. Sarah smiled.

"Markus, Darian, go get the leaf for the table and all the extra chairs from downstairs." She was back to business, barking orders. "You two," she addressed Alex and Sage, "Go get cleaned up. And Sage, I don't care who asks you how that happened tonight. You will not repeat any part of what you said that led her to hit you, or you'll begging for the Creator's blessings, understood?"

His eyes widened.

"I was doing laundry." The laundry room in the basement was the door closest to the barn. "Be thankful she drew blood before I could." Just the mere tips of Sarah's fangs peeked out from her glossy lips. "You better clean up your mouth and fast, or you'll be living in that barn." Sarah spun on her heel and headed into the kitchen. Sage didn't wait around to face Markus's accusing glare. He was gone in a flash.

Darian started towards the basement door, whether to pursue Sage or just to fetch what Sarah had asked, Alex wasn't sure, but she stopped Markus from following, just in case.

"Who else is coming tonight?" she asked grabbing his arm. "And should I have gotten people presents? Do I need to dress up? Because I don't—"

"Shh," Markus soothed pulling her into his arms. "I might have slipped up this evening, but give me a little credit, please."

She tried to return his smile, but his words, which so closely echoed Sage's, sent a pang of guilt through her.

"I took care of gifts for both of us. Until you have children, it's traditional to give gifts to your parents and your mate." Her heart sank further. "But I knew you'd feel badly if you didn't have something to give me in exchange, and Ellie told me modern human couples often exchange a gift on their wedding night. Since you won't technically be my mate until then, I figured we could wait. As for our parents, my father is getting a large enough bottle of expensive Irish whiskey to shut him up until after we've said our vows, and our mothers are both getting . . . some kind of scarf. Okay, Sarah actually took care of those."

Alex began to laugh, but then his words sank in. "Our mothers, plural? You invited my mother to a holiday gathering of vampires, in the middle of the night, just days after the shock of losing her husband? Markus, what were you thinking?" She had stepped out of his embrace to glower at him.

"I was thinking she could use some company, some cheer, and a good meal," he said eyeing her. It was no secret Alex got her emotional eating, or lack there of, from her mother. Neither woman had eaten more than a few mouthfuls of dried cereal since the returning ceremony, or funeral, as her mother called it. "My mother explained to her we all work nights and suggested she catch a few hours sleep before they pick her up. It'll be fine. She's not the first human any of us have interacted with. Although she is the first to be invited into the Regan's home. You, technically, weren't invited." He kept a straight face waiting for her reaction.

She relented and smiled. "No, I was dragged here. Will she at least be allowed to leave at the end of the evening?"

"If she behaves better than you did the first night," he said with a wink.

She swatted at him. "What should I wear?"

Markus pointed to their room. "All taken care of."

"My fashion fairy godmother strikes again?"

"No, I didn't want to bother Sarah more than I had to," he answered glancing toward the kitchen. There was something more to his words, but he seemed reluctant to explain. "I asked Ellie to help pick something from your wardrobe thinking she could use the distraction, but, well, let's just say she was unenthused by her choices. So she ordered some things online. Rocky picked them up this morning. They're on your bed." Markus read her expression. "I know nothing about fashion, but I know you, and angry with you or not, Elizabeth wanted you to fit in and look nice."

"Probably just so she can feel less guilty about slaughtering me in my sleep later today."

"Perhaps." He feigned indifference until her glare wore him down. "Look, the bottom line is you have something to wear that fits the theme and suits you. Trust me. Now go change before everyone gets here. It might look bad if you're wearing Sage's blood on your jeans."

She glanced down at her leg. He took the opportunity to kiss the top of her head. By the time she looked up, he was gone.

"Stupid vampire super speed," she muttered as she lugged her sore body up the stairs.

Almost two hours later, Markus burst through the door.

"What's taking so long? Everyone's here already. Sarah's getting impatient."

Alex had been standing in front of the full-length mirror on the back of the closet door. As promised, she was surprisingly pleased. She had purposely avoided unwrapping the tissue paper covered pile on the bed until after she indulged in a long shower, styled her hair, and even applied a touch of make-up. When she could postpone it no longer, she had plucked at the tape and watched with apprehension as the paper fluttered to the bedspread. But all was well. There were a few moments when she fumed realizing Ellie had ordered her junior's sizes, but standing in front of the mirror in the dark fitted jeans, silver sequined tank, and white cashmere shrug, she had to admit everything fit perfectly. This was more than she could say for most of her wardrobe. It was amazing that with the right fit and a few feminine touches, she actually felt, not boyish or childish, but womanly. She liked it.

"I look pretty good," she said turning to Markus who couldn't help but laugh.

"Almost perfect," he said turning her back to face the mirror.

"Almost?" She became suspicious as he reached into the pocket of his usual black cargo pants. He was sporting a crisp white button down with a silver gray tie, but from the waist down was warrior as usual. She looked down at the clunky toe of her blue Doc Martin boots peaking out from under the cuffs of her jeans and smiled. They were well matched.

When she looked back up, Markus was reaching around her neck with a silver ribbon. A beautifully ornate charm was attached. He tied the ends behind her back so it rested on her clavicle. She was speechless at first, but then spun on him.

"You said no gifts tonight."

"It's not a gift. It's an accessory to your outfit. And a family heirloom. My father gave it to my mother their first Creator's Day together. Maybe wearing it will win you some points with him." He winked.

"Or maybe he'll think I'm not half as good for you as Diane was for him, and he'll despise me more for it," she moaned turning back to the mirror to take a closer look. The elder Markus had been rather blunt about his feelings for her, or more particularly for her and Markus's impending mating.

Markus leaned over and rested his chin on her shoulder. "I doubt it. He went out of his way to give it to me for you to wear tonight." He met her shocked expression in the mirror and nodded to confirm.

She ran her finger over the half-dollar sized charm. It was an oval of tiny white flowers that seemed to be carved out of ivory, encircling a small silver dagger whose hilt and blade made a cross in the center.

"The silver and white, what does it mean?" She had guessed after seeing her outfit and then Markus's, both matching Sarah's color scheme, that the colors were symbolic.

"The silver represents us, vampires. The white is for the Creator. But this symbol, you'll see it tonight on the tables, too, it represents more than just our relationship with the Creator. It's representative of our roles in the coven and in our relationships with each other. The moonflower," Markus said running his fingertips over the delicate white ring, "appears beautiful and fragile, like our females might appear at first glance. But as you know," he said with a smile, "our females are also our protectors. They can be just as deadly as the males when they need to be. Moonflower is poisonous, a self-protection that allows it to grow strong and reproduce. That strength ensures there are always new warriors—males—ready to fight off the prey foolish enough to threaten our protectors. My father thought if any female in the coven ought to wear this symbol around her neck, it ought to be the mate of the lead warrior. Perhaps because we have a history of mating the most beautiful and fiercest protectors."

Alex spun around and tugged Markus into a deep kiss. Before he could get his cool hands fully under her top, she chuckled and pushed him away.

"What?" he asked, uncharacteristically breathy.

"Any chance there's another one of these for Sarah?" She pulled him to the door. "Because right now she feels pretty fierce, and I have a hunch it's aimed at us."

Markus rolled his eyes, but he quickened his step when he heard Sarah's voice calling from the foyer.

Alex stopped him, though, before they even reached the top step. No longer absorbed in his embrace, she was able to take stock of everything else she was sensing.

"Who else is here? There are at least four people, er, vampires, I've never met. You said—"

"Calm down," he whispered. Everything they said could be heard by those below. "Two are likely Sarah's parents."

"Sarah's parents are still alive?" she interrupted. Most of her conversations with Sarah had centered on the males' pasts, or learning about the coven, or her gift. Alex felt selfish realizing she had never once asked about Sarah's family.

"Yes, of course. They live in New Hampshire with a small group of elders who grew tired of the city." Markus stopped.

Alex's eyes narrowed. "And the other two?"

"Well, Vivian. I mean, even Sage knows better than to think he'd ever feed again if he didn't spend our only holiday with his partner." Alex's lips pressed into thin, hard lines. She knew who the final guest was. "And Cormelia's here. I thought it'd be nice for you to finally meet her."

"And you planned on telling me this as I was shaking her hand?"

Cormelia had been Markus's feeding partner for close to three centuries. She was the female who kept him alive after his first love, Alia, died. She was the female he knew best, the one who could comfort him when no one else could. She was also the female who'd healed the wounds inflicted on him as Alex's punishment when she had argued with the Regan, wounds Alex herself had no means of mending. Alex had spent the five months since she and Markus met teetering between intense jealousy and absolute reverence for a female she'd never seen. And Markus hadn't had the forethought to mention she would be there until she was less than twenty feet away. Alex was about to lay into him when Sage appeared at her elbow.

He was wearing pressed black dress pants and a silver grey button-down, untucked. He had no tie and wore his sleeves rolled. The only bit of white he wore was the undershirt visible only because he had his top button undone. It was clear he was honoring his own species, or more likely himself, above the Creator.

"Not true," he said listening in on her thoughts. "All my best parts are covered in white. What better way to pay homage to the blessed, virginal Creator."

Alex was too busy swallowing the bile that rose in her throat to comment, but Markus got in his face.

"Sarah hears you say that and you'll be staked on the front lawn at evening's end baring your 'best parts' to the world—and the sun."

"Yeah, well, I'll have company if you two don't make an appearance pronto. I was given permission to drag you downstairs if necessary. Any takers?"

Markus shoved him into the wall and held his hand out to Alex. Despite her earlier anger, she gladly took it.

"I'll pass, thanks. Nice face, by the way," she whispered as they passed. "The swelling almost camouflages all the ugly." Once she was on the stairs in earshot and eyesight of the others, he couldn't retaliate.

Or so she thought. A carefully focused wave of anger shot at her from behind causing her to slip from Markus's grasp and trip down the last three stairs. Nearly all the guests, who were gathered in the large open foyer for cocktails, seemed to see. She spun around and was a split second from projecting Sage down the entire flight of stairs when she felt a hand, no larger than her own but immensely stronger, grasp her forearm.

"Not worth it," chimed a melodic voice. Alex turned to see a small-statured young female standing at her elbow. She was no more than three inches taller than Alex's five-foot frame, tiny by vampire standards, but she was certainly a vampire. Despite her size, her grip was like a vice, and through her forced smile Alex could just perceive the tips of her protruding fangs. These might have given away what Alex already sensed quite clearly through contact: She was as furious with Sage as Alex. So why was she holding her back? Alex looked back up the stairs where Sage had frozen. She had enough control these days to hit Sage with a wave of emotion strong enough to knock him out without any chance of accidentally harming the female trying to restrain her, and would have if the female hadn't whispered in her ear.

"The Regan and Sarah are right behind you, watching. Besides," she flashed a wicked grin, "I daresay I have more effective means of making him pay . . . later." She spit the last word in his direction.

Alex's fists relaxed as she sensed Sage's emotional cringing at the comment he overheard either aloud or in one of their heads. The dark haired female relinquished her grasp as Sage began trudging down the stairs. At the bottom he crossed his arms and stared at them both.

"Alex, Vivian. Vivian, Alex," he muttered as means of an introduction.

"Charming, isn't he?" Vivian said clasping Alex's hand as her visage reverted to a more natural smile. "It's taken far too long to finally meet 'the other woman,' and we have loads to talk about, but I think your soon-to-be mate wants to introduce you to *his* other female first." Vivian winked and began dragging Sage toward the Regan and his father, Ardellus.

Markus stepped in front of Alex looking relieved. "For a minute I thought you were going to . . . right in front of everyone, including *your mother*."

She shrugged. "Yeah, well, for a minute, so did I."

"I don't know who's more foolish, him for dishing it out, knowing she'll catch him, or her for putting up with it just so she can punish him time after time," Markus said watching Sage and Vivian from across the room.

"No relationship is perfect."

They were Alex's words, but another, quieter voice had spoken them. The female who had come up beside them was striking—in her plainness. She was absolutely ordinary in a way that made her stand out from the others. The vampires Alex had met thus far had all seemed too beautiful, too strong, too dynamic. But Cormelia had the same quality that first drew Alex to Markus, that allowed her to open up to him, to fall for him. Both were more human than one could expect a vampire to be.

"Alex, I'd like you to meet Cormelia," Markus said. She sensed he meant it; he was thrilled to have his two females finally together.

"I, um," she stuttered searching for the right words to convey what she wanted this female to know. When they didn't come she simply reached out and took Cormelia's hands in her own.

"She's normally more loquacious than this," Markus told Cormelia.

"Hush," she said to him, squeezing Alex's hands. "She's speaking volumes. And you're welcome," she replied to Alex. "It's been my pleasure, but now it's my pleasure to give him up to you."

Markus understood what Alex was doing but not how Cormelia had interpreted it so keenly. Alex understood; Cormelia was emotionally intelligent and intuitive.

"You won't give him up completely, I hope." Alex knew there'd be times Markus would need more than she could provide. Besides, the thought of leaving Cormelia without a feeding partner after the centuries of devotion she'd shown Markus would be unconscionable.

Cormelia's cheeks blushed as she released Alex's hands and straightened the front of her white woolen dress. "Your mating is unique in that sense, but I suppose that job belongs to whoever you choose to be Markus's commendatrix."

"His what?" Images of whips and leather popped into her mind before she realized she had misheard, but far too late to keep Sage from hearing, or Creator forbid seeing, what had crossed her mind. Darian elbowed him hard after the Knower sprayed an entire mouthful of whiskey down his front just feet from Alex's mother. When Sage leaned over and shared Alex's misunderstanding, all was forgiven. Darian roared with laughter causing half the room to stop to see what was so amusing. Centuries would pass before she lived this one down.

Undeniably crimson, she turned back to Markus and Cormelia whose sympathetic smiles seemed slightly less mocking.

"A *com*mendatrix, meaning entrusted one, is a female chosen by the female being mated to serve as her mate's protector should something happen to her. In turn the mating male chooses a commendator, a warrior or other male to serve his female should he die," Markus explained.

"Like your kind's best man or maid of honor, only with feeding responsibilities," Cormelia added.

"Well, that's a no-brainer. Of course I choose you. I mean, if you're willing. If you haven't gotten sick of him over the last couple lifetimes," she added teasingly.

"If you train him well, he's quite tolerable," Cormelia replied. Then in all seriousness, she took both Alex and Markus's hands. "I'd be honored to."

Alex thanked her and was about to ask who Markus had chosen, when he abruptly changed the subject.

"Our mothers are starting to exchange embarrassing baby stories about us. Should we go attempt to save what remains of our reputations, before they dig deep into their purses and start pulling out the naked photos?"

"You were a little old to be running around naked by the time photography became commonplace, weren't you?" she laughed.

"I was," Markus answered straight-faced. "But you weren't. And yours is the mother who spent the last three nights unpacking a lifetime of photo albums."

She considered this a valid point.

"If you'll excuse us, Cormelia, but Sage already has enough new ammo to use against me for one night."

As the night wore on it became apparent to Alex that the celebration would continue into the daylight hours. Vivian had found Alex later that evening and dragged her away from Markus and the males to chat with her, Ellie, and Cormelia. She explained Creator's Day was a twelve-hour celebration from midnight to noon. It was a way of recognizing both their strength and their limitations. Another rich tradition. Another fact Markus had failed to mention.

By the time the others began settling down for the afternoon, Alex felt dead on her feet. As she leaned on the counter in the kitchen helping Sarah dry the dishes, her eyelids were drooping. She startled when someone took the dishtowel from her hands.

"Why don't you go sit in the living room with your mother and rest," Cormelia suggested.

Alex yawned and nodded. She hugged Vivian and Cormelia, and thanked Sarah again for such wonderful food. She even managed to get Ellie to nod at her after thanking her again for helping with her wardrobe. She would have preferred to go curl up on Markus's lap where he no doubt sat on the couch in Darian's office. He, Darian, Sage, and the elder Markus had retreated there an hour ago and were likely talking shop despite the holiday. She wouldn't have been bothered by the talk of patrols and security, but she thought Markus might not be comfortable with such displays of affection in that setting.

She headed instead into the living room where her mother sat chatting easily with Markus's mother Diane and the Elder Regan, Ardellus. Sarah's parents had already gone to bed in Markus's old room, and Rocky and Ellie had retreated to the basement to do Creator knew what for a few hours before Sage and Vivian would be occupying the room next door.

"Speak of the devil," Ardellus said as Alex crossed the room to join her mother on the white couch facing the blazing fireplace.

"Are you still telling stories, Ma?" she asked plopping beside Ellen and squeezing her leg.

"We're swapping tales, actually," Diane answered. "That's what parents do for fun once they have children," she said with a wink.

"Well, I hope it's the . . . " She paused, unsure if titles were inappropriate to use in front of her mother. "I hope it's Ardellus's turn, then. I rather enjoy hearing about Darian's mischievousness."

Ardellus shot her a warning glare. "You seemed to get into nearly as much trouble—in far fewer years I might add."

She laughed, not denying it.

"Yes, but she'll tell you it was all the fault of her older brothers' influences," Ellen teased.

"Actually, I was going to say that rigid, overbearing fathers tend to spawn rebellious young," Alex said smirking, her eyes never leaving the Elder Regan's, whose brows shot up. She was pushing the boundaries because her mother's presence let her get away with it. They both knew it. She was rather enjoying it until she caught the changed timbre of her mother's voice.

"You'd be right to blame your father, probably for far more than I will ever know." What began as bitterness became instant remorse. "Excuse me." Her mother stood and walked to the far end of the long room. Alex followed.

Ellen stood looking out onto the snow covered yard. Alex brushed a hand over her shoulder, but let it drop. Her mother's feelings were intense enough without the added contact.

"Mom, you can miss him while still being mad at him for not telling you as much as perhaps he should have. God knows I do," she whispered. "But please don't be mad at him for the decisions I'm making." Beneath the grief and the anger, Alex could feel the current of fear, fear of more loss, more pain. She felt helpless, but she couldn't lie and tell her mother those fears were baseless.

"Alex, I know in the end he had you convinced that all of this is the right thing." Ellen's gesturing made it evident her mother had not been as oblivious to her fellow guests and their strange traditions and appearances as Alex had hoped. Ellen had drawn the connection between her daughter's new companions and the little Alex had told her earlier that winter about her role and the danger it brought.

Alex was hyper aware of Ardellus's eyes on her back. She'd been forbidden to tell the secrets of the coven, as well as Seers, to anyone else, including her mother. He listened to assure she had and would continue to obey.

"I'm sorry I can't explain more, but you have to trust him, trust me. It *is* the right thing."

Ellen turned to face her daughter, resting her hands on Alex's small shoulders. Alex wondered if she had learned this from years of dealing with her husband, or if Tim had perhaps told his wife more than she admitted. Once the contact flooded Alex's sense with her mother's emotions, none of that mattered.

"I want so badly for that to be true," Ellen said. "I need it to be true. I just hope you live long enough to prove me wrong."

The breath escaped Alex's lungs like she'd been punched in the gut. Ellen dropped her hands and strode from the room and up the stairs. She'd be staying in Alex's room, where she would lie in bed unable to sleep due to the knowledge she had not been told, would not be told, but knew instinctively. Her daughter was in danger. It was possible, likely even, that she'd bury her youngest child just as she had buried her husband and her two older sons.

Alex leaned against the wall and allowed her weak knees to give out beneath her. There was a whispered exchange on the far side of the room. Diane left, leaving her alone with the Elder Regan. She took a few steadying breaths and opened her eyes to find Ardellus standing before her.

"Shall I get Markus?"

"No." She tried to spring up but managed it only with a firm tug from the Elder Regan. "And please don't tell him, or the Regan, for that matter."

Ardellus released his grip when she seemed steady, but he never freed her from his knowing eyes.

"She's already mourning you, along with her mate, because she feels you pushing her away."

Alex shook her head. "That's ridiculous. I spent the last four days with her. If she feels I'm pushing her away, it's because of all the secrets I'm forced to keep from her."

"And yet no one has asked you to keep secrets from Markus, or your Regan, or your friends. No one but you, Seer. Yet there seems to be quite a bit about the night of the ball that you aren't sharing."

Alex averted her eyes to which Ardellus nodded.

"So is your mother's fear a product of being human and knowing less than we do, or is it because she's your mother and therefore knows you better than all of us? If it's the second, Alexandra, it will only be a matter of time before Markus and the others feel the same agony as your mother. Knowledge is a strong weapon against fear, one that unfortunately can't be afforded to your mother. You'll both have to suffer that, I'm afraid. But you have a choice whether you alleviate the others' pain and worry."

"You're assuming knowing the truth is always better than being left ignorant." It was a sentiment she didn't share when it came to the prophecy, because it was too ambiguous to *know* anything for sure.

Ardellus shook his head and ran his fingers through his neatly trimmed salt and pepper waves, a habit he passed down to his son.

"After six and a half centuries, I don't have to assume much, Child."

CHAPTER 3

For the first time since the ball, Alex awoke slowly, peacefully. Not rattled awake by a nightmare or shaken by her half-conscious sobs. The weight of Markus's arm draped over her stomach was comforting, though surprising. She had expected him to linger only until she had fallen asleep before he headed in to work. Neither Diane nor Ardellus had repeated the conversation she had had with her mother, but her and Alex's tense and tearful goodbye that evening was enough for Markus to realize all wasn't well. He was the one who insisted Alex rest for a few hours before beginning any preparations for the fast approaching mating ceremony. She hadn't argued. She had needed his company and his comfort as much as she needed the rest.

But there was something else she needed. She was sure of it now that she had slept. Now that she lay in bed, the only one in the house awake, and still felt the heavy, nagging exhaustion. It wasn't caused by her injuries, or the interruption to her schedule, or the large number of senses in the house. It was the increased strength of her power, the strength she gained from her father's parting gift of essence, that tipped the scale. She had found a passage in her family's histories that confirmed what her body had been telling her the last couple days. It was rare, but it had happened before to a few other Seers whose powers were nearly as strong as hers.

She needed to feed.

"Hey, sleepy," she said squeezing Markus's hand. "You planning to go in for your patrol?" She brushed her fingertips gently up and down his arms until her sense of him strengthened. When he was fully awake his eyelids fluttered open. He smiled.

"Not now. Not unless you like your mates extra crispy," he croaked.

She bolted upright. Her eyes darted to the window. Sure enough, a faint glow outlined the heavy curtains.

"I slept through the entire night?"

Markus glanced over her shoulder at the clock on the nightstand. "And half the day, too. Don't give me that look. You needed it."

"Maybe, but I also needed to be planning our mating ceremony. Now I only have one full night left." She was working herself into a panic.

"Don't worry about it." Markus sat up. His voice was strangely tense. "Darian's got everything under control."

She was sure he meant Sarah but didn't see the need to correct him. The details were unimportant. Surely there were still things she had to do herself. She began to rattle them off, but Markus leaned over and kissed her.

"Everything. I promise. Which leaves plenty of time to practice for the honeymoon," he said pulling her onto him. "I missed you being home the last few days." Alex felt him harden under her. She almost forgot why she had roused him, but her body's need was even greater than its desire.

"Wait, Markus. There's something I need first." She was actually quite sure it could be done during intercourse but knew he'd require convincing first.

"I know what you need," he purred nibbling her earlobe, which suddenly connected directly to lower regions.

"Oh hell." She'd explain as they went. She rolled into him and returned his playful bites, edging herself closer to his neck. "I need this. I need you," she finally managed between nips and kisses.

"I know. I need you too," he replied sliding between her thighs.

"No, Markus, all of you."

He mistook the comment as a criticism or a challenge and grabbed her by her hips, pulling himself deeper inside her than seemed possible. She had no breath for explanations now, yet the more her body ached for his, the more her need for his essence overcame her. The only sound she managed to emit was a whimper. She'd have to take what she needed on her own terms and explain it all later. She slipped her hand beneath the pillow. She had just found the haft of the knife he kept for safety under his pillow when he pulled out and flipped her onto her stomach.

"You asked for it," he teased grabbing her hips and pushing himself back inside her. "Now quit your whining and take it."

Realizing this new position would thwart her plan, she found her voice. "Markus, no," she said more forcefully than was probably needed. She used his moment of surprise to twist out from under him.

"Whoa, hey, calm down!"

Alex took a second to catch on. She had sat up with her hand still on his weapon.

"I thought you liked that position."

She stifled a laugh. "I do; I love it. . . . Okay, no, I don't, but I love that you love it."

"Then why are you attempting to stab me with my own knife?"

"I wasn't. Well, I was, but not for the reason you think."

Markus fell back onto the quilt and rubbed his eyes with his right hand while soothing other areas with his left. "Am I still dreaming? Are you?" he asked rolling over to face her. "What the hell are we talking about?"

She smiled at him sympathetically. Perhaps she ought to have stuck to the script she had so carefully planned over the last couple nights.

"Feeding. I need to exchange essence with you, and I'm not talking about during our mating ceremony," she continued when he began to interrupt. "The last couple nights, as the essence you gave me the night of the ball to heal my injuries began to wear off, I've started to feel cranky, and tired, and less in control of my gift."

"That's because of you're still healing. I'd feed you again, but I don't think it's safe."

"It's not my injuries, Markus. Well, the fact I need more so soon might be exacerbated by my injuries, but not my need to feed—to exchange essence. That's because of my increased power. It won't go away after I heal. And it is safe. It's in my histories, and I double-checked with Christo. Or his son, Rick, to be precise. Past Seers whose powers have been strong fed from vampire mates, too. It's even documented in the coven's medical histories."

Markus's jaw flapped as he decided what part of this to address first.

"You went to Christo without Darian's permission? How did you even—"

"I called Rick. Your mother gave me the number. I didn't tell her why I needed it, just that I had a private medical question. I'm not entirely sure she doesn't think I'm knocked up. She took my drink away at least twice at the party. As for Darian, I don't need *his* permission to ask about *my* family's medical history."

Markus just shook his head. She knew he was torn between fear, likely of hurting her, and elation.

"Christo, er, Rick said it's safe?"

She nodded. Then she addressed the final emotion he was feeling, one she knew he'd never admit to.

"He said you could still feed Cormelia, too. I won't need much once everything settles down. And you might need more than I can give, especially if either of us is ill or injured. Rick said we'll have to play it by ear for a while. He told me just to listen to my body."

Relieved of his final fear, Markus's worry lines eased. His playful smile began to twitch at the corners of his mouth. Before she knew it, he was on top of her again, and there was no wriggling free this time. She gasped as he entered her hard and fast. Her whole body shivered as she felt the tips of his fangs brush her neck. He whispered into her goose pimpled skin.

"What's your body telling you now?"

Her response was her short nails digging into his shoulders. He wasn't being gentle or gentlemanly, like he often was when they made love. She didn't care. She wrapped her legs around his back so she could once again take in all of him. She tried to hold back, to prolong it, but she knew he was getting what he wanted. He wanted to be in control. He wanted her to completely lose control. So she gave into it, into him, into her body's every reaction. Just as she arched her back and opened her mouth to cry out, he brought his pierced wrist to her lips. She felt the pinch just above her collarbone at the same time she swallowed the first mouthful of his sweet, completing essence. She may have whimpered again. Markus won. She had never been so happy to concede.

The second time Alex woke up she was certain it was evening. She sensed others awake. Darian was in his office. Rocky and Sage were in the kitchen. Sarah and Ellie were still asleep, though, which meant one of the guys was cooking. For the first time in a week the smell of food was tantalizing. And she was ravenous.

Throwing back the covers she rolled onto her side to sit up. Her body ached all over. A few aches lingered from the injuries she sustained the night of the ball. But there were also new aches in new places. These were much more tolerable, almost pleasurable because of the sweet memory of what caused them. She smiled at Markus where he slept. She was tempted to lean over and kiss him awake but knew where it would lead. There was too much to do and only one night left to do it. Her first task, though, was to attack a plate of bacon and pancakes smothered in butter and syrup.

"I hope you made extras. I'm starving," she said a few minutes later when she plodded barefoot into the kitchen. She was past worrying about looking presentable for her housemates. She had thrown on the first two articles of clothing she found on the floor: a pair of sweats and a t-shirt that turned out to be Markus's and fell nearly to the floor, the wide collar slipping off one bony shoulder.

Sage had been stabbing Rocky with the spatula for plundering the mound of bacon spread on paper towels by the stovetop. Rocky jumped back and turned to her with a strip of meat hanging out of his toothy grin. One glance at her and his expression shifted.

In a flash he was bearing down on her. One hand roughly tugged at her loose collar, the other forced her chin to the side. She blanched when his fangs sprang with a guttural growl.

"Rocky!" Darian had entered the kitchen just in time to witness this. He shoved the young vamp away, sending him crashing into the counter. "What the hell's—" He stopped, finally glancing where Rocky, too angry to speak, was emphatically pointing.

Alex reached up and touched her neck feeling the two small scabs and the sore surrounding area. No doubt there was already a bruise dark enough for vampire eyes to discern.

"Let her explain, please." Markus was out of breath. He obviously had flown down the stairs at the sound of trouble. He stood half naked at the entrance to the kitchen cautious of coming closer.

"It's you who needs to explain, I think, Warrior," Darian spat at him.

"It's in Alex's histories," Sage interrupted. Darian spun on him but allowed him to elaborate. "She's the one who should have explained this to us—before walking in with fang prints on her neck."

"I don't need to ask permission to exchange essence with my mate, especially since it's perfectly safe . . . and necessary." She yanked her shirtsleeve from the Regan's grip to cover herself. She puffed herself up to continue, but Sage cut her off.

"It's also illegal," he reminded her, deflating her argument. "It didn't occur to you to check first with the one person who could pardon your mate from that mandate?"

She turned to Markus with a dawning understanding of the shame and regret he was working to repress. Her anger abated. Rocky and Darian had acted on instinct. Rectinatti didn't feed from humans. It was probably the most sacred coven law. And she had walked into the kitchen mindlessly flaunting the evidence of her mate's transgression.

"But," she began more mildly than before, "as you've been telling me for months, I'm not a regular human. My sense isn't the same, nor is my body anymore. The added power my father gave me caused even more changes. I needed to feed. I will need to feed from now on." She explained to them as she had to Markus earlier, reiterating at the end, "Markus didn't do anything wrong."

Rocky pulled in his fangs, his shock and disgust replaced with curiosity. Darian's emotions were a little harder to sort out. He stammered deciding where to begin. Ironically, he chose the same place Markus had.

"You went to Christo's? Did you take her?" he questioned Markus.

"I called, and no. He didn't know until earlier today. Again, my body, my family's medical history, my call—one I should have made a long time ago. Rick and Christo's knowledge might have helped me through my transition, through the weeks after it." Darian's eyes flitted to the scars on her wrist, exactly where she wanted them. "They have a whole volume on Seers, Darian. Did you even know that?"

The Regan stepped closer, jaw set, but she held her ground. She was right, and the better part of him knew it.

"No, I didn't," he admitted. "And I'm sorry if not going to them caused you more suffering than necessary. But this," he snapped and gestured to her newest scar. "This you should have come to me about." He turned to Markus. "Rocky's reaction is the same you're going to get from half the coven. To them, she's a human and you're the lead warrior, for Creator's sake, the person I put in charge to protect humans from being fed on. Could you have at least chosen a vein a little less conspicuous?"

Markus shifted on his bare feet. "Sorry, Regan. I wasn't thinking at the time."

"Sure you were, just not with your head," Sage cracked. Rocky attempted to stifle his laughter at the sight of Darian and Markus's glares.

"Enough." She stepped in before Sage continued. "We'll be careful next time," she told Darian. "Until then I've got cover-up and scarves. It's winter; no one will think anything of it. Now can I eat? I'm starting to understand where vampires' insatiable appetites come from." She was already reaching around Sage to pile a plate full of food.

"It's not from the feeding, sweetheart, but from the related activities." Sage tried to slap her ass, but Markus flashed across the kitchen and nearly broke his wrist.

Darian called over the ensuing scuffle. "Keep it down, and get this cleaned up before Sarah wakes. Then go to work. The only activity on Alex's agenda tonight is a talk with me, alone. Neither of us need or want your running commentary, though I've a sneaking suspicion you've already given your opinions on the topic."

Sage shrugged. Alex found her mouthful of food hard to swallow as she took in Darian's searching stare.

"It's time. Come see me when you're cleaned up."

She nodded, but Darian didn't see it. This was an order given by the Regan, not a request made by a housemate. He didn't have to wait for her response; she had no choice but to obey.

Alex headed upstairs to shower, leaving her loaded plate mostly untouched following her exchange with Darian. The males ate in silence. Markus caught Rocky glancing up the stairs numerous times. He ought to have been grateful for the young vamp's concern. Instead it annoyed him.

"What's she got to tell him that I didn't already account for? I was with her almost the whole night. And I told him everything."

"He does believe you," Sage responded to a part of Rocky's

comment he chose not to voice. Markus smirked. Sage's gift was aggravating when wielded on him or Alex, but it was interesting, even amusing, when applied to other victims. "I think it's the parts of the evening you weren't with her, or weren't conscious, that he'd like elaborated on," Sage finished.

"He can't punish her for screwing up a few things, not after the night she had had. Besides, mistakes aside, she saved lives."

"She sure did," Sage muttered in a tone that confirmed he knew far more than he was saying—and disapproved of a good part of it.

"You're a great mentor," Rocky accused. "If you won't stick up for her, I will." Rocky stood.

Markus yanked him back into his chair. "If anyone is going to get slapped around standing up for her, it'll be me, thanks. He wouldn't even let you through the door. As lead warrior I have a right and a responsibility to be there. I can handle both without your help."

Sage shook his head. "Your last night of freedom and you're fighting this idiot for the opportunity to get beaten on her behalf. You two should do a Dumb and Dumber remake."

Rocky cracked a smile. Markus wasn't in the mood, but he appreciated Sage's attempt to lessen the tension.

"With Alex's track record, you really ought to have two commendators, because you and the *first one* will likely die at Darian's hand before any Vengatti get to you."

All right, I get it. Now, knock it off, Markus thought to Sage. He wasn't stupid. He knew why Sage pushed this line of conversation. The cleansing ceremony was tonight. He needed to ask.

But he had spent the last week second-guessing his decision—decisions. Both were critically important, and both hinged on his ability to trust someone else with Alex's well being, her future. Rocky wouldn't have been Markus's first choice. But Alex trusted him unequivocally. That ought to have been enough.

Sage threw his hands up. "You can't clone yourself, you egotistical bastard. Get over it, and ask him."

Rocky looked between Markus and Sage waiting for one of them to explain. Markus caved.

"I have a favor to ask you. Two, actually."

"Shoot," Rocky answered.

It wasn't really the response Markus, as lead warrior, would have liked to receive from the wet-behind-the-ear twenty-six year old. He took a calming breath. "I know you still want to be a warrior," he began. He saw Rocky's face fall at his intonation. Sage narrowed his eyes realizing Markus intended to screw with the kid. Good, they both deserved it. "But there's been a little in-fighting among the other guys about you."

Rocky nodded. His voice was tight as he replied. "Sure, I understand."

"I agree with them." Markus paused here. Sage mouthed 'prick' at him behind Rocky's back. "The warriors are right that you'd be good on regular patrols." Rocky's head jerked up hopefully as he caught Markus's smirk. "And Remalt's right that you'd make a great assistant to help bring the coven up to date on the latest security and surveillance technology. And you can have either of those jobs, if you want them, but—" He held out his hand to stop Rocky, who was practically bounding out of his seat to respond. "I'd prefer you accept another assignment, one more important to me and the coven. I want you to be the warrior assigned to Alex. You'd be her partner and her protection. You two fight well together . . . and you care enough about one another to keep each other safe." It was hard to admit the truth, a truth that made him as jealous as it did confident that this was the right choice.

Rocky looked flabbergasted. He appeared to understand the gravity of what Markus was asking, but couldn't grasp why he was being asked. He was looking to Sage, his mentor, who to some might have seemed the more obvious choice.

"It was decided we spend enough quality time in each other's heads. That and Markus thinks I'm a surly S.O.B. who wouldn't be gentle enough with Alex's fragile disposition."

Rocky laughed at this, which was only half true. Markus worried more that Alex would meet bark with bite and kill the two of them by knocking out Sage while he was driving ninety miles an hour on some back road on the outskirts of Bristol.

Rocky finally gathered his wits enough to reply. "I'll do it. I'd be honored, but that's only one favor."

Markus sighed. "Yeah, well, the second one became a little more complicated six hours ago when I discovered she'd need more than protection if I died first. Ellie is not going to like this one," he said shaking his head.

"You're asking me to be your commendator . . . tonight? The

cleansing ritual starts in, like, hours," Rocky sputtered unable to locate a clock. "And yours, I imagine, will be a little more complicated than normal."

Markus held out his left forearm where there should have been a scar, a small mark made just below the wrist on the eve of one's mating. Though he'd been mated once before, there was nothing to see.

"Part of it's been done already. Darian and Sarah convinced me to remove it when we moved from Ireland. They hoped a new country might change my mind about re-mating." It hadn't. Nothing had until he met Alex. He thought the pain he'd have to endure during the renewal ceremony that evening was unnecessary considering how he suffered for centuries after losing Alia, but he'd endure it without complaint for Alex. She had a pull on him he couldn't explain.

"A new country wasn't drastic enough. He had to wait until we unearthed a forgotten species," Sage heckled, apparently uncomfortable with the serious tone Markus's thoughts had taken. "Your bigger concern ought to be the smell. You willing to reek of baby-vomit if Markus kicks the bucket and leaves you to exchange essence with her?"

Markus kicked Sage's shin under the table. "She's not a regular human, and I don't, and won't, smell like a Vengatti."

Rocky bit his bottom lip. "But she's not a vampire, either, and you do kinda smell funny this morning. Not sour milk, but not normal. And I don't think a shower or Alex's cover-up idea is going to mask that come tomorrow. Maybe I could pick you up some cologne as my first official act as commendator."

"Is that a yes?" Markus asked between gritted teeth. He was torn between slapping him and shaking his hand.

"Of course. But maybe I ought to ride into work with you. Someone needs to tell me what the hell I'm supposed to do tonight and tomorrow. The last mating ceremony I went to I was five."

"Sage has been to a few in his lifetime, I suspect. He'll have to do. I need to stick around and assure you still have a job tomorrow and I still have a mate."

Sage grew serious for the first time all evening. "Good luck with that." He grabbed the keys off the counter and headed to the door. Markus knew it'd be useless badgering him for information. Sage was a lot of things, but he was loyal and kept his word. If Alex convinced him not to say anything, to let her tell her own tale, in her own time, he wouldn't go back on that. Sage turned around before he reached the door. "So long as she tells the *whole* story, she'll be just fine."

Markus sighed. If Alex was planning on withholding information that could save her own skin, it would be because she thought she was saving someone else pain. He had a hunch he was the someone else.

CHAPTER 4

"Come in, Alex," Darian said before her fist even touched the dark wood of his ajar office door. Countless times before she'd barged in unasked for and unannounced. Tonight she decided to play nice. She could only expect him to excuse so much in one evening.

"I have a right to be here, too, Regan." Markus stood in the doorway, arms crossed.

"If you're here to listen and advise as my lead warrior, by all means, come in." Markus stepped in without hesitation. He hadn't gone a step when Darian flashed into his path. "But if you interfere with my obtaining the information I need or with whatever I decide to do with such knowledge, it may be the last time you enter as lead warrior. Are we clear?"

"Crystal. There's no need to keep reminding me, Regan. I don't easily forget information pertaining to the security of my role or the safety of my mates." Markus emphasized the 's' in mates.

The temperature in the room plummeted. Alex fiddled with the scarf she had put on to hide the marks on her neck. Both males probably already had Markus's first mate, Alia, on their minds as Markus prepared to re-mate the following night. Darian clenched both fists at the sly reminder of his role in her murder. It was Darian's attack on a Vengatti village that was being avenged the night Alia was killed. More intense than the Regan's anger, though, was his remorse. Markus's was quick to follow. They held each other's gaze, as if waiting for the other to crack first and apologize. Instead Darian nodded. Markus shrugged. They both moved to their usual places,

Darian leaning on his desk, Markus sitting in the armchair across from the couch where Alex always perched. She slowly made her way there giving them time to settle their nerves.

"I should start with my father," she began. She had days to think about how best to explain this to Darian and to Markus, who refused to let her tell him until the Regan knew.

"Rocky told me all that. Just skip to the ball."

"No, Regan. If you're going to understand, really understand, I need to tell it all. Please."

Darian threw out a hand in concession and let her begin. She started with the story of what had happened to her father at her childhood home. Some of which was confirmed, some implied, and some pure speculation based on her knowledge of her father and his gift.

"It seems two young Vengatti showed up at his door. What they planned to do to him, Creator knows, but the intent was clear. They wanted to draw me out during daylight hours. Lucky for me, and him, I suppose, to some degree, they underestimated him." Alex paused trying to sort some things out for herself. "I don't think it was luck he was lucid, though. I think that was due to great effort on his part. I think he always had the means of breaking through whatever it was that left him in a haze most of the time. But it took most of his energy just to focus. Using his gift to influence them into leaving was more than his body could handle. Sage recognized the symptoms, those of one's body battling an imbalance of physical strength and power. And he was right about it being a trap, too." Darian looked smug, but she shook her head. "If I hadn't gone when I did, Regan, I wouldn't have the strength or the knowledge I do now." They knew her father had led her to the book of Seer histories. She then explained how her father had fed her his power through his essence.

"Sage said he's never heard of a Knower doing that," Markus noted.

"The Knower gift often isn't hereditary," Darian reminded him.

"Right. But I found in my histories that with Seers the ritual is extremely valuable. It doesn't just strengthen the receiver's power. It strengthens the bloodline." She looked to Markus. "It means if we have young, there's a greater chance they'd get the gift. It might even give them a better chance of surviving their maturity, but no one really knows. So many Seers died in battle, far from their young, few ever got the chance to perform it." Until she had read this passage, Alex hadn't really thought about the fact having children would mean suffering the fear and anxiety she had sensed so strongly from her father. Now every time she thought about having young with Markus, a part of her recoiled at the memory of such crushing pain. He must have seen a shadow of this in her expression. He crossed over to the couch and squeezed her hand.

"There's time to talk about that later. And it'll be your choice, always, alright?"

She nodded but needed a moment before she continued. Rocky had already explained about Leonce's text made to look like it was from Ellie. Alex admitted she had used her gift to convince him to let her go outside. Rocky knew it, too, but he hadn't used it as an excuse when he explained to Markus and Darian how she escaped his protection.

"Is there anyone you didn't use your gift on that night?" Darian asked. He was still sore over being influenced and then knocked on his ass—twice.

Alex grimaced. "I'm getting there." He didn't yet comprehend her meaning but urged her on.

"Once I was out of the crowded hospital, alone, I was able to release the added power my father provided. It was amazing. It is amazing. The surety with which I'm able to sense others' emotions, even the complex ones that I can't put names to, is intense. And hard to handle. Sarah's Creator's Day party, the ceremony tomorrow, those are pretty uncomfortable." Markus glared at Darian, but from the look the Regan returned, it wasn't a good time to ask for an explanation. She continued. "It's not like when I first matured. It's not overwhelming, because I'm not scared of what I might do anymore. As soon as I accepted the added power, I knew I had absolute control over what I released, how intense it would feel to others, and who would be affected by it. As long as I knew the technique and had a little practice, I could execute it flawlessly. No mistakes. Nothing unintentional." She stopped to let this sink in. Darian's popping neck veins told her he saw where this was headed. Markus, bless him, was looking for loopholes.

"But as soon as you acquired the new power, you knocked yourself out. And you did it a second time at the ball."

"The first time was just my body adjusting to my power. You said when my gift first matured my blood pressure jumped all around. A sudden change could have caused me to faint."

Markus shuddered, though he'd heard this before. "They could have killed you so easily," he murmured.

"And rob Leonce of the chance to play with me before my death?" She smiled trying to brush off his fear.

"Get to what happened at the ball." Darian could be held off no longer.

That didn't mean she couldn't try. "You mean why I passed out again?"

"If that's important." The tension in his voice seemed to ripple the air in the space between them, a few short feet.

"It's not. It was merely exhaustion and inexperience with pulling back a projected emotion," she admitted. She braced herself. This was the part Darian needed explained. This was the part crucial for him to understand if he was going to help. It was also the part in which her actions were least likely to be accepted.

"Rocky got me close enough to sense the crowd. He could see what I could only sense—that the elders and young from our coven were struggling, even though we outnumbered the Vengatti. Rocky told me I had to act fast. I could easily discern the Rectinatti warriors and males. They were unified; they wanted to fight to defend their families and their Regan."

Darian nodded. She sensed the pride and gratitude he felt for the males, who despite their fear and, in many cases, lack of training and weapons, stayed to fight.

"I thought I could feel out the Vengatti males as easily and knock them out without any fear of unintentionally hitting our males."

"But you couldn't?" Markus asked hopefully.

She sighed. "I could. Only what I sensed from them shocked me."

"I think disgusted is the word you're looking for," Darian said.

"Yes, most of them were thoroughly enjoying inflicting pain and fear. Some sick S.O.B.'s were practically getting off on the mere thought of the carnage they hoped to cause." She shook her head trying to rid her memory of these feelings.

"Most." Darian spat out the word like it was a foul morsel he had almost ingested.

She nodded to confirm, hoping it would give him a moment to brace himself for the details.

"I also sensed others who felt much the same fear our coven members felt. Fear for loved ones, family and friends. I felt their desire to protect them; it was the yoke of their obligation. They didn't want to fight; they were being forced to." Darian was gritting his teeth, his nails bit into the wood of his desk. She barreled on before he lost it. "I only knocked out our own coven because I knew they couldn't see what I could sense. An armed Vengatti would have looked like a threat—"

"Because they are a threat!" Darian roared, unable to hold in his fury any longer. "With us out, they could have killed you and slaughtered the entire coven." He closed the gap between them to tower over her.

"The fact that they didn't proves I was right. You need to trust my sense, Darian."

"It's your judgment I'm questioning. Your recklessness is going to get you, and who knows how many others, killed!"

"My sense is going to get me killed," she said shooting to her feet to meet his rage head on, "because I can't stand by while innocent people are forced to kill and get killed."

"Stand down, Seer." Markus was addressing her as he would one of his males, pushing her back from Darian. She read in his eyes and sensed through his touch, however, his concern, as her mate, that she would push the Regan too far. She nodded and sat back down.

"What's done is done, Darian. You can decide what to do about it later. Right now she needs to tell us the rest." Markus waited until Darian took a step back before joining Alex on the couch. "What happened once we were all out?" he asked.

"I knocked out everyone but them. There were about two dozen, maybe a few less. One of them, a slightly older vamp, seemed to have their respect. He spoke for them; most stayed to listen. He asked why I did it, and I explained. I also urged them to take notice of one another, to realize how many of them stood together. I told them if they were willing to stand up against those in their coven who had forced their hands, that we'd help them."

"What did he say to that?" Markus asked.

"He was skeptical, but also intrigued. I wouldn't be surprised if we heard from him."

"That just proves how naïve you are. And arrogant. You have no authority to make offers to anyone, the enemy in particular." The

Regan pounded his desk.

"If those twenty males were our enemies, you're right, I'd be dead. You're the one who wants to take stock in the prophecy, Darian. It says, 'Victory for all,' not 'Victory for the Rectinatti.' I'm doing what I'm supposed to do."

"It was written by a Rectinatti Knower. All means the coven."

"It was stolen by a Rectinatti Knower—or at least half of it was. It was written by a Seer. All means all, and I'm pretty sure a union between the Vengatti and Rectinatti is about as in need of binding as they come."

This surprise staunched the Regan's anger and left both he and Markus speechless.

"Sage wanted me to tell the whole story, yes? If you'll listen, I'll fill in the gaps." Alex didn't have vampire hearing, but when Sage inundated her with emotions from halfway across the house, she tended to pay attention. Knowing when to listen made it easier to eavesdrop.

Darian was already pulling the aged book from out of the climate controlled glass covered bookcase.

"There's no line about a union."

"Not in your version." She had come prepared for this. She dug into the back pocket of her jeans and took out the folded piece of paper she had tucked in just prior to meeting Markus outside Darian's door. She unfolded it and took one last look at the prophecy in its entirety. Almost. Then she handed it over to her Regan.

Darian scanned the creased notebook page greedily at least twice before reading it aloud so Markus could hear as well.

"*The last of three will yield more power than them all.*' Your father gave you the second half of that line when you first came to us last summer," Darian recalled. Alex nodded. They'd already speculated on the possible meanings of that one, but more and more it seemed pretty obvious that all meant all Seers, not just all of her siblings. It was daunting to consider, so she didn't linger on it. There was plenty else in the prophecy to worry about.

"*Where essence is strong, marred by one whose emptiness is blinding.*' Leonce is your only blind spot, but what's the emptiness?"

"His soul?" she speculated, only half kidding.

"Humph," was Darian's only response to her attempt to lighten the mood. "*And before the turn, battle-worn, she'll bring about his fall.*' You nearly killed him before you matured," Darian passed this one off as being self-explanatory.

"But he's still alive and still in power, so was it really a fall?" Alex wondered, partly because it was true and partly because poking holes in the whole thing made the line she omitted less frightening.

"As far as we could tell, he was out of commission for awhile," Markus said. "Who knows what that did to his power within the coven? If you're right about how large a faction isn't loyal to his cause, a few months under another's rule could have done irreparable damage. It doesn't take much to turn an already divided group against its leader."

Alex ignored the 'if,' and nodded along with Darian.

"*From which will then be born to us a unity in need of binding.*' Humph," Darian repeated before rattling off the remainder of the lines, which were far less cryptic than those preceding them.

"'*A unique warrior, against reluctance, will heed the call,*
Tis' she who Sees a way, through vision without eyes,
To victory for all.'"

Darian scanned the prophecy a final time, reading it aloud again, though in a more fluid, poetic style. He paused after the final line on the page. His piercing glare was enough to inform her he hadn't been fooled. She could live with that, but Markus needn't know.

"Trusting my judgment any better now?" she asked quickly to prevent Darian from confronting her about the missing line.

"Was that your plan? You and Sage thought you could dazzle me with a few more scraps of prophecy, and I'd let you off the hook for allowing two-dozen Vengatti to go free? I'm a bit better with timelines than you, apparently. Perhaps it has something to do with my having been around a few *hundred* years longer. This—" he said strangling the piece of paper, "wasn't in your possession until after the ball."

"I never said it was the reason for my actions." She was careful with her tone. "I'm just offering it up as evidence that perhaps I was right."

"If this is your idea of evidence, be glad you're not on trial." Darian slammed the paper onto his desk. "Now what the hell do I do with you? And what the fuck am I supposed to tell my father and the Elder Council? Hey, gentlemen, new policy, we're now giving amnesty to anyone Alex's gut tells us is 'not so bad'?"

"I'll explain it to them, too, if you want," she offered.

"You're kidding? After the last Elder Council meeting you attended? I'd rather bring one of the Vengatti you let go to help me explain."

"Sorry," she answered with equal sarcasm. "By the time we got to the exchanging numbers stage of our relationship, Sage was awake and ready to rip their throats out. Or mine."

"That would have been a pity," he snarled so sincerely that she flinched.

"Darian." Markus's own calmness came across as a reprimand to the Regan. "You don't need to decide how to handle all this tonight. I assume you don't want to change any plans for tomorrow evening?"

Alex nudged him. He made it sound like a challenge, one she feared Darian would jump on, revoking his permission for their mating.

"Absolutely not," Darian replied with a smug grin. "If anything, this knowledge strengthens my resolve. Tomorrow night just became more important than ever."

"What is he talking about?" she whispered to Markus, suddenly aware there was a crucial bit of information about their mating night that no one had yet to mention.

"Later," he mumbled to her before continuing with Darian. "Fine. Then you'll have plenty of time while we're on our honeymoon to mull it over. In the meantime, there's a lot left to do before the ceremony." He stood clutching Alex's hand and made to leave.

"She doesn't need to be at tonight's warrior meeting. She'll stay here. With me." Darian had stepped forward and grasped her other arm.

"Fine." Markus looked at her apologetically. "Sorry, Babe, but I'm late, and I need to save my skin for later tonight. You'll be all right. Darian won't want to leave you any more bruised for tomorrow than I already have." He leaned into kiss her so deeply she couldn't help close her eyes. She felt the Regan's hand leave her arm and suspected her soon-to-be mate had slapped it away. After, Markus paused just long enough to shoot Darian another glare before disappearing from the room.

"Wait," she called after him. "What warrior meeting? And what's later tonight?" But the front door closed before she even finished.

She turned to Darian.

"Sit. I'm sure he'll explain all his cryptic comments on the honeymoon, if not before. *He* doesn't tend to withhold important information from *you*."

Alex sat and put her head in her hands. His attempt at a guilt trip was exceptionally effective tonight. She was already feeling what he wanted her to.

"In addition to the torturous hours I was forced to spend studying literature, including more poetry than I ever want to lay eyes on again, I have had the pleasure of translating a fair number of these prophecies." Darian thumbed through the yellowed papers. "This one, made when the coven was still in Rome, warns against an open alliance with the humans. It ends by foretelling the death of the Regan's daughter at the hands of a greedy human." He flipped a few more pages. "This one warns of a traitor. It ends by foretelling the death of a Regan." Another page. "Corruption ending with an infertile Regan. Murder of innocents . . . a plague. Birth of a Knower . . . death of a warrior. See a pattern, Alex?"

She looked up. "Everyone dies. Comforting. Thanks."

"That's the point. Everyone dies. The daughter of that Regan? Killed by an angry mob after she attacked them with her fangs. They burned her thinking she was a demon. The Regan? Died when his thatch roof caught fire during midday. We all die, because that's part of life—not because some fool writing a prophecy decides he'll be taken more seriously if he predicts impending doom."

"Maybe Seers' prophecies aren't written by fools. Maybe ours don't all end in doom and gloom."

"Or maybe you're back to lying to me and deceiving your mate to 'protect him' because you're not ready to face the truth."

"Well, is it exaggerated bullshit, or is it truth, Darian?"

"It's what you make of it," he said echoing Sage's words.

"Then I choose to make nothing of it. So there's nothing to tell."

"There is. I want the last line." He held the paper out to her.

She was about to hum a little Rolling Stones, but reconsidered. If he wanted it badly enough, he'd badger her until he got it. There was a greater chance of Markus discovering it that way than if she just gave in here while he was away.

"Fine. 'And her just demise.'"

Darian repeated the prophecy again in its true entirety.

"The last of three,
  will yield more power than them all.
Where essence is strong, marred
  by one whose emptiness is blinding.
And before the turn, battle-worn
  she'll bring about his fall.
From which will then be born to us
  a unity in need of binding.
A unique warrior
  against reluctance will heed the call.
Tis' she who Sees a way,
  through vision without eyes,
To victory for all,
And her just demise."

"Yup. Victory for all. Death for me. The meter still sucks; it's all over the place. But at least you can be happy with the rhyme scheme now."

He put down the paper and searched her face. "I think you of all people know this doesn't make me happy. Nonsense or not, it's hard to ignore, because it echoes a fear we all had already. You were the one earlier who said your gift draws you into dangerous situations. Being honest with yourself and with us about that is a start. Reading your histories to learn everything you can about your gift, taking your training more seriously—those are important, too. And if you think Christo's family has more to offer, I'll see to it you get it."

"Thank you."

"But, Alex, I'd like you to reconsider telling the others."

"Others, plural? Should I have a t-shirt made: short, sassy, and destined to die young?"

Darian was running his hands through his hair. "I'm serious, Alex. As your mate, and as someone who has lost a mate once already, Markus deserves to know. And as your partner, Rocky ought to be told, too, especially since Sage seems to know. The three of you shouldn't be worried about hiding secrets from each other when you're out on patrols. As for Sarah and Elizabeth, that's your call. But on rough nights it might allow you some compassion and patience where otherwise there would be little."

Alex lowered her voice to match Darian's quiet volume. Both females were awake and in the kitchen, likely sharing coffee and conversation, something Alex had often done with Sarah in the fall.

"Did I do something to upset Sarah? She seems . . . distant. And I do have a habit of shooting my mouth off and not even knowing it."

Darian chuckled, but Alex sensed the tension behind it. "No. Sarah's just . . . a little on edge, and might be for a while. Helping Ellie, and you, if you'll let her, would be good for her."

Alex shrugged. She didn't know what to say. In some ways Darian was right. Not only did Markus and her housemates have a right to know, since it was absolutely affecting her outlook and her attitude, but it might actually be easier for her if they knew. She'd have understanding; she'd have help.

"Interdependence," she breathed closing her eyes. How many times had they explained the concept to her? To them, it was a necessity and therefore second nature. To her, it seemed at best a hindrance, at worse a terrifying web of people she could hurt. In her mind the word spread like a string tying together all those Darian mentioned. Rocky, her best friend and strongest ally had just been asked to be her commendator should anything happen to Markus, who was soon to be her mate, after a ceremony overseen by Darian, her Regan and Markus's best friend, which would be translated by Sage, the coven's Knower, her mentor, trainer, torturer, and confidant. The wispy word swirled on connecting her also to the others—Sarah, Cormelia, her mother—an unbroken strand. It was time she stopped seeing it as a tangled snare and started accepting it for what it really was—a safety harness, a net ready to catch her after each fall.

She opened her eyes to find Darian watching her closely.

"You get used to it. You might even find it has some pleasant perks," he said eyeing the scarf.

She pulled it off and snapped it at him. "You're as bad as Sage."

"Perhaps, but I'm not the one about to get a tongue lashing for my bedroom behavior." Darian flashed behind his desk and straightened his wrinkled rugby shirt just as Sarah entered.

"Sorry, Darian, but Alex—" Sarah stopped short.

Alex was fumbling with the scarf but hadn't moved quickly enough.

"She's all yours," Darian said to a still stuttering Sarah. "She can explain that to you on the way to her mother's."

Sarah shook herself free from her shock. "And how is she going to explain that *to her mother?* Or to half the—"

"I'll handle tomorrow. If it can't be kept from Ellen, Sage can always tweak her memory when it's all over."

Alex jumped up. "Absolutely not! He even thinks about it and—"

"Enough." Sarah cut her off. "We'll think of something in the car. Let's go."

"Wait. Now? The mating ceremony—"

"Is in twenty-four hours. And tonight's ceremony is equally important."

Alex's expression must have been as blank as her understanding.

"Markus didn't explain this either? Incredible. Do you two talk or just—"

"Sarah," Darian interrupted in a soothing voice. "It's early. You've got all night. Besides, I'm sure your explanation would be far better than anything Markus or I could give. And Vivian and Cormelia can help."

Sarah took a deep breath. "Sorry. I'm fine, Darian. I promise. You can throw away the note you just wrote under the desk to Alex. She knows better than to influence me without my knowledge or permission." She looked at Alex to confirm.

"True. A smart woman doesn't bite the hand that feeds her, or more importantly, dresses her." Alex winked at Sarah.

Darian smirked. "No, just the neck of the one who undresses her, apparently."

CHAPTER 5

"What's your tolerance for pain?" Vivian's bubbly voice almost convinced Alex she was kidding. Then she caught Cormelia's cringe and Sarah's sigh.

"Has Sage told you nothing about her? Please don't ask her questions like that."

Alex laughed at the way Vivian shrugged off Sarah the same as Sage often shrugged off Darian.

They sat in the living room of her mother's cottage. Ellen was sitting at her side, taking in stride all she had heard and witnessed of the ceremony the three other females were performing on her daughter. Sarah sat on Alex's left explaining what Cormelia, with Vivian's help, was doing and the significance of it all.

Cormelia had just swabbed the inside of her left wrist with alcohol, a modern-day precaution. The traditional ceremony only called for the bathing and oiling, which Alex had already undergone. At first, the idea had seemed incredibly awkward. But when the three female vampires had crowded into the cottage's small upstairs bathroom, softly incanting the traditional blessings, while caressing her body with warm cloths, cautiously due to the number of bruises that still besmirched Alex's otherwise unblemished skin, her embarrassment vanished.

Bracing herself for the final part of the ritual, she found Cormelia's cool touch comforting.

"It's only for the ceremony. It doesn't need to last beyond tomorrow," Cormelia said.

Alex glanced at Sarah's pale left arm. After explaining the ceremony, she had shown Alex the faded white mark, which after close to three hundred years was still discernable even to human eyes. Just below the wrist, no more than two inches across was what had originally looked to Alex like a figure eight. When Sarah lifted her arm in a gesture she equated with one about to take an oath, it was clear it was not a number. It was the symbol for infinity, the same never-ending loop Cormelia had rubbed into her shoulders upstairs.

"Unum solum est finis. Duo simul manere ad infinitum." One alone ends. Two together continue forever.

"I want it to last," Alex said determined.

Vivian nodded to her from the door to the kitchen before heading back in the direction of the acidic scent. Cormelia squeezed her hand before following.

"It's pine pitch, right?" she asked Sarah. The whole house smelled like Christmas.

Sarah nodded. "The essence of an evergreen." Another symbol of the vow she'd make tomorrow—to be Markus's for eternity.

"I want it to last, Sarah," she repeated.

Sarah smiled. "We all do."

Sarah had understood her double meaning and replied with her own. Her emotions, though, made Alex wonder if she knew even more than she let on.

She wished she had spoken to Darian sooner or just listened to Sage. She was sure she wouldn't see Markus until the mating ceremony, wouldn't have a chance to be open with him. She could promise him eternity, because she would love him no matter how long she lived. But was it fair to ask the same of him, knowing that his love could be burdened so soon with grief?

"Sarah." She sat up as the thought occurred to her. "Why doesn't Markus have one of those marks already? How can he even mate me tomorrow if he promised himself to Alia for eternity?"

"Alia?" Ellen had been a quiet observer most of the evening, but Alex's first sign of nerves seemed to rouse her. "Was that Markus's first wife? The one that passed away?"

"Yeah, Mom, but . . . " Alex turned to Sarah. She wanted answers, but having her mother there complicated matters.

"Oh, shoot," Sarah exclaimed suddenly. "Vivian, I never got the ribbon from Diane."

Vivian came out of the kitchen and exchanged a quick glance with her. "Right. Should I go next door and get it?"

"You can't go in the house. Not if the guys have already started. Some things are a little silly, but they're tradition," Sarah explained apologetically to Ellen. "Would you mind going with her? As a guest, one who's unaware, I'm sure Diane wouldn't keep you out."

Ellen smiled and stood. "Sure." She went to the front door and took her jacket from the coat rack. "Anything other than this fictitious ribbon I should ask for?"

Sarah blushed and immediately apologized, but Ellen waved her off and closed the door behind her.

Alex shook her head. "I've told you and Darian before, she's not stupid, and she's incredibly intuitive. If you insist on keeping things from her, you're going to have to do better than that."

"Darian insists on keeping things from her. I agreed not to say anything explicit. I never promised him I'd be subtle about such secrecy."

"So you agree with me, that she ought to be told?"

"This may seem ironic coming from one whose entire species is kept secret from yours, but I don't believe secrets, in general, are healthy. Unfortunately there seem to be an awful lot of them buzzing about lately. If I tried to convince everyone I knew was hiding something to come clean, I'd hardly have time to sleep." Sarah's eyes never left Alex's.

Impossible.

Sarah grinned and gave in. "You and Sage aren't known for having quiet disagreements. And I'm not known for taking Sage's side in an argument, but—"

"I know. Darian convinced me earlier. But it's too late now. I guess it'll have to wait."

"At least until we're done, which from the sound and smell of things we will be shortly. While they finish up in there, I'll answer your questions about Markus, if you'd like."

Alex nodded. "Thank you."

———◆———

"Come on. You've wanted to hit me for two years. Here's your chance. Do it now while they're upstairs. Neither of us really want an audience for this part, right?"

Rocky didn't respond. He'd been standing in silent disbelief since

Sage and the elder Markus had explained what this part of the ceremony entailed. When they had both left the basement to see what brought Vivian and Ellen to the house, Markus hoped to seize the opportunity. Rocky wasn't making it easy.

"Eighteen?" he finally spoke.

Markus nodded. "One for every year we were mated." Rocky still looked uncomfortable. "It's only a pine switch, Rocky. It's not like that bloody thing Darian uses. It's symbolic. It's not going to hurt near as much—" Did he really have to explain this? Rocky nearly lost his partner just weeks ago. They had only been together a year, but it had nearly killed the kid to contemplate a life without Ellie.

"I know," Rocky said. "That's why I don't get it. Haven't you suffered enough over the last two hundred and something years?"

"Two hundred and eighty-two. Two hundred and eighty-two years she didn't get to live. I mated her forever. The only reason I'm being allowed to break that vow is that we hadn't had young yet, hadn't been given a chance to give back to the coven. That's the law."

"Well, it's a stupid one. One of the more stupid ones actually, and trust me, that's saying something."

Markus had almost forgotten Rocky had once been apprenticed to his father, a coven lawyer. He couldn't picture the stocky warrior behind a pile of law books. "Be that as it may, it's tradition to pay reverence to a lost mate before re-mating. I owe it to Alia's family. And I owe it to Alex—to be able to start fresh with her."

"Couldn't Sage or the Regan—"

"Enough." Markus grabbed the pine rod out of the young vamp's hands and whipped a few fast strokes at his calf. Rocky yelped, more in surprise than actual pain. "There. Now you have a better reason to hit me back. So do your job—and pray to the Creator you never have to be on the receiving end." Markus shoved the whip back into Rocky's hand and returned to his spot gripping the edge of his father's workbench. He wasn't really angry with Rocky. He couldn't imagine having to do this to another male who'd lost a mate. But it had to be done. And cruel as it seemed, he knew Rocky responded to shame and guilt.

It worked. The young vamp dealt the blows without another word. The silence was fine by Markus. He had better things to think about. Eighteen years with Alia. Good years. Happy years. But nothing compared to an eternity with Alex.

"Second window from the left."

She startled even at the soft sound of Cormelia's voice. Alex had thought she had made it downstairs and to the front door undetected. She was just wrapping her scarf around her neck when Cormelia's comment alerted her to the female's presence. She sat by the fire, mere glowing embers, wrapped in an afghan that had been left on the couch.

"I just wanted some fresh air," Alex said, her hand on the door.

"I know what you want," Cormelia said warmly. "Go ahead. I'll stay here in case anyone notices you're gone and worries."

"Thanks . . . for everything." Cormelia nodded as Alex backed through the door and closed it quietly behind her.

Outside she pulled up her sleeve to let the biting winter air cool the burn on her wrist. She had hardly flinched when Cormelia poured a fine stream of searing pitch onto her skin in a perfect figure eight motion. Not once, but three times.

"Once for you. Once for your mate. And once for the Creator," Cormelia had explained.

"Are you sure you want it to be permanent?" Vivian had asked a minute later when the pitch began to cool. Alex nodded unable to unclench her teeth. Vivian smoothed a thin cotton cloth over the hot sticky pitch. Alex realized what she intended to do a split second before the female tore away the cloth, taking with it the burned layers of skin. That time Alex couldn't help but cry out.

Even covered in a soothing salve and bandaged tightly, she felt the heat in throbbing waves. The cold air felt good. But that wasn't the real reason she was skirting along the property line shared by her mother's cottage and the elder Markus's and Diane's beach house. As Cormelia had expected, she was hoping to find Markus. She wanted to tell him the final line of the prophecy. But that wasn't all. After hearing from Sarah the additional ceremony Markus had undergone to be allowed to mate again, she wanted more than anything to thank him, and if he'd allow it, to comfort him. She knew this night would bring back painful memories for him, but she had no idea the extent of it until it was already underway.

At the edge of one of Diane's gardens, dead and brown for the winter, she scooped up a few small rocks. She took one in her left hand and launched it at the second window from the left. It clattered on the pane. She waited. After a minute she aimed another stone. As soon as it left her hand, the window flew open. The rock went in— and then sailed back out. It barely missed her head. A face appeared in the dark opening.

"Front of the house, idiot," Sage whispered down at her.

She squeezed the remaining rocks in her hand, ready to ricochet them off Sage's skull.

"Better not," Markus breathed into her neck.

She jumped, but then turned to him in relief.

"Why not?"

"He'll just wait until they're out of your hands and then slam the window closed. Then somebody will have to explain to my parents how their window got broken and to Vivian how his neck got broken."

"Mmm, true. Much easier for me just to do this." Even she heard the satisfying thud that meant Sage had been rendered temporarily knocked out by her projection.

Markus cringed. "Isn't that risky the night before our mating ceremony? He's likely to get revenge sooner rather than later, and he's unlikely to give a damn who's around to witness it."

She shrugged. "Not my biggest concern right now. Can we walk?"

"Sure." Markus instinctively reached for the hand closest to him, but caught himself. He flashed to Alex's other side so they could hold each other's right hands.

"Good move. I don't want to add any more blood or ooze to your sweatshirt." This wasn't exactly how she planned on broaching this subject.

"The girls explained to you?"

"Sarah did. Markus, thank you, for doing all this just to mate me." She conveyed her sincerity through a soft influence. She was miffed when he laughed.

"*Just* to mate you? You make it sound like I played human piñata for a Cracker Jack prize. Mating you tomorrow is worth a whole lot more pain than Rocky managed to inflict. Though get him pissed enough and the kid's got a solid swing—and more pent up aggression toward me than I realized." He shrugged his shoulders and winced. Seeing her flinch at his show of pain, he rubbed the back of her hand with his thumb. "Alex, I should be thanking you. You're the one who agreed to all these crazy traditions, which no one even had the courtesy to warn you about before tonight." He grinned down guiltily searching for forgiveness. She had more than that to offer but wasn't sure he wanted all the extras.

"There hasn't really been time," she said offering them both a reason.

"That's a poor excuse," he said.

"Yeah, I know, and it's only half true anyway. But I'm still hoping you'll forgive me for not telling you right away."

"You mean what you were hiding from me and Darian earlier tonight?"

She heard him straining to keep his voice even. She squeezed his hand. "Darian wasn't the only one who figured it out, I guess."

He nodded and waited for her to continue.

"The last line of the prophecy. It doesn't end with 'Victory for all.' It ends with predicting my death once the conflict between the covens is over."

Markus remained silent while he took this in. "Are you sure?" he finally asked.

"I'm sure what the line says: 'her demise.' But what else it could mean, I don't know. Darian claims all the prophecies predict the death of someone important in the coven so that they're taken seriously. Only half, he claims, actually proved true. Sage thinks even those that came true were because the one being prophesied about followed the path the prophecy lay out—and therefore made it true. Me? I don't know what I believe, except that I'm going to do everything I can to assure it doesn't end that way. Not for a very, very long time."

Markus nodded. He let go of her hand, but it didn't help. She still sensed all he was feeling.

"Are you scared?" he asked.

She stepped closer and rested her hands on his hips. "A little. A lot. Mostly of losing you, of hurting you."

His hands remained at his sides. "And that's why you didn't tell me?"

"I know you're angry. And I understand that. I chose to keep this from you even after you told me how much it hurt you when I did it last time. I was weighing the greater pain. When I first heard it, the prophecy seemed worse. Be honest, Markus. If I wasn't the coven's Seer, if I didn't have to know about some of the greatest dangers out there in order to do my job, would you choose to tell me about them?"

Markus rested his hands on her shoulders. His face softened. "If you know I'm angry, you also know how hard I'm trying not to be. And you also probably sense that I understand your fears, because I share them."

She chuckled. "I do now. Sometimes when I'm babbling I manage to miss things. Speaking of which, the first layer of guilt is linked to your anger. What's the second one all about?"

Markus stammered. Her suspicion piqued.

"Spill."

"I wasn't supposed to tell you," he began. "But clearly you weren't exaggerating earlier this evening when you said your gift was intensified."

"Did you think I was?"

"No. It's just given me a stronger reason to disobey the Regan." He didn't defy Darian often. That he was willing to this night had her on edge. She urged him on. "Our intimate mating ceremony . . . it's not going to be so small or intimate anymore. Darian invited a few more coven members since he wasn't able to present you the night of the ball."

Some of the comments Darian and Markus had exchanged earlier were starting to make sense. Markus began rubbing her shoulders in an attempt to relax her instantly tense muscles.

"Define a few."

"Well, most of the warriors, for starters. That's why you couldn't attend tonight's meeting. They're traditionally part of important ceremonies, but some weren't warriors when Darian and Sarah mated, so they needed a crash course."

"The last time they were a part of a mating ceremony was Darian's?"

"I'm lead warrior, Babe. It's an honor. I couldn't really say no to my own males."

She nodded. This wasn't so bad; she liked most of her fellow warriors. A few even liked her. "Who else?"

"You know . . . important coven members."

"The Elders." She should have expected as much.

"And their mates."

"The rest of the first families?"

"Not all of them."

"How many total, Markus?" Her patience waned as her fear waxed.

"You promise not to leave me at the alter?" He was only partially kidding.

"I promise. I can't guarantee I won't leave Darian's unconscious ass alone at the alter as soon as the ceremony's over, though."

"That would be a bad idea in front of two hundred coven members, half of whom aren't too thrilled Darian's letting me mate you to begin with."

"Two hundred!"

"Shh, everyone else went to bed early. You'll wake them. I'd like a few tension free moments together before we get called back to our respective holding pens."

Alex laughed at his word choice and shared his desire. The plans for the next night were set. There was nothing she could do to change them now.

"He really does always get what he wants, huh?"

"One way or another." Markus nodded.

"It's aggravating," Alex said stepping even closer to him.

"You get used to it after . . . an eternity?" He lifted her left hand and interlocked their fingers so both their bandaged wrists lightly touched. Sarah had explained how Markus had removed his original scar from his first mating. This was the second time he'd be promising someone eternity. She squeezed his hand hoping it'd be the last.

"I hope it didn't hurt too badly. With a little extra essence it'll be gone in no time." He kissed her neck, a little overly eager to work on that essence exchange.

"I hope not. If I had to suffer through that much pain, it better last."

Markus's playful attitude turned icy. He stripped off her bandage before she could pull away. "I told them to do it lightly. Cormelia—"

"Would have denied me the chance—as asked. Vivian, thankfully, gave me the choice. I asked that it be permanent. Insisted, actually."

"That wasn't supposed to be an option. This looks awful."

Alex jerked back her wrist. She had done this for him, and all he could say was that it disgusted him to look at it? "I didn't think it was meant to be a fashion statement."

"Alex. No. I didn't mean that." He tried to pull her back into his embrace. "I meant it looks painful. I appreciate your wanting to do this for me, for us, but you don't heal the way we do. I didn't want you to suffer another injury you'll need to recover from."

Sensing he was genuine, she gave in. She let him pull her against him as he rewrapped the wound.

"You're just afraid it'll impede your honeymoon plans." She pouted. Markus loved that she didn't know where they were going, because it drove her nuts. Her only clue was it was some place Sage thought she'd appreciate. This wasn't comforting.

"Hmm. It might," he said wagging his brows. He was walking backwards, pulling her toward the dunes leading to the ocean. "We've got almost an hour before dawn. Maybe we should go see."

"Or maybe you could pretend to have an ounce of propriety and escort your female back to where she belongs. Then return to the house—before your mother has an absolute conniption." The elder Markus slammed the front door before Alex had even turned around to face him. Which was fine; the skin on her cheeks burned nearly as hot as her wrist.

Markus rolled his eyes in the direction of the house.

"So I guess this is good day," she said.

"I'll walk you back."

"It's okay. Go calm your mother, although I don't sense she's nearly as bothered as your dad. Then you might want to make sure I didn't do any long-term damage to Sage. I've never kept someone that confused for so long."

Markus's jaw dropped. "You can do that? For that long?"

"Apparently I can now. No need to tell him how long it was, though, okay?"

Markus laughed and leaned down to kiss her long and hard. Finally pulling away, he locked his gaze with hers, his green eyes twinkling. "I can not wait to mate you tomorrow."

CHAPTER 6

Legs shaking, Alex squeezed Rocky's right arm for support, wrinkling his neatly pressed tunic with her sweaty palms. He was immensely proud to be wearing the traditional ceremonial dress of a warrior for the first time. Not that he told her. He was a guy, after all. But when he knocked on the door of the third floor room of the coven's club where the females had been helping Alex dress, it was evident. The white tunic shirt had been ironed and starched. The black pants had a crisp crease up the center. His silver dagger didn't have a fingerprint on it where it hung perfectly straight from a black leather belt on his left side.

And here she was feeling like she could vomit on the both of them at any second.

As they turned the final corner entering the hall that led to the grand lobby where the ceremony was to be held, he tried to distract her. "Having a hard time in those heels, huh?"

"The heels I can handle. The two hundred plus vampires about to watch me attempt to walk in them are my bigger concern."

"Ah, come on. There were more there the night of the ball and you did okay."

She knew she'd need to fill Rocky in later about what had happened that night, but this wasn't the place. "There's a lot to be said for fear induced adrenaline," she mumbled instead as they reached the doors.

Rocky chuckled. "Well, then, you'll be fine," he whispered knowing there were guests close enough on the other side to overhear. "Just keep in mind at least half the room only likes you a smidge more than the Vengatti do."

She squeezed harder. "Not helping, Rocky."

He shrugged. Before he could reply further, the hall grew quiet; the crowd on the other side of the door hushed. Alex faintly heard music playing. The hymn had clearly crescendoed and was coming to an end.

"That's our cue," he said. His hand hadn't reached the handle before she bolted through the door to his right, her hand over her mouth.

She had just flushed and stood up when she heard a commotion outside the stall.

"Give her a minute. You can't just barge in on her."

"Actually, I can. She's in the males' bathroom."

Alex felt the heat creep up her pasty cheeks. In her haste she didn't waste time to read signs. Leave it to Sage to point this out—rather loudly.

She looked down at her dress, desperately hoping the white wrap Cormelia had expertly tied together with a single length of silver ribbon was still clean and securely in place. Miraculously, it was spotless and as elegant as it was before hanging her head over a toilet. She blotted her face with some bath tissue and took a steadying breath before opening the door.

Sage was leaning on the sink across from her smirking. Rocky stood beside him, arms crossed.

"Could you move, please," she croaked, her throat sore from being sick.

"I could move faster if it weren't for this headache. I slammed my head onto the floor at some point last night, Seer. Remember? No matter; I've got a bottle of aspirin here somewhere." He patted his pockets, finally pulling out what Alex needed. She grabbed for it, but he held it above her reach. "I didn't hear the magic words," he taunted.

"Please. Thank you. I'm sorry. You're wonderful. Now give me the friggin' pills!"

Rocky shushed her pointing to the ajar door, but Sage chuckled and handed her the plastic bottle. Alex pried off the childproof cap and shook three extra strength aspirins into her palm. Staying sane and alert meant blocking at least some of what she was sensing, and that would lead to a serious headache in a short span of time. She popped all three pills in her mouth before realizing she had nothing to swallow them with.

Sage shoved something in her hands and she gratefully swilled it—then choked, sputtered, and coughed as he took it back, downed a swig himself, and returned it to his back pocket, all while wearing a shit-eating grin.

"Enough, Sage." Rocky pointed to the door. "Get out."

"Better to smell of fine Irish whiskey than vomit. Unless, of course, Darian smells it and realizes I've been raiding his stash again. Speaking of the Regan, your sense might have missed it among the crowd of other impatient people waiting for you, but mine's working just fine. He wants me to tell you 'Now, Alex.'" Sage disappeared, leaving the door into the hall swinging behind him. He was likely already back at the Regan's side ready to translate the Latin ceremony into English for those, like her, who needed it.

But she figured he was in her head anyway. "Tell the Regan to keep his fangs in. I'm—"

Rocky clamped his hand over her mouth. She hadn't exactly meant to say it aloud or with quite so much volume. She felt a wave of anger that wasn't Sage's.

"When I agreed to keep you alive, I kind of hoped it meant I'd get to fend off some Vengatti, not our own Regan," Rocky hissed in her ear as he took his hand away. Alex managed a watery smile. She couldn't have been more happy with Markus's choice of Rocky as both her commendator and her partner. But she had to admit, she wasn't making this first role as easy as it seemed. Rocky rolled his eyes. "Just look extra nervous and contrite. And a stumble for good measure couldn't hurt."

She raised her brows as he began to open the door.

"Trust me. I'll catch you." With that he swung open the door.

When Alex first agreed to mate Markus, she had pictured a small ceremony with him in Sarah's living room with their housemates as the only witnesses. When she learned it was being moved to the club, she envisioned the lounge where Sage had subjected her to numerous torturous midnight lunches to accustom her to larger crowds after her gift matured, with perhaps a few of Markus's closest warriors as added guests.

What sprawled before her, now, was the dream of every little girl who hoped for a fairytale wedding with all the frills. Alex had never understood those girls.

Until tonight.

The wall-to-wall marble floors of the spacious room were polished to a glassy sheen. The wood paneling on the walls was lit softly tonight, the elegant sconces dimmed warmly, while the drops of the glittering chandelier cast prisms that danced across the high ceiling. Directly below that was a wooden structure that had been erected especially for this night, a two and a half foot platform on which the ceremony would be performed. Surrounding this stage was a semi-circle of chairs in perfect rows. Every one seemed filled, but Alex couldn't be sure; she couldn't see over or past what lay directly before her.

Lining a path to the altar were the two-dozen other warriors, half on each side, evenly spaced from where she and Rocky stood to where Sage, Darian, Cormelia, and Markus awaited. Each imposing male wore the same black and white regalia as Rocky and Markus, with one exception. The honor guard were all armed with rapiers, the same as Darian had worn to preside over her father's returning ceremony. Each held the thin gleaming blade before him in both hands, blocking the aisle. Rocky stepped forward, regardless, dragging her with him. When the two were practically touching the first pair of blades, the line fell into motion in pristine precision. Pair by pair the warriors sliced the blades through the air until the tip hovered just over the floor. Then in a second sweeping motion each swung it to the side with one hand, pointing the way down the aisle. As they fell to their knees, they brought their free hands, in fists, to their hearts.

No one needed to explain this tradition. The warriors were pledging to their leader and his mate their allegiance and protection. Some deep part of her recognized her desire to stop and thank each one of her new brothers along the way, but Rocky led her forward with purpose, and the rest of her remained too stunned to do anything more than blindly follow.

It wasn't until they reached the final pair that Alex looked up. Her eyes met Markus's immediately. His broad smile mirrored what her own heart felt. Eager to have her hand in his, she stepped ahead of Rocky, misjudged the stairs in her heels, and fell forward. She caught herself with her hands on the top stair. Only then Rocky's hands grasped her bare arms—a bit too late to be considered 'catching her.' She shot him an accusatory glare as he steadied her on the platform.

He shrugged. "It worked," he mouthed before turning to bow to the Regan and then to Markus. Alex copied him, before remembering she was supposed to curtsy. Vaguely aware the other guests and warriors were tittering, she looked up at Darian who was pitifully repressing a grin. His anger was gone. Rocky had been right. Alone, puking, cursing, and sassing the Regan seemed crass at best. Reframed, a weak stomach, wobbly knees, and a bit of humiliation could be downright endearing. If that was all Darian wanted from her this evening, perhaps letting him get his way wouldn't be so bad. And if in the end she were mated to Markus for eternity, she'd say she got the better end of the deal by far.

Darian cleared his throat to quell the noise of the crowd and began the ceremony. He paused every few sentences for Sage to translate for Alex, her mother, and any other coven members present who were not fluent in Latin. Alex tried to focus on the words, but emotions, her own mostly, kept getting in the way. It was too soon after her father's returning ceremony not to be reminded of the last time she heard Darian and Sage speaking in that pattern.

Hoping contact would help her concentrate, she reached out to take Markus's hand. He squeezed it gently, focusing his joy and serenity. Her sense of him began to ease her nerves, but he released her hand too soon.

"Not yet," he mouthed when she met his eyes.

She nodded and tried in vain to refocus. A moment later Markus was turned to face her with Cormelia at his side. Cormelia's right hand was placed gently behind Markus's left, which was raised like he was being asked to take an oath. Sage heard this observation in Alex's head and rolled his eyes. Right, their vows, an oath, same idea.

"Yes, I do," Cormelia answered to some question Alex hadn't heard, or registered, at any rate.

Suddenly Alex felt Rocky grabbing for her wrist and gently tugging her into place, a mirror image of Markus and Cormelia. This time she listened for Sage's translation. Instead, Darian addressed the crowd in English.

"Cormelia has shown Markus loyalty and companionship for . . . a very long time," he began. If he was editing for her mother's sake, Alex thought he could have been a bit subtler. "She was an obvious choice. It might seem Markus would have had a harder time choosing a commendator for Alex, since she has been with us such a short time. But in that time there has been one other male who has shown her acceptance, friendship, protection, and more patience and understanding than I can fathom." Darian paused to smile at Alex and Rocky while the guests chuckled. She returned the expression genuinely. She realized what Darian was doing. This larger ceremony may have been planned so he could get his way and introduce her to the coven. But he also seized the opportunity it provided to reintroduce Rocky as a coven member with renewed status.

"As our newest warrior, Rocky has already accepted the role of Alex's guardian, a job I wish him the best of luck with."

Alex had only been informed of this hours ago herself on the way from her mother's to the club. She was thrilled. Though as Rocky replied, she wondered if having an eager-to-please rookie as her guardian might be less desirable than she originally assumed.

"I like a challenge, Regan."

Darian waited until the renewed round of laughter, particularly from the warriors, died down before continuing in a more serious tone. "Markus also ask that you accept the added responsibility of serving as Alex's warrior should there come a time when he cannot. Do you accept?"

"I do, Regan."

Darian nodded, then turned to Alex and Markus. "Join hands and repeat the pledge to one another after me—in English, if you must." He muttered the last to her, but she was too eager to continue to sneer at him.

Rocky and Cormelia dropped their hands as soon as Alex and Markus's open palms touched. They stepped back as Darian began reciting. With Markus's hand in hers the rest of the room fell away. This was what the night was about, the two of them making formal the vows they had informally given to each other a hundred times in a hundred different ways.

She wasn't surprised when Markus's voice spoke the vows in English in unison with hers, his loud and clear, hers shaky and hoarse.

"Before our friends, family, coven, and Creator, I pledge to you my body to protect and cherish, my blood to strengthen and nourish, and my spirit to comfort and guide. These I give willingly, completely, and unconditionally, from now until eternity.”

Markus pressed his hand hard into hers as if he wanted to leave a lasting imprint before he had to turn away. He faced the Regan who had stepped forward on the final line. She saw the small ceremonial dagger he held in his right hand and followed Markus's lead offering her left palm to him. With a gentle push Darian pierced Markus's hand, then Alex's, and finally his own. Alex hadn't expected this final gesture, but was surprised when the other guests gasped.

“If any couple deserves the blessings of the Creator, bestowed upon them through the bloodline of a Regan, it's you two,” he said quietly. He held her hand carefully as he squeezed his fist over it, mixing a few drops of his own blood with hers. He repeated the gesture with Markus before licking closed his wound and nodding to them to perform the essence exchange, the final act of the formal mating ceremony.

“Darian, I—” Markus couldn't manage more, so she finished for him.

“Thank you.”

Markus recovered and lifted his palm towards her lips. She carefully followed suit, closing her eyes as his blood touched her tongue. As one they began to take in each other's essence, simultaneously experiencing and exchanging their love for one another. Alex was reminded they had an audience only when Markus tugged his hand away to lick closed the cut on his palm, something he had apparently done to her hand moments earlier. He was grinning as he used his other thumb to wipe what she guessed was a smear of blood from her chin.

One of the warriors let out a hoot. A half a dozen others followed. Darian finally silenced them with a glare after one distinctly called out ‘atta girl.’

After a few final words from Darian and a purposely PG kiss, the guests erupted in applause. The worst of it, and the best of it, was over. She didn't blush when Markus swept her down the stairs so she wouldn't trip, or when one of the warriors, who were once again creating an honor guard, blew her a kiss and winked lasciviously at her as she passed. Whatever else the night brought, she'd have Markus by her side.

That bubble was quickly burst. Her first dance with Markus ended before her excitement had settled enough for her to enjoy it. They hadn't exchanged more than a few words; they hadn't needed to. Their collective joy flowed freely between them.

But it wasn't joy she felt as the song ended and he placed her hand in his father's. The elder Markus appeared amused by her stuttering as his son left her alone with him on the dance floor. Alex felt only slightly better when Markus returned with her mother as the music started.

"Is this tradition?" Alex asked as the elder Markus began leading her around the dance area. His moves were stiff, not from age, she presumed, but from centuries of soldiering.

"Yours, from what I was told," her father-in-law answered. Her confusion must have been evident. "Your mother told my mate it was tradition for human brides to dance with their fathers. She worried ignoring his recent return would only emphasize his absence."

"Oh. Right." She had thrown herself into the vampire's traditions as a means of dealing with her grief. But it had been years since she'd held out hope of having her father walk her down the aisle or dance with her to some sappy song that would make them both cry. Even on a good day after his gift had ruined him, those actions would have been too demanding. She'd mourned the loss of those fantasies long ago. The lump she swallowed now was just a memory of that pain.

"I don't presume to replace him tonight, Alex, but you are family now. When Darian asked, I didn't hesitate to accept." He looked down at her with the same bright green eyes he shared with his son. With her small hand in his large rough one, he was telling her he accepted her and her relationship with Markus.

She nodded. Her eyes scanned the room for Darian. It startled her to think he had discussed this with her mother. The elder Markus followed her gaze.

"You don't give him enough credit."

She stumbled as she looked back up at him. He deftly caught her and continued across the slippery marble.

"You're wrong. My independence causes us to butt heads far too often, I suppose, but I respect him—deeply."

"I don't doubt that," Markus replied. "Although learning what that looks and sounds like in the coven would be a wise move on your part." Alex maintained eye contact despite her desire to look away from his reprimand. "I was more referring to the fact that you don't seem to grasp just how much he respects and cares for you in return. Do you have any idea the significance of the blessing he bestowed upon you and my son tonight?"

"No. I guess not," she answered honestly, though it cost her something to admit it.

"No, you couldn't. I doubt anyone under Darian's age could, because they wouldn't have been around the last time such a blessing was given—to the Regan and his new mate on their mating day. You made it quite clear you weren't happy with him planning all this without informing you, when you should have been thanking him. Such ceremonies, such blessings, are rare, not to mention usually reserved for the coven's heir. He took a risk so openly supporting your union; I hope you understand the responsibility that comes with that."

She might have argued that the responsibility now owed to Darian was likely the exact reason the Regan had bestowed such a blessing. But that would have been a lie. At least in the moment, Darian had wanted nothing more than to see his best friend happily mated once more.

She was still silent and scarlet when the elder Markus handed her to her next partner. Rocky, either having overheard some of what passed between her and her father-in-law or just seeing it in her expression, wasted no time in trying to cheer her up.

"So, Mrs. Markus, how does it feel to be living the dream of thousands of girls who grew up in the nineties?"

"Huh?"

"Oh, come on, you know vampires take their father's first name as their family name. It didn't occur to you until now that you just married Marky Mark in a ceremony officiated by Vanilla Ice?" he said referring to Sage's marked brow that signified his gift as a Knower and strongly resembled the shaved brow of the one-hit wonder from her childhood.

She was glad Rocky was as good a dancer as he claimed, because she spent the rest of the song laughing, first at his comment, than at the glacial stares they were getting from both Sage and Markus. When the song finally ended, though, she was eager to return to Markus's waiting embrace.

"Any chance we can start the honeymoon now?" she whispered as he pulled her close to kiss her again.

"Not quite yet," Markus chuckled. "You've got one more dance to go. This is your presentation, too, remember?"

How could she forget? Markus took her by the hand and led her to the table where Sarah sat with Darian, her parents, Ardellus, and an older female Alex didn't know, but was presumably the elder Regan's feeding partner.

Sarah stood and took Darian's hand as they came around the table to stand before the newly mated couple. Markus bowed to both of them. Alex remembered this time just to curtsy. Sarah held out Darian's hand and spoke loudly enough to be heard over the murmuring crowd.

"As our newest member through mating, we feel it fitting Alex be presented tonight also as our Seer and a protected, trusted, and loyal servant to this coven. Though, we did see fit to make a slight alteration to the traditional dance. Darian," she nodded to him, as the guests smiled, some even sincerely.

Since Alex was the first female Seer, it'd be the Regan himself, and not his mate, with whom Alex would dance. He took her hand from Markus's and led her back to the center of the floor. He gave her a quick nod before grabbing her waist and starting in on a quick waltz. Alex was uncomfortably aware that there was more attention on her and Darian than there had been during any other dance. The reactions to seeing the Regan making physical contact with a Seer were mixed.

Darian raised a brow quizzically as she scowled.

"You ought to be flattered by how protective of you they are," she whispered in answer to his unspoken question.

"Perhaps you ought to be flattered by how much they respect the power of your gift," he returned with a grin.

"You'd think after the ball they'd have figured out I don't need physical contact to knock them on their asses."

"Let's not remind them of that, shall we?" His tone was sharp as he spun her so fast it took a moment for her vision to clear. She considered reminding him she couldn't walk, never mind dance, at vampire speed, but caught herself. There was something else that needed to be said.

"Darian, I wanted to thank you . . . for everything tonight. My mother being allowed, the honor guard, giving Markus and me your essence—"

"Don't forget failing to inform you of the two hundred extra guests you'd be sensing."

She laughed. "I didn't forget. I just have no intention of thanking you for it until I'm sure I can make it through the night without vomiting on one of them."

Darian leaned in and dropped his voice. "Promise to give me a heads up, and I'll point you in the right direction."

"No need. Sage is easy to spot even in a crowd of other super-sized vamps."

"Your sense must be overwhelming you if you think Sage is your biggest problem here tonight," he said as the song came to an end. He lightly kissed her hand as the room erupted in polite applause.

She searched the room for Markus as soon as Darian released her hand. "I don't know about that," she said more to herself than the Regan.

Sage had Markus by the scruff of his neck, leading him to the bar where the majority of the warriors were waiting, shots in hand. The Knower turned and blew her a kiss that hit her with a wave of knavish pleasure. She considered flattening him from across the room, but Darian intervened.

"Later, perhaps. For now, I'd like to introduce you to a few other coven members."

"The same members you just implied would rather stick a finger in an electrical outlet than shake my hand?" she asked after breaking her gaze away from Sage, who was already pressing the third or fourth drink into Markus's palm.

"You've never heard the expression 'know your enemy'?"

"As they're my own coven members, I think the more modern term would be frenemy."

Darian didn't even try to comprehend. He started across the floor expecting her to follow.

"Darian, wait." She wobbled in her heels as fast as she could to catch up. His furrowed brow made clear what her garbled sense struggled to decipher. "Oh, right. Sorry, Regan." Few coven members called Darian by his first name outside the house. "I was just wondering if you could take my arm." She hated to ask, but knew the physical contact would help make the next few hours bearable. If she couldn't be holding Markus's hand, Darian's arm would have to suffice. "Please."

He seemed to understand why she was asking. He nodded and offered her his left arm. She clutched it firmly and allowed her sense of him to drown out some of the rest.

"Ready?" he asked when she had steadied herself.

"Smile and nod, right?"

Darian grimaced as she repeated the plan they had originally agreed on for the ball. Apparently inciting memories of the recent disaster wasn't what the Regan wanted.

What felt like an eternity later, he steered her towards yet another table of guests. She gazed longingly back at Markus and grit her teeth as she watched Sage fill his glass again with what appeared to be a never-ending supply of whiskey. Darian chuckled as she squeezed his arm.

"I thought he was looking forward to getting rid of me for a week? Markus will be lucky if he can walk, never mind drive us anywhere tonight."

"He never planned to. You're leaving tomorrow at sunset. Today you're staying here, as are many of the guests, including Sage. I think you can surmise what the Knower's plan is," Darian said with a grin.

She would have commented that it would take a lot more than whiskey to keep either of them from making love on their mating night, but Darian stepped closer to the table he had been approaching and not so lightly squeezed her hand, a reminder that even a muttered comment would be overheard. Alex reapplied her vapid smile as the Regan began another round of introductions to another group of vamps who wouldn't shake her hand and in turn whose names she didn't even bother to listen to, never mind try to learn.

She was startled when a familiar name caught her attention, shocked when the older vampire extended his palm to her.

"The elder Abram, of course, you also remember meeting," Darian had been saying.

"Oh, yes." She released her grip on him to shake the gentleman's hand. A second glance around the table and she realized she should have remembered most of these names and faces. It was filled with the heads of the first families whom she had met at the disastrous Elder Council meeting that fall. Perhaps her mind had purposely blocked out the powerful males who had spent the final hour of the meeting glaring at her and Rocky after being assured both would be 'taken care of' by the Regan for their transgressions. Alex involuntarily squirmed feeling the ghosts of Darian's blows to her back.

The Regan plowed on as if he hadn't noticed. "I was planning to get in touch later this week, Abram, on Alex's behalf." She looked at him curiously, at which he rolled his eyes, annoyed with her lack of a poker face. "Abram is Christo's father, Rick's grandfather. As head of the family, it is his permission you require to read their family's histories of past Seers."

Her head spun back to the Elder. "You're Rick's grandfather? That explains the questions the night you met me." She remembered Abram as being more curious and less hostile than the others. "You treated the last Seer, in Ireland, right?"

Abram nodded. "For a short time. I was still young when he . . . passed."

"Was killed," Alex corrected. Darian nudged her foot. She wasn't supposed to have read the coven's histories—even the sections about her ancestors. "It was in the Seer's histories my father left me. No Seer has ever just 'passed.'" She thought she'd done an adequate job of covering, but from what she sensed from Darian, he liked her sharing this information even less. She quickly realized why as a dozen faces turned in her direction. Damn vampire hearing.

"I would have thought those had been lost after the coven left Ireland," Abram said.

"You knew they existed?" Darian asked.

"Of course. At the time I was even privy to a little of what they contained."

"I wish you would have shared that earlier, Abram."

"I wished you would have asked earlier, Regan," Abram replied unruffled. "I had expected a call shortly after I heard the first rumor you had discovered a Seer. I'm not sure I could have been any more help than your medic. The outcome of the maturity process is nearly impossible to predict or alter, but there might have been something in our records that could have made the transition a little easier."

Though her inclination was to tell Darian, "I told you so," she sensed that wasn't the wisest course of action. She figured her chances of reading those histories would diminish greatly if she couldn't keep the Regan's temper in check.

"It's over now. And Briant did great. He saved me and Darian that night."

"You saved me that night," Darian interrupted, loud enough for the nearest eavesdroppers to hear.

"Right, well, he sewed you up after the fact. Point is, Abram has information I'd like to read." She kept her voice down and turned to the Elder. "If you're willing to share it."

"Though it wasn't his place, especially without the Regan's permission, Rick was right in telling you that what we have we are willing to share. We wouldn't have such records had your family in the past not been willing to entrust their care to us."

Alex thought she sensed an edge to this comment, but she didn't particularly care whether it was aimed at her or Darian. She wanted more information; Abram had it.

"Thank you. And please pass along to Rick that I'm still willing to allow him to examine me and draw blood in exchange."

"What's he want with your blood?" Darian asked.

Abram groaned. "The boy's obsessed with some modern branch of medicine he studied at the human college."

"He majored in genetics," Alex explained. "He's trying to isolate the differences in DNA between the species. Since you all keep telling me I'm not quite human, I figured I'd give him the chance to scientifically confirm or deny it."

Darian looked to Abram who simply shrugged. "Fine, so long as he's discreet about his findings. I'll be in touch to work out the details."

Abram nodded. Alex tried to focus her sense. There was something Darian wasn't saying or something he didn't want Abram to say. Before she could confront him, though, he drew her attention to where it had wanted to be all night.

"You should probably go save your mate from drowning in alcohol. Sage is having too much fun, and at this point it's a waste of excellent whiskey."

She smirked. "Perhaps I should deal with both of them as they dealt with me, by disabling the enabler." Alex was remembering the night soon after her transition when she and Rocky had a few too many. She ended up sick as a dog; Rocky ended up with two broken ribs at Markus's hands for letting her get that way.

Sage hit the floor before Darian puzzled out her plan and grabbed her arm to stop her. More than a few heads turned, first to the Knower who was sprawled awkwardly on the marble, then to Alex as a number of them caught Darian's expression and pieced together the rest.

"Release him, now," he spat in her ear, "before the rest of the coven—and your mother—figure out what just happened."

She pulled back the emotion she'd slammed into Sage. With fewer injuries and plenty of essence, she was able to do it this time without the risk of it rebounding. There was a tense moment as Sage sat up rubbing his head while Darian still held her bicep in a death grip. Then Vivian, appearing at Alex's side from who knows where, took her other arm and led her from the Regan to where the warriors were gathered. She laughed and spoke to Alex in a volume meant to carry.

"I think that's our cue to cut off our males, huh? Welcome to being the protector of a warrior. Our biggest job is protecting them from themselves."

Alex laughed along with the other guests, hoping hers didn't seem too forced. By the time they had crossed the dance floor most everyone had resumed their previous conversations.

Sage scowled down at both of them, but it was Vivian he addressed first. "Nice save—at my expense."

"And Markus's, but you both deserved it. No harm done really." Vivian smiled up at him and put her small hands on his massive chest. Alex was amazed to feel his anger dissipate so easily with her touch.

"I'm still plenty pissed with you," he hissed hearing her thought.

"Feeling's mutual. But I'm guessing you got that." Rocky, not Sage, had admitted one night after training that being hit with anger or even fear was more painful than being knocked out by confusion. Knowledge she pocketed until tonight.

Markus slid off his stool, hoping to intervene before they could continue. "Hey, let's not—" It was all he got out before staggering sideways. Luckily Rocky was close by and grabbed him around the waist before he could topple over taking Alex with him.

Sage laughed as a few other warriors muttered "lightweight" or "cheap date" under their breath.

Alex crossed her arms over her chest as she addressed them. "Mission accomplished, boys. The boss is officially hammered. Now go slink back to your own mates before he and Sage aren't the only casualties of the evening."

One of the twins, Dalton or Donel, she could never tell them apart, turned to his brother and chuckled. "Want to guess who wears the pants in that mating?"

His brother laughed. "Maybe Markus would have better luck in those heels than Alex did."

Markus swallowed the last of the water Rocky had given him and slammed the glass down on the bar. "I'm drunk, not deaf, you two." He took an unsteady step toward them, hand on his dagger, and they scrambled, as did the rest of the warriors, save Sage and Rocky. Finally Markus turned to her apologetically.

"Don't bother," she said. "We're even. Only I can't carry you to bed the way you carried me."

"We got it," Rocky said grabbing Markus by one arm. He looked to Sage to grab the other. She knew Sage wanted to refuse, but one look from Vivian and he relented.

Alex watched warily as Markus's color went from flushed to pale to a very unhealthy yellowish hue as the elevator carried the four of them to the top floor.

Outside a pair of large, intricately carved wooden doors, Sage punched a six-digit code into the security panel on the wall. Alex heard the click and stood stunned as Sage and Rocky dragged Markus into the most luxurious room she had ever seen.

"We're staying here?" Though it was only technically one room, it had to be as big as an entire floor of the farmhouse. The sheen of the soft lighting hit the fur, silk, and crushed velvet covering various pieces of furniture throughout. Her body didn't know whether to squirm, blush, or giggle. It resembled what she pictured a high-end historical brothel to look like or perhaps the bedchambers of some flamboyant European king.

Sage snorted. "Perhaps in his youth, but I wouldn't try calling Darian flamboyant to his face these days, especially not after he and Sarah gave up their suite tonight so you newlyweds could . . . well, whatever. Such a wasted gift, Markus won't remember where he passed out come sunset."

Markus groaned in response.

"Oh, yes, he will," she said recovering. "Rocky, put him in the tub." Rocky looked unsure about following such an order. She reassured him. "He'll thank you later, trust me." She winked at him as he shook his head in disgust.

Sage laughed at the sound of Markus retching in the distance. "Good luck with all that." He was already heading to the hall when Rocky returned.

"He, ah, asked you to give him a minute," he said with a sympathetic grimace. "If you need me tonight, Ellie and I are staying in another guest suite down the hall, last door."

"Thanks, Rocky, but I doubt I'll need *you* on my mating night."

"I meant in case of an emergency."

"I know what you meant, otherwise I would have slapped you. But I'm in the club, with the lead warrior. I think we're good," she teased.

Rocky's reply was far graver. "You're in a building Leonce has already managed to infiltrate once before, with a warrior who currently wouldn't know his weapon from his woody."

Alex wasn't sure who jumped the most at the cracking sound. She and Rocky both turned to see the haft of one of Markus's knives sticking ominously from one of the bedposts, a direct line of nearly thirty feet from the bathroom. She tried not to laugh at her partner's suddenly pale complexion.

"Thanks for taking your responsibility so seriously, but like I said, we're good." She leaned forward and whispered in his ear. "I'll do my best to see he has more pleasant things to remember come tomorrow." She patted Rocky on the chest before turning him around, pushing him out into the hall, and closing the two doors behind him.

She kicked off her heels, finally, and padded across the dark wood floor to the door of the bathroom. Markus was propped against the marble wall of an oversized glass shower looking marginally better after purging his system. She sashayed across the cool tile and rested her hand on the shower knob.

"Is this payback?" He referred to the night shortly after her transition when he had dumped her fully dressed into a cold shower. She had needed the jolt, but it didn't mean she wasn't going to enjoy getting even.

"Oh, yeah." She turned the handle all the way to cold and then stepped out of range. Markus flinched but made no move to turn it off. She started for the door, calling over her shoulder, "When you're sober enough to appreciate it, I'll be more than glad to share a drink of a different sort."

Half an hour later the door to the bathroom opened. Markus stood stark naked, water still streaming down him in rivulets that followed the contours of his taut muscles. With the bright light from the bathroom shining behind him and a mischievous fire lighting up his already bright green eyes, he was as striking as any depiction of the god of war for which he was named.

"Am I allowed out now, or am I still being punished?" The clarity of his speech and the jauntiness of his stance proved he was sober. Other parts of him made it clear his mind was exactly where hers was.

She slid off the bed where she'd been waiting for him and rested one arm on the bedpost. "Oh, you can come out, but I can't promise I'm done punishing you."

Markus flashed in front of her causing her to gasp. He tugged playfully at the silver ribbon Cormelia had used to transform the simple square of white silk into an elegant gown.

"You're torturing me right now still wearing this dress."

"I was given strict orders by the females not to touch the ribbon. They said that was traditionally the male's job."

Markus's fangs snapped to full length. "They were right." He lifted her easily and laid her on the bed. Then he grazed his fangs along her neck, down the curve of her collarbone, following her cleavage to where the ribbon crisscrossed under her breasts. With a quick snap the ribbon released. The white cloth that had served so well as her mating night dress slid off her bare body becoming their mating day bed sheet.

CHAPTER 7

Markus awoke late afternoon with Alex's small warm body draped over his. Not wanting to waste an inch of the luxurious space Sarah and Darian had graciously lent them for the day, he and Alex had made love in more than a few places. It took him a moment to remember where they had finally collapsed in blissful exhaustion. Just as he recognized the feel of the down pillow beneath his head and realized they had made it back to the bed, he also recognized what had woken him from such a deep, contented sleep.

"Fine, I'll do it." Two male voices could be heard just outside the door. His males, his warriors, who had strict orders not to come to him for anything short of an absolute emergency until after he returned from his honeymoon. That's why he'd left Sage in charge. Of course that in itself could be seen as an emergency by some coven members. If the Knower had sent these warriors to him for some bullshit reason, he swore to the Creator he'd rip out one of Sage's fangs and use it to pierce his—

There was a soft knock on the door. "Markus, sorry to bother you, but—"

"You will be sorry," he muttered. He was carefully sliding out from Alex when her hand pressed into his chest.

"Don't." She sat up startled. She had obviously been awake long enough to sense him and his males. "Something's wrong."

He looked down at her and could see the worry in her face. It jolted him into action. He closed the bed curtain to give her privacy and flashed to the door.

Neither warrior seemed surprised to see him standing before them stark naked. They seemed more concerned about his reaction to their interruption.

"What happened?"

Liam, the younger but brasher of the two warriors before him, took the initiative. "A package was delivered at the main entrance about an hour ago."

"Bomb?"

"Ah, no. A mating gift."

Markus stepped forward ready to strangle the two of them when he felt the clashing sting of calm Alex hit him with. He was about to clarify that pledging his body to her hadn't meant he was volunteering to be a pincushion for her projections, but was staunched by the expression she wore as she came to stand by his side.

"Let them finish." She squeezed the sheet she had wrapped around her chest tighter as if to brace herself for what they were about to hear. Markus wanted desperately to know what she sensed from them, but then another speed bump arose.

Liam's jaw had dropped as he took in Alex's neckline. Not thinking either of them would be around coven members for a couple weeks, especially half-dressed, Markus hadn't worried about which vein he drew essence from. In the heat of the moment, he hadn't been particularly gentle or neat about it either. Both the bruises and the blood were still visible on her pale skin.

"It's necessary and legal," she said also seeing where his gaze had landed.

"And none of your business or any of the other warriors until I choose to explain it to them. Got it?" Markus demanded.

"Yeah, sure," Liam said snapping out of it.

"So?" Markus was losing patience.

"Right, the package. It was from the Vengatti. From Leonce."

Alex gasped. He shared the sentiment, but pressed for details. "How do you know?"

Tadas, Liam's partner produced a large envelope. "Besides the smell?" he asked handing it to Markus who crinkled his nose at the odor.

"It was addressed directly to Alex, and the return address—" Liam stopped. There was no need for him to continue. Markus growled as he read. There was no need to ask if the package contained anything dangerous. Leonce had intended for this package to pass all their security measures, which meant it contained dangers of a different sort. He handed it back to Tadas.

"Go wake the Regan. Give him this and ask him to meet me in his office as soon as he's dressed."

"Wait." Alex reached forward and grasped the corner of the envelope. "It was addressed to me. I want to see it."

"No," he said, "we need to make sure it's safe." He knew as soon as the words left his mouth it was a mistake.

"Bullshit. They wouldn't have brought it here without ensuring that." She glared at him. "We're mated now. How 'bout we both agree to cut the protective crap and stick to being honest with each other."

Her pain stabbed him. He wondered if she even knew she was hitting him with it. She had to know his desire to keep her from suffering more was the only reason he could ever lie to her. She'd done it herself more than once. But now wasn't the time for finger pointing.

"I'm sorry. You're right. At least allow me to get dressed so we can look at it together."

She nodded. Tadas reluctantly released the envelope, which Alex carried over to the settee in front of the fireplace.

Liam caught Markus's eye and shook his head emphatically. Alex sensed whatever warning he was trying to give and spun to glare at him. The warrior dropped his gaze to the floor.

"Tadas, the Regan. Liam, Sage, and Rocky, too, I suppose. Actually have Rocky meet me here." Both warriors nodded and took off down the hall. Markus closed the door and turned to face his mate.

"I really am—"

"I know," Alex cut him off. He bit his tongue to keep from saying more. Though her foul mood was contagious, he knew it sprung from the fear of what she'd find in the envelope she held in her shaking hands.

He went over to the far corner of the room where he knew Sage and Rocky had brought up the two suitcases that had been expertly packed by Sarah and Ellie for the honeymoon. He grabbed the first outfit he could find for each of them. Returning to where Alex sat, he handed her her pile.

"These aren't mine," she said looking at what he held out.

"Mating present from Ellie. She ordered them the night she bought your creator's day outfit."

"What'd she do, replace my whole wardrobe?" Alex snatched the pile with one hand and dropped it next to her.

He glanced at the overstuffed suitcase full of her new clothes. "Your winter wardrobe at least."

She made no reply, nor any move to dress, so he threw on his own clothes and sat beside her.

"It's been opened."

He nodded. "They would have had to open it to swab it for chemicals, poisons."

"Right." She slipped the inside package from the envelope. It appeared to be a wedding album. He could only imagine the images the bastard Leonce had filled it with.

Alex opened the cover. Just a short note was scrawled across the page.

'May your new union be as joyous as your parents' . . . '

She looked up at him dreading as he did what lay on the pages following. He reached over and squeezed her hand. Together they turned the page. It was cruel but better than he could have hoped for: a newspaper clipping announcing the marriage of Alex's parents was centered on an otherwise blank page. Where her father's face should have appeared in the photo next to her mother's, a hole had been burned.

The opposite page held another note in the same sickeningly neat cursive.

' . . . and may your young live as long and find as much success.'

Markus knew what to expect on the next two pages, but nothing could prepare a sister from seeing the images the enlarged photos captured. The first was the most gruesome: the burned corpse of Alex's oldest brother, Dave, still smoking in the remains of his burned out sedan. Markus saw Alex swallow hard to fight the bile that rose in her throat. The second image was likely equally as painful. It depicted a beaten and bloodied Levi, her middle brother, alive and huddled on the dirty floor of what appeared to be a cell, no doubt the room in which he spent the better part of a decade. But knowing Alex, what bothered her most as she shook beside him streaming tears, were the captions scribbled under each: *'Davidian, the foolish martyr'* and *'Leviathan, the cowardly traitor.'*

He tried to pull the book away, to keep her from turning another painful page.

"No, I need to see what I'm up against."

"You know what you're up against: a cruel vindictive bastard who knows causing you pain is the best chance he has of getting you to do something foolish."

"I couldn't care less how he defines foolish!" she raged, jabbing her finger at the word beneath her brother's burnt body.

He cringed. "I didn't mean—"

"Turn the page, Markus. Now."

He took a deep breath and flipped the page again. He expected some image meant to represent Alex, the last of the three Crocker children. Instead there was a photo, very recent by the quality and color, of an older couple beaten so severely there was little chance they had survived. He didn't understand, even after reading the caption.

'And finally, Alexandra, the bleeding heart savior—off to a promising start . . . '

At first Alex didn't seem to understand either, but after reading the caption again, she pulled the book closer, examining the male corpse whose face was distorted with swelling and encrusted in blood.

"Oh, Creator, no!" She dropped the book on the floor and sprinted to the bathroom. Markus made to follow, but Liam stepped in front. He and Rocky had entered the room just as Alex reacted to whatever it was she saw in the picture.

"There's one more page," his warrior whispered picking up the album and handing it to Markus. "One you need to see."

He nodded and flipped the final page. Beneath the phrase *'. . . but still so far to go'* were the pictures of every living being Alex loved, each with a target carefully drawn over the face. The oldest were an old black and white picture of Darian and Sarah, and a blurred photo of Markus talking with Sage. A colored snapshot of Rocky with Seamus and a few other young coven members outside a human club made Markus swear. He had hoped Rocky's youth would provide anonymity for him as he protected Alex, but, of course, Seamus's turning traitor had stripped Rocky of that advantage. It was the last image, though, that Liam pointed at, a picture of Alex's mother. Ellen was leaving the downtown post office where Alex had convinced her to set up a p.o. box. It was time-stamped just two days ago.

Hearing the doorknob turn, feeling her fear and pain wash over him again, he ripped this last image from the page and jammed it into his back pocket. Rocky saw it and frowned, but remained silent.

"What's on the last page?" Alex returned to the main room looking clammy and pale. She clutched the sheet around her shoulders now with both hands. "There was another ellipsis. What did the final page say, Markus?" Her tone was stronger than her raspy voice. She had been physically ill after seeing the image Markus still didn't understand. He began to ask her about it, but she cut him off. "The last page. Then I'll explain."

He held open the final page. She nodded as if she expected as much.

"The male in that picture is the leader of the group of Vengatti I let escape the night of the ball, the ones being forced to fight. He was the one who asked me why I did it. He was the one I encouraged to seek our help. I'm guessing the female is his mate."

Markus glanced to Rocky and Liam to gage their reactions to this information. Rocky ground his teeth, but Markus knew he was more pissed about not being told or trusted to help her in the first place. Seeing Liam's look of disgust, though, he prepared to lay into them both.

"They did that to one of their own? And to a female, a protector?" Liam said before Markus had managed a word.

He smiled grimly at his warrior's reaction. His focus was where it should be. Still, Liam was known for shooting his mouth off.

"Another detail you'll both be discreet about until I can tell the others."

Rocky nodded.

Liam shrugged. "I doubt they'll be shocked to hear the Vengatti are sick fucks."

"I think you know that wasn't the detail I was referring to, and I'd appreciate it if you'd watch your crass comments around my mate."

Rocky snorted then tried to turn it into a cough. Even Alex managed a weak smile at the irony of scolding a warrior for using language she was far too often guilty of herself.

"My apologies," Liam managed without too much of a smirk.

"And for what it's worth, if Alex let them go for a reason, I trust it. If the Seer can't judge character, who in the coven can?"

Rocky looked at Liam with a raised brow. His expression mirrored what Markus was feeling. Liam never struck him as bright. In fact, he half expected him to flunk out during his initial probation year. He wondered if he'd misjudged him. He nodded and then dismissed him, telling him to find Tadas and stick close in case they were wanted for further questioning.

"Alex why don't you—" The look she gave him stopped him short. He changed course fast. "Take a quick shower and get dressed. Rocky will wait outside and bring you to Darian's office as soon as you're ready."

"Nice save." She leaned in to let him kiss her damp forehead. "How did you once describe me to Darian? Trainable? I guess you're trainable, too." She smiled, but it didn't fool him.

"Their deaths weren't your fault, Alex," he whispered as he held her face in his hands. "Your father, brothers, that couple—they died because of Leonce's choices, the Vengatti's choices, not yours." He felt her jaw muscles tighten as she fought back further tears.

"There's no target over my picture, Markus. If he can't have me, he wants me to suffer. He's going to keep at it until everyone I love is dead. My choice not to give up puts you all in danger."

"We all made that choice, most of us long before you were born. Your choice gives us a hope and chance of finally putting an end to this."

"Right, by fulfilling the prophecy. Not really the end I hoped for." She pulled away and disappeared again into the bathroom.

"Shit." He hadn't wanted to remind her of another terrifying discovery as a means of alleviating the pain of this new threat. Rocky looked askance of both their reactions. "She'll tell you if she wants you to know," Markus whispered. "But don't ask her, especially not today."

Rocky nodded. Markus knew he could trust him to obey, if not out of respect and obedience to him, then out of loyalty and friendship to Alex.

When Alex came through the double doors less than ten minutes later, Rocky didn't seemed surprised. He also didn't comment about her hair still dripping or her shoelaces being untied. And she doubted he even noticed she had dressed so quickly she managed to make even her new and properly fitting clothes look rumpled. All of those would have made for much too light and easy conversation. Instead he still seemed to be stuck on her last words. She knew he'd keep his promise to Markus, but he shouldn't have to. His picture was on the last page, too.

"Let's take the stairs. It'll give me time to explain."

"Let's take the elevator. It'll give you time to talk and tie your shoes, without the added risk of you falling and knocking out your front teeth."

She swatted at him, but couldn't help smiling. Rocky was good at breaking her mood swings. He continued that streak after she shared the prophecy with him on the way downstairs.

"I'm with Sage; it isn't worth the paper it's written on. Although, it is too bad it was written by a Seer rather than a Knower, like we first thought. It's one less thing we can rag on Sage for," he said as they turned the corner into the hall where Darian's main office was. She smiled, but it quickly faded.

Approaching Darian's door she realized she shouldn't have rushed. She wasn't ready to face the others, to listen to them strategically analyze the words and pictures that to her were so steeped in emotion. She reached out and touched Rocky's sleeve. He stopped and turned to her.

"Give me a minute?" she asked pointing to the row of benches that lined the opposite side of the wide hall. He nodded and sat next to where she slumped over, head in her hands. She actually grinned a few minutes later when he tried to comfort her by awkwardly patting her back. Ellie's influence, no doubt. She sat up ready to take the final steps towards the office when she heard Markus raise his voice.

"She needs to be told about us for her safety. Surely you can make an allowance under such circumstances."

"You know I can't," Darian snapped back.

"Fine. Then you can play dumb while Alex and I tell her."

Alex's confusion evaporated with the heat of her anger as the snippets of conversation began to come together.

"That picture was taken just days ago, Darian."

There were no recent pictures on the pages Alex had seen except those of the Vengatti couple. And only one important person's photo was missing from that final page.

She stormed into the office, strode directly to Markus, and slapped him across the face with all her strength. Despite his greater size and tolerance for pain, he flinched. She realized she likely hit him with her anger, too, and wasn't sorry.

"Six months and you never once lied to me before. You nearly left me when I did it to you. And then in the twelve hours since we've been mated, you've done it twice!"

"Alex, look, I—" Markus stammered. For once the others remained silent. "I was feeling the fear and pain you were projecting. I couldn't stand for anything to make it worse. I just reacted . . . stupidly. I'm sorry."

She nearly hit him again. "If I was projecting an ounce of my fear and pain on you, you wouldn't be standing. Did it occur to you those could have been your own emotions?"

"Yes," he answered quietly.

"But they weren't. Not all of them," Sage interrupted. She spun on him, but he didn't let her start. "Your essence carries some of your gift, Alex. Exchanging it with someone makes your connection to him stronger. And, occasionally, it can make your partner have a connection to you, one he or she couldn't normally ever have."

She was too dumbfounded to speak, but Markus wasn't.

"You mean *I* was sensing *her*? Like a Seer does?"

"It wears off quickly, and no matter how much essence you could take from her, you'll never be able to do more than sense her emotions," Sage explained.

"You say that like I'd try to take her power," Markus snapped.

"You wouldn't, but others would. I imagine that's why it's not mentioned in either of our histories. It'd be better if it never was." Sage looked to Darian who nodded in agreement. When he turned to her, she was surprised. Until then it hadn't occurred to her she was now responsible for not only protecting, but also maintaining her kind's written histories. She nodded as well.

Sage didn't want to discuss it further. Alex thought she knew why. Vivian. This must have been why he never mated her, why he was careful to only exchange essence with her as needed. He snarled at her line of thought and stepped toward her threateningly.

Darian cut them off. "Is whatever private argument you're having really what you want to focus on right now?"

"No. I want to see the picture."

The Regan hesitated only briefly before pushing it across the desk. She had heard enough not to be shocked by the date, but the time rattled her.

"It was daylight."

"Every coven keeps a few young warriors trained to manage daylight duties," Darian replied. His matter-of-fact tone boiled Alex's blood.

"Markus is right," she said sliding the picture back at the Regan. "I'm telling her, whether you grant your permission or not."

The sleep-deprived Regan leaned over his desk narrowing his bloodshot eyes. "Don't you think you've bent enough coven laws lately, Seer?"

"You're right." Markus came up behind her. She momentarily considered slapping the two of them until her mate continued. "So don't force our hands into bending or breaking another." On the word 'our' he rested his hands on her shoulders.

She looked back offering the forgiveness he sought through his reassuring touch.

"I can't give you permission to tell a human about our kind. And I can't pretend this conversation never happened." Darian was remorseful but bound by his office.

Markus thought for a moment before speaking. Trusting in his experience, Alex waited for him to take the lead.

"No more than I can sit idly by while the Vengatti place an immediate threat on an innocent human, whose current living situation endangers two prominent coven elders—my parents. All I'm asking is for you to let me do my job, as I see fit."

Darian sighed. "Fine. You have my permission, Warrior, to take the steps *you* deem necessary to protect the human and our coven members."

Alex threw her hands up. "What the hell's the difference between that and—"

Markus covered her mouth. "Plausible deniability," he whispered in her ear.

"You mean it'll be your ass on the line if anyone finds out."

He just shrugged.

She turned back to Darian. "What about the rest of you?" She pointed to the last page that lay facing up on the desk between them.

"Let's just clarify to prevent future disasters," Sage interrupted.

"Just because your mug isn't on that page doesn't mean that book isn't a direct threat to you, too, sweetheart."

She wanted to kick his shin, but Markus maintained a firm grasp on her shoulders.

"He's right, Alex. But to answer your question, we had already put together a plan for tightened security at the house, travelling, and for patrols. We'll follow through with those as scheduled."

"Good."

"They are good. And each measure has been meticulously thought out to maximize everyone's safety. There are plenty I don't particularly like, and even more you're likely to disapprove of," Darian addressed her. "But you will follow each to the letter without complaint, since nearly all of them only became necessary after your previous lapses of good judgment, and many of them have been designed specifically for your safety."

She felt like she had been slapped.

"That's not fair, Regan." Darian's eyes shot to Rocky who had spoken up quietly from his spot near the door. "It was Seamus who leaked information to Leonce, not Alex. And most of the security features Markus and I are installing at the house should have been in place for years—for your safety and Sarah's."

She heard Sage chuckle and could sense Markus's amusement as he still held her by the shoulders. Darian's scowl softened.

"Probably right, but it doesn't change the fact that had I given in to my initial desire to lock her in the basement back in July, I could have saved us all a lot of headaches."

She knew he was teasing, mostly, in order to lighten the atmosphere. She wanted him to know, though, that she took both his request and his concern seriously. She reached forward and flipped back two pages in the book to the picture of Levi, beaten and captive.

"If you were that kind of Regan, you wouldn't care whether or not I followed your safety measures, and I wouldn't care whether or not I survived to help you. But you're not, and I do."

Darian grinned. "Excellent. So do you want to hear the new rules before or after your honeymoon?"

CHAPTER 8

There had been no honeymoon. Both Alex and Markus had made it back to the room they shared after their mating ceremony and turned to the other to break the news.

"I don't think we should go."

They had smiled at their nearly simultaneous declarations, then spent the next hour lingering over passionate make-up sex, though without further feeding.

In the month since their mating they had seized every opportunity to make love. Leonce's mating gift had only intensified what both of them had felt since hearing the prophecy, a desperate desire not to waste one moment together. It had been an unnecessary reminder that even forever could be fleeting. Alex had been careful, though, to exchange essence with Markus only when she absolutely needed it. Being new to her gift, though, it was still more often than she would have liked. Markus caught glimpses of her emotions far too frequently, and many of those emotions hadn't exactly been light and pleasant.

It wasn't just the added security measures that bothered her. Alarms had been added to every egress of the farmhouse and the adjoining barn, each with their own code that needed to be punched in at something close to vampire speed, so that she was constantly setting them off. An additional warrior now stood guard on the property at all times, an additional sense for her to have to block or tolerate even in the middle of the day when she should have been able to get a little peace. The property itself now had a high, heavy security gate at the entrance and an electric fence had been installed just inside the natural tree borders. As complete overkill, motion detectors were set five feet inside the fence line, precariously close to her running route, in case a Vengatti vampire could manage to jump the twelve-foot wires without electrocuting himself. It was just a matter of time before she veered too far to the right and set that off, likely ending her running routine indefinitely. All in all, though, she could have dealt with the lack of privacy and feelings of confinement had they not been piled onto to the laundry list of other issues.

Her mother, as it turned out, was easier to deal with than Alex believed she'd be, but even that had a hitch or two. Markus had recruited his mother, Diane, who'd become Ellen's fast friend in the weeks since she'd moved into the cottage, to help him and Alex explain why she now needed a guard if she left the property. In an attempt to follow coven law, they told Ellen as little as possible, not even mentioning the word vampire. But she was sharp, and Alex knew she figured out more than she admitted. She had the feeling her mother wanted to pretend it all wasn't possible. Having been through the same discovery just months ago, Alex understood that reaction. Ellen was willing to agree to their safety measures, with no further questions—until she discovered it meant she could no longer work. It turned out Alex's proud streak wasn't entirely inherited from her father.

"That's all taken care of, Mrs. Crocker," Markus had explained. "An account's been set up for you to cover all your expenses."

"Please, Markus, Ellen is fine. What is not fine is your . . . friends paying for my living expenses."

"But it's our association to you that prevents you from safely working as you'd wish," Markus argued.

"These Vengatti, as you call them, have taken enough from me already. I won't let them dictate my life. I won't let them win that way." Ellen's eyes shone with tears, but she blinked them back as she pushed her chin forward.

Alex had shot Markus an I-told-you-so glance, which was no help at all. Luckily, Diane came to the rescue.

"Markus, I'm starting at the Regan's soon to make meals and help with the house work until things settle down and Sarah's . . . more up to it. It's quite a crowd to take care of; I could use an extra hand." Diane turned to Ellen. "The Regan pays well, as he should for good care, but it'll mean working nights with me."

Ellen knew Diane didn't need her help, but being offered a job and companionship from a friend was a far cry from being forced to accept charity and protection from strangers. She had agreed. Alex and Markus both sighed in relief. Not only was Ellen now spending her nights with plenty of protection, she would also be happier than if she were to sit at home and mourn. Crocker women don't handle sitting at home well, which was why it was the perfect punishment for Alex.

The first warrior meeting since the ball hadn't gone as horribly as Alex had feared and Darian had hoped, but its result was lingering. Markus called the meeting the night after they had returned from the club in order to address the latest threat and rearrange patrols to include the added security details for Ellen, Darian, and Sarah. He brought the album from Leonce along and allowed it to be passed among the warriors as he spoke. At first, Alex was upset with the decision, which he had not okayed with her ahead of time. She already felt many of her fellow warriors treated her position among them as a joke; to them she was a little girl trying to play with the big boys. Feeling their growing sympathy, compassion, and protectiveness as the book changed hands, her frustration increased. But as Markus brought their attention back to another matter of business for the night, she realized he had strategized deftly.

"I hadn't planned to do this to my mate so soon after our union, but it needs to be done, and as lead warrior it's my job to do it." Markus paused and glanced at Darian, who hadn't had the time to decide for himself exactly what to do about her actions at the ball. Markus had to inform the warriors about the conversation Alex had with the small group of Vengatti, though, in case one of them came forward for help. He hoped turning it into a public reprimand would appease the Regan's bloodlust. Darian nodded for his lead warrior to continue, but Alex knew he was making no promises this speech would suffice.

"While the blame for the ambush at the ball lay with the Vengatti and the traitor Seamus, there were some poor decisions made on the part of our newest trainee that in some ways exacerbated the situation." By then all eyes were on Alex whose cheeks burned like hot plates as Markus told them what she had so recently told him and Darian. Though their emotions varied greatly at different parts of the story, by the time Markus finished nearly all lingered somewhere between acceptance and sympathy. She could have lived without the second, knowing it stemmed from feelings of superiority, and was actually grateful when Markus ended with a stern threat with which they were all sure he'd follow through.

"We're a family working together within the larger coven for the good of all," he wrapped up. "No one of us has the right or the burden of acting on our own, even for the best intended reasons. The next one of you to play vigilante on my watch is going to suffer a hell of lot worse than a month of unpaid desk duty, rookie or not. Clear?"

Everyone one of his warriors, including a humbled Alex, had voiced their agreement. Only Darian remained truly aggravated with her as the meeting was adjourned and the other warriors filed out. Some stopped to welcome Rocky as the newest rookie. A few brave ones razzed Markus about his new eau-de-human scent, which he'd also had to explain. Not nearly enough shot Alex nasty glances as they left, something Darian felt he needed to make up for.

"You're not off the hook yet," he had growled as he swept up the stairs.

She expected as much, but five weeks of dragging out his decision just to keep her on tenterhooks or perhaps in hopes of keeping her indefinitely in line was maddening. Almost as maddening as spending a month on desk duty at the club in close vicinity to his taunting. He'd been spending more time at his office there since the disaster at the ball, hoping his more visible presence would quell some coven members' fears. Although he claimed he preferred to work in the more laidback environment of home, Alex thought he got an awful lot of enjoyment out of flaunting his authority at the club.

"If you've decided to take on the job of Sarah's secretary in addition to Markus's, you'll need to do more than sit on her couch and read romance novels," Darian started in on her the minute he walked into his mate's office.

"I'm not anybody's secretary," she snarled back. "And I'm researching my power, not reading romance novels, though I might as well be for all the use my gift is getting these days."

"Hmm, maybe another month or two of 'researching' and you'll finally learn to control your emotions." He sat on the edge of Sarah's desk and sneered at her. "You seem a little short-tempered lately."

"Must be contagious. How's that new guard working out?" If Alex's mood had soured over the last month, it was nothing in comparison to Darian's. He had nearly bitten the head off the last three guards who'd been assigned to him in the club. Markus was praying the fourth would last more than a week.

Darian began to stand up, undoubtedly to snap his fangs in her face, but Sarah stood and shoved his shoulder back down.

"Alex, why don't you take a walk. Go grab us a snack. I've got a craving—"

"For something with cheese?" she chuckled. Sarah had been on a cheese kick for weeks. It was one of many signs Alex had pieced together lately. Sarah simply smiled. Alex checked her phone yet again, hoping she had missed a message from Sage saying he needed her to help a victim or to convince some human that he didn't see what he really saw. The screen was blank. Figured, he'd called on her only twice in almost a month. "Yeah, okay." She grabbed her coat from the rack by the door and headed into the hall with a wave over her shoulder to Sarah, ignoring the Regan's growl. It was most likely aimed at his guard waiting just outside the door, anyway. She gave the male a sympathetic smile on her way past.

One good thing about working in the club every night was that her fellow coven members had become accustomed to her. She was no longer a curiosity. Her scent no longer startled everyone she passed. In turn, she had grown even more tolerant of their hyper-speed movements and the comments they whispered at volumes too soft for her to hear. She knew most of the guards, mostly retired warriors, and the regular visitors, mostly first families, by face if not by name. She waved to a few as she made her way to one of the side exits that would dump her out on the bitter cold streets half a block closer to where she thought the nearest convenience store was located.

She pulled the cords of her hood tighter as she blinked against the icy early February wind. Between the blowing snow and the slippery sidewalks, she hardly looked up as she bustled toward the glow of the twenty-four hour Quick Mart, but her sense told her the streets were quieter than normal. It felt good to be away from the club, where even on slow nights, the stinging buzz of all the vampires' emotions in the enormous building left her drained by night's end.

The one human clerk in the small convenience store hardly

registered with her sense. He must have thought she was high when, wearing a glazed grin, she threw two bags of cheese twists, a cheese stick, a bag of M&Ms, and a regular Coke on the counter.

Her serenity evaporated when her phone began buzzing in her pocket. She knew from the Eye of the Tiger ringtone that it was Rocky. She flipped it open as she handed the clerk her bankcard. Before she could spit out a greeting, he was barraging her with questions.

"Who are you with? What'd they need you for? How come you didn't text?"

She cringed. Aggravated with the Regan, restless with her 'job,' and lost in her thoughts about what she'd recently read in her histories, she had left the club alone—breaking half a dozen of the new rules set in place for her safety.

"Answer me, Alex." Responsibility had turned Rocky into a tyrant, and while Markus had grown fonder of him for it, she had not.

"Um, I kind of forgot." Silence, very likely fury-induced silence. "I left to get a few snacks for me and Sarah." A low growl. "If it's any consolation, I'm still in sight of the club." She looked out the window. For a human, this was a lie, but she guessed the guards patrolling the perimeter could see her . . . if they knew to look.

"Don't move. Liam's patrolling outside the club tonight; I texted him your position. He'll be there soon."

If she could have growled like a vampire, she would have. "Friggin boots," she grumbled scuffing the linoleum floor with the heel of the Docs Rocky had micro-chipped months ago for their plan to rescue Ellie. This initial move had given them the idea to put tracers in Alex's other shoes. It was the one security measure she had not been okay with, one she had fought vehemently against, arguing it implied a complete lack of trust on the part of her mate and best friend. One instant of thoughtlessness tonight would leave them both feeling smug and vindicated tomorrow—assuming their anger had worn off by then.

She took her items from the counter and stuffed them into her pockets. She headed onto the sidewalk out of view and earshot of the nosy clerk.

"Any chance we could not mention this to Markus?"

"No chance in hell—he already knows. I included him in the text to Liam, so Liam wouldn't think the order was optional."

"Super. Dinner ought to be fun with the whole house pissed at me."

"I'm not pissed, Alex. I'm worried. Of all places to wander off unprotected, you pick the one area of Bristol the Vengatti know to look for you."

"Sorry, Rocky." And she was. She hadn't left deliberately, but even if she had, that wouldn't have occurred to her. Inside the club was so safe, which of course was why Markus wanted her there every night; she'd been able to let her guard down over the last month. "No worries, though, I can sense—" She was about to say Liam. But it wasn't just a fellow warrior who was rushing her. There were two senses, coming from two directions, at speeds she couldn't escape.

She saw the blur in front of her, felt the sting on her upper arm, and reacted with a forceful projection. Two bodies collapsed around her. One she recognized.

"Oh shit."

"Alex, what's wrong?"

She didn't take the time to answer. The phone dropped to the sidewalk as she whipped out the knife Rocky had given her without Markus and the Regan's permission. Thank the Creator for his foresight. Too bad he couldn't also have erased the nightmares she had after using it to kill two Vengatti last fall. Her hand shook violently. It would have to be a last resort.

She placed her hand on Liam's arm and tried to lift the confusion she had slapped him with. Her eyes darted between him and the Vengatti warrior just feet from her. Though she'd been training with Sage since the ball, selectively removing her gift was still not a talent she'd perfected yet. One instant of inattention and she could lift it from both fallen males—or worse, just the Vengatti. The shouting from the fallen phone wasn't helping her focus.

"Rocky, shut up!" she spat. Liam began to stir. "Liam, get up! Please." She tugged at his sleeve as he sat up. Liam took one look at her and snapped to his feet, knife in hand. He spotted the still body right away.

"He alive?"

She nodded. She tried hiding her own knife, but Liam's eyes went to it. He shook his head at her and began dragging the Other back into the narrow alley between the store and the nearest building.

"Wait!" She was on her feet, too, reacting the instant she sensed it.

"Please tell me you don't want to save this bastard, too?"

"No," she sneered. "He's all yours. While you're there maybe you can slit the throat of his partner who was two seconds away from ambushing you in that alley. I knocked him out, too. You're welcome."

Liam chuckled at her attempt to appear blasé as she sheathed her own knife and brushed her bangs from her eyes. He disappeared into the alley, body in tow. She was picking up her phone, which was ominously quiet, when the blue lights lit up the pavement. Liam was at her side before the cruiser had rounded the corner and screeched to a stop.

"Pretend I just hit you in the nuts," she hissed to him.

"What?"

"Do it, or I will." As the officers stepped from the vehicle, hands on their weapons, she started in on him at full volume. "Smooth, jackass. Someone called the cops over your little 'surprise.' Officers, is there any chance you can charge this idiot with stupidity?"

The two young policemen relaxed at hearing her lay into Liam, whose indignant expression fit her story just fine.

"We had a call that there was a possible assault on a female in the area. Is everything alright, Miss?" the darker haired officer questioned.

Alex glanced back quickly to the convenience store clerk who was peering nervously from behind the counter. She began to calm him and the officers as she explained.

"Yes. Genius here is a friend. He recognized me and thought it would be a riot to sneak up behind me. I assure you he'll rethink repeating the stunt if he ever wants to have sex again."

She looked to Liam. Her gift could only get them so far. Luckily, he had caught on and cringed.

"I should've known better than to mess with an East Bristol chick. They're all ball-busters—literally." Liam adjusted himself, faking a wince. Alex hid her surprise as one of the officers, obviously a local, laughed. "Sorry if we scared the clerk in there," Liam finished.

"It's alright. He calls at least once a month with some story. This was one of the few believable ones," the first officer responded, his hand no longer on his weapon. "So long as no one's hurt too badly." He nodded to Liam.

"I'm married with two little girls. If my masculinity can handle princess parties, it can handle just about anything," the hulking warrior replied. Alex rolled her eyes. It was a good thing she hadn't let up on her influencing. If she didn't buy that, they sure as hell wouldn't.

Both officers shook their heads and wished them a good night as they headed back to their car. As soon as it was out of sight, Liam pulled out his knife again and began dragging her quickly towards the club.

"Princess parties, really? That's the lie you chose? And how'd you know I was from East Bristol?"

"I remembered your sweatshirt the first warrior meeting you attended. Besides you do fit the profile—mouthy and tough." Alex stomped on his foot, but his steel-toed boots kept him from missing a beat. "And the princess parties are true, but, ah, that can stay between us right?"

She howled, humor and hysteria combining as her initial shock wore off. When she caught her breath, reality began creeping in again. She knew it was the least of her worries, but asked him anyway. "I'll keep quiet about that if you don't mention to Markus about my knife, or to Rocky about my failure to use it." She was already in for a night of lectures. She didn't need to hear the 'hesitation will get you or your partner killed' one—again.

Liam shrugged. "You knocked out two Vengatti and took care of the cops; that's good enough, Seer. Of course, had you been wearing a lighter colored coat or if humans could smell blood, we'd have been screwed. But as it was, not too bad."

As they entered the club, she looked to where Liam had pointed as he spoke. In the chaos since the attempted attack, she had forgotten about the stinging in her arm. She realized now the Vengatti male had clipped her triceps with his blade. The warmth running down her frozen fingers was a trickle of blood.

"Oh crap." All she needed was for Markus to walk in the building and smell she'd been injured.

"It doesn't look deep. I can clean it, if you'd like."

She looked up thinking the voice she heard was addressing her. Instead she saw Abram standing beside the fuming Regan. She knew why Rocky had hung up; he must have called the club for back up. Word traveled fast. Darian nodded, and Abram approached one of the guards by the door to get the first aid kit that was kept on hand there. The Elder beckoned her to a nearby bench. She knew it was best to obey. She slipped off her coat and pulled her sweatshirt over her head. Abram tore off the bloodstained sleeve of her long-sleeved tee with little effort. She thanked him as he cleaned the wound, but when he pulled out a needle and suture thread and started for the cut, she pulled back.

"I thought you said it wasn't deep."

Abram looked up surprised. "It's not, very, but it will require a few stitches to heal properly." He saw her hesitation and stopped. "I can go upstairs and get an anesthetic from the medical office, if you'd like."

"No. Do it now, please."

She turned to glare at Darian who had spoken for her.

"Not a word from you, Seer. A few stitches are the least of your worries."

She started to argue, but Abram pulled her right arm toward him, turning her away from the Regan. He pinched her elbow once and gave her a quick look that implored her to hold her tongue. She nodded and squeezed her eyes against the pain, which he tried to lessen by working at speeds no human doctor could. When he finished placing the final bandage and helped her back into her sweatshirt, she whispered another thanks. He seemed to understand it was for more than just the medical treatment.

"Good luck," he mouthed as she turned to face Darian who was already addressing Liam.

"Markus and Rocky are already on the scene. Go fill them in." Liam nodded and headed back outside. "You and I will wait for them in Markus's office." Darian grabbed her by the scruff of her neck like she was a misbehaving pet. "Maybe tonight the significance of what you've been staring at for the last month will finally sink in."

She had no idea what he was referring to and didn't care. The harder he shoved her along the corridor, the less contrite and more furious she became. She finally stopped walking and attempted in vain to shake him off.

"I put up with the stitches, because I accepted your initial anger," she said continuing to try to break free. "But there's no reason to manhandle me. It was an innocent mistake. Now let go."

Darian scoffed and squeezed tighter. Alex snapped. She used the physical contact to hit him with a powerful projection. She had expected, desired, his yelp. What she didn't expect was his shock or the jolt the projection gave her. She thought her days of having her gift rebound on her were over.

"What the hell was that?" Darian was looking at his palm. He grabbed her with his other hand and slammed her into the wall. "Is this innocent, too?" He shoved his crimson hand in front of her face. The skin appeared burned.

She stared. "I didn't mean to do that."

"When were you and Sage planning to mention this?"

He didn't understand. "I didn't mean to do it, because I didn't know I could do it, Darian. I don't even know how I did it." Her breath was coming in gasps. Only part of her fear was caused by the Regan's temper.

"You want me to believe your histories didn't mention *this*? Bullshit."

"It's not," Sage said upon arriving. He edged his way between the Regan's fangs and Alex's face. "She's read her histories forward and back. They're only slightly more instructive and detailed than ours."

Before more could be said, Markus and Rocky appeared. Markus gave her a quick once over to assess her injuries, before misdirecting his anger at Sage.

"I asked you to take care of the clerk and the two cops."

"It's done," Sage snapped back. "It seems your mate has rendered my talents 'redundant.'"

Alex glanced at him, but quickly averted her gaze. He'd just stood up for her against the Regan's wrath; she couldn't repay him by commenting on his jealousy. Of course hearing this in her head was nearly as bad. He gave her an icy stare before stepping to the side, leaving her once again unprotected before the Regan.

Markus nodded. "Alex, go wait in my office." Had she sensed chivalry, rather than a desire to get her out of his hair while he handled the situation, she might have refrained from snapping at him too.

"Keeping me in that damn office every night while the rest of you are out doing real work is likely what led me to forget the dangers outside these walls."

Markus's voice was tight as he turned on her. "After all you've lost, I didn't think you needed more injuries to be reminded of that."

Alex recoiled as if he had slapped her. He opened his mouth, but she didn't want to hear an apology she couldn't accept.

"Injury," she corrected. "This," she said pointing to the tender skin on the nape of her neck, "is from somebody's temper issue."

Darian snarled, but Sage actually chuckled.

"Yeah, yours. That's a burn, not a bruise."

"What?" She reached up and felt the flesh on the nape of her neck, hot and tender like a severe sunburn.

"A concentration of power and energy strong enough to scorch the one touching you isn't going to leave your own skin unscathed."

"Right. Silly me. It's all about balance, isn't it? Creator forbid a new part of my power develops without some added pain or danger. Remind me to thank her later."

"Shut up!" Darian swung so fast she had no hope of avoiding the blow herself. Sage must have heard it coming, though, and managed to tug her back by the hood. Not quickly enough. The back of Darian's hand grazed her cheek with enough force to split her upper lip.

For a second, everyone froze. Then everything happened at once. Sage pulled her behind him, whether to keep her from retaliating or to protect her from future blows, she didn't know. Rocky flashed in front of Markus, pushing hard against his shoulders and talking a mile a minute in a volume too soft for her to hear. Alex appreciated her mate's instinct to protect and avenge her, but was thankful Rocky had intervened. He was undoubtedly trying to talk the lead warrior out of a career-ending mistake. Darian didn't move, but looked posed to strike as soon as he decided whom to hit first.

If she hadn't been so drained from everything that led up to that moment, she may have reacted sooner. As it was, it seemed like an eternity before she could pull herself together enough to influence them all. She kept the burst short, a jolt of calm that would cause them pause—long enough she hoped to prevent the situation from escalating.

It worked. At least until Darian became further infuriated that she was breaking yet another of his rules. He stepped toward her.

"Darian, wait. Whatever you want to do to her, it's your right," Sage cut in. Alex fleetingly worried where he was going with this, but he continued. "But at least let her understand why. It's not her fault nobody warned her about making such comments, particularly to you, now." He shot a scathing look at Markus. "Don't pile on your added anger because of your and Sarah's situation. At one time or another, every one of us has had a reason to feel the same as she's feeling."

Darian held Sage's gaze. She was certain he was silently communicating some threat to his Knower, but she interrupted regardless.

"What situation? Is something wrong with Sarah or the babies? What does that have to do with my comment?"

"Nothing is wrong, and I intend to do everything in my power to keep it that way, therefore it has everything to with your comment!" Darian roared.

She staggered backwards at his intensity, then looked to Markus for an explanation.

"Did you say babies? How do you know?"

"I'm not oblivious, though you apparently think so, since you never bothered to fill me in when I came back after my father's death." After returning from her mother's following her father's death, Alex had begun noticing the changes. Sarah began allowing her and Ellie to help out more while she snuck away for midnight naps. Then she began wearing Darian's button downs untucked over a pair of leggings. When the insatiable cravings set in, Alex was certain. Besides, she was a Seer.

"Even if I didn't notice her dipping her cheese sticks into the tub of cream cheese, I can feel her emotions—and yours," she said to Darian. "There's nothing else that could make you both so happy and simultaneously so afraid. I figured after the last time, you just wanted to be sure, and you'd tell me when she was further along. But I still don't understand—"

"We didn't tell you, because we don't talk about it! Our young are gifts granted to us by the Creator, when she sees fit. We respect that power by not anticipating or expecting such a gift until it is granted to us. In the meantime, I will by no means tolerate you blaspheming her with a complete lack of gratitude for the gifts she's given you. And not just your power, either," Darian gestured to the others, "but also your life, your friends, and your mate."

"I'm sorry."

"You will be." Darian made to grab for her, but Markus sidestepped Rocky and caught the Regan's arm.

"Did you hear what she said? Babies. Twins. Are you sure?"

She realized Markus hadn't known. *Oh, Creator.*

Darian hadn't known.

"P-pretty sure," she stuttered. "In the last week or so I've been able to sense them, just flashes, but I can tell them apart because they're different genders." She looked to Sage for confirmation, but he just shrugged. He couldn't hear them yet. Darian saw their exchange and stomped his foot so hard the floor shook.

"Enough! I heard her, and you heard me: we don't talk about it. But since you stupidly disregarded that in a transparent attempt to distract me," he said to Markus, "you can watch as I enforce the rule about respecting the authority of both our Creator and your Regan. My office, now."

"No, Darian." Just as he made a final attempt to grab her, another defender interceded. "You will not lay another hand on her."

Darian closed his eyes and ran his unburned hand through his hair before calmly addressing his mate.

"You weren't here—"

"I still heard it. None of you were being quiet. Alex didn't understand the gravity of her words. She does now. They won't be repeated." Sarah stopped.

Alex knew this was one of those times when Sarah's words served as both comment and threat. She nodded and repeated her apology.

"And now that everyone in the house is on the same page, there'll be no need to discuss the related topic again, either. Is that clear?" Sarah looked at them one at a time until each nodded in compliance.

"That still doesn't excuse her leaving the club." Darian's voice remained tense.

"I asked her to get me a snack. You were there." The three warriors all dropped their jaws. "True, I didn't mean she ought to traipse across Bristol—there are vending machines in at least three hallways." Alex blushed; she'd forgotten about those. "But I also didn't think to stop her when she took her coat, an obvious sign she meant to go outside. And neither did you."

Darian clenched his jaw.

"If we temporarily and quite innocently forgot, surely she could have, too. Let's call it even, shall we?" Sarah turned to Alex calmly. "Any chance you still have that snack on you?"

Alex couldn't help but smile as pulled the cheese stick and two bags of cheese twists from her pockets. When Sarah had taken them and headed back toward her office again, Alex reached into her coat and pulled out the bottle of soda. She held it out to Darian.

"It's still cold. It'll feel good on your hand."

He didn't even look at it. He was busy studying her. When he decided she hadn't meant it to be either a joke or a taunt, he replied. "I plan on drinking heavily later tonight, but none of it will be that crap. Keep it." He turned to the others. "Markus and Sage, I want the report on how those Vengatti got that close. Rocky, stay with the Seer."

He swept off down the hall. Sage followed at a safe distance.

Rocky waited until both were out of sight before turning to Markus.

"Sorry."

"For what?" Markus whispered. "Darian's mood? You did exactly what you were supposed to tonight. If you hadn't called and put her on guard, she might not have reacted quickly enough."

Though he maintained a stoic countenance, she felt his emotional shudder, and it nearly broke her. She held it together long enough to assure Rocky.

"He's right. I owe you big time, Rock-o." She attempted a grin. "Sorry I nearly gave you a heart attack."

Her partner attempted to look stern. "I'll accept your apology after you admit the tracking devices were a good idea." His mouth began to curl as she scowled.

"They were a good idea," she finally conceded through clenched teeth. Both males' expressions softened as they led her to Markus's office.

———◄●►———

Alex walked into the office ahead of him. She headed right for the icepack in the small freezer of the mini fridge he kept by his desk. Markus intended to follow, wanting a few private words with her before facing the Regan. Rocky tugged his sleeve, though, and motioned for him to stay in the hall.

The young warrior hesitated briefly before beginning quietly enough that Alex wouldn't hear. "It might not be my place to say this, Markus, but it's been a month. Her punishment is technically over, and my security work with Remalt wrapped up last week. I believe her that tonight was an honest mistake, but maybe she had a point earlier, too. Maybe being here every night isn't a good idea.

Maybe—"

"Later." Alex had turned to watch them. If her ears weren't keen enough to catch the drift of their conversation, her sense was. "Give us a minute, alright?"

Rocky nodded and stepped back so Markus could close the door behind him. In the privacy of his office, he could finally drop the warrior role and react as he'd wanted to since the second he'd seen her following the attack—as a mate.

She startled when he flashed in front of her. No, she flinched. Did she really think he could strike her? He knew she'd been sensing his anger, only some of which was aimed at her, and even that she knew the reason for.

"Sorry. I'm just on edge."

He actually laughed. She apparently sensed his hurt and shock, too.

"You're a little too good at that now," he said brushing aside her bangs. "It's like having two Knowers around."

"Creator forbid. I can hardly handle one." Alex dropped the hand which had been holding the ice pack to her lip and looked into his eyes. She was seeking assurance that they were okay . . . or perhaps an apology. Either way, he provided it by leaning over to gently lick her cut lip. The venom stopped the bleeding allowing him to kiss her. He continued the trail from her mouth, to her cheek, ear, just under her jawbone. She stopped him when he got to her neck. Pushing him away, she turned to face the wall of pictures.

"Darian said earlier that I didn't understand the significance of what I was seeing in here every day," she began. "He meant these pictures, didn't he? You didn't tell me the truth about them."

He sighed. "Not all of it. They *were* all my warriors. But at the time I didn't think you needed to know the rest."

"Markus." She was frustrated, but he shushed her.

"Let me finish." He walked to the wall. "I put these pictures up for me. To remind me what's at stake behind every decision I make in here and out there. To remind me of the debt I owe to my warriors and my coven. These pictures are of warriors who have died since I've taken over as lead warrior. I didn't tell you, because I didn't want you look at the last four and feel guilty every night. And I know you enough to know you would. But perhaps I should have explained it for other reasons." He didn't have to be more explicit than this.

She felt his fear, and from the way she still shook, he guessed she had felt a good deal of her own over the course of the night.

She ran her hands over the final frames, those of the warriors who had died in the attempt to rescue her brother and the two who died the night of the ball. She stepped back to look at the others and shook her head.

"You and Darian told me that only seven coven members had been killed by the Vengatti since he took over. There are fourteen pictures here, and your father was still lead warrior that first decade, wasn't he?"

"Yes. We don't include the warriors. Not that they don't count. They do. But because of their willingness to die for our cause, lumping them in with the other Vengatti victims feels wrong. They didn't die as victims, they died as warriors. With me they count more."

Alex nodded, and for a minute they both stared at the photos, lost in their thoughts. Eventually she started back towards his desk. He saw her stagger just in time to catch her.

"What's the matter?" he said stretching her out gently on the floor.

"I'm fine," she said fighting to get up. "I'm just tired. I used my gift a lot tonight, and whatever I did to Darian was intense." Her hand clenched into a fist to stop it from shaking. "I could use a nap. Let Rocky take me home."

He shook his head. She was only telling him part of it. She also needed to feed. With her fresh wounds, he hadn't been able to smell it earlier, but it was clear.

"I'm taking you home; you need essence. Rocky," he called into the hall. The warrior poked his head in the door. "Tell Darian." He saw the young vampire's expression and understood the sentiment. "Sage is with him. He won't let him kill the messenger." What Darian would do to Markus later was another story.

"You could text him," Rocky suggested.

"You want to be extracting that expensive new phone you just gave me from halfway up my colon?" he asked sweeping Alex off the floor into his arms.

"Hey," she groaned. "Sudden movements and nasty visuals are not helping the nausea right now."

"I'll take the weak-stomached Seer over the enraged Regan any night," Rocky offered. "Better her vomit than my blood down my shirt."

Markus pointed to the door. "You disobey an order and you'll have both. Go."

Rocky flashed from the room as Alex's color went from gray to green. Markus plopped her in front of the wastebasket just in time. He couldn't help but chuckle.

"Is this a delayed rookie P.O.P.?" She had panicked and overreacted when attacked. Puking would complete the acronym. "Or does your tendency to vomit increase in tandem with your power?"

She wiped her mouth on her already bloody sleeve and glared. "You sound like Sage."

It was not meant to be a compliment.

CHAPTER 9

The two aspirin stuck in her throat even after downing a glass of water. Alex felt hung over as she plodded out of the bathroom and headed into the hallway still wearing her pajama bottoms and one of Markus's t-shirts. The previous night had taken a toll on her strength. Not to mention her sleep.

Her nightmares had returned. Not those of being attacked by Ty or Leonce. Not those of watching her brothers slaughtered. But those of her holding Leonce's ankle as she used her gift to force him to thrust the knife into his chest. As always the Vengatti Regan's face morphed into someone else. Today it was Darian's limp body she saw fall to the ground just before she felt the wave of sickening satisfaction wash over her. Her heart was pounding each time she awoke with the fear of the previous fall resurfacing. She was in better control of herself, though, than she had been just after her maturity when she feared her own power. As she lay in bed she tried to reason logically about what she had managed to do the night before. The problem with reason and logic, however, was that both required knowledge, and when it came to her gift, she still had reasonably little. That needed to be remedied and quickly.

Heading down the stairs, she wasn't surprised to hear Markus's voice. The last time she had woken him with her tossing and turning the light peeking in around the curtains was beginning to fade. He had likely gotten up as soon as he had soothed her back to sleep by gently twirling her hair between his fingers. He seemed to have lost that calming manner in the intervening hour.

"That's not what you said last night." His voice was rising. "You agreed she doesn't belong there."

Alex stopped on the bottom stair to listen.

"You didn't let me finish. I was implying she belongs back out on patrols," Rocky shot back. "How many other warriors could knock out two Others without so much as throwing a punch? It's a waste of her strength."

"Is it her sitting at home that bothers you, or you having to be here with her, Rocky? You accepted this position. I'm sorry if it isn't turning out as glamorous as you'd hoped."

Rocky's temper flared. "I hoped that by protecting Alex, I'd be helping her help others. That's kind of the point of being a warrior, isn't it? So let me ask you, Markus, are you doing this to protect Alex because she's so valuable or because she's your mate? Because it seems to me, locking her up isn't helping anyone but you."

She dashed into the kitchen in hopes of diffusing the situation. By the time she arrived, though, Markus was too close to Rocky's face for her to squeeze between them.

"The only one in danger of being locked up is you, Warrior."

"Markus." She didn't say anything more as she ran her hand down his arm, calming him against his will. A new wave of aggravation arose from him, aimed at her. Fortunately, she didn't have any fangs for him to rip out.

"I appreciate you speaking up on my behalf, Rocky, but perhaps you ought to let me speak with Markus and Darian about it before risking your own neck." She sent him a warning shot before continuing. "Besides, I'm not up for patrols tonight. I'd like you take me to Rick's clinic later to read what he has about Seers. It'd be better if only one of us actually needed medical attention."

Rocky was wise enough to back down, despite liking her alternative plan for the evening even less than staying home.

"Fine. Sorry." He nodded to them both before leaving the kitchen. Markus wanted to stop him, but she stepped in the way. She watched over her shoulder until the door to the basement was closed.

"As his boss, you don't need to answer him, but as my mate, you do need to answer me. I overheard enough to figure out I'm being kept home. Is this your decision or Darian's?"

He sighed. "Honestly, both. Darian asked me as lead warrior to 'handle you' so last night wouldn't happen again. And, yes, I seized the opportunity as your mate to keep you safe."

"Despite knowing Rocky's right?" she asked. "I'd be just as safe and twice as useful back on patrols with him and Sage."

"Sage has a new partner," Markus argued.

She snorted. "Don't you mean partners? According to Liam, Sage is quote: a partner whore who goes through warriors faster than a vamp-tramp goes through males. Luckily, Vivian was around to explain that one."

"I'm going to kill that mouthy son of bitch." Sage, who had apparently been listening from the living room, stormed across the foyer, grabbed the keys from the dish, and slammed the front door behind him as he left the house.

Markus was laughing harder than the analogy warranted. She raised a brow.

"He's scheduled to go out with Liam tonight," he finally choked out.

She cringed. She wouldn't have risked repeating it if she had known. Markus seemed unperturbed by the fact Sage would likely be beating his partner senseless before patrols. Luckily, Liam was almost as tall and as big as Sage.

She touched Markus's cheek to return him to the current conversation. "You remember what you told me last night about the warriors on your wall?"

He nodded, suddenly sobered.

"Rocky and I each owe debts to different coven members for different reasons, just as you do. You can't keep pushing us aside to protect us. We want a chance to repay the coven. We know the risks, even if one of us occasionally suffers from momentary brainfarts." Markus smiled until she finished. "We're willing to die, too."

"Not on my watch." He pulled her close, so tight it felt as if he wanted to pull her right into his body, as if by engulfing her he could protect her.

"I know, Markus. I do."

Finally he released her and stood with his hands on her shoulders. His green eyes were overly bright. She spoke so he didn't have to.

"I'll sit out for a week or two to appease Darian. But by then Sage'll have run through the rest of the warriors, and Rocky will have had his share of twiddling his thumbs. You need to promise me you'll at least be open to discussing it then."

Markus raised his brows like he was surprised by this demand. Then he remembered who he was dealing with and capitulated.

"Fine. Two weeks, and then we'll discuss it."

"Thank you." She stood on tiptoes to give him a kiss. When she started to the fridge he grabbed her uninjured arm.

"My turn. I was straight with you. Now I want to know why the sudden rush to visit Rick. You've had weeks since Abram gave his permission. Why now?"

"Darian was supposed to take me. I'm tired of waiting of for him." She was looking at her feet, wiggling her toes in her socks. He didn't buy it. He waited for her to admit it. "Alright, I was a little freaked out after last night."

"A little? Do you know how many times you woke up today?"

Alex glared at him. "Yes. And you know I do."

He rested his hands on her shoulders. "I'm sorry. I guess I just don't understand. You seem more shaken by what you did to Darian than by getting attacked yourself last night."

He was right. He didn't understand. But she knew part of being mated was helping him to understand, even if she'd rather not discuss it.

"I expect the Vengatti to be a threat, to try to hurt me and my family. I didn't expect that I'd be the one hurting people."

"It was an accident."

"Is that supposed to be comforting? It means either I have no control over it and could hurt any one of you at any time without meaning to, or it was a slip of a greater power I'm just developing and haven't learned to handle yet, one that could potentially seriously injure someone I wanted to hurt."

"That's a good thing. It's another weapon in your arsenal."

"Yeah, one that leaves me too weak to get away or fight a second attacker."

Markus shook his head. "It was the first time. All your powers left you weak when you first developed them."

Alex shrugged. Maybe he was right. Maybe she could come around to seeing it as an asset if she knew for sure what she was doing, if she knew she wasn't the first one to have done it. "We'll see what Abram has to say."

"Do you want me to come with you?" He stroked her hand in a comforting gesture.

"No offense, but not really. I don't know what I'll learn, but I know I'll want time to process it on my own first."

He nodded. "Okay, but promise me we'll discuss it when I get home."

"I gave you two weeks," she argued playfully.

"That was to give Darian time to defuse. If it was just my decision, and you were feeling one hundred percent, you'd have been right there with Rocky demanding instant agreement." His gaze dared her to refute him. She didn't. She couldn't.

"Fine. We'll discuss it." She allowed him to pull her into his chest again. His hands slid under her shirt as they kissed. Hers found their way around his back, eager to make up for last night when she had realized she was too exhausted to enjoy the usual perks of feeding. She reached around with one hand and was fumbling with Markus's belt when he suddenly pulled away.

"If Sarah catches you two christening her kitchen and starts having contractions, I swear to the Creator, I will flay you both alive." Darian had entered the kitchen without either of them noticing. Alex tried to sense if Sarah had heard, expecting to feel her fury both about the newly weds' attempt to make love in yet another room of the house, and at Darian's reference to her pregnancy.

"She left with Ellie and Dalton an hour ago," Darian said guessing what she was doing. "But that's not the point." He stared until Markus spoke.

"Sorry, Regan." He kissed Alex on the forehead and headed to the door.

She wanted to kill him. He planned to leave her alone with Darian, in this mood? After last night? As she shot Markus a look across the foyer, the Regan watched. He was mentally smirking, even if his expression remained neutral.

"I have no intention of hurting her, Markus."

Her mate ground his teeth as his eyes lingered on her lip. "You mean hurting her further?"

"Go to work." Darian pointed to the door.

Markus hesitated just long enough to be defiant. "Yes, Regan." The door slammed behind him rattling the dishes in the cupboards.

"He was far more compliant before you arrived," Darian said shutting a cabinet door that had popped open.

"How boring," Alex replied.

"I like boring. I hope you'll be good and boring after you get dressed and meet me in my office." He filled his mug with coffee and left the kitchen without even glancing back.

She'd been accused of and guilty of a good many things in her twenty-six years. Boring was not one of them.

It was over an hour later when Alex pushed open Darian's door and stood waiting to be invited in. She had dawdled purposely while getting dressed. That and her opening the door without knocking were her silent acts of defiance. It was typical Alex. Her grudging acceptance of her subservience wouldn't get in her way of letting him know when she was pissed.

"Come in. Sit," he ordered masking his amusement. If she wasn't stewing in her own emotions, she would have figured out he was toying with her. As it was, he'd keep up the charade a while longer.

She entered and went straight to her usual spot on the couch, completely ignoring the desk chair he had pointed to. He stood up from behind his desk and came around to the front. Taking the straight back wooden chair himself, he dropped it inches from her knees. When he sat, his own shins nearly touched hers. Alex had mastered the flat affect, but she couldn't control her increased heart rate and breathing, two signs any vampire could easily detect. Signs of fear.

He scraped the chair back six inches. He had meant what he said to Markus about not hurting her again. Darian had gone too far the night before. Sage had later reminded him of how new everything was to her, how fast her life, her body, and, lately, her gift had changed. Her ever-growing power must have been as frightening to her as it was fascinating to him.

"Alex, I—"

"Sorry, Regan, I—"

"Go ahead."

"No, it's okay. You go."

He caved and let her see him laugh. "I was going to apologize." She sat up straighter, her fear replaced with a smug grin. He clarified before she got too cocky. "Not for the stitches or for dragging you down the hall. You were stupid last night and deserved to be reminded of it." She opened her mouth to speak, but he continued. "But I shouldn't have struck you. I knew no one had explained to you. Even if they had, you have a right to decide what you believe. You don't, however, have a right to speak about the Creator in such a manner in front of me or Sarah. Is that distinction clear?"

"Yes," she answered shortly. But instantly followed it up. "Just so you know, I wasn't saying I didn't believe in a Creator. I'm just not sure I buy that everything good or bad that we face in our lives can be attributed to a deity. Isn't it possible for there to have been a Creator, but for there also to be chance, or choice, or just plain shit luck?"

Darian leaned back in his chair and examined her, wishing for the thousandth time that he had her gift, so he could read her. She seemed serious. She wasn't mocking him or his beliefs. In fact she seemed genuinely confused, or desperate even. And why wouldn't she be? If their lives were predestined, the chance of changing the prophecy was slim to none. She wanted to believe she had a hand in what happened to her.

"It's possible, likely even, but I also believe what I told you last night. Certain gifts and certain burdens are bestowed on us by the Creator for reasons we might not always understand."

Alex shrugged. "Maybe, but if I give credit, I also need to lay blame. I'm not sure I want to go down that road right now."

He nodded. It was true she had lost more than her fair share in her short life. Despite being smart and insightful, she was too young to see far enough into her future to understand it would likely balance out.

"Was your apology going to be any better than mine?" he asked.

She grinned. "Nope. I didn't mean to zap you . . . " she paused for a minute like there was more to say about that, but she didn't say it. She powered on. "And I already copped to the complete brainfart of leaving alone. The rest I'm not all that sorry about—especially after I learned you're partially to blame for me being stuck here with nothing to do."

From theologian to punk in under sixty. Perfect.

"Not nothing. I actually have a favor to ask." It was the real reason he had called her in here tonight.

She paused. He knew she was sensing him, trying to read him. It would have aggravated him, except her sensing the emotions behind his request was easier than having to voice them.

"It must be important if you pretended to bring me in here to apologize as a cover. We all know how much you love saying sorry."

On second thought, it was still aggravating. He shot her a glance, but she held firm. She knew he needed her gift and was enjoying the sudden shift in the balance of power. He grit his teeth and began.

"You mentioned last night sensing how scared and anxious Sarah is."

"How scared and anxious you both are, yes."

He clenched his jaw and ran his hand through his hair. "Sarah's my concern at the moment." Alex nodded sincerely. He had hoped her love of his mate would be enough to convince her. "I want you to ease her fears as much as possible, to keep her as calm as you can—"

"Without her knowing or noticing," Alex finished.

"Yes."

"Darian, I promised Sarah the same thing Sage did: privacy and immunity. She's my friend, one of the few I have. Manipulating her emotions without her knowledge or consent is wrong."

She was right, yet he shook his head. "Sarah would consent to anything that led to a different result than last time. But if she knew, it wouldn't have the same effect. When you influence us in an obvious way it catches our attention. It reminds us how we should be feeling, or at least how *you* think we should be feeling, but it doesn't change our mood unless we let it. But you have the power to influence us without our knowing, the power to change our mood in a more permanent manner, right?"

"Sure, but—"

He was a little startled by how quickly his Seer agreed to this statement, and a little disconcerted by the idea she could have done it a hundred times without any of them apart from Sage knowing. It was good Alex was fairly moral and Sage loose-tongued.

"Then do it. Not just for me, or her, or the . . . " *Babies. Twins. Oh, Creator, keep them safe.* "But for the coven. We need an heir, the sooner the better."

"You planning on croaking soon?" She attempted to tease him, but her concern shone through.

"And leave you without anyone to fight with? Not likely." She smiled, then waited for a more serious answer. He sighed. "The coven thrives on stability. A Regan without an heir in a time when tensions with the Vengatti are rising makes members uneasy. Add to that Sarah's last miscarriage and my near demise last summer, and speculation begins to sprout up. A million 'what ifs?' are thrown about. Those already in power get desperate to find strongholds so they can keep it. Those not in power seek ways to obtain some. Unease and uncertainty can lead us to do to things we'd normally never consider."

"Like Seamus did?" she asked quietly.

He nodded. "Like that. It's more likely, though, that they'd stir up trouble within the coven than seek status outside it."

Alex considered this. "So my influencing Sarah behind her back is justified by the fact it might stave off a future coup?" Both her brows raised. "You really need to work on a better excuse than that, because if I get caught, I fully intend to drag you under the bus with me."

Realizing she had just agreed to it, Darian grinned. Alex stood and headed to the door, not waiting to be dismissed.

He flashed to block her exit. "Going somewhere?"

She pretended she hadn't startled. "Keep your fangs in; I'm taking Rocky."

"Pardon me?" He snapped his fangs to full length as he leaned over her short stature. He was only partially playing. The other part of him was losing patience with her attitude and the stubborn streak that left her unwilling to lose such battles. He growled for good measure. She blinked.

"May I be excused, Regan, to visit the elder Abram's as you promised me last month?"

"Certainly. I'll get my coat." He headed down the stairs to the foyer, leaving Alex stuttering in his office.

"Wait. What? No. Rocky's taking me," she called in his wake.

Darian took the keys out of the porcelain dish by the door and headed into the frigid night knowing his Seer would reluctantly follow.

CHAPTER 10

"Ridiculous." Alex craned her head to catch a better view of the estate they had just passed. Shore Side was technically part of the city of Bristol, but it was far from the reality of the rest of the old mill city. The houses were nearly all sprawling mansions on lots the size of small city blocks. And though most didn't actually own shorefront property, the community sat high enough above sea level and the rest of the city to have priceless ocean views. She had grown up hating her peers from this part of Bristol simply because of the assumption they all were entitled twits who didn't know hard work from a hole in the wall. She should have out grown such petty prejudices years ago, but she couldn't help comment as Darian wound his way through the prestigious neighborhoods.

"If you need an intercom to call your kids to dinner, I think it's a sign your house is obscenely oversized."

"My mother called us to dinner, same as yours," Rocky spat from the back. Darian had insisted on driving, so Rocky was left to ride in the rear.

With her back to him and her mind on what she was hopefully about to learn, she'd lost track of him for a bit. She tuned in now. He had been anxious ever since she mentioned wanting him to escort her. She understood that; Christo ran the clinic. Rocky would almost certainly have to face the male who had defended his youngest son, despite his guilt, leaving Rocky to serve a sentence he didn't really deserve. Rocky's debt had been repaid by Ellie's father after her rescue, but that didn't make walking into his accuser's house any easier. And that wasn't the only thing bothering her BFF as they drove deeper into Shore Side.

"You lived up here?" she guessed.

"Yup. On the bay side. We'll drive past it on the way home." He said this with a cold detachment she knew was just for show. The Regan knew it, too. She caught him glancing into the rearview mirror. It was obvious he felt as much pity for Rocky as she did.

She began to apologize for her comment and for not anticipating how uncomfortable this would be for him, but Darian cut her off. Perhaps it was for the best. Rocky didn't seem to want to discuss it.

"While you already have one foot planted firmly in your mouth," Darian began, "perhaps I should remind you Abram is an Elder, and you are a guest in his home. I don't care how chummy you've gotten with Rick in your phone conversations. You will remember they are Abram's family histories and it is Christo's clinic. Understood?"

"It was Rick who I agreed to let examine me, though."

"Alex." Darian pounded the steering wheel.

"Okay. Yes. I understand."

At the next driveway Darian pulled the truck up to the gate. It opened for him almost instantly, though she saw no one in the dark yard.

Rocky must have seen her searching. "They have one of the most advanced security systems in the coven, nearly all automated. The camera at the gate scans license plates; the reinforced steel entrance to the clinic has a camera linked to all the rooms. Christo and Abram can open it with a voice command, so they're not interrupted during surgeries. This whole estate requires only one retired warrior as a guard—and usually a trainee or two."

Alex was impressed and started to ask him how he knew all this, but Darian was already getting out of the parked truck and looked back impatiently at the two of them. When they reached the entrance to the clinic, which appeared to be an entire wing of the huge mansion, he turned to Rocky with the keys.

"We'll be an hour, at least. You can take the truck if you want."

Rocky shook his head. "I'm good, thanks."

"He's trying a case tonight at the club. You shouldn't punish her for his mistakes. Sarah said she's sent you three letters since your sentence was revoked," Darian said quietly. Alex knew Rocky heard in the Regan's voice the same compassion she sensed from him, but there was a wall of bitterness and hurt in Rocky that Darian's words couldn't break through.

"I said I'm good," he snapped. "I'm going to check in with whoever's on duty. Alex has my number when you're ready to leave." With that he took off into the dark yard leaving the Regan still holding his keys. He let him go without a word. Alex wondered if Rocky knew he had gotten a better father figure in Darian than he ever had in his own father.

"His mother's reached out to him?"

"Not your business, Alex."

She might have pointed out that Rocky seemed to think it wasn't the Regan's business either, but decided against it. "I'm his friend, Darian."

"Then if he wants to talk about it with you, he will." Darian reached for the handle, but the door swung in.

"Regan, what a nice surprise." The tall, lanky male with curly black hair bowed deeply. "Come in," Rick said standing up and beckoning both her and the Regan into the long industrial lit hallway. Once the door was shut and the lock clicked, he turned to her.

"Alex, I presume?" He flashed a warm smile. She was surprised to see his front teeth overlapped in the center; vampires rarely had noticeable flaws.

"Yes. It's nice to finally meet in person, Rick." She held out her hand as a test. He passed with flying colors. He not only took it, but pressed it briefly to his lips before releasing his hold.

"The pleasure's ours. We're thrilled you finally decided to take us up on our offer."

"Your father's here?" Darian asked. Alex sensed Rocky wasn't the only one who wished to avoid a direct confrontation with Christo. Darian had orchestrated the deal that ended Rocky's sentence two centuries sooner than expected.

"Ah, not presently," Rick said leading them down the hall. "He had to make a house call. My grandfather's here with me tonight."

"He's missing dinner with the Elders?" Darian asked as they entered a large room not unlike an ER. There were three examination tables, each with a full array of equipment surrounding them. Cabinets full of medical supplies and a large sink lined the far wall. From a door on that end, Abram emerged in his usual shirt and tie, but without the blazer he wore in the club.

"I much prefer our young Seer's company to that of my fellow Elders, Regan. A few thousand years of combined life experience leads to some deadly boring conversations."

Alex laughed. "I would think you'd have some good stories to tell about each other after all that time."

"Oh, we do. The problem is we've all heard them more times than we care to recall." Abram took her hand as he finished and kissed it gently. She blushed, though perhaps that was due to the lingering look he gave her bruised cheek and cut lip.

"I was thinking, Elder, we could start with the examination. Alex might feel more comfortable asking her questions with that part over with," Rick said to his grandfather.

Abram shook his head. "Don't let him fool you. He's more interested in quelling his own curiosity than he is with your comfort."

Rick shrugged, a guilty grin playing on his lips.

"That's fine," she said sliding her coat off her sore neck and arm. Rick handed her a gown and went to fetch his clipboard. With her hand on her zipper, she turned to Darian. "Um, do you mind?"

He cracked his knuckles and took a step closer in response.

"Alex," Abram cut in. "We prefer to draw blood the old fashioned way, with a syringe in your arm." He nodded pointedly to her lip. "I'm sure you understand the Regan's need for knowledge supersedes individual privacy."

She felt her cheeks flush, but knew it was repressed anger not embarrassment. She tried to remember what she'd been telling herself all week.

"I had no intention of staying to watch your examination. Rick can and will fill me in after," Darian said.

"Of course, Regan," Rick answered quickly.

"The answers I seek are the same you want," Darian told her. "And they're to be found in the past. I'll be with Abram when you're done."

"Editing out the unpleasant bits," she mumbled under breath.

The Regan grabbed her injured arm, his large hand squeezing the wound. She refused to cry out, but had to clamp her jaw tight to refrain. He spoke so close to her ear that she could feel his hot breath on her cheek. "If you have a problem with something you've learned recently, I'd suggest you keep quiet about it until we're home. Or better yet, learn your place and hold your tongue altogether."

He didn't wait for a response before heading out through the door Abram had entered. The Elder followed in similar silence.

Rick waited a long moment before he spoke, and even then it was in a whisper. "Please tell me you plan on taking his advice. I hear he's a bit more lenient than his father, but . . . "

"He's not his father. Or his grandfather. I know that." She was convincing herself. Rick didn't understand. "Have you read the histories, Rick, of my ancestors, I mean?"

"Yes. I had merely skimmed them in my training, but after you called, I read through them thoroughly."

"And Darian, has he read them?"

Rick hesitated. "He hasn't, but after your mating ceremony he contacted Abram. They discussed what's in them at length." He paused. "After that, I was told not to meet with you without one of them present." Rick was going as far as he could to confirm the suspicion he had just heard in her voice without endangering himself.

"Thanks. I'm sorry if I got you in trouble with your grandfather."

He waved it off. "It was my fault. I knew the Regan should have been informed of your feeding and your wish to read the histories. But I feared his . . . relationship with my father would prevent you from getting what you deserved, what you needed." Rick reached forward and touched the spot on her neck where Markus had fed from her. Despite Darian's mandate, in the heat of the moment Markus had bitten this more visible spot on a few other occasions. At this point, she doubted the scar would ever fade completely. But she wasn't ashamed of it, and therefore felt no need to hide it any longer.

"I take it feeding is going well?"

"Markus isn't thrilled with his new scent, but the other, ah, perks, seem to make up for it." She grinned. It faded, though, as she remembered the less pleasant side effect. It was one of the questions she wanted to ask about. She explained the flashes of her gift Markus had experienced, and how Sage had explained the possible reason.

"I think he's right. It's not mentioned explicitly in our records, either, but it's hinted at in a few places. But, Alex, Markus needs to feed frequently to stay strong for his job, and you need it to maintain your gift, particularly these first few years. Don't hold off feeding because of an occasional discomfort. The dangers far outweigh a few unpleasant flashes."

She nodded. She and Markus had both already come to the same conclusion.

As Rick began the examination, regular conversation ceased. He listened and observed intently as he completed a study of her breathing, heart rate, reflexes, strength, speed, and agility. He also tested her hearing and vision, took a urine sample, and finally asked to draw blood.

"When was the last time you exchanged essence?" he asked swiping an alcohol pad over the crook of her elbow.

"Markus fed me last night after I was injured and did whatever I accidentally did to Darian."

Rick stopped short with the syringe. "His hand? You did that?"

Alex hadn't realized the burn to his hand was still visible, but then Rick had just told her that her vision was no better than an average human's. "Yeah." She pointed to her neck. "My gift got the better of us both."

"I guess that explains why he struck you." She didn't correct him before he continued. "If that was why you rushed over this evening, you won't be disappointed. There was something about it in the earliest book, dating back to the first Seer."

"Timian." Alex remembered the passages she had read with Sage when the Rectinatti first took her in. "The coven histories didn't mention—" She caught herself.

"Darian allowed you to read—"

"No. Well, just a few pages about Seers, but I wasn't supposed to share that."

"Share what?" Rick smiled. "Anyway, they wouldn't. The coven's histories are kept vague for a reason, there are too many copies floating around. Each first family has one. It's dangerous to have too many details in there. Besides, most Regans don't love having to write detailed accounts of the decade's events for each first family to add to its copy. Family records are more secure and therefore more detailed. I had asked Abram about that part of the records. The Latin was older, and I had trouble translating. He said one of Timian's sons was the only Seer to ever have been able to do it."

"Do what, though?" she asked, eager to understand.

"Corporeal transformation, at least that's how I translated it. It means, like you, he was able to go beyond sensing and manipulating emotions, to be able to use that energy to create a physical reaction."

"I don't understand. How?"

Rick chuckled. "Good question. Your gift is more mystery than science, Alex. I can point out what you already know—even in an ordinary human or vampire, emotions create physical responses. We blush when we're embarrassed, cry when we're in pain, our heart rate and breathing quicken or slow. As a Seer, everything tied to emotion is intensified. How you can focus it and project it—or harness it into a weapon—most likely can't be explained by science."

Alex looked at the needle still in his hand. "But you intend to try."

"I like a challenge." Rick stuck her vein. When he withdrew the needle a small bead of blood welled up. "May I?" he asked holding out a finger.

She knew what he was asking, and though it was odd, it didn't bother her. "Sure."

He stuck his finger in her blood and brought it to his lips. She waited for a reaction.

"Strong for a human, but otherwise normal," he provided before jotting down more notes on his paper.

"Is that it?" she asked pulling down her sleeve.

"Just about." Rick went to the cabinets on the far end and came back with a jar of some kind of salve and a bottle of pills.

"What's—"

"Shh," he quieted her. "I just thought being a little more comfortable might keep you from losing your temper when I bring you upstairs. Abram told me you weren't given any painkillers before or after your stitches. That's common for warriors, but it seems a bit harsh for a human female." Rick shook two pills from the bottle, then looked back at his chart. "Is the weight on these charts from Briant accurate?"

Alex sensed his disbelief. "Yes. I had some . . . issues when I first matured."

"I know. I read his notes." He didn't say more but handed her just one of the pills. She found it hard to swallow. Rick then rubbed the salve around the stitches, into the back of her neck, and even put a small amount on her lip and the surrounding bruises. She sighed in relief as the pain dissipated.

"My father doesn't believe in most of the herbal remedies anymore, but the potency of Abram's salve even he can't deny. He keeps the recipe close, but you can stop by here or his office in the club anytime, okay?" Rick returned the jar to the cabinet and held the door to the house open for her.

"Unfortunately, with my track record, I'll probably take you up on that." She grabbed her coat.

She followed him down another similarly cold hallway, passing a few more plain doors of surgical and x-ray rooms on each side. Rick opened the final door at the end.

"Wow." Her eyes widened. The main house was as impressive as the outside suggested. The hallway they had entered was as wide as a school corridor with a silk rug running down the middle as far as she could see. Nooks were cut into walls for sculptures and decorative vases. Between each nook hung more artwork than Bristol possessed in its one museum.

"Abram has spent his life practicing medicine, but his passion is art," Rick explained seeing her gawk.

"It's beautiful."

"A bit ostentatious for me. But I'm told I've no eye or appreciation for it. I can't tell one naked marble bust from another. I prefer my males warmer and softer, myself." He winked.

"Vampires can be gay?" She clamped her hand over her mouth a moment too late in complete mortification. "I'm sorry. That was totally tactless. I just—"

"Spend your days around warriors who could make Clint Eastwood look effeminate?" Rick laughed. "It's okay. We're a rarity, but there are a few of us in the coven. If you and Sage feel ostracized, you ought to see the rest of the warriors on the nights my partner and I show up for our mandated patrols. Your mate actually took pity on me a few years ago and said, since I was needed in the clinic, I could be excused from serving. I declined. It's healthy for his males to have to rub shoulders with us every now and again."

Alex was indignant. "Good for you. Take names next time; I'll gladly zap a few of them for you." She wiggled her newest weapon, her fingers.

Rick stopped outside a set of double wooden doors, still laughing at her.

"Thanks, but I doubt that'd help my reputation any. And you need to be careful with that." He motioned to her neck and hand. "Even after you gain greater control over it, it'll always leave a mark on the point of contact, and it will always require enough energy to leave you spent. It needs to be a last resort."

121

This was one time Alex wished she had been wrong. Or maybe not.

"Rick," she stopped him from opening the doors just yet. "Corporeal transformation, does that just mean I'm turning my own emotions into a physical response?"

"Yes, basically."

"So, I wouldn't need to sense my victim in order to do it, because it has nothing to do with the victim's emotions?"

"I don't think so, but is that ever an issue?" Rick's curiosity was piqued.

"Could it ever be strong enough to kill someone?" Alex knew they'd soon be interrupted. She could sense Abram and Darian listening in behind the door. She needed an answer to this before the Regan decided Rick had learned too much already.

"Maybe. But it'd have to be intentional, Alex. You don't need to fear hurting someone by accident," he assured her. A few hours ago, this was all she needed to hear. Now it was a secondary comfort.

"What if I did want to? What if my hatred of my enemy was severe enough?"

"Then, yes, probably, if it were aimed at a vital organ. But, Alex . . . " He bit his lip. He was conflicted over whether to tell her the rest. He needn't be. She knew it. Balance was biting her in the ass again.

She finished for him. "Something that strong could kill me too."

He nodded.

"Last resort then, I promise." When her words didn't work to ease his anxiety, she touched his arm and gently eased it for him.

"That's amazing, you know."

She smiled. "Some people disagree, especially when it's done to them without their permission."

"Well, then, let's refrain from using it on some people, particularly those much larger and higher-up than you, shall we?" Rick said with a wink before opening the doors.

Alex was drawn instantly to the tall shelves of old leather-bound books like a child to a wall of brightly colored sweets. Abram's library, with its scent of dust, ink, and aging paper, did for her nerves, what her influence had done for Rick's. She was ready to face the Regan as she turned to the sitting area on the far end. She headed for the empty chair, but Darian slid over and patted the spot next to him on the perfectly worn leather couch. She obeyed, despite knowing he just wanted her in arm's reach in case she got out of line.

"Anything interesting?" he asked Rick as she sat.

"Not yet, Regan. I'll run a few tests on the blood and urine, but otherwise, aside from her strong essence, she'd appear to be a normal human."

"Appearances can be deceiving."

"I agree. She's far more wonderful," Rick replied with a warm smile aimed at Alex. She smiled back, both at Rick's charming compliment and at the Regan's less-than-pleased reaction to it.

Abram read the Regan's scowl and sent Rick back to the clinic. When the two doors closed behind him, she turned to Abram. If she was going to get answers and honestly voice her concerns, she was going to have to ignore Darian's presence.

"Where do we start?" she asked.

Abram smiled. "With your questions. This is to help you understand yourself and your gift."

"Well, Rick answered the question I was most concerned about— what I did last night. I'm not the first to have done it."

"No."

"And you agree with the rest of what he told me?" Rocky's comment about the intercom system hadn't gone unnoticed. Darian might not have felt the need to watch her examination, but she suspected both he and Abram had listened.

The Elder smiled. "I do. Especially the part about it being the most dangerous power you've developed so far. Now that you know you have the ability, you need to choose to control it."

"Choose to?" She couldn't help sounding defensive.

"Yes. Separating your gift from your emotions is a choice. You don't zap everyone around you every time you feel something, do you?"

"No."

Darian scoffed.

"Okay. I occasionally lose my temper and project on someone, but that's different."

"How?" Abram asked. "We occasionally react dramatically when we're angry or scared, and it might feel like we lost control, but really we've just allowed our emotions to cloud our judgment. You chose to hurt Darian last night, just as he chose to strike you back."

She and Darian exchanged glances.

"That answer should be comforting, but it's not. Trusting my gift, as erratic as that can be lately, would be more assuring than trusting my temper," she admitted.

"We were all hot-tempered in our youth," Abram said grinning at the Regan. Alex knew there was a story behind it, more than one most likely.

"Yes, but we grew out of it quickly, or had it beaten out of us." Darian was glaring at her.

"From what I've heard, it took Ardellus the better part of a century to tame you. Unfortunately for everyone, my father only had fifteen good years to work on me."

Darian was on the verge of snapping until her final words. "It is unfortunate," was all he said.

She knew they were close to the topic the Regan wanted to avoid, but she needed to know. "That's my next question. How did my brothers and I end up full-blooded Seers? How did my father have some power, but not enough to be discovered? And what happened to his ancestors in between?"

"Slow down, Alex. That's more than one question, and ones that, until recently, I thought you already had the answers to." He looked to Darian, who nodded, granting whatever permission he sought. "Ardellus had me trace your family as best I could shortly after you were brought to the coven."

She spun on Darian. "I asked you if you knew Abram had these books, and you said no."

"Because I didn't," he snapped.

"Well, your father sure as hell did."

"Alex," Abram cut in. "That temper we spoke of, if you'd like answers, it needs to be controlled."

She took a deep breath and nodded for the Elder to continue.

"When we left Italy for Ireland, the coven had a Seer in its possession." Alex bristled at Abram's word choice, but let him continue uninterrupted. "He died in battle when his two sons were both young. The oldest son died during his maturity years later. It was around then that the first of the famines was hitting the country. The youngest boy, Timothy, snuck off one night leaving behind a note saying he was off to find the rest of his family. He took with him a satchel of food, hard to come by at the time, and a few stolen trinkets from the Regan's home, enough perhaps to pay for passage for his mother and two older sisters to America."

"His family was human?" Her disbelief caught Abram and Darian's attention. They exchanged a look as she fought back her anger.

"Yes. Timothy's father had fallen in love with a village girl. They married and had children. When the boys, both Seers, were old enough to be weaned, he sent his human wife and daughters to live with relatives in the country. Timothy and his brother were raised and trained within the coven."

Alex started to say something, but stopped herself. She'd hear the rest first. "Please, continue."

"A year after Timothy left, we received a note from a country priest saying he had succumbed to illness and wanted to make amends for his theft before receiving last rights, a Catholic ritual."

"Yeah, I know what it is," she said staving off any further unnecessary explanation. "But he didn't die, did he?"

"Apparently not. There are records of a Samantha, Mary, and Timian Crocker leaving on a ship for America the same month the letter was received. Mary and Samantha were the names of his sisters. Timian was an easy change from Timothy, and as much a taunt as their new last name."

"New?" she asked.

"The Seers had gone by Viden in both Italy and Ireland, Viden being a twist on the Latin word for seeing. After witnessing his father's bloody body brought back from a skirmish and watching his brother die, my father and I unable to help him, Timothy had taken to referring to his gift as a crock."

Alex thought for a moment about all this, adding it to the little she knew of her family's history in this country. "So was he my great grandfather or something? Wouldn't my grandfather had to have been a Seer too then?"

Abram once again looked to Darian. It was he who answered her. "You know Seers who aren't killed can live as long as vampires, Alex. Did you ever meet your grandfather, or any of your father's relatives for that matter?"

"No. My grandfather died when my dad was a teenager. Wait. Darian, you're not saying . . . No. He couldn't have been. It's not possible."

"Timothy Viden was Timian Crocker. The name reappears in different decades in employment registries, property listings, tax records—all with various dates of birth. But there are no death certificates, no headstones, no death benefits filed for. As far as we can tell, there has only ever been one Timian Crocker in America, Alex—your father."

She stood up still shaking her head. The room spun, so she sat back down only to feel her whole world spinning. Could she really have known her father so little? Could he have kept something so crucial from everyone he loved? But then, who would have believed him if he told them?

"And my mother?" she finally spoke.

"Seems to be exactly who she says," Darian answered. "If your father was a direct line, she wouldn't have needed the gift in her blood, as I originally thought. Not that she couldn't be related to another line of Seers. She could have been a female descendent from one of the other Seers who died. That would explain the strength of your gift."

She narrowed her eyes. He was testing her to see what she knew. Fine. Play ball.

"I think we both know the likelihood of a female descendent surviving to pass on the gift through her bloodline is slim. Mary and Samantha must have been overlooked by your father. Either that or they were very, very lucky their father knew to hide them away."

The Regan nodded. His suspicion was confirmed, but instead of guilt or remorse, he was angry with her.

Before he could respond, Rick's voice came over the intercom system.

"Elder, I'll be needing your assistance. A call just came in that we have two injuries arriving shortly—Vengatti related."

Abram stood immediately. "If you'll excuse me. I need to see what this is about."

"Of course." Darian was also on his feet, worry on brows. "Keep me informed."

"Yes. Feel free to stay awhile and finish your conversation, by then we should be able to fill you in." Abram disappeared from the room. Darian took a moment to shift his focus back to Alex.

"How long have you known?"

"I deciphered that part of my histories two weeks ago." She had read and reread the passage, hoping she'd interpreted it incorrectly. She couldn't believe, didn't want to believe, that a coven renowned for its so-called righteousness could have killed innocent humans, babies, simply because they were born girls without a useful gift.

"How long have *you* known?" she spat at Darian.

"There were hints in our histories. That's why I had Sage choose the passages you initially read carefully. I didn't know for sure until Abram confirmed it when we spoke after your mating ceremony. Is this the real reason you've been so angry with me lately? It has nothing to do with you feeling cooped up by the new security measures, does it?"

Alex was still digesting his initial comment. "Sage knew?" she roared. "Did Markus?"

"No."

That was a small amount of comfort.

"Why didn't you come to me when you first found out? Why didn't you allow me to explain?"

"What is there to explain, Darian? Your ancestors killed mine, for no better reason than because they didn't trust them to keep your secret. How would you have liked me to address that? 'Pardon me, Regan, but if I pop out a human baby girl, do you plan on drowning her in Bristol Bay?' Or perhaps I should have asked your father why he didn't follow tradition and force my grandfather to mate a vampire, for all intents and purposes to be raped by a female he didn't love just to assure the coven would continue to 'possess' another Seer or two without the inconvenience of human offspring."

"Stop!" Darian's fists were shaking by his sides.

Alex, who had stood to face him as she shouted, took a step back. When he spoke next, however, his voice was soft if not steady.

"Do you really think my father or I capable of such things?"

"No." She wiped the tears from her cheeks. "And that's part of the problem. I want to rage and scream and tear at the bastards who could have done such things, the bastards who were easily as twisted as the Vengatti. I want to be sickened by the idea that I trusted you all, I mated one of you, I fed from you. But I can't. Because I, of all people, know that's not who you are, any of you. I love you all like family, though my histories tell me how wrong that is."

"But it is history, Alex. It's the past. That's why I didn't tell you. It'll never repeat itself, and knowing it does you no good." Darian was calm now, but she wasn't.

"Then you should have trusted me to see that, to see past my anger to what I'd witnessed firsthand. It's my history, Darian. My father."

"I didn't know about your father until after his death. And even if I had, when would have been a good time for that conversation? When you were first brought to us and were terrified we were going to kill you? Or when you started falling for Markus, who I knew would be crushed if you ever left? Or after your father just died and you discovered your histories, histories I soon discovered he had likely translated, histories I knew would paint us as the monsters he believed us to be?"

"When have I ever changed my beliefs because an authority figure told me to?" she challenged.

Darian actually laughed. "Never." He took a deep breath and stepped closer. She remained still as he rested his hands on her shoulders. "I'm sorry, Alex. I'm sorry my kind hasn't always been as good or as moral as I may have made them out to be. And I'm sorry that I wanted your trust badly enough to betray it. You know I don't see you as merely a weapon against the Vengatti, and I'm certainly not foolish enough to think I possess you."

He had added the extra contact so she'd have no doubt. She nodded. He let one arm drop, but squeezed the other a little tighter.

"But I am your Regan," he continued. She knew this was coming, here or at home. Good reasons aside, her outbursts wouldn't be forgotten. "Since physical pain doesn't seem to deter you, it seems I have to revert back to coven tradition. You speak to me again like you did tonight, in front of anyone, but especially in front of an Elder, and I will have Markus beaten—publically—while you watch and take in the emotions of everybody present. Understood?"

She opened her mouth to argue, but Darian closed it with his other hand.

"Starting now. So be sure you want to say whatever it is that comes out of your mouth next." He slowly withdrew his hand.

"Sage is here. And I think he's badly hurt." It wasn't what Darian expected. It wasn't what Alex had planned, but as the realization hit her, it was what she blurted out.

Both of them took off from the room before exchanging another word.

CHAPTER 11

Abram and Rick were already examining a young female whom Liam had carried in and laid out on one of the examination tables.

"We gave her this to knock her out—a little late for Sage, but it worked nonetheless. He treated her neck the best he could as I drove." Liam handed a syringe to Abram as Rick gently removed a bandage from her wound. Seeing how much blood soaked the female's blouse and hair, Alex marveled she was still alive.

"He did well," Abram commented, after sniffing the victim. "With what they drained from her, she wouldn't have made it here otherwise."

"Where is he?" Alex asked. She could have sworn from what she sensed Sage was injured, too.

"In the car. I couldn't carry them both. And he insisted he was fine," Liam said.

"I am fucking fine," Sage growled trying to shove off Rocky who was trying to assist him. He was holding something to a wound on his abdomen. Alex knew he was lying just from Rocky's face, which was a white as Sage's.

"Yeah? Then why are you holding in your own intestines right now?" Darian asked rushing to his other side.

Rick looked up, and his eyes widened. Even Abram took a second glance. Alex turned back to her mentor to see what she missed. As it hit her, she clamped her mouth closed and swallowed hard against her reflex to vomit. What she had thought was a bloody rag being used to staunch the bleeding was in fact a protruding intestine. The room spun. How the hell was he still standing?

Abram pushed her into a chair as he swept past, needle in hand. "Put him on this table. I'll administer the anesthesia so we can begin surgery right away."

"I don't need any of that shit. Just stitch me back up." Sage tried to push Darian away with his one free hand.

"It's a little more complicated than that, Warrior. Now lie down and give me your arm," Abram ordered.

"Like hell."

"Sage!" Darian snapped.

This wasn't going to end well. Sage was the worst of the bunch when it came to admitting fault or defeat. Rocky seemed to be thinking along the same lines. She watched his hand curl into a fist. She wasn't sure whose head he heard it in, but Sage turned to Rocky with a growl.

"Don't you—"

Too late. She acted before Rocky could. Darian and Rocky were close enough to catch him. Rocky even had the wherewithal to put his hand over the wound to keep anything else from spilling out. His bloody hand was the last thing she remembered before coming to on the floor of the hallway.

She sat up and slowly opened her eyes allowing them to adjust to the light. Someone held out what appeared to be a bedpan for her. She startled. For a moment she thought it was Sage. Then the face of another tall, blond warrior came into focus.

"A weak stomach as well as a big mouth. Not great traits in our line of work," Liam said. "Trust me on the second one, at least."

She looked up and took in his swollen left eye. Sage had apparently informed him whom he had to thank for it.

"Sorry about that. I didn't realize he was in earshot when I repeated your vamp-tramp comment." Her voice was raspy. She tasted vomit and wrinkled her nose. "Did I throw up before or after I fainted?"

"They were pretty much simultaneous." Liam was pacing in front of the door.

"Is he going to be okay?" she asked.

A new voice answered. "He damn well better be, or I swear to the Creator I will revive him just to kill him a second time." Vivian had stormed in the main door and was furiously heading to the operating room. Despite her comment, Alex sensed her trepidation.

"Vivian, wait." Markus flashed before her. "Let me go in and see if they're ready for you yet."

Markus was short for a warrior, but even he towered over the tiny Vivian, which was why it was so astonishing to see him flinch at her reaction.

"Move," she said her fangs snapping into place. "Or I'll move you, piece by piece if necessary."

He stepped aside. Vivian disappeared into the room. Markus picked Alex up off the floor and squeezed her hand. It was supposed to feel reassuring, but the worry that his contact conveyed left her more concerned.

"What happened, Liam?"

"We got to her too late. She had been nearly drained. I went to secure the alley, to make sure it wasn't a trap. Sage bent down to treat her. She seemed unconscious when we first approached. He must have put his knife down beside him so he could try to stop the bleeding. All of a sudden I heard her scream and saw him collapse holding his gut. When I got there she was sitting up, thrashing the knife around. I disarmed her and used the tranquilizer from the medical kit to knock her out. Then I got them both back to the Jeep. Sage threw a fit, saying he was fine, and insisted on treating her while I drove. He did, too, with one hand holding in his insides the whole time. It was amazing . . . and disgusting."

"And stupid. You should've knocked him out, too," Markus said shoving Liam in the chest.

"There was only one tranquilizer. What did you want—"

"Abram said she would have died on the way over if it hadn't been for Sage," Alex jumped in before either of them let their emotions get the better of them.

Markus turned to her and shook his head. "Great. Now Darian will have to be the one to finish her off. And her mate and sisters will blame him instead of the Vengatti scum who're really responsible."

"You don't think she'll recover?" Liam was shaken by the idea.

Markus sighed. "I think what she did to Sage is probably a good indicator."

"But she was injured and terrified," Alex argued. "She probably thought he was the Vengatti who attacked her."

"Let's hope so."

Inside the clinic Rocky stood with Vivian by Sage's side. There were tubes and machines all around him, but he was resting. Alex must have been out longer than she thought. His surgery was over. Vivian had been called to feed him once he awoke to speed his recovery.

"The stubborn bastard was right," Rocky said when Alex asked him for details. "Nothing inside had been punctured. It really was just a matter of cleaning everything and sewing it back in. Not that he'll be recovered anytime soon, but it could have been worse."

"I don't understand how he stayed conscious," she said shaking her head.

Rocky shrugged. "Adrenaline, stubbornness, stupidity?"

"The last two for sure," Vivian said, holding Sage's limp hand. Suddenly it contracted.

"Thanks, Babe." At least that's what Alex thought he mumbled before Vivian slapped him hard across the cheek. Rick rushed forward to stop her, but she didn't try to strike Sage a second time.

"You arrogant S.O.B.. You promised me you wouldn't do this to me again." With that Vivian bit her own wrist and shoved it into Sage's mouth.

He opened his eyes enough to glare at all of them as they laughed, but he eagerly drank his partner's essence without any attempt to argue.

"She's awake."

Alex followed everyone else's eyes to the male standing at the foot of the furthest bed. From his agony, she knew this had to be the female's mate.

"Monica, can you hear me?" He had rushed to her pillow. The others tensed waiting for her reaction. It was then Alex noticed the restraints on her arms. "Monica, you're okay." He was desperately trying convince himself.

She opened her eyes and looked at her mate. There was recognition, but nothing else. "You're here?" she croaked. "Great timing, Jonathan. Where were you earlier? Banging one of my sisters? Go away."

"What are you talking about? Monica, you know I'd never—"

"Go away!" She tried to claw at him, but the restraints kept her arms pinned.

Abram took the male by the shoulders and steered him back.

"Give her time. Let her recover, if she can."

"If?" he shouted. "Is that why he's here? Is that why you called the Regan?" He turned to Darian with a look of hatred. "You're here to kill my mate?"

"No." Darian spoke calmly, but his agony was plain from the stiffness of his gait, the intensity of his gaze. "My being here was a coincidence. I hope as you do that she recovers. But, Jonathan, if she doesn't . . . "

"She won't." Alex knew she had tears streaming down her face. She didn't bother to hide them. What she was saying was horrific. She was causing each and every one of them varying degrees of agony, yet she knew it was better to say it now. She had fooled herself when it had been her brother, and it cost two warriors their lives—and nearly killed her and Darian. She wouldn't let someone else live with that guilt.

"How do you know, Alex?" Darian asked her.

"Because I can sense what I did with Levi. There's a void where all her goodness should be. There's nothing left to recover. It's not coming back. I'm sorry," she said turning to the male whose tears had begun to spill over. "But postponing it won't help."

"You're lying!" he screamed at her. "You're wrong. You make mistakes. You knocked us all out at the ball. You don't know what you're doing or what you're saying!"

"I didn't make a mistake at the ball. And I'm not making one now," she said wishing it weren't true. She wiped her face on her sleeve.

Darian pulled her close. "Get control of your own emotions. Make contact. Be sure. Because you do know what you're saying, don't you?"

"Yes, I do." She pushed back her damp cuff and pulled in a steadying breath. Closing her eyes, she forced out everyone else's emotions. When she opened them, she walked directly to the female who thrashed on the bed. She didn't make eye contact. She couldn't look at the victim she was about to condemn, afraid the once innocent face would lead her to ignore what she was about to sense. She gripped Monica's wrist and focused her gift. Hatred. Pain. Anger. Fear even. But no love, no concern for her mate, who was now being restrained by Rocky and Liam. When Monica's emptiness began to resonate through her, Alex jumped back terrified of what would happen if that were all she could feel. She ignored the snarls coming from the female and turned to her mate.

"The female you loved is already dead. They killed her. The Vengatti killed her." Facing Darian she nodded. "I'm sure. I'm so sorry, but I'm sure." And with that she left the room. She couldn't stay and feel anymore than she already felt.

CHAPTER 12

The office door was closed as it had been for the last three nights. Both Sarah and Markus had warned her not to bother him. Darian had had similar stretches after the other times he had been forced to put a coven member to death. He'd come out when he was ready to move on, they said.

Still, she paused as she passed on her way downstairs. Someone ought to at least ask how he was feeling. She could at least offer to ease some of what he felt. Selfishly she also wanted to ask if it ever got easier, because she had a feeling it wouldn't be the last time she was asked to use her gift in such a way. But she knew the answers to all these questions. And she was pretty sure asking the Regan to voice them would only serve to redirect some of the anger he felt towards her. So she didn't knock. She did, however, release a small burst of comfort. He growled loud enough for her to hear, for her to know he felt it. But he didn't bother to mask his gratitude as well.

"You dare get out of that bed, and I'll have Sarah handcuff you to the frame," Vivian was saying as Alex reached the foyer. It was sensing her newest friend arrive with Sage that pulled Alex out of her own room willingly for the first time since returning from the clinic. Vivian was already heading out of the living room and back toward the front door, though.

"You're not staying?" She tried to hide her disappointment.

"Three days by his bedside is more than I can handle," Vivian said smiling. Alex knew she was lying.

Jerk, she thought, hoping Sage could hear.

"Missed you, too, twerp. Looking forward to training tomorrow?" Sage called from the living room.

"If he thinks—"

"He won't. He just likes to threaten me," Alex promised. "We'll see he heals up okay."

Vivian nodded. "I should be used to it," she whispered. "But it's been a while since Markus or another warrior came pounding on my door like that." She shook herself as if she could fling off her fear. "I know better than to panic. He's too damn stubborn to die."

A grunt came from the other room. Alex hoped Vivian heard in it what she felt. She smiled and blew a kiss in his direction, so Alex guessed she had. She gave Alex a quick peck on the cheek, too, before bustling out the door.

Alex poked her head around the doorway to the living room. Sage was leafing through the stack of books Sarah had put on the coffee table next to the cot. It had been set up on the main floor so he wouldn't have to do the stairs just yet. A water bottle and a vial of pain meds remained untouched.

She sighed. She had secretly and selfishly enjoyed the privacy and quiet of the last three nights as her sense of Sage had been dulled by whatever drugs Abram, Rick, and Christo had forced into him.

"Feel free to take a few yourself," he said in response to her thoughts. So much for privacy.

She smiled. "I'm good. I'm not the one stewing in my emotions for once."

He raised a marked brow.

She crossed the room to sit on the arm of the chair facing his bed. "Yes, really," she answered the sensed skepticism. "You're out of the loop for once, Knower. Darian and I had it out the night you were injured."

He took less than a minute to pull the memory from her mind. "So everything's rainbows and butterflies between you two now?"

She shrugged and pointed upstairs. "Hard to know, but it can't be worse. At least everything's out in the open now. No thanks to you or Ardellus, I might add."

"Knowing the truth isn't the same as forgiving, though, is it?" Sage asked ignoring her last comment.

"Darian's not like his predecessors," she whispered. "And I'm not like mine. I won't run away."

"That's my point. If the truth won't change the outcome, let it be." Sage picked up a book and pretended to read. She knew this was a sign for her to leave, but she couldn't help comment on the guilt she sensed.

"I don't suppose telling you what I told Markus, and myself, and would tell Darian, if he'd leave his office, will help, huh?"

"Nope. Because in my case you'd be wrong. Liam and I should have been there."

"You're a Knower, not a clairvoyant. How were you supposed to know the Vengatti would be there at that time?"

Sage rolled his eyes. "You made the warriors' schedules for the last month. You know how it works. We are scheduled to be in certain neighborhoods, at certain times based on when our coven members need us. Monica was one of three females who did secretarial work for a group of the coven's lawyers with offices downtown. Three nights a week the warriors clear the neighborhood just before two when they wrap up work. We were five minutes late."

Alex remembered Liam's black eye and how he got it and swallowed hard. If that was why they missed saving Monica, she was nearly as guilty as Sage was for repeating the comment that pissed him off to begin with. And Markus, arguably, should have ordered Sage not to act on it. But that kind of what-if thinking was foolish.

"The Vengatti attacked Monica. End of story." It was the same argument Markus made to her when she felt responsible for what happened with Ellie and the attack on the ball.

"Yeah, well, enjoy forgiveness while you're young," he sneered. "It isn't granted so freely after a few centuries on the job."

Someone behind her vehemently agreed. Alex turned in the direction of her sense. Markus stood in the doorway to the living room. Seeing Sage home and recovering alleviated some of her mate's concern. What remained was his rage.

"Leave us alone, please, Alex."

———◆———

"An entire year?" Alex asked incredulously. She had stopped midstride and pulled her winter running hat back so she could see him clearly, as if her impeded vision had messed with her hearing.

Rocky shrugged. "That part's more symbolic than anything else. His salary will be paid to Jonathan and his family for restitution. But at Sage's age, it's not like he doesn't have enough in savings to cover his own expenses for a year. The rest is going to hurt a lot more—both the physical blows and those to his pride."

As they ran, Rocky had been explaining what he overheard the night before after Markus had thrown her out of the living room. In addition to the year's lost salary, Sage would be submitting to a warrior's disgrace, the only punishment less severe than being let go. As soon as he was recovered, he would be whipped in front of his fellow warriors and then demoted back to rookie status. It was a long fall for the warrior who had been second only to Markus just a week earlier. He'd spend the next year or more of patrols letting less experienced, less knowledgeable warriors call the shots.

"Wait." She had resumed her stride as a new, somewhat selfish thought surfaced. "If Sage doesn't have any more status than we do, what does that mean for our chances of returning to patrols?" With her blind spot for Leonce no longer a problem—or at least reduced to a degree that she could perhaps argue it was no longer a problem—she had assumed Markus would reinstate her and Rocky on patrols as soon as Sage recovered.

Rocky thought about it for a minute and then turned to her with a grin. "Now would be a good time for you and Markus to pop out a kid or two. Stay at home Seer, stay at home mom, same difference, right?"

It was a good thing he flashed back to the porch at vampire speed, or Sage wouldn't be the only one recovering. As Rocky entered the door, Markus exited.

"Up for another lap?"

She shook her head gasping for breath. "Just finished five miles—with sprints. But I'll walk a lap with you if you want to talk." Markus had taken a page out of Darian's book and locked himself in the basement room he used as an office last night. He never made it to bed, so when she awoke needing a run, she'd dragged Rocky from his warm covers, much to the chagrin of his snarling partner, Ellie.

Markus wrapped his arm around her and headed back into the dark night. "It's been awhile."

"Since our last stroll, or since we've really talked?" she asked looking up at him.

He smiled. "Both. You never really got to fill me in about what you learned at Abram's before . . . "

"Yeah, before." She sighed and then began with what she learned about her father and the coven's treatment of Seers.

Markus stopped as she relayed her exchange with the Regan. "Wow. Babe, I'm sorry. But you know Darian wouldn't do that; he wouldn't hurt an innocent. You can feel how much he's hurting now."

"I know. I just said that, didn't I?" She cursed realizing Sage was right the night before. Knowing and forgiving were different. "Sorry. It's just crazy to think those things were happening, if not in your lifetime, than certainly in your parents'."

Markus's jaw tightened. "Most certainly. He knew. He remembered. And he said nothing."

Alex put the pieces together. "Your father knew mine. He would have helped train him. He would have remembered when he deserted." She snorted. "I guess that explains all the Seer insults." And why he worried so much about her mating his son; he was waiting for her run, as her father had, after every conflict she faced.

"I could kill him," Markus fumed.

"But you won't. Just as I promise not to pick a fight over it with Ardellus. It won't do anything to improve their view of my kind, my father, or me. So why bother?"

Markus raised a brow. "Who are you, and what did you do to my mate?"

She swatted at him. "I'm trying to work on my 'coven-loving' interdependence crap. Not that you're making that easy."

"Me?" he asked. "You mean because of Sage?" His dander went up instantly. "A female died. You had to condemn her. Darian had to finish her off. It's the least we owe to her family."

"You don't see anything wrong with beating and humiliating a warrior, who's served over two and a half centuries, for an act of violence the Vengatti committed?"

"I'm not saying Sage killed her. But he played a role. That is part of being interdependent, part of being a coven member and a warrior. Those females and their families trusted us to be there to protect them. Sage broke that trust."

"By five minutes, Markus." She stopped and tugged on his sleeve to turn him toward her. "That could have been caused by traffic, following a lead somewhere else in the city, anything."

"But it wasn't." The flames that flickered behind his green eyes dared her to contradict him. "They need to see him pay."

"What they need is to respect and trust him, so he can do his job. You need him Markus. The coven needs him. If they didn't, you'd have let him go. If you want to heal the family and the coven, let's work on a way to solve the real problem, rather than creating new ones."

"Is this just about Sage?" He held her gaze; he'd picked up on her passion, and it tamed his anger.

"No." She sighed. It sucked when he was as intuitive as she was. "I want to be out there doing what I'm meant to do. And I want to know the coven I'm doing it for shares my goals and my morals."

He put his hands on her shoulders. "I do. Darian does. We all do. But our laws and our traditions, and yes our punishments, aren't going to change overnight. No one's going to mistake Sage or you as the enemy. You'll both be out there soon enough fighting the real problem. Okay?"

She nodded and leaned in to kiss him before they headed back to the house. "How about I tell you what else I learned from Rick and Abram so we can make 'soon enough' sooner?"

He huffed. "I heard you telling Rocky as you were tying your shoes before heading out. But as you told me, it's a one shot deal. If you used it against Leonce, you'd be a sitting duck for any other Vengatti around."

She cursed herself under her breath for not keeping her doubts to herself. "But the point is I *can* use it against Leonce. I no longer have a blind spot. And as *you* said, my gifts always drain me more when I first use them."

Markus crossed his arms. "You do realize rushing back to be an active warrior means there's no bowing out of watching Sage's punishment?" He knew such an event would be harder for her than the average warrior to watch.

She scowled at him but didn't back down. "You're cruel, on both accounts."

"Sorry, Babe, but it comes with being a warrior. It's a punishment for him. It's a deterrent for the rest of you."

CHAPTER 13

Alex felt Darian before she heard his teeth grinding together or saw him glaring at her from the door to his office. She was sitting at his desk. In his chair. Without his prior knowledge or permission.

"Sorry. I just wanted to check email." She was already out of his seat and edging around the opposite side of the desk from where he now approached. He didn't look as disheveled or exhausted as he had when he had first emerged from his office two weeks before, but he didn't exactly look cuddly either.

"I've told you before to stay out of here when I'm not home."

She wanted to inquire what other unsavory details the many old books in the room hid, but reminded herself she'd pledged to move on.

"I didn't realize it'd take so long. I figured there wasn't much sense in lugging it to my room for just a few minutes."

Darian lifted the razor thin laptop with one finger, but didn't comment on the lame excuse.

"Maybe it's time you take your next paycheck and get your own."

Alex raised a brow. She couldn't remember the last paycheck she'd earned. She'd lost a month for acting on her own at the ball. Then she'd zapped him the night she was officially fired as Markus's secretary. She figured she'd see thirty before she saw another paycheck.

"That's my way of telling you that this is your last week of docked pay." Darian sat heavily in his desk chair and crossed his arms.

"Oh. Thanks. Does that also mean I'm going back to work?"

"You're training every night. And you're on call if we need you. Neither of those is exactly easy."

This was true. Sage had been carried out of the warrior meeting last week, bleeding and semi-conscious, after accepting his punishment. It had been even worse to witness than imagined as she'd sensed the collective shame and sympathy of his fellow warriors. Even Rocky had assumed it'd be a week before Sage returned from Vivian's where he had asked to recover. They had been less than pleased two nights later when he returned and dragged them both from their lovers' arms into the freezing barn for training. Pain and dependency on his mate made Sage even surlier than usual. Alex had spent the last week slathering on arnica and Icy Hot like most women wore moisturizers in the New England winters.

Darian eyed her rubbing her hip, the site of her newest bruise, and grinned.

"Glad my pain amuses you. If you start paying me by the bruise, I'll have that computer in no time." She shook her head and started for the door. She'd wait another week until Sage was ready to return to patrols before pleading her case.

"Alex." She stopped and turned around. "I'm paying you for your other work, too. You are still keeping up with that?" He nodded his head in the direction of the bedroom where Sarah was taking a late night nap. She looked quite obviously pregnant now, making it harder not to mention it.

Alex nodded. "It's helping, isn't it? She's gotten to where just a slight influence soothes her for hours."

He smiled. "I'm not sure if that's her feeling less anxiety the further along she gets without complications, or you perfecting your power. Either way, I'm happy and grateful. Thank you."

"Anytime, so long as she doesn't catch us." She winked and was about to leave, but sensing his improved mood, paused. "Regan, could I possibly ask a favor in return?"

His teeth resumed their grinding. Using his title in a polite, deferential manner had given her away.

"You can ask."

"And you'll listen? And talk it over with Rocky and Markus before deciding?"

The vein over his temple was pulsing. "Do they already know about this favor?"

"I mentioned it at breakfast. You had just left."

"Convenient. And how did they react?"

She hesitated. "They were . . . agreeable."

"Humph. That sounds promising. Take a seat and spit it out—before I throw you out," he ordered calling her bluff. "Agreeable my ass."

She swallowed, forced a smile, and sat on the edge of the couch, leaving a clear escape route should one or both of them lose their temper requiring her to flee.

Two mornings later Markus stood in the foyer unhappily kissing her goodbye.

"Be safe." The words sounded more like an order he'd bark at his males than a goodbye said to one's mate. He'd had a rough night. Two humans had been brutally attacked. Covering it up required Sage's assistance far sooner than Markus would have liked. She understood his desire to want her close after that, but it was too late to back out.

"You agreed to this. Both of you." Alex glanced at Rocky who stood at the door squeezing the keys to the Jeep in his fist.

Neither answered her as Darian entered the foyer leading Sarah from the living room up to bed. The truth was neither had ever thought Darian would allow it. They had both believed that giving in to her request to help her old friend Peter for a few days was harmless, since it would never pass the Regan. Alex herself thought Darian would blow a fuse when she had first asked. He had rattled off every safety concern he could conceive of, each of which she had a planned response to. At the last minute, he caved. At first she feared she'd accidentally projected on him. When it didn't wear off she figured maybe deep down he felt guilty about dragging her from her old life and denying her so many of the freedoms to which she was accustomed. As he smugly addressed her, she realized he had another reason.

"Enjoy, Seer. I'm sure it'll be great to see your old colleagues. And the kids—how many are at East Bristol Middle these days? About 800? What fun."

Sarah rolled her eyes and nudged him up the stairs. Alex refused to react. She kissed Markus good day and headed out with Rocky into the bitter predawn air.

She could panic once they reached the highway.

Torie took a steadying breath. Only one more double period until she'd be free. Then she could find some solitude in a back booth of one of her usual haunts until dusk, at which time she'd head home. Until then she'd have to pretend to be intimidated by the thugs who thought they ruled the world, because they had somehow won the popularity lottery that was eighth grade. Because standing up to them was the equivalent to standing out, the one thing she couldn't afford to do. She slammed her locker door, startling a few of her peers. It wasn't tolerating some annoying human teens that was eating at her. It was the fact her whole family needed to remain silent and obedient just to postpone the inevitable—all because of her.

Earlier that morning when she couldn't find her favorite pair of jeans on her bedroom floor where she thought she left them, Torie had padded down the hall to the laundry closet. Sure, the last few tiptoed steps might have been considered sneaky in a normal household, but Torie's home life was far from normal. If her parents wanted to hear her, they could, no matter how quiet she was. So she had assumed the conversation she heard coming from the kitchen of their apartment early that morning wasn't any more confidential than usual. It hadn't occurred to her that her parents could have been too upset to listen for a nosy teenage daughter.

"He was a bloody mess, beaten to within an inch of consciousness . . . just left there to watch her die."

Torie heard the strain in her father's voice. His disgust shook her more than his description. Unfortunately she had overheard too many descriptions of battered humans, so she knew instantly he was relating some horrific scene he'd witnessed the night before.

"Are you sure—" her mother began.

"It was definitely some of ours, Jess. The alley reeked of Vengatti males, two of the younger ones."

"Maybe you should report them to the warriors. If they're being careless—"

"Careless? You're worried about exposure? I'm a little more worried about the fact our young are torturing humans for sport. He wasn't even fed from, Jessica. They kept him alive just so he could watch, helpless, as they drained his daughter. She couldn't have been more than eighteen."

From where she had become paralyzed along the wall of the darkened hallway, Torie couldn't see her parents, but she was certain she wasn't the only one with tears streaming down her cheeks.

"What did you and Charlie do?" her mother whispered.

"What could we do? We left the girl's body and dropped the male in Rectinatti territory. We figured one of them would find him and call an ambulance—after their Knower had the chance to modify his memory. That poor bastard—"

Torie heard her mother shushing him. It was futile. She knew what her father had been thinking. With their own Knower busy leading the coven most nights, the Rectinatti Knower was left cleaning up after Vengatti atrocities. It was a gruesome job. One that would be Torie's burden in less than a decade unless something drastic changed her fate.

She plodded down the hall to her last period English class with low expectations, both of her future and of learning anything nearly interesting enough to take her mind off of it.

"Damn him." Alex rubbed her temples to ease her headache. Darian had been right.

Being in a school with so many emotional teenagers was about as pleasant as kicking a wasps' nest. The fact they were human did not make up for the fact they were bundles of hormones teeming with emotions. Completely blocking them was impossible. The best she had managed was to dull her sense of the students enough to focus on her teaching.

As she prepared for the start of last period, she felt she had done a decent enough job. She was rusty, but she hadn't completely lost her touch in the classroom. The students, who had somehow managed to scare off the teacher hired to replace her, had seemed pretty mild to this point. Perhaps, though, this had a little to do with her new perspective: anyone not trying to rip her throat out with two-inch fangs seemed pretty tame these days.

Rocky's head thudded on the table as the warning bell jolted him awake. He had stationed himself in the back corner of the classroom because he was too big to fit at a student desk and too intimidating for her to want him sitting in the teacher's chair at the front.

"Is that it?" he asked after yawning. Despite his initial curiosity about human public school, the change from his nocturnal schedule was not going well.

She rolled her eyes. "There's one more double block," she told him.

Rocky groaned. "And to think I complained about being home-schooled. I actually feel bad for these human brats."

"Hey," she reminded him in a hiss as the first few students sauntered in, "watch the 'human' comments."

More than any other class all day, she sensed this crew was feisty, but it was last period. Who could blame them? She was ready to escape herself. The class finally settled, and remained relatively quiet as Alex ran through the roster.

"Victoria Ventura," Alex called the final name expecting the same unenthused response. But there was only silence. Then a few giggles.

"Sweet, maybe we scared off Freakenstein, too." A skinny redhead spoke in a stage whisper she clearly intended the rest of the class to hear.

"We're not that lucky. She dropped her stuff off then left. She's probably crying in the bathroom because her boyfriend quit." A boy in the back held up a pink spiral notebook like it was a nasty specimen from science class and let it drop back onto the desk.

Rocky startled. Alex wondered momentarily if he had been drifting back to sleep again, but then, she, too, was on alert. What she felt from him was not annoyance at being woken, but disbelief and sudden protectiveness. As his eyes scanned the room, Alex rattled off a lecture about respect. She assigned fifteen minutes of silent reading and headed to the door leading to the hall. Rocky flashed to her side faster than should have been feasible.

"Act human, will you," she warned. "What's up?"

He sniffed the air and pointed around the corner. Alex realized she was sensing somebody from the same direction, sensing strongly someone's shock, fear, and anger.

"The girl?" she asked him in a whisper.

He nodded. "Vengatti, for sure. Her notebook reeks."

She sucked in a breath. Her body had tensed at the word, prepared for battle, just as Rocky was. But as her sense, and her common sense, kicked in, she realized they were being ridiculous. This girl wasn't one of the vampires hunting her. She'd had nothing to do with the destruction of Alex's family. She wouldn't technically even become a vampire for a good five or six years. She was just a kid.

"There's nothing we can do now. Go back inside and keep the others from killing each other. I'll go get her back in the classroom."

Rocky grabbed her sleeve. "Are you nuts? Did you hear what I just said? She could be calling in half her coven as we speak."

"It's the middle of the day. No one she could call in would pose much of a threat. We'll get through the next hour and then go straight home. I promise." She tugged her arm free and headed down the hall trying to decide the best thing to say to the child of her enemy.

Torie didn't look up when she heard the footsteps approaching. She knew who it was. What she didn't know was how she knew, how she was suddenly hearing this small, strange female's every thought. Torie knew what she was, or more precisely, what she would become. Her parents had explained early on what the two scar-like lines on her eyebrow meant. This was her 'gift', the reason she'd one day be of great value to her coven leaders—who would no doubt force her to be a part of their twisted brutality.

But none of this was supposed to happen until her late teens or early twenties. And even then her power was only supposed to work with eye contact or physical touch, something she wasn't about to attempt with the human who had brought a Rectinatti warrior as her protection.

She kept her long dirty-blonde hair curtaining her face as the short substitute teacher in combat boots crouched down beside her. The woman looked over her shoulder at what she was reading and wondered how Torie had heard her assign those pages from her position in the hall.

"I didn't think your senses enhanced until after you matured," she said. Torie couldn't help but grin. She liked adults who were straightforward with her.

"They don't." Torie looked up, brushing her bangs to make sure they were still over her eyes. "You're just annoyingly loud." Torie didn't explain what she meant by this; liking was different from trusting.

"Listen, Victoria—"

"It's Torie," she cut her off.

"Whatever. I don't care who or what you are outside this building, but in this building, I'm just another teacher, and you're just another student. So unless you want your parents woken from what I'm sure is a very sound sleep to take a phone call saying you're suspended and they've got to pick you up—which I'm guessing would pose a problem for them at one in the afternoon—you'll get your butt back in there and act like any other student."

Torie was impressed by the woman's fearlessness, especially since it didn't seem to stem from having a warrior right down the hall. Her thoughts hadn't strayed to him once. Whatever gave her confidence was internal.

"You want me to act stupid and obnoxious?"

The human attempted intimidation by narrowing her eyes and putting her hands on her hips. Torie stood to full height. Just as Torie suspected she would, the woman cursed silently. Apparently she had grown used to being towered over by male warriors, but being dwarfed by an eighth grader who wouldn't even get her fangs for another seven years was aggravating. She glared at Torie and pointed back to the classroom.

"Get rid of the thug warrior first." She tried to say it with the same smug tone, but the female seemed to sense Torie's fear. Her scowl melted into a reassuring grin.

"He only looks like a thug. He's more of a puppy dog."

They both looked down the hall to where the warrior with his arms crossed over his chest filled the doorway. Torie couldn't be sure, but she thought she heard him growl.

"Fine, just keep him on a tight leash." She pulled back her shoulders and stuck out her chin as she headed back into the room, carefully avoiding contact with the large male. Had he been human, he would not have noticed her hand shaking as she clutched her textbook, and he may not have detected her fear. Being a vampire, she was sure he did. She couldn't understand, though, how the human female knew everything she was feeling. What was it about this woman?

Midway through a dreadful lesson on theme, it hit her. Humans weren't allowed to know vampires existed. Unless, of course, they were gifted and could be of use to a coven. Like a Seer. This tiny female, attempting to teach twenty-five bored teens, was the infamous Alex Crocker. Torie hadn't seen it, but she knew this woman's picture had been passed among the matured members of her coven with the promise of a lifetime of rewards for the vampire who could bring her or her remains to the Vengatti Regan. No one had succeeded yet, and a few had died trying. She was the most hated and hunted member of the Rectinatti coven.

Which meant she had to be good, both at what she did and in her intentions. Torie had found her escape route.

——◢◆◣——

When the two-twenty bell rang, the Vengatti female had dashed from the room. Rocky was torn between pursuing and getting Alex back safely to the farmhouse. Luckily the second desire won, with a little unknown influencing from Alex. She had no intention of hunting a teenager—of either coven.

"I'm guessing we won't be returning tomorrow?" she asked as they crossed the icy parking lot.

His growl she expected, but when his hand went to the band of his jeans, where she knew he hid a concealed weapon or two, she startled. Then she followed his gaze to the tall blonde leaning on the side of their Jeep, black book bag by her boots.

"Go ahead, Warrior," the girl said. "But you might want to look around first. How do you think it would look to the rest of these humans if a grown man attacked a young girl in a school parking lot?"

"I don't attack females." Rocky spat each word through clenched teeth. Torie had unknowingly hit upon his sore spot. He had a serious knight-in-shining-armor complex and was as disturbed as Markus when he heard about the human girl the Vengatti killed the previous night. Odd as it sounded, his anger over this was probably the one thing keeping Torie safe.

"So he'll help?" Torie asked as Alex finished the thought.

She was so used to Sage commenting on her thoughts, that it was a moment before she realized what Torie had done. The pieces fell together. She had been sensing Torie's emotions as strongly as she sensed Sage. Not having met an unmatured vampire before, she had passed it off as a quality of all vampire young. But that didn't make sense. Until a vampire had reached maturity, their essence was only slightly stronger than that of a human. There was no reason for Torie's sense to be so strong. Unless she wasn't a normal vampire.

"Look who's talking about normal, Seer," Torie mumbled, obviously still hearing the thoughts in Alex's head.

But you're years from maturing. How can you hear me so clearly and consistently?

"You tell me. I'd only had a few flashes before you showed up," Torie responded. Alex sensed a hint of bitterness, but underlying it was desperation, fear, and confusion. The young girl was struggling to make sense of this sudden manifestation of power. Alex sympathized. It's enough for most teenagers to deal with their own thoughts or emotions. Adding those of another, a stranger who was supposed to be an enemy, would be unsettling, if not terrifying.

"What the hell is going on?" Rocky asked. "I feel like I'm listening to you and Sage."

Alex looked at Rocky and nodded. Then she turned back to Torie. "Seers and Knowers sometimes make a connection. No one seems to know exactly how or why, but something about the similarity of our gifts makes it intense and virtually instantaneous. I connected with our Knower right away, but we thought it was because I was so close to maturing—weeks, not years. I guess it doesn't matter, because it seems to be what you've done."

Rocky finally caught on. "No way."

Torie rolled her eyes and pulled back her bangs, just briefly, to let him see the lines in her brow that marked her as a Knower.

"Why are you showing us this?" he asked. "It makes you a target—an even bigger target."

Alex was about to snap at him, but Torie proved she didn't need anyone to speak for her.

"I couldn't help being born with this, any more than I could help being born into the Vengatti coven. We're not all monsters, believe it or not." She crossed her arms defiantly.

"I believe it," Alex said.

"I know. I know who you are. My dad . . . he was at the ball. You let him go. You saved him. I want to take you up on the offer you made him and the others that night. I want . . . I need your help."

Rocky scoffed. "Don't buy it, Alex. Mommy and Daddy aren't too innocent. I could smell you a mile away."

Torie shook her head. "My parents only feed from humans when they have to, and never enough to do permanent damage. *They've* never killed anyone."

Alex sensed the accusation in this last statement. Torie might have been young, but she knew enough about Alex to throw this fact at her.

"I killed in self-defense," she admitted. "But only when it was necessary. No vampire ever needs to feed from humans. The Rectinatti feed exclusively from each other, and they only take what's willingly given."

It was Torie's turn to look away. "The Rectinatti don't have to fear for their lives from their paranoid, violent leader—who, as you know, is my coven's only other Knower."

Alex felt Torie's fear and her shame, and she finally understood. "If they didn't feed, they'd be suspect. And if Leonce read your parents' thoughts, he'd find out about you."

Torie nodded.

Rocky's jaw dropped. "Leonce and your coven don't know another Knower was born?" Keeping a secret like that from the leaders of a coven was nearly impossible. It was also gravely dangerous. Alex rubbed the scar on her neck from the night Leonce had attacked her. She knew even then, before he'd continued to hunt and torture her loved ones, she'd rather die than be forced to serve him.

"Exactly," Torie said concurring with her thoughts. "My parents have barely been able to cover for my lack of interaction up to now. I was shy. I went to public school, so I had to sleep nights. I got sick easy. They're running out of excuses. And I'm running out of time."

Alex looked at the young girl in front of her. Her soft features made her look younger than eighth grade, despite her height. But her serious expression and intense emotions belonged to someone with many more years' life experience.

"You won't be presented until you mature. That's not usually until almost twenty."

Rocky and Torie both shook their heads.

"Vengatti young start being trained to hunt and feed before they turn. And because their leaders like to assure they are all brainwashed well, they're trained by the Regan's warriors, not their parents," Rocky explained.

Alex looked to Torie to see how she would react to this unflattering description.

"No, he's right," she said. "I need to disappear—soon. Before it would be suspicious and put my parents in danger."

No one said anything for a minute. Torie scuffed the frozen

blacktop with her boot. Alex looked to Rocky for an opinion, but he just stood staring, shaking his head. She sensed his strong confliction.

"And you want us to what? Take you home like a stray dog?" he asked finally.

Torie ignored his tone and turned to Alex. "I'd stay and refuse Leonce, if it'd just be me in danger, but he's crueler than that. You know he is."

She did. Leonce would show no mercy until he got what he wanted. And then what? She could only imagine the things he'd do to this girl, the things he'd make her do to others.

"Call Sage," she said to Rocky. "I'm pretty sure he's half awake already." She could sense Sage, even from this distance, and, from his suspicion, she guessed he had been trying to get in her head. In order to protect the girl, she had been blocking him from hearing her thoughts ever since Rocky realized Torie was Vengatti.

"What the hell did you two idiots do?" Even without enhanced hearing, Alex and Torie heard Sage's greeting to Rocky.

"Nothing," Rocky replied with feigned innocence. He held out the cell so Alex could hear Sage's response.

"Yeah? Ask Alex how her head's feeling. She's been blocking me ever since she realized I was awake. Remind her it only works completely if I'm trying to keep her out, too."

Alex cringed. She could block his emotions until her head exploded, which it felt close to doing at any minute, but unless he worked equally hard to sever the connection, he could still capture scraps here and there. He had apparently heard enough to know he wasn't going to like what she was hiding. She grabbed the phone from Rocky.

"We need your help. Shut up and meet us as soon as it's dark enough. And go out through the barn so Markus doesn't freak." The last thing she needed was her mate showing up on high alert the minute he smelled Torie.

"Any other demands, princess?"

"Some aspirin…please."

CHAPTER 14

The early winter sunset meant they had only had a few awkward hours to kill before Sage's arrival. Torie had led them to a quiet Internet café near the state college. Alex sucked on an iced-coffee hoping the caffeine and sugar would ease her aching head. Rocky was staring at his cell muttering to himself. He apparently was expecting Markus or Darian to call any minute to tell him he was fired and would be executed at midnight. Torie avoided conversation with either of them by pulling out her math homework. Alex was almost relieved when she sensed Sage close by. She looked expectantly at the door. Torie followed her gaze, her anxiety intensifying.

"He's not as gruff as he likes to come across," Alex said to her.

Torie tried to hide her gulp as Sage walked into the small café, his large frame hardly fitting through the door. Like Torie, he wore his dirty-blonde hair longer in the front to obscure the marks on his dark brows. The similarity didn't seem comforting to the young girl as Sage's brooding grey-blue eyes pierced Alex across the room.

"Sure," Rocky said reading his partner's expression. "He looks almost cuddly tonight—like a poisonous cactus."

Alex kicked him under the table. "There's no such—" She stopped and clutched her chest. Emotions hit her like a tidal wave. She looked up and realized Sage had made eye contact with Torie. She was guessing by Torie's shock and Sage's righteous anger (aimed entirely at Alex) that the two Knowers had made the same connection each had made with her.

Sage stormed the last few yards and grabbed Alex roughly by the arm.

"Outside. Now. We need to talk."

She slapped her hand over his and zapped him with what was intended to be a wave of calm, but she wasn't sure she hadn't projected her anger at being assaulted by him instead.

"Back off and calm down," she said releasing her hold. He pulled his hand away, but the glacial stare lingered. "She can hear my thoughts just as well on the sidewalk, I'm sure. And I'm guessing from what you two are feeling, she'd be able to hear yours now, as well." Neither he nor Torie denied it. "Good, then let's be polite and talk about her to her face. You can ream me out in private later."

"I intend to—but it won't be in private."

She knew that was coming. There was no way of bringing a new member into the coven without the Regan being informed. And hiding a former Vengatti was out of the question.

"It's all out of the question," Sage said. "Sorry, kid, you're on your own." He turned and started to leave.

She's terrified, Sage, Alex thought, forgetting Torie could also hear. Sage was already answering some unspoken comment of Torie's.

"I'm sure you would, but it doesn't change anything," he said to her, but Torie wasn't listening. She was pissed at Alex's word choice.

"Don't be dramatic. I'm not terrified," she spat.

Alex was ignoring her, pleading with Sage through her thoughts to at least let the girl explain.

Sage pounded the table. "Stop! All of you." He took a breath and became aware of the scene he was creating. The attempted grin he gave to the customers who had looked up seemed more like a sneer. As he slid in next to Rocky, he pulled a bottle of aspirin out of his coat pocket, poured a handful into his palm, and popped them into his mouth, chewing them like mints. He handed the bottle to Alex, who accepted it gratefully.

When he swallowed, he spoke in a softer voice. "If we're going to have this freak-show conversation, we're going to do it aloud."

"Finally, thank you," Rocky said. The three of them glared at him until he returned to fumbling with his cell phone.

Alex tried to hide her smile. Sage agreeing to have the conversation meant she had already half-convinced him. Besides, she could always *make* him agree, though that would have unpleasant consequences later.

"Very unpleasant," he warned.

"That lasted long," Rocky muttered.

They all ignored him. Sage turned to Torie. He seemed to be putting together the pieces from what he had heard in all their thoughts.

"You really think you can give up your coven, your family—sever all ties and never look back, never once contact them again?"

Torie held his stare. When she responded, it was clear Sage wasn't the only one to use silent pauses to gather information. "My parents would want this for me; they've always wanted this for me. Besides *I'll* be leaving by my own choice, to keep them alive, to keep Leonce from using me to kill innocent people. My case is nothing like yours was."

Sage clenched his fists at her words. Alex and Rocky exchanged a nervous glance. This young girl was walking on thin ice reminding Sage of his own split with his family, a story she must have pulled pieces of from his thoughts.

"Why can't her parents make the switch, too?" Alex was curious, but also hoping to diffuse the tension.

"It's not just my parents who are in danger. It's my grandparents, uncles, aunts, baby cousins. Leonce will punish me by hurting anyone he thinks I care about. Most don't even know what I am—and many wouldn't want to leave even if they knew. Like Rocky implied earlier, our leaders do a good job making sure every family has some reason to hate humans and to hate the Rectinatti. One of the males you killed this fall was my uncle. He left two little boys behind. Everyone made it sound like he was a hero."

Alex's heart sank. This was what she feared the night she had been forced to slit the throats of the two Vengatti males who were attacking her, Rocky, and Sage. She had told Darian then that it felt wrong. Hearing this intensified her remorse.

"They attacked us," Rocky spoke up in her defense.

"Sure, and you were just innocently strolling by our homes," Torie countered.

"Trying to find the female they kidnapped." Rocky leaned threateningly towards Torie. He had pressed his lips into a thin line, but Alex was sure, had he opened his mouth, his fangs would have been showing. That female was Ellie, his girlfriend and feeding partner.

"Calm down, and retract the dental work, now." Sage yanked him back against the seat. "She's just making a point. Each side finds ways to feel justified."

Torie nodded.

"Then how does she leave without putting her family in danger?" Alex asked.

Torie met Sage's stare. "I need to have a tragic and untimely demise."

Sage shook his head. "It won't work. Accidents require evidence, proof. And I hope you're not dumb enough to think we'd kill an innocent vamp or human to fill in for your remains."

"And I hope you're not biased enough to believe just because I was born a Vengatti that I'd ask you to," Torie sneered right back at him.

Alex found humor in these two Knowers pretending to be tough as nails while debating morality issues. Sensing neither of them appreciated the comparison, she changed the subject.

"You all disintegrate. Why do you need remains? Wouldn't her clothes and book bag suffice?"

"Not our young," Rocky explained. "That's only after we mature. It's something to do with the strength of our essence."

Torie crossed her arms tightly over her chest and dropped her chin. Alex knew it was to hide her quivering lip. Sage glared at Alex, as if this were all her fault. She turned away from both of them to look out the café window at the falling snow illuminated by the streetlights. Her gift was no real match for life's toughest emotions. She could alleviate Torie's despair and abate Sage's anger. But if she couldn't change the situation that caused them, what was the purpose? Gazing out into the night, she envied the people on the sidewalks whose greatest worry was slipping on the icy puddles.

Her head snapped back to meet Torie's hopeful gaze. The young girl nodded. She and Alex both met Sage's glare. He sighed in defeat.

———◄●►———

"Anyone else think we should check with Markus or Darian *before* doing this?" Rocky asked. Torie looked to his partners, worried his comment would have them thinking twice. Neither Alex nor Sage reacted, though by hearing their thoughts Torie knew they shared Rocky's concern.

Torie stood with Alex and the two males on the bank of the river that ran through the center of Bristol feeding into the bay. There was a layer of ice over its surface. It looked deceptively safe, which was why every other winter someone lost his life trying to cross it. Bodies were rarely found. Winter searches were dangerous, and the current this close to the ocean was swift and strong. This year it was going to be a foolish teenage girl, walking home alone in the dark at the start of a nasty snowstorm.

"Better to ask forgiveness than permission," Alex finally answered Rocky. Torie chuckled; she liked that line. Alex seemed to sense this. "Don't even think about using that on one of us later, got it?" she said turning to her.

"Uh-huh."

Sage turned to Torie holding a rock the size of a basketball. He made eye contact and held it. It was uncomfortable, but she knew if she couldn't answer the question forming in his head with absolute certainty, he'd walk away.

"You're sure about this?" He was thinking of the million reasons not to help her. She kept thinking of the one good reason to follow through. It was the right thing to do. For her, sure, and her family. But also for the people she didn't want to hurt but knew she'd have to if she remained with the Vengatti. And for the people she could help if the Rectinatti could learn to trust her and were willing to train her. They did it for the human. Why not her?

The human willingly runs into danger to help other humans as well as her coven. And she's old enough to understand the responsibility that comes with her gift and her place among us. Sage answered Torie's unspoken question in matching silence.

I'm running to keep myself from becoming one of those dangers. And I've kept what I am a secret since I was four in order to protect my family. I know a little about responsibility.

Sage held her gaze. *I'll buy that. But you're still a kid; I'm not sure you can really understand what you're giving up until it's too late.*

"I'm sure," she answered aloud. The certainty of it stole her breath away. But Sage seemed to understand the difference between pain and doubt.

He nodded, took her coat from her and wrapped it around the rock to give the divers something to find. He hurled the boulder to the center of the river where the ice was thinnest. It crashed through the surface leaving a hole large enough for a slender teen to have fallen through.

Sage turned around to climb the steep bank. "Let's go. We need the snow to cover our tracks and our scent."

Alex stayed by her side as she watched the inky waters churn under the broken surface. Torie knew the Seer felt her fear of facing an unknown future and her grief about leaving behind everything she knew. Never was a long time for a vampire. She turned to Alex who seemed to know what she was wondering.

"I can ease it, Torie, but you have to feel it eventually."

Torie wiped the hot tears from her icy cheeks. "Does it ease on its own—after awhile?" She had heard enough of Alex's and Sage's thoughts to know she wasn't the first to suffer a painful split from loved ones. All of them, even Rocky, had been forced to start over. Torie knew Alex felt all their pain as each remembered, so she knew the answer she'd receive would be accurate, as well as honest.

"It eases, but, from what I can tell, it'll never be easy." She faced Torie. "But, then, you already knew that, didn't you, Knower?"

Torie sniffed, swallowed down the last of her tears, and nodded. There was a lot she knew that she wished she didn't have to. It almost made her envy her clueless classmates. The kids who attempted to make her school years miserable would be the humans she would now grow up to protect—from dangers unknown to them, but all too familiar to Torie.

They had all climbed back up the banking, Torie taking a different path so her scent wouldn't be linked to theirs in case someone came across it before the snow masked it. Alex met her at the top and started to the Jeep with her and Rocky. She hadn't reached the passenger's door when a hand clutched her collar.

"You're riding with me." Sage dragged Alex to the side of Markus's truck before she had time to react. "Project on me and you'll face the Regan alone." He had heard the threat in her mind and volleyed a far more terrifying one in return.

Alex nodded and then assured Torie, whose fear had increased as Rocky had blindfolded her. It was a small gesture of precaution they hoped would slightly abate Markus and Darian's safety concerns. "We'll be right ahead of you the whole way," she promised as Rocky shut the door for Torie.

Once on the road Sage started in. "It didn't occur to you to just walk away?"

"She followed us. And I'd already connected with her. Should I have left her, not knowing whether she'd have a twenty-four hour insight into our coven?"

"That might save your skin with the Regan, but I know damn well that didn't occur to you before you called me. If it had, you would have known my showing up would only increase that danger. Why the hell didn't you call your mate?" He pounded the steering wheel, and she flinched.

She glanced at the screen of her phone, which she had silenced. Thirty-three missed calls, seven voice mails, and four texts. All from Markus. That was one reason. Where she was concerned, Markus didn't always act rationally. It might have worked in her favor. Him seeing how important saving Torie was to her would have been the only thing able to sway him to help her without the Regan's approval. Or it could have been disastrous. He could have feared for her safety and snapped the girl's neck the moment he smelled her near Alex.

Her other reason, of course, was what had Sage aggravated. She'd called him because she hoped, out of all the males, he would understand Torie's plight and take pity. Aside from Alex, only he could understand the fear of feeling one's gift for the first time and the anxiety of wondering how it would be accepted and used by others. He had, and now he hated her for inciting such emotion in him.

"She's holding it together pretty well," she said as her thoughts and sympathy drifted back to Torie.

"You think? An hour after she sensed someone for the first time, she kissed her entire life away. How do you think that's going to feel come morning?"

"I suppose that depends on how the rest of the night unfolds. Do we have a plan?"

"We? I plan on doing and saying as little as possible short of keeping the kid from getting killed."

"I could call—"

"Absolutely not. Are you insane?" Sage had heard the rest of her plan and squashed it before it even had time to formulate. "You need to get it through your thick skull: Sarah is off limits from now on."

"Alright. I get it. I just thought, you know, dealing with a kid and all, it might be beneficial to have a female's perspective."

"What are you?"

"To Darian? An aggravating gnat that he's going to be sorely tempted to smoosh between his fingers the second I step out of the truck."

Sage snorted but didn't disagree. He also didn't offer any useful advice as he sped on toward home. She knew he would help, but how far was he willing to go for a Vengatti? How far would he be able to convince Darian to go? Even as a child and a Knower, she was still the enemy—at least she'd be seen that way by the rest of the Rectinatti coven.

Almost all the rest.

Looking over her shoulder, Ellie saw the snow picking up outside. Sarah had started a fire in the living room fireplace and opened the shades and curtains so they could watch it fall. It would have been beautiful on another night.

"Gifted or not, that human needs to be put in her place. If Darian won't do it, I will."

"Elizabeth." Sarah spoke her name as a chastisement. She'd been wonderfully supportive since Ellie had moved in after being rescued from the Vengatti, but her anger at Alex was one emotion Sarah hadn't understood or accepted. Ellie did her best to repress it. When she couldn't ignore or avoid the Seer, she attempted to be cordial. But there were certain things she wouldn't tolerate.

"What if it were your partner she was constantly endangering or dragging into trouble?"

Sarah actually laughed, one hand on her expanding belly. "Rocky may give into you quite easily, but I don't think too many others in the coven drag him anywhere he doesn't feel he ought to be, Alex included."

"Who's to say she isn't making him 'feel' he ought to help?"

"I trust her. She wouldn't use her gift on any of us like that."

Ellie scoffed. She might have said more, but Darian appeared in the entrance glaring at her. If he worried she knew what task he had recently set the Seer, he had reason to, but she would keep his secret. Tonight she wanted to be sure his anger was aimed entirely at Alex. She only broke his gaze when her phone started ringing.

"Speak of the little—" She pressed talk. "What do you want?"

"Are you in the room with Markus or Darian?"

"Answer my question, or I'm handing the phone to the Regan." Darian was already standing over her with his arm outstretched.

"Ellie, please, it's related to Mallory. Turn down the volume and go in the barn—without the others."

Her breath caught. "Hold on." She stood up and faced the Regan. "I'll be more than happy to help you beat her, but right now I'd like to talk with her privately. Don't follow me, and don't have me followed." She motioned to the yard where she knew one of the warriors was patrolling. Darian glared. "Please, Regan," she added hoping it would suffice. As the daughter of a Regan herself, she'd grown up giving orders to everyone except her parents. It was a hard habit to break. But then if it weren't for that status, he wouldn't have even considered the request.

"Fine," he spat. "So long as you both know I expect to hear the whole story eventually."

Ellie nodded and flashed out of the room. In the barn she shut the door and stood in the dark staring at the phone. Having spent so many weeks in near pitch-blackness during her capture, her eyes had taken time to adjust to the bright lights of the farmhouse. She hadn't minded the headaches. The pain from the light sensitivity had been better than the pain and fear she felt whenever she closed her eyes and relived what she'd experienced in that cell with Mallory. Her captors had done their best to destroy Ellie's spirit, her sanity; Mallory, a perfect and complete stranger and an enemy by coven, had assured Ellie survived intact. Because of her, Ellie was okay with the darkness tonight.

"You found her?"

There was hesitating silence on the other end.

"No, Ellie, that wasn't what I said. I'm not even sure if who we found knows Mallory or where she might be. I just thought—"

"You manipulative little wench. You did it again, screwed with my emotions to get what you wanted." It was good the human was still miles from the house. She ached to tear into her flesh.

"I can't do that over the phone."

"Fuck you. You know what I mean." She was about to end the call when Alex cried out.

"We're bringing home another Vengatti girl. I need your help. She needs your help. Ellie, please."

She brought the phone back to her ear. "Why? Why would I help you—or her? Why not call your mate?"

"Markus has never known the Vengatti to be anything but ruthless. You have. I have. The girl we're bringing home, Torie, is only thirteen. She's a Knower. If she stays with them she'll be forced like Mallory was to do things she doesn't want to do, things she knows are wrong. I know you don't like it, but because of your position, Darian listens to you. That's all I'm asking. Just get him to listen."

Even through the phone she could hear the Seer's desperation. She just couldn't trust the motive behind it.

"I'll make sure the girl is safe and has a chance to explain herself. I won't step in on your behalf."

"I'm not asking you to." Alex's tone was sharp, but softened as she finished. "Thank you. We'll be home in under twenty."

The call cut off. Ellie slid down the door until she was sitting on the floor with her back to it. How many hours had she sat back to back with Mallory just to feel the warmth, to hear the heartbeat of another living being? Mallory had risked everything to keep her alive. Despite all that happened to Ellie, to her coven members, at the hands of those monsters, Mallory had been proof good and evil had little to do with which coven one was born into. If this girl was half as good as Mallory, Ellie would see to it she was protected. Neither the Seer nor the Regan would stand in her way this time.

The warrior Jaron met them in the driveway as they stepped out into the blinding snow. His eyes were downcast, hands buried in his pockets.

"I'm supposed to—" He stopped when he looked up and saw Torie, blindfolded, duck out of the car. "Oh. Well, I'm supposed to cuff her, too."

Alex started to protest, but Sage cut her off. "I think I can handle a teenager, thanks."

"I've got orders, Sage."

"Yeah, well, I'm amending them."

Jaron cleared his throat softly. "You don't have the authority to, especially after . . . "

Alex held her breath as he let the sentence trail off. What they didn't need was Sage dismembering a fellow warrior before even making it into the house. His fangs were clearly visible, but he backed down.

"Hands in front. And no tighter than necessary," he barked.

"Miss Elizabeth already gave that order. It's just a safety precaution. They're cold, but they won't hurt, okay?"

Torie understood she was now being addressed and nodded. Her unabashed bravery was crumbling as they approached the biggest hurdle of this ordeal. Alex put her hand through one arm.

It's us he's angry with. Be honest and polite, and it'll be just fine.

Torie nodded again. Jaron caught it and eyed her and Alex suspiciously as he led them through the drifts of snow. Alex held her breath as she came through the door into the foyer. A welcome sight greeted them. Sarah stood with Ellie at her side wearing a warm smile.

"You can remove the blindfold now, Torie," Sarah said.

Torie looked like her prayers had been answered when she heard the voice of another female. With her cuffed hands she swiped off the bandana they had used and searched for the source.

"It is Torie, right?"

"Y-yes."

Sarah saw her shivering as the melting snow dripped from her hair. She turned to glare at Rocky, Sage, and Alex. "I'm sorry none of them thought to give you a blanket or one of their coats. You look cold, and hungry, I bet. Have you had breakfast?"

"I . . . " Torie was struck speechless by such hospitality. She wasn't the only one.

Sage recovered first. "She goes to school with the humans. She's on their time."

"Dinner then. Come with Ellie and Jaron and me into the kitchen. Jaron, she'll need those removed."

"But the Regan—"

"Jaron."

"Yes, Madame Regan."

Hearing this form of address, Torie's eyes turned to saucers. Sage nodded, likely confirming that she'd heard correctly. She swallowed hard then headed into the kitchen turning back just once for reassurance.

Sarah paused at the door. "I wouldn't keep him waiting longer than you already have. Best intentions aside, when your Regan calls you personally, it is wise to answer it." With that she swept into the kitchen leaving all three of them checking their phones.

"Blessed Creator. It was me." Rocky's olive skin had turned a sickening shade. "I thought it was just Markus again."

"*Just* the lead warrior and your boss?" Markus had appeared out of nowhere and was breathing down his youngest warrior's neck. "You better have more satisfying answers to the Regan's questions. Go. Now."

Both Rocky and Sage disappeared. Alex waited to see if Markus would follow as fast. He didn't.

"Markus, I'm sorry, but this was the right thing to do. You agreed, if any of them approached us—"

"That we would take them to a safe location for questioning. The Regan's residence wasn't exactly where I had in mind," he snapped. Taking a slow breath, he settled himself. "I know you meant well. I was there when Ellie explained about the girl. I'm not mad about that. Stumped at what on earth we're going to do with her, but not angry."

She raised a brow. He was angry—at her—and knew she could sense it.

"You called Sage. You wouldn't even take my calls. It was more than an hour after we discovered Sage left before *Rocky* texted to say you were okay. And after the false text supposedly from Ellie last December, I wasn't even sure I could believe that."

Alex wrapped herself around him. It was the quickest way of conveying everything she wanted him to understand. He surrendered to her and returned the embrace. But when he pushed her back and grabbed her by the shoulders, his grip was as firm as his tone.

"You can't keep doing these things. You need to trust me, as a mate and as your boss. If you'd involved me from the start—"

"You'd be the one about to take a beating. You still might if you both don't get your asses up here." Darian stormed back into his office.

Markus picked her up without warning and obeyed. When she was righted, she was next to Rocky who still appeared peaked. It was wrong for him to be here at all. She started to explain, hoping to exonerate him, but the Regan's fangs snapped by her face.

"Rocky will explain. Sage will listen to ensure no one's being toyed with. And if I grant you permission to speak, you will answer what I ask and say no more. Understood?"

Alex paused just long enough to see his fist curl.

"Yes, Regan."

"Good. Rocky, every detail, every decision, and every reason behind it."

Rocky nodded and started the story at the beginning of last period. He hadn't gotten far when the Regan interrupted.

"Why not take her number, come home, and seek permission? You are familiar with the concept, yes, Alex?"

Sure, it seemed logical standing here in his office.

"They had already made a connection," Sage interjected hearing her flounder. "Going home would have given the girl an hour to pluck important information from her head."

Darian, like Sage when he'd first heard this excuse, wasn't buying it. "If you worried she was the type to 'pluck information' from your head to share with her coven, you wouldn't have wanted to bring her here at all. Am I right, Seer?"

"Yes."

"Then why were you once again making crucial coven decisions *on your own?*"

"It was the right thing to do." It was a whisper. She already knew what the Regan's response to this would be.

"And I'm not nearly intelligent, experienced, or compassionate enough to have come to that same conclusion?" he raged. "I needed to be manipulated by my houseguest, silenced by my ward—"

"I'm not—"

"Shut your trap and let me finish or you will be again," Darian snapped at Rocky before continuing. "And lied to by my Knower."

"It was more of a carefully manipulated truth," Sage said, unable to resist.

"Use that expression again in the next century, and I'll rip out your fang and use it to tattoo those words across your ass."

Alex stifled a laugh, which became a grunt as Rocky elbowed her roughly in the ribs.

"We'll see how funny you two clowns find your punishment. Finish the report, Rocky."

Rocky made it to the end with only a few questions from Markus about the precautions that were taken both in faking Torie's death and in bringing her back to the farmhouse.

"You both blocked her the whole way here?" he asked Sage and

Alex at the end. Alex felt he knew the answers to his own questions but was asking them to assure the Regan heard them.

"Yes, but she'll need to be trained to block us in return. Otherwise, it's possible she'll still catch glimpses of important conversations now and then," Sage answered.

"You don't think distance will break the connection?" Markus continued trying to find an easy solution.

Alex shook her head. "Doesn't work for Sage and me, at least not locally. And we can't send her unaccompanied to Canada or California." She'd also been considering Torie's options as Rocky reported. There were few that were feasible. "She's still a child. She needs a parent figure. Someone who can keep her out of trouble and help her with her gift." She looked at Sage beside her. "She's already in your head. Wouldn't it be better to have her close, to keep an eye on her?"

It took him a minute to register her suggestion. "Me? You're joking. I don't do young. I can hardly stand you and Rocky, and you're supposedly adults. I'm for option A. Put her on the first flight to some Vengatti-free village in Europe and hope to hell the connection breaks midway across the Atlantic."

"If it doesn't?" Darian asked. "Who in the coven can I trust with whatever thoughts of mine, yours, and Markus's go through Sage's head for her to hear and possibly repeat? And among them, who is going to be willing to take in the daughter of our enemy? You don't think these things through to the end, Alex. This is another mess you made that I'll have to clean up. How am I supposed to face my mate, or myself after I'm forced to ki—"

Alex's knees shook. Markus grabbed her elbow as he cut off whatever gruesome idea had flitted across Darian's mind.

"You couldn't. You won't. Because it'd be wrong, Darian, by every measure." He grabbed Alex's hand in his and watched her face as he spoke again. It was partially a suggestion to the Regan, partly a question posed to her. "We'll take her in. We'll vouch for her, be responsible for her."

She sputtered. "Markus, I'm hardly twice her age. I can't be her mother."

He squeezed her hand. "No more than I can replace her father. That's not what she's going to need. You know teenagers, and you know what it's like to start over, to lose family, to have a gift that doesn't always feel like one. And I know the rest—about our coven and hers, about how to protect her, hide her, keep her safe. Who better to help her through this?"

She wasn't sure how to respond. Wanting to help Torie was a bit different than wanting to raise her.

"How are those turning tables treating you, twerp?"

"Go screw, Sage."

"Tsk. Tsk. What a bad example you're setting for your young."

She shot him a few silent statements instead, which only had him laughing harder. "Her hearing won't be good enough for a few more years to have heard your first comment, but the slew of curses you just shot me through your thoughts, she definitely heard."

Markus squeezed her hand and grinned. "You are going to have to watch that. And not just for Torie's sake." He glanced quickly at Darian. Sarah had implied the week before that the first one to swear in front of her young would have his, or more likely her tongue cut out and served to her for supper.

"Yeah. Right."

"I suppose I should meet her, huh? If we're going through with this," Markus asked.

"Hold up. I haven't agreed to anything yet. You've accounted for your decisions. I want to hear from her. Rocky, go get her."

"Yes, Regan." Rocky darted from the room.

Alex looked at Markus again. Though their engagement and mating had happened considerably faster than the average human relationship, she still didn't think there was much he could do that would surprise her. His latest decision had. She was trying to puzzle out his real reasons for it when Sarah entered with Torie.

"Thank you, Rocky," she said before he could reenter with them. "You and Sage can clear the driveway while you wait. I told you all during the last storm, I don't want it blocked, just in case."

Rocky looked relieved to be dismissed. He avoided Ellie's gaze as he slipped past her. Sage hadn't moved more than a step before Darian intervened.

"No. You I want to stay."

"I doubt shoveling snow is all that mentally taxing, Darian," Sarah cut in. "He can listen from there. If something urgent needs to be brought to your attention, he'll be back here in a heartbeat. Ellie, you're also not needed here. It'll be easier for Torie and Darian to talk with less of an audience."

Neither Sage nor Elizabeth moved, despite Sarah's tone. Darian's glare went from his mate to Alex.

"I didn't involve her. I knew better." Sage coughed. "Ok, Sage knew better."

"That's right. You called me, so I could take the blame for that, right?" Ellie sneered.

Before she or Darian could respond, Sarah stepped forward. "No one involved me. I chose to involve myself. It is part of my duty as the Regan's mate to see to the welfare of the coven's females and young."

"She's not exactly—"

"Out, Sage."

The Knower didn't wait for Darian to contradict his mate again. He disappeared through the door. Ellie gave Sarah a final pout and Alex one last death glare before sidling out herself.

Sarah began with introducing Torie to Markus, who shook her hand warmly, and Darian, who did not. Torie seemed unsure of what the proper response to meeting the Rectinatti Regan ought to be. Mixing the vampire world she was born into and the human world in which she lived most days, she began with a bow and ended with, "Hi."

Darian glared. The rest of them chuckled. Sarah crossed the room to squeeze his shoulder in a manner meant to calm him. She then led him around the desk where she took the nearest wingback chair. He took her cue, sort of.

"Sit," he ordered the room at large. Alex nodded and led Torie to the couch, sitting next to her but not so close as to make her uncomfortable. When Darian made it clear he planned to remain where he was, leaning against the desk, Markus took the final seat next to Sarah.

"Let's start with your full name."

"Victoria Ventura," Torie answered softly.

"Your real name," Darian demanded.

"Darian, that's the name—" Alex stopped when he spun on her.

"My earlier mandate remains. Stay silent or get out."

She nodded and avoided the exasperated look her mate was giving her. Darian turned back to Torie.

"My father's name is Jason, but, she's right, I've never gone by that." Her voice was stronger. Alex appreciated her trying to help, but knew it was dangerous.

"And you're thirteen?"

Torie looked in her lap. "I will be next month."

"But—" Alex cut herself off before Darian ejected her. Torie was in eighth grade. She'd heard them all night referring to her as a teenager and never corrected them.

Torie heard this and explained. "Vampire young are bigger than human kids the same age. My mom lied when I started school, so that I'd blend in better. It worked until I grew half a foot last year." She glanced at Alex. "I didn't correct you, because I knew if you heard I was only twelve, you and Sage wouldn't believe I was old enough to know what I was doing."

It seemed silly that one year would make such a difference, but it did. Alex had taught both seventh and eighth grade and knew they were worlds apart maturity wise.

"Please, I was more mature than most human eighth graders by the time I could talk."

"Alex." Darian pounded his desk. Torie flinched.

"Darian has a thing about only hearing half the conversation," Alex explained.

"The Regan has a rule about transparency and more than a few about respect," he corrected sharply.

"Sorry, sir. I just . . . I can hear her like she's speaking aloud, like you all should be able to hear her. It's weird and hard to think you can't."

Darian saw her rubbing her temples, just as Sage did when his gift distracted him, just as Alex did when hers overwhelmed her. His fists relaxed. Alex still comforted her, not knowing if Torie had seen it.

"Hey, you're doing fine. He knows it's hard. They all do. They helped me through it just recently. They're still helping me through it."

Torie was fighting back tears. She just nodded and swallowed hard.

"I'll let you rest soon. But I have a few more questions. Can you do that?" Darian's voice was gentler now than Alex had heard it all night.

Torie nodded.

"Sage and Alex explained to me why you came to her for help, why you left. I know you think you're mature enough to make that decision—"

"I am mature enough. I already decided."

"Let me finish." His voice was sharp again.

"Yes, sir."

"I need to be certain you understand the consequences of that decision, which you're right, has already been made." He paused long enough to shoot Alex a look. "I also need to know if you're able to understand the responsibility you're accepting by asking to stay with this coven."

Torie waited until she was sure he wanted her to speak. "I know that by tomorrow morning I'll be on the news, breaking every coven rule about staying under the radar. If I go back after that, Leonce will wait just long enough for the cameras to go away to kill me, or if he figures out what I am, to kill or maim someone I love. I know he'll be watching them for weeks, months even. I know that means I can't go back. I can't even send them an email to tell them I'm okay." The tears came now despite Torie's best efforts. She wiped them away angrily. Alex reached over slowly, not to startle her, and rested a hand on her knee.

"That'll be the hardest part, Torie, but there's more to it. Your new life won't be easy either." Sarah was only trying to be honest, but Alex didn't think all this needed to be said tonight.

"Because of my gift? That would have been hard no matter what coven I was with. At least if you let me stay, I won't be forced to use it to hurt people or to cover up for those in my coven who hurt them. Right?" She looked nervously between the four adult faces in the room.

Darian sighed. "I think Sage and Alex would argue that using their gifts to clean up after what the rest of your coven is doing isn't much easier."

"No, but it's better than being forced to be a part of it," Alex interjected. Darian nodded and didn't bother to scold her for speaking out of turn.

"But it's more than just that," Sarah said. "You and Sage made a connection to her right away that allowed you to know her—and trust her intentions. It was your certainty that convinced us. The rest of the coven won't have that luxury."

"You mean because the rest of the coven doesn't particularly trust

Sage and me. She can't help being gifted. She's trying to change being Vengatti. That ought to count for something."

"Of course it counts," Sarah said.

"Good, then let's not pile on any more worries for her tonight." Alex turned to Darian. "The connection's made. It was no one's fault, and it can't be undone. Tell her the rules, make her aware of the responsibilities, but first assure her that you'll keep her safe. And keep in mind she's a kid, please."

"And one who looks like she's had far too much for one day," Markus spoke up. They all turned to Torie whose hands shook in her lap. She looked pale under the curtain of blond hair that she'd let fall to hide her tears. "Come on, kid. The rest can wait."

Markus slipped his hand under her elbow and helped her up. She was nearly as tall as he, but looked like the child she was as she covered her face in his chest. Alex stood to follow, but a tug on her arm told her that was wishful thinking. She might have feared what was to come, but was too enamored with watching her warrior mate melt for a child who had awoken as their enemy and headed to bed as their responsibility.

It was after midnight when Alex escaped from Darian's office, the last to be released from his haranguing of her, Sage, and Rocky. She had been awake for over thirty hours. When she saw Markus sitting in a chair in the doorway to the guestroom, she wanted to collapse into his arms.

"You look like you're about to keel over," he whispered.

She leaned against him, resting her head on his shoulder. "She's asleep." It wasn't a question. She had sensed when Torie's exhaustion had finally over-taken her other emotions. Rocky and Ellie had given up their room, at least for the night, so that Torie wouldn't have to sleep in Rocky's old room in the basement.

"She calmed down after she left the office. She wanted to stay awake to get on our time, so Sarah and I explained how you and I had offered to vouch for her and therefore would be in charge temporarily."

"Temporarily?"

He nodded. "Sarah suggested we wait awhile before making anything official. I agreed, and Torie did, too. Waiting will give everyone a chance to adjust. She needs that even more than we do."

Alex nodded. "But I think she'll be okay. She seems pretty smart and tough. I'm glad you talked to her."

"Me too. She's a neat kid. And, yes, smart and tough, a little like someone else I know, only politer." Alex swatted him. "When she fell asleep in her hot chocolate, though, Sarah and I insisted she at least take a nap. Tough or not, she was spent."

"And now you're guarding her. The way you guarded me after I tried to run away that first day."

Markus stroked her cheek. He heard the tension in her voice. "Hey, I fell in love with you watching you cry yourself to sleep. It's a precaution. Darian will lift it when we're sure she's not going to freak out like you did and do something stupid."

"There are so many misconceptions in all that, I don't even know where to begin."

"Then tell me what happened in there, instead." He nodded to the office.

"You didn't hear it all?" Darian hadn't been quiet.

"Not all of it." He smiled. "I'm hoping the fact he hasn't dragged me in there to be beaten on your behalf yet is a good sign."

She cringed. "He took another two months of my salary . . . and yours."

"That one's new." Markus was nonplussed.

"Sorry."

He shrugged. "As far as punishments go, it's a gift. He knows I can afford it. It's only a punishment at all because it bothers you. That can't have been all, though."

"It was for Rocky. And really it's more than he should have gotten." She watched to see if Markus would support her on this. He nodded. He'd come a long way where Rocky was concerned.

"I'll see what I can do in a few days when things have settled down."

She smiled and squeezed his hand, but she sucked at poker faces. He waited patiently for the rest as if he knew it somehow involved him, too.

"He's attempting to teach Sage and me a lesson about the importance of interdependence within the coven." She paused. Markus seemed to know where this was headed. Apparently this punishment wasn't a new one.

"He banned you from feeding. For how long?"

"Well, since it was the second time in recent months we each had an issue with the concept, two weeks."

"For both of you?" His voice rose. She tried to quiet him. "But Sage has two and a half centuries on you. Can you even go two weeks?"

She shrugged. It had only been a little over a month since she began feeding. She hadn't gone more than a few nights without exchanging at least a little essence with him, but part of that was for pleasure. She had no idea at what point it would actually become painful, but guessed it would be well within two weeks. She'd have to be careful not to use her gift more than necessary. That meant no blocking, which meant no peace and no privacy—for her or Sage. Of course, Darian knew this, too. It was the perfect punishment for the Seer and Knower to have to suffer together. If they didn't kill one another in the next two weeks, they'd make themselves miserable refraining from it. The Regan was undoubtedly patting himself on the back for thinking up this one.

"I'm going to talk to him." Markus pushed her off his lap to stand.

"Not tonight." She held a hand against his chest, soothing him. She didn't hide what she was doing. He let her do it. "I'm going to take a nap, too. Wake us up before dinner, and we can all go down together."

"Like a family?" Markus asked lightly, a tone that clashed with his emotions. His question answered her earlier one about what had made him so eager to accept responsibility for Torie. Her brows shot up. They'd been mated less than two months. Not once had the topic of young come up.

"Considering Darian's mood, I was thinking more like the Titanic," she replied hoping to delay it awhile longer. "But whatever floats your boat."

"English teacher humor? That's really your response?" He teetered between amused and annoyed.

"For now. Torie isn't the only one who needs time to adjust. We've got forever, remember?" She held her hand up for him to see the scar that remained on her wrist, just as she'd wanted it to.

He raised his left hand to match hers. "From now until eternity."

CHAPTER 15

"Presumed dead. An adept presumption, though perhaps a bit early." Leonce tossed the previous day's paper onto the coffee table.

Ty merely cracked his knuckles. Coven member or not, he didn't give a rat's ass whether some snot-nosed kid had disappeared or drowned. What he wanted to know was who was involved.

"Ah, yes," Leonce said catching some of his thoughts. "Last seen at East Bristol Middle School. Why does that name ring a bell?"

Ty rolled his eyes. The only thing he wanted to ring was her neck. Leonce knew damn well it was the same school they'd first attempted to snag Alex Crocker from the previous June.

"She hadn't returned. We checked," he assured the Regan.

"Hadn't, perhaps. But hasn't?" Leonce challenged.

Ty sighed. "I suspect she has." He tossed another section of the paper toward his boss. "A posting for an English teacher popped up last week. According to what we learned about her last year, I'd say it was her old job."

"And you think she was ballsy enough to return?"

"When has she ever lacked in that department?" Ty spat. "I'd stake a fang she was there the day this female disappeared. The storm covered all the scents, but I don't believe in coincidences where the Seer is concerned." He rubbed his knee, which frequently still throbbed after a night on patrols, a constant reminder of the debt he still owed her. He planned to repay it as painfully as possible. "Seems your mating night gift hasn't had the effect you hoped."

Leonce raised a brow, but he couldn't deny it. The threats hadn't spurred her into any drastic action which would make her a more visible target. And the only time she was spotted outside the Rectinatti's careful web of protection, two more of his warriors ended up dead.

"This is a far bigger problem than a few warriors killed doing their duty," Leonce said.

Ty clenched his teeth. The Regan never liked to get his hands dirty. He never had the proper respect for those who did, either. He was a master manipulator, but knew little of soldiering or leading troops. If he had, their warriors might not have been decimated in December. Ty had argued vehemently against attempting an attack on the Rectinatti ball with a group of mixed males. For a successful slaughter of the magnitude Leonce was looking for, every warrior and every male needed to be fully engaged.

"Charlie swore none of the males let go that night considered the Seer's proposal. Perhaps he was right, and this girl left of her own accord. Or perhaps he was wrong." Leonce dropped the paper onto the table. "Bring him in again, and the girl's father, too."

"To what end? If they are involved, they'll die before telling us where to find her."

"Does that prospect bother you, Warrior?"

Ty shook his head. "Not really, though Charlie can be useful at times. My real problem, and yours, too, is that two more of our males will be dead while that Seer still lives. She's meddling with more than just my warriors, now. She's made it clear she wants to turn as many of our coven members as possible against us, against you. If she were unbound by her own coven, she'd likely have lured more to their side already."

Leonce sat down and rested his elbows on his knees. His fingers drummed together as he considered this comment.

"I wonder how many Rectinatti know she's taking in Vengatti young and letting our warriors go free," he finally said.

"I'd hardly call them warriors." They were a misfit bunch of two-faced cowards.

Leonce raised a brow. "Would the distinction matter if it were one of our coven members releasing nearly two dozen Rectinatti?"

"No." Ty saw where he was going with this and grinned. "I'd burn the bastard for the traitor he was."

Leonce stood up. "Perhaps we ought to leave this problem in the hands of those a bit closer to it."

Ty couldn't agree more. It was time to let the Rectinatti take out their own trash.

Alex scrambled to change the channel as Torie entered the kitchen with Ellie looking for lunch.

"It's not on there anymore," Torie said. "I got bumped off the six o'clock news by a toddler who died of carbon dioxide poisoning in Shore Side. Guess a drowned East Bristol tween can't compete with that." She smiled a bit too nonchalantly to be believed.

The adults had all gone out of their way to occupy her mind in the last four nights. Ellie had helped her order an entire new wardrobe, for which Torie kept insisting she'd pay Markus back. Finally frustrated with trying to convince her she didn't have to, he'd asked Sarah for a list of chores Torie could help with around the house. Alex had enlisted her in creating a curriculum for her. She couldn't return to any public school in the area, so Alex and the others would have to homeschool her. Even Sage had spent a couple hours each night answering her questions and attempting to teach her to block her gift. Alex knew he had a selfish reason for these lessons, but so did she. Having a teenager privy to one's every thought could cause some problems.

Currently, though, she was the one invading Torie's privacy, sensing her emotions and calling her bluff. "Just because the news isn't covering it, doesn't mean anyone else has forgotten." She reached out to stroke her arm to soothe her, but Torie jerked back.

"I know. I wasn't about to parade around Bristol."

Alex raised a brow. "I meant your family, and I think you knew that." She didn't reprimand her for her attitude. She'd had plenty of her own temper issues when her gift was new, or newer.

Torie's lip trembled. She'd held it together pretty well so far, but her pain and fear were always close to the surface.

Ellie saw this, too, and glared at Alex as if she'd beaten the tears out of Torie. "She's not the only one who's getting stir crazy. I noticed you took a nice hour long run this morning. Must be nice to at least have that freedom."

"I didn't make that rule," Alex said. It had been Darian and, to be fair, Markus who decided it was too risky for Torie to be seen in the yard. With all the trees save the scrub pines bare, glimpses of the yard could be seen from the road. All it'd take to cause chaos was one passing driver to think they recognized the face from the evening news. The long blonde hair and striking blue eyes in the yearbook photo the school had provided the reporters were distinguishing features. Until that image had time to fade from the public's mind, Torie was stuck inside. Alex just hoped Markus and Darian realized that for the general public that meant about twenty minutes after the last tweet, because if they were judging off a vampire's memory instead, Torie would see two hundred before she saw the sun again, and by then it would be a little too late.

The tears spilled over, then. Alex cursed herself realizing Torie had heard her latest musing. She started to apologize but Torie brushed it off.

"You're right. And Markus has already thought of that. He thinks my coven will figure out you were somehow involved. He's scared they'll try to find me in order to find you."

"Really?" she asked with a grin. "He told you all this?"

Torie shrugged sheepishly. She'd quickly become enamored with Markus. She had a healthy respect for his authority, but unlike with Darian, who frightened her, she had warmed enough to Markus to ask him questions and respond to him playfully at times. She apparently also felt comfortable enough to pluck his thoughts from Sage's head.

"I didn't mean to hear it. You won't tell him . . . or Sage, will you?"

"Not tonight, but try to be more careful. Sage believes in an eye for an eye, so unless you want your own undies aired at dinner each night, you'll learn to keep a lid on that laundry basket of other people's secrets, okay?"

Torie nodded, though her next comment proved she clearly missed the point. "You're not scared?"

Alex snorted. "Sure I am. But one, it's nothing new, and two, I haven't been lead warrior for decades. I don't analyze every situation for its every possible threat."

"Clearly," Ellie mumbled from where she was making a salad on the other side of the kitchen.

Alex tried to remember she needed to be a role model and responded calmly. "Do you have a suggestion, then? One you're willing to present to Markus and the Regan?"

Ellie turned around, whipping her red hair, her own identifying feature, over her shoulder. She was examining Torie. A grin spread across her face. "Actually, I do."

A few hours later Alex and Torie sat on the front steps drinking in the freedom of fresh air with their hot chocolates. They were still sipping when Markus, Sarah, and Darian returned from the club. Darian and Sarah were deep in a discussion that Alex sensed bordered on an argument, but Markus noticed them right away. His arms crossed as soon as he shut the door to the truck's cab.

"I thought I—" He froze midway through the reprimand. Flashing to the stairs, he took in what he was seeing. "Torie?"

She stood and twirled once. Her long blonde hair gone, the short black bob with a few streaks of brilliant blue bounced as she spun. She had replaced her blue jeans and snow boots with a pair of combat boots, black jeggings, and a fitted long sleeve tee that bared just a glimpse of her midriff. All this, in combination with the touch of make-up Ellie had taught her to apply, had completely erased her lingering touches of childhood. This Torie was all teenager. She became an increasingly nervous teenager as Markus remained silent, and the Regan and Sarah joined him in gawking.

Alex provided some aid. "Ellie and I helped solve your problem of Torie being recognized. I'm guessing from your gaping it was successful?"

"Very," Markus said, recovering. "The difference is . . . stunning."

Torie blushed. "Red carpet stunning, or just been hit by a taser stunning?" she asked.

"Honestly, sweetie, a bit of both," Markus answered, to which both Alex and Torie chuckled in relief.

Torie turned to her. "That's not so bad, then. My dad would have killed me if he came home to this." Alex smiled. Sarah and Markus were recovered enough to recognize the reference as a reminder of her loss and also both smiled at her. Darian, though, was still glowering.

"If I ever come home to something like this as a father, I will skin whoever is responsible with my own fangs." He bared his teeth at Alex for emphasis before entering the house.

Torie blanched, but Sarah patted her arm on her way by. "I rather like the blue, myself," she whispered with a conspiratorial wink.

"Coven colors, it is a nice touch." Markus nodded. "But just for future reference, I draw the line at tattoos and piercings." He pointed a finger at Torie and slapped Alex playfully on the rear before heading inside.

Six more days. Oh, Creator. Alex let her head fall to the kitchen table. "Rocky," she mumbled with her cheek smooshed into the wood, "can you get me a coffee? And some of those aspirin on the counter, please?"

He had been eyeing with a blend of apprehension and annoyance the organic Fruit O's in his cereal bowl, Ellie's idea of getting him to eat healthier. He seemed to welcome the distraction and turned to the counter behind him.

"Ah, Alex, I know that in a glass blood and wine might look alike, but please tell me you didn't think two bottles of Merlot was going to ease your thirst?"

She glanced at the two empty bottles on the end of the counter near the coffee maker. She couldn't deny she'd considered other means of dulling the discomfort caused by Darian's mandate banning her and Sage from feeding, but she'd learned her lesson concerning mixing alcohol and her gift months ago.

"Not mine. That much alcohol would kill me."

"That was the result I was after, but no such luck." Sage stumbled into the kitchen and snagged a steaming cup of coffee right from Rocky's grasp. "What?" he snapped. "I might not be an infant in the essence arena, but I imagine smelling my partner's scent on another male is just about as miserable as being denied blood mid-screw. Thanks for not even trying to block that this evening, by the way. It's just what I needed to wake up to."

She was too aggravated to blush, too tired to bother responding, and too weak to block anything from anybody. All of which he knew damn well. Still she was puzzled.

"Markus fed from Cormelia." She knew, because she made him. This was her punishment, not his. One of them needed to be thinking clearly.

"Who had exchanged essence with Vivian the night before." Markus's tone was contrite as he entered the kitchen rubbing the kink from his neck. He had hobbled to the nearest couch after she cut short their early evening romp. "Sorry, Sage, I hadn't thought of

179

that."

The Knower growled but said nothing. Alex sensed the reason for his sudden silence. Darian and Sarah were waking upstairs. Sage wouldn't give the Regan the satisfaction of complaining about his punishment. She was miserable enough not to care.

"Rocky, the aspirin, please."

"He's nobody's gofer boy anymore. Get it yourself."

"Oh, joy, Ellie's blessing us with her presence for breakfast," Alex mumbled as the redhead strode past. Given her lack of control and Ellie's itch to get into it with her, a catfight would almost certainly have ensued if Darian hadn't entered in a mood of his own.

"Why aren't you dressed?" he asked Alex.

She looked down at her sweats and long sleeve workout shirt. Unless Under Armour made an Emperor's New Clothing line, she was pretty sure she was dressed. Torie giggled at the unspoken remark. Even Sage smirked. Darian caught this and spun on him, too.

"And you?"

Sage raised an arm and sniffed the pit of his usual grey t-shirt. "I'm good. Smell better than most of those old coots."

"You smell like a barroom and Alex's blood. Change. Now."

Sage peered over his shoulder at the smear of blood she had wiped on his shirt during the previous night's training. Exhausted and unfocused, she had wrapped her hand around his knife trying to disarm him. Markus had healed her cut, while lecturing them both about the dangers of using real weapons for training. Neither had listened, too preoccupied with the sight of blood.

"Yeah. Right. If it's not enough to satisfy them, why give them any ideas, huh?" Sage winked at Alex before sauntering toward the basement where his bedroom was. His lack of urgency further infuriated the Regan. It wasn't until she realized who Sage had been referring to that she understood Darian's foul mood.

"You're taking me to the Elder Council meeting? You were serious about that? After last time?" Her mouth hung slack in disbelief. The night she brought Torie home he had thrown out any number of threats, one of which had been that he'd changed his mind and would be dragging her along to explain her actions at the ball and concerning Torie.

"It won't be like last time." This was another threat—and a promise that consequences would be severe if she was unable to comply.

"No, it won't. I'm in better control than I was then. And I know that what I did was right."

Darian's brow shot up.

"But I'm also willing to admit and accept responsibility for the fact that my methods were unacceptable by coven standards."

He crossed his arms. "Leave it at unacceptable. Period."

"Fine." She would play the game, by the rules the council kept, knowing he hated it as much as she did. She tossed the rest of her yogurt; her appetite for food decreasing proportionally with her need for essence. As she grabbed the bottle of aspirin and started for the stairs, Darian caught her arm.

"Are you really in better control?"

She tried to read him, but, of course, her sense was shot, the very reason he was asking. So she'd try being frank, and hoped he'd reciprocate.

"If you're asking whether your punishment is proving effective, yes. I accidentally zapped Markus so hard he fell out of bed this evening." She didn't mention it was because he wouldn't allow her to suck the blood from the nail marks she left on his back during foreplay. There was frank, and then there was over-sharing. "That said, if my looking and smelling weak and miserable will help tonight, I'll make it work. But just to be safe, it's probably better if you don't allow any physical contact—at least not with anyone you like."

Darian actually released a snort of amusement. "Fair enough. Go get dressed. And look presentable. Nothing with a drawstring, please." He eyed her sweats. She knew he was remembering the pajama pants she refused to take off after she nearly killed herself draining her own essence last fall.

"It's not that bad. Not yet," she said as she headed to the stairs.

"Hold it together tonight, and at least attempt to conciliate them, and we'll discuss shortening your sentence—before you hit Markus in some limb he actually needs to lead my warriors."

So much for not over-sharing. Markus must have beaten her to the punch. She started up the stairs without turning so he couldn't glimpse her grin.

That's right, Regan. You'll catch more flies with honey—or in this case, blood.

When they arrived in the club lobby Darian turned to Sage with a silent request. *Go read the temperature of the room.* For the benefit of anyone in earshot he added aloud, "Tell them I'll be there shortly."

Sage looked at Alex, who was trying to hide her hands, which had starting shaking like a stroke victim the minute she entered the building and was inundated by so many senses. Without her usual hoodie with its front pocket, she floundered.

"Wouldn't the Seer be better for that job?" It was a sick joke. Despite her attempt to play it cool when the Regan had questioned her back at the house, Sage knew she was hours away from breaking down and begging for essence and days past when she should have. It was beyond punishment at this point. It was dangerous—and not just for Markus's malehood—for all of them and for her.

Darian was finally beginning to see this. His eyes darted to her hands, as well. "You've been at this a bit longer," he said. *How badly does she need it?*

"Quite a bit," he answered to both.

"Fine. Then do your job. And bring Markus back with you."

"And Vivian?" he asked with a half-assed grin.

"Isn't required," Darian said. "Alex, come." The Seer snapped out of her daze and stumbled along behind him without even contemplating a snide remark about the command that sounded like one usually given to a well-trained pet.

Crap. She's worse off than I thought. Of course, aside from the turncoat teenager back home, no one could hear the thoughts in his head.

He made his way around a back hallway where the first families had a private lounge. He hoped a few of the Elders might have been lingering there. Walking into the meeting room would provide him little opportunity to do what Darian asked. As much as he hated admitting it, Alex was best suited for that job. His gift required contact, which few members willingly provided. But get enough of them in a crowded space . . .

"Hold up." He flashed to the elevator just as the doors were closing and stuck his boot in the shrinking gap. He grinned as the doors reopened on six startled faces. "Sorry, gentlemen, but since we're heading in the same direction . . . " *I'll just take advantage of a few of your meager minds.*

He squeezed in among them using the excuse of his size to bump into far more of them than was necessary. His initial glimpses of *'big brute,' 'still unmated—no wonder,'* and *'necessary evil, I suppose,'* were undoubtedly referring to him. He'd likely have to engage them in some form of conversation to turn their thoughts back to the meeting. Necessary evil, indeed.

'If anyone in the coven is responsible for the girl's death, surely it's him, not the Regan or the Seer.'

Sage's sense perked up. He still had one shoulder lightly brushing Dante's back. The ancient coven lawyer was agitated and rambling in his head a mile a minute.

'Crazy to blame the human for Monica's attack. Then again, if Antonio's right, she made the warrior's schedules. She may have known who was being protected. But knowing and sharing are not the same. He's got no evidence. Of any of his allegations. Not that the burden's on him to provide much. Once the allegations are made, though, there's no turning back. It's dangerous. I told him as much, warned him. It's all I can do. If he's hell-bent on trying her, let it be on his head.'

The doors opened and the others filed out, including Dante. Without the connections, Sage stood frozen by his own thoughts.

"Hey, there you are. Where are Darian and Alex? Rocky and I—"

Sage grabbed Markus by the wrist and yanked him into the elevator before the doors could close again. The lead warrior began to pitch a fit. Then he saw Sage's expression.

"What's happened?" Markus pointed toward the door, though they were already back on the main floor where Darian's office was. "What'd you just hear?" His voice was rising, shaking, the way it only ever did when Alex was involved.

"The shit's about to hit the fan, Markus. And you need to keep yours together, or there'll be two of you on trial."

"On trial?"

"Come on." He grabbed Markus's shoulder and shoved him down the hall. "I'll explain everything—after you feed your mate."

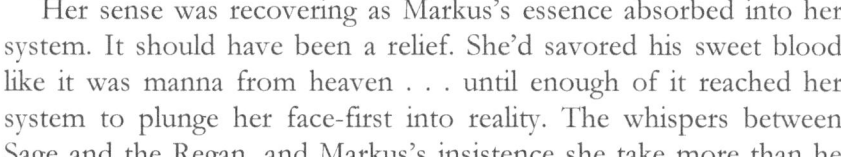

Her sense was recovering as Markus's essence absorbed into her system. It should have been a relief. She'd savored his sweet blood like it was manna from heaven . . . until enough of it reached her system to plunge her face-first into reality. The whispers between Sage and the Regan, and Markus's insistence she take more than he ought to give without receiving some in return all accompanied emotions she couldn't sort out until they hit her like a Mac truck.

They'd explained—minimally. Antonio was out to prove himself and tarnish the Regan, both at her expense. They'd comforted—weakly. He'd never follow through; it was far too great a risk of his reputation if he failed. Mostly, they warned. Darian was still at it as they stopped one corner shy of the corridor the meeting was to be held in.

"I know you trust your sense, Alex, but tonight you need to trust us. Say nothing unless I ask or Sage gives you the okay." She agreed, but he continued as if she'd argued. "I mean it. If you say too much, or Creator forbid, lose control and use your gift on them, I might not be able to stop this." It was the closest he'd come to admitting what she thought she was sensing. She needed confirmation, needed to know what she was facing.

"Stop what, exactly? What aren't you telling me, Darian? What's at stake?"

He studied her just a moment before deciding if or how he'd answer.

"Everything, Alex." He looked at Sage and then at Markus. "For all of us, everything." And with the weight of those final words on his broad shoulders, he strode ahead.

At the door, Markus made a final plea. "Maybe it's better if she's not there." He had stepped to the Regan's side, pushing her behind him.

Darian shook his head, a sentiment Alex shared. "It's better if we face it. Knowing what we're walking into gives us an advantage Antonio won't be expecting." He looked his lead warrior up and down. She peeked her head around Markus's shoulders and nodded emphatically to confirm his suspicion. Darian saw it. "That said, probably best not to have both you and Rocky in the room. Too many reminders of Alex's influence. Go see if Nicolo can step in for you tonight."

Markus snarled. "Nice try. I'm not leaving her alone with them."

"She won't be alone. She has Rocky, Sage, and me. But I can't protect you both. And quite frankly, where she's concerned, I don't trust that you won't need it."

"I know the risk I'm taking. But remember, you already pledged your trust and protection to her in front of all of them the night we mated. And if not to her, than certainly to me, you owe as much. I won't so much as speak her name once this is settled, but tonight I'm calling in Alia's debt."

Darian nodded. "I'll do everything I can, but do not interfere. You may be my best warrior, but Antonio and whoever else is in cahoots with him won't be playing by the rules of war. This will come down to who's the better manipulator. And I'm better trained at that game, Markus." He plastered a cocky grin on his face and entered the room to greet the council as if he'd just been discussing nothing more important than the phase of the moon. The Elders greeted him in turn.

"Blessed Creator, let's hope so," Markus whispered before staggering Alex with a peck that might have appeared innocent if she hadn't been able to feel the passion and terror behind it.

Darian stood as soon as she and Markus had sat in the empty seats next to his. He apologized for the delay, blaming her female grooming proclivities and human speed for making him late leaving the house. It was an artful start, disarming most of the all male, all vampire crowd at her expense. She faked a smile and guilty shrug before he continued.

"Since we didn't have a full meeting last month and much has happened since the last one, most of it involving our Seer, I hope you won't object to her presence? Good," he plowed on in a manner that made it evident he was only asking out of a vague sense of propriety.

"Excuse me, Regan," Antonio broke in regardless. "But if your intention is to let the one you say is responsible for the latest disasters explain them to us, then, yes, I actually do object."

Darian maintained a nonplussed appearance. "I never said she was responsible. I implied she was involved, a fact she will confirm when given the opportunity. The two are very different. After all, we were all involved to some degree, unless you were among the few able-bodied males who left the ball before the fighting broke out—thanks to Alex's ability to forewarn us."

The unspoken accusation of cowardice had more than a few of the Elders bristling, particularly those who had also left. Alex nudged the Regan's toe under the table, a subtle, silent suggestion to move on.

"But her help with that was already explained at the emergency meeting the night after her father's returning ceremony. She was home mourning, of course, after yet another loss suffered at the hands of the Vengatti." A well-played recovery, Alex thought. "But I felt strongly about her being here tonight as we discuss the rest of that night and some follow-up events. She does, after all, have a unique and valuable insight into things."

Darian had laid it on thick, but she sensed many of the council were in agreement or at least open-minded to the idea. If Antonio could read them nearly as well, perhaps he wouldn't proceed with whatever plans Sage had overheard. She watched as he scanned the faces and his scowl morphed into a smug grin. His eyes locked with hers.

"You're that good aren't you? You've got them all convinced. Between your gift and the charming flaunting of your human flaws— tripping up the stairs on your mating night, constantly rolling the cuffs on that oversized sweatshirt you traipse around the club in, given to you by some human ex-boyfriend, no doubt—how could anyone find you anything but innocent?"

Alex opened her mouth, but Darian's foot and Sage's sense stomped on her comment before it escaped.

Markus jumped in instead. "That sweatshirt belonged to her brother, who was . . . killed by the Vengatti when she was still a kid." Alex had an inkling why he paused. Using the word burned would be dancing a little too close to the fire they were hoping to extinguish before it ever really ignited.

"Personal tragedies aside," Ardellus chimed in, "I find her far from innocent, though far less devious than what you seem to be dangerously implying, Antonio. If she's here to admit her role in recent events, as Darian said, I suggest we hear her out."

"You're right about the dangers," Antonio said, ignoring the Elder Regan's suggestion. "Isn't it true, Abram, that she could be influencing us as we speak, and we'd never know?"

"More than likely, yes," the healer replied. Antonio puffed up. Abram met Alex's eyes and smiled, though, as he happily deflated him. "Though if you're implying she's doing it now, I'd say she's rather botched the job. From my limited observations, she's gotten far better than that." Most of the rest of the Elders chuckled, but unfortunately Antonio would have the last laugh despite Abram's best intentions.

His blush of embarrassment became the ruddy glow of victory. "Exactly my point, Elder. Who's to say she hasn't been that way all along? Who's to say Seamus, the male who was killed as a traitor, was really to blame for all he was accused of?"

"He did," Rocky roared. "He admitted everything. How else do you think I could have killed him? He had been my best friend, Dad!" He swore and kicked the wall behind him. Alex knew he was more pissed he had lost control than angry with his former father.

"A lot has changed since those days," Antonio said. To the Elders it was a reminder he had severed all ties with his son. To Rocky it had to feel like a twist of the knife that never quite left his chest after his father's abandonment. But nothing compared to what he said next. "Besides, you had a lot to gain by believing he was guilty, didn't you?"

Rocky lurched forward, but Sage thankfully clotheslined him, slamming him back against the wall.

Alex had had enough. There was no way this was going to end as Darian wanted. He was right. They had to face it, whatever it was. She planned on doing it with dignity, before Antonio systematically smeared the reputations of every person she cared for and respected.

"Elder Antonio," she said her voice surprisingly steady. All heads turned. Darian and Markus both spoke her name, Darian as a warning, Markus as a plea. "I'm sorry," she told them both. "But if he means to accuse my family, friends, mate, and Regan of being accessories to something, I'd like to at least know what that something is. That is your intention, Elder, yes?"

Antonio stuttered. It was a small victory.

"No."

"Oh, my apologies for interrupting then." Alex folded her hands on the table and looked to him to continue. It was one innocent gesture too much.

He stood. "I do, however, intend to accuse you."

"Careful, Antonio," spoke the Elder named Dante, the one whose thoughts Sage had overheard. "Some things can't be unsaid."

"I've no intention of eating my words and every intention of being careful where our coven is concerned."

"That's my job." Darian pounded the table as he stood.

"It's your job to enforce the laws, of course, but I believe it is the duty of any coven member who suspects another of having committed such an atrocious crime to bring it to light, and to trial."

"Atrocious crime?"

"Trial?"

"Antonio, you're not—"

The uproar was instantaneous as those in the room collectively saw where he was headed. Alex accepted for the first time what she knew as soon as Sage had hinted at it back in Darian's office. She was being accused of the coven's greatest crime. Antonio wanted for her the punishment Seamus had escaped when Rocky mercifully slit his throat in December: to be burned to death as her family and friends were forced to look on. She silenced them all with a quick burst of her anger. It was the exact action Darian swore her not to take. He wasn't angry now, though, not with her. He was ready to face this fight, as well.

"As you all witnessed at my mating ceremony, I'm not a dancer. Stop waltzing around the issue, Antonio. If you've got the guts, say it."

"Very well then," he said pulling his shoulders back. "Alex Crocker—"

"Alex Markus." Markus stood so suddenly and spoke so violently the whole room started. "She's my mate, with my name."

"This is one charge where mating status doesn't matter, Warrior."

Alex knew as much, but was relieved to hear it confirmed. Markus wasn't. He grabbed her hand and squeezed it so hard she feared he'd break it. She'd never tell him, though, because she was more afraid he'd let go.

"It matters to me. If you plan to charge her with a coven crime, you'll use her coven name, my name."

Antonio continued as if the interruption never occurred. As the rest of the room collectively held its breath, he leaned forward, both hands on the glossy surface of the table.

"Alex Timian Markus, you are hereby charged with the crime of treason."

The crack of the wood splitting between Antonio's hands as the handle of Markus's knife vibrated above it was the last she remembered of the chaos that ensued.

CHAPTER 16

"Still no luck?" Rocky heard Sage's voice upstairs. He couldn't help gravitate towards it as the Regan answered.

"No. And Dante was my last resort. As expected, he respectfully declined the offer, feeling his duty as an Elder is to remain as a juror."

Rocky heard the cacophonous crashing and figured the Regan had just swept the contents of his desktop into the far wall of his office. He stopped a few feet from the ajar door to listen to the rest.

"Might be to our benefit. Dante didn't jump on Antonio's offer to help prosecute. He didn't agree with the charges. That's two votes she can count on, maybe three," Sage said.

"Are you counting my father or Abram as the maybe?" Darian asked in a biting tone.

Sage didn't answer, at least not with any response Rocky could hear. When Antonio argued Alex couldn't be held in the same house as her mate, Ardellus had been a little too willing to take her to the cell in his brownstone, a damp hole in his basement, far worse than the clean concrete block at the farmhouse.

"Have you told him yet?" Sage asked as if he heard Rocky's thought and was forced to remember who was occupying that cell in her place.

Darian scoffed. "He'll be able to feed from Cormelia later tonight. I'm not giving him any more bad news before he's healed."

Rocky ground his teeth so hard he felt the grit of enamel between them. His father's insistence the lead warrior be beaten for attempting to 'maim' him was the final straw. Rocky had informed Antonio, quite loudly, that had Markus intended to hit him, he would have. Darian agreed but silenced Rocky before he became the third casualty. Markus and Alex had already been knocked out. Sage had stuck Markus with one of the tranquilizers the warriors kept in their first aid kits to keep him from doing irreparable damage to his career and reputation. Ironically it had been Markus who knocked Alex out. When he saw Sage approaching with his hand on a pair of cuffs, he mistakenly thought the Knower planned to apprehend his mate. He tried to push her aside to protect her, but in his fury he pushed a little too hard. Alex tripped over her chair and slammed her head into the table. Her limp body hitting the ground was the last image Markus remembered before the drug kicked in knocking him unconscious.

He awoke in the cell in the basement convinced he'd killed his second mate. It took all three of them to keep him from ripping his wrists to shreds. Finally, Sage was able to transfer to Markus's mind a memory of Alex coming to, alive and well except for an egg on her head. Luckily her fear for herself and her mate wasn't something Sage's memory showed. When Markus accepted the memory as real, he curled up and wept. Convinced he was no longer a threat to himself, Darian had sent Rocky and Sage away. The Regan himself had kept watch over his friend all the next day, only to have to beat him to within inches of his life the very next night.

Markus hadn't so much as whimpered at that. When Antonio came to witness the brutal punishment, which the Regan had insisted on lest there be accusations of leniency (and also because he refused to spare Antonio's genteel senses), Markus stood in the center of the cell with his hands chained above him. He held the Elder's gaze until he physically couldn't hold his head up any longer. When Rocky and Sage were finally allowed to free his wrists, they laid him on his stomach with his shirt folded under his face. So far as Rocky knew, he hadn't moved yet. Since the assault had been committed against a first family Elder, the usual twenty-four hour period between the time a punishment took place and when a male was allowed to feed from his protector to heal had been doubled. Rocky heard Sarah tell Ellie that both Cormelia and Vivian were already on their way to the farmhouse to help him.

Darian and Sage were silent, except for the clinking of ice on glass, which told Rocky they had already broken into the Regan's supply of whiskey. He was just about to sneak back downstairs when Darian cleared his throat.

"Will he drink from her willingly?"

"It's not like last time," Sage answered. "He's still got someone to live for."

"For now," Darian breathed. It was barely audible from the hall. "But if we can't find her a lawyer—"

"Hold that thought. We've got company."

Rocky turned to flash down the stairs only to slam into Torie.

"Mother—" She cut herself off rubbing the growing lump on her forehead.

"Fucker," Rocky finished, nursing his own egg. His cursing elicited giggles from the tall tween. He shrugged. "Go big or go home," he said helping her to her feet.

"This from the male who's been lurking outside the door for a good ten minutes." Sage had sauntered into the hallway where he stood glaring at them. Darian leaned on the doorframe with his arms crossed. He shot one scathing look at Rocky before addressing Torie.

"What do you want?"

Hearing his harsh tone, she stepped farther back towards her room. With neither Markus nor Alex to care for or comfort her, and the rest of the house in foul moods, even Rocky saw she was falling apart.

Damn it, Sage, help her out, he thought hoping Sage would listen.

Sage sighed and turned to Darian. "Give her ten minutes to talk to Markus. It might do them both some good."

Darian raised a brow, likely worried about the same thing Rocky was. Markus's back was shredded to bloody bits the last anyone saw him. Even if he'd begun to heal on his own, it wouldn't be pretty.

"She as good as witnessed it through my thoughts. If for that reason alone you owe her a chance to check on him," Sage responded.

Darian pulled the keys from his pocket. "He looks worse than he is, Torie. He'll be okay as soon as he feeds."

"I've seen worse." She said it with such assurance that all of them blinked. "At least listening to Sage's thoughts I knew you didn't enjoy it like Leonce does." She started down the hall, then turned around biting her lip. "What will happen to Alex if you can't find her a lawyer?"

"We'll find one." Rocky had cut off the Regan before he could respond. "My fath—the Elder Antonio thinks he can win this without a fight. He's wrong. Alex was a warrior even before she was a Seer, Torie. She proved to all of us that you don't have to look the part to finish the job. It's time my father learned that, too."

He strolled down the stairs, grabbed the Regan's other set of keys from the dish in the foyer and headed out into the night. When it came to choosing between 'go big, or go home,' he chose both.

The Regan's truck got Rocky past the guard at the gate. The front door key he had in his pocket the night he'd been taken into custody got him into the house. That was a bit of a surprise. He half expected to find his father had changed the locks on him. Stepping over the threshold, though, everything easy ended. He stood in the foyer, fists clenched into balls, waiting for his heart to stop pounding on his rib cage as if it wanted nothing more than to escape. He considered the idea himself.

"Sly! Norman just buzzed. He said—" Maria stood at the top of the grand staircase peering past his shoulder as if expecting someone else to enter behind him.

"The Regan's not with me." Her eyes widened. "He knows I borrowed the truck. I can't afford one of my own yet. And it's Rocky, now, not Sly."

"Oh, right." His younger sister avoided his gaze as she came down the stairs. They hadn't seen each other or spoken since the night he barged in and interrupted her from being raped by another first family male. It was the night this life, the one of grand stairways and marble floored foyers ended for him. "Mom's not here," she said finally reaching the landing. She stopped there, her hand remaining on the railing. "She met Dad at the lounge for lunch. They'll be back soon."

"I'm not here for a social call," he said.

"Why are you here?" Her right foot searched for the bottom step behind her.

"Seriously, Maria? You think I'm here to hurt you or trash the house?" She stepped further back. He'd been yelling, but there was no containing his hurt and rage. "I gave up my entire life for you. You're welcome by the way." He stormed across the foyer, snarling when she recoiled as he passed. Halfway up the stairs he realized he was stomping like the petulant, entitled male he was when he last left here. He cursed himself and flashed into his father's office.

Maria appeared by his side. He startled. She had been a few days yet from maturing last time he saw her. He wasn't used to her matching his speed.

"It's not fair to blame me entirely. And it's certainly not fair to blame Mom. You shouldn't ignore her letters. All of us made poor decisions that night and in the weeks following, you included."

He used all his will not to slap her. He had saved her. He remained silent to protect her reputation, while ruining his own.

"Would you rather I—"

"You didn't ask then," she cut him off sharply. "It's a little late now to ask what I was willing to sacrifice for you. Besides, I get the impression you're happier in your new life than you ever would have been if you stayed."

It was true. Even when he was still serving his sentence as the Regan's ward, he was more content and felt more useful out on patrols than he ever had studying law in a stuffy office. Yet here he was. He didn't respond as he headed for the closet closest to the door. Sure enough, hastily thrown in a cardboard box in the back corner, were the collection of coven law books he had copied by hand in his halting cursive. He pulled out the box and kicked the door closed with his boot.

"Why do you need those?" Maria asked recognizing the books right away. "I heard you're a warrior now. I heard . . . I heard you were partners with the girl dad's trying for treason."

"Still am. That's why I need these. Thanks to Dad, there isn't a lawyer in the coven willing to defend her."

"So you're going to?" She covered her mouth after hearing her own disbelief. She mumbled an apology, which he waved off.

"I'll do whatever it takes to save her." He started down the stairs. Maria flashed to the step in front of him, forcing him to stop.

"Is she innocent, Sl—er, Rocky?"

He nodded. "She's made mistakes, but she's no traitor."

Maria seemed to be steeling herself for something. "Can I help this time?"

Rocky sighed. Her silence, when he was accused of attacking the other male unprovoked, had kept him from proving his actions were justified. As she had just said, her willingness to help came too late.

"You weren't involved. You don't have anything that can help her."

Maria glanced up the stairs in the direction from which they had just come. "But I can get it," she said. "You know how soundly he sleeps. His office is unlocked all day. He has to have witness lists and evidence he plans to use. It could help you with her defense."

Rocky shook his head. "Those things all have to be disclosed anyway."

"But his notes don't, his questions for each witness, his strategy."

It was so tempting, and in some ways fair. An experienced lawyer wouldn't need such things. An experienced lawyer could anticipate strategy and create one of his own. But Antonio had gotten to all the experienced lawyers and convinced them it would be a career crusher to lose. Rocky had no career to crush, but he also had no experience. He would be floundering. He thought of Alex, of how small and frail she looked just before Darian had closed the heavy metal door on the cell at Ardellus's, locking her inside the cold dark room. He thought of Markus, a grown warrior, openly weeping out of relief that his mate was alive and fear that in two short weeks she wouldn't be.

Then he thought of his father, willing to sacrifice his own son to salvage his power hold in the coven, and now willing to condemn an innocent human in order to increase it.

"No," he said to Maria. "I won't become him to beat him. I won't lie and manipulate those I care about to win. I'm doing it my way. The right way."

"The righteous way." She smiled despite the tears brimming. "Of course you are. And I hope you win, not just for the girl's sake, but for yours." She stepped up next to him and pecked him on the cheek. "Thank you," she whispered.

Better late than never.

Sage dropped the plate onto one of dozens of books Rocky had spread across the coffee table in the basement family room. The kid looked up bleary-eyed from one of the larger tomes.

"Thanks." He devoured the first sandwich Sarah made him in a matter of seconds. The second he actually chewed. "Didn't realize how hungry I was," he said between bites. He hadn't slept or eaten since he returned from his father's the previous night.

"Any luck?" Sage asked. He had tried that morning to help Rocky look for anything useful. He'd finally retreated to his room for a little sleep after hours of unsuccessful searching.

"No." Rocky bit off a corner of bread with more violence than rye normally required. "I think he's right," he said after swallowing. "The only case law I can find supports his motion."

Antonio had learned of Rocky's intention to defend Alex mere minutes after Rocky left his former home. By sunrise he had filed half a dozen motions with Ardellus, who as Elder Regan, would serve as judge. Rocky had twenty-four hours to draft a response to each of them. He didn't need Sage or Darian telling him his father was hoping to overwhelm him with the sheer volume of paperwork and legal jargon. He surprised them both by quite deftly sorting through the pile. Four of the motions were minor issues no one saw any reason to appeal or protest. One was a farce. Antonio wanted Rocky removed because he wasn't fully trained and, as such, would leave Alex with grounds for appeal if she were convicted. Sage was pleased with this attempt. The fact Antonio had enough concern about Rocky acting as her lawyer to contest it had given the kid a fair amount of confidence and perhaps a bit too much cockiness.

"Nice try," Rocky had scribbled across the top. Once convicted of treason, a vampire, or in this case Seer, maintained no legal rights, including those of appeal. Since traitors were executed less than twenty-four hours from their conviction, this made sense. What was the point of being acquitted once you were dead?

The last motion was causing him more serious problems. Antonio had motioned Alex be tried in absentia. Surprisingly, he hadn't argued that her ability to influence jurors and witnesses without anyone's knowledge made a fair trial uncertain at best. This would have been true, but unprecedented. Ardellus would be deciding the law, not enforcing interpretations previously established, which was always a risk. So Antonio went with the surest bet and pointed to the physical dangers Alex posed. She'd amply proved she could knock the entire courtroom unconscious the night of the ball. Not to mention her zapping the Regan had been witnessed by just enough coven members for the rumor to spread. There were numerous cases in coven law where a defendant was denied the right to be present for his trial due to the danger he posed to others. Back before the days of titanium shackles and tasers, most violent criminals were beaten and drained into submission then locked up while the jury of Elders decided their fate. The council tended to be fast and efficient in such cases. Nearly all the accused were executed within a night of their crimes.

"She didn't resist arrest or threaten anyone like the other cases, though," Sage pointed out.

"The concussion I gave her might have explained that."

Sage and Rocky both spun around at the sound of Markus's voice. He stood in the doorway grasping the frame with one hand. His other arm was on Cormelia's shoulder.

"Hey, you're not, ah . . . " Rocky struggled to finish. Sage knew why. He too was running through the mental list: trying to kill someone or yourself, bawling, bleeding, or incarcerated.

"Resting," Cormelia finished. "I said the same thing, but he insisted on thanking you first, before I took him upstairs."

Markus smiled at her. At least Sage thought he was trying to smile. The pain, both mental and physical, warped it into more of a cringe.

"You see her yet?" he asked Rocky. Markus couldn't, even with his punishment over. Only her legal team would be allowed to visit before the trial. For now that meant only Rocky. The kid averted his glance guiltily, though it wasn't at all his fault.

"As soon as I finish these, I'll deliver them to Ardellus by hand. I should be allowed to see her then."

Markus nodded. Cormelia had her hand around his waist trying to lead him away. They'd all agreed behind his back to tell him as little as possible. He'd worry enough without obsessing over details he could do nothing about. He started to walk with her. It was a painful undertaking from the looks of it. He stopped after a few steps.

"You'll tell her . . . " He trailed off.

"I'll tell her everything she needs to hear—even the gushy shit—and none of what she doesn't," Rocky said.

Markus shifted his narrowing gaze between the three of them. "I suppose I'm getting the same degree of censorship?"

"Damn straight," Sage answered. "And if you keep eavesdropping, Cormelia's agreed to take you to live with your mother and father until the trial."

"And my father?" Markus asked. For the first time in days he was thinking about something other than Alex. Sage thought it healthy, but Cormelia disagreed.

"Is as capable as ever. As are your warriors. The coven and the city will manage without you for a few more nights."

"Alright. Alright." He winced as she pushed a hand into his healing back to lead him up to his bed. He glanced over his shoulder at Sage one last time. *She's really okay for now?* he asked.

Sage nodded.

Promise me you'll tell me if that changes, if she needs me.

Knowing a nod wouldn't suffice for such a promise, Sage raised his fist over his heart.

Rocky waited until he heard Markus and Cormelia reach the upstairs foyer before commenting. "Whatever you pledged him, count me in. We're getting her out of this alive, one way or another."

"Let's try to do it legally, shall we? Otherwise we'll all end up dead, or worse, hiding with Alex for eternity on some deserted island."

Rocky didn't laugh, a sign his father was already getting to him. "If I can't so much as win one bloody motion, the only one that really matters, I might as well stick my head in the sand for eternity."

Sage pursed his lips, debating whether to offer it as a life raft so early in the game. He swore never to tell Alex it even existed. Markus had heard of it long ago, but either forgot about it or thought of it only as a dangerous aid some pregnant females dabbled with. And Darian wouldn't suggest it, having been the one who outlawed it. Though any female dumb enough or desperate enough to toy with it was usually punished far beyond the slap on the wrist he could dole out.

"Why is it so important to you that she be there?"

Rocky looked bewildered. "Why? Because they need to see the face of the person they're accusing, condemning. Because it's far too easy to sentence a discmbodied idea to death than it is to look in the eyes of a twenty-six-year-old female and tell her you're about to burn her alive. Creator, Sage, how can you even ask that?"

He nodded. It was exactly the answer he expected, but he had to check. If Rocky felt he needed Alex's gift to beat his father, he wouldn't have made the offer. Since it never crossed Rocky's mind, he did.

"What if there was a way to turn off her gift for the night of the trial?"

"I need her conscious and preferably lucid enough to testify, Sage. You can't knock her out or shoot her up with a sedative."

"No needles necessary. I believe the witch has managed to

produce the inhibitor in pill form in recent years, a vast improvement over the vile tea she sold me when I first moved here two centuries ago."

Rocky stammered for about ten seconds. Then, always one to roll with the punches, he checked his watch. "If we're going to get to her shop before she closes and still have time for me to draft the response before it's due to Ardellus, we should probably get going. I'll grab my gun and meet you at the Jeep. You can explain on the way."

CHAPTER 17

Torie had been singing the lyrics to her favorite song in never-ending repetition. She hadn't made any progress learning how to block, so the best she could do was fill her thoughts with something mundane. When Rocky switched on the radio, though, and she inadvertently began singing to the current song instead, the ruse was up.

Sage slammed on the brakes so hard she rolled out from under the blanket she'd been hiding beneath and smashed into the back of the seats. Before she could even brace herself, he'd thrown the Jeep in park and flashed to the rear.

"Get out. Now." He didn't grab for her. Having to crawl out in his direction under the power of her own wobbly legs was far more daunting. When she finally managed, he stepped close enough that the toes of his boots rubbed hers. "Give me one good reason not to put you over my knee and beat you senseless."

She couldn't remember what her response to this was supposed to be. Instead she infuriated him by thinking of another reason: that most modern humans driving by would likely call the police if he tried. He didn't seem too concerned as he spun her around and pushed her hands onto the bumper. Fear and adrenaline finally kick-started her brain.

"My pocket! It's in my back pocket."

He snarled, but yanked out the folded piece of paper. She tried standing up, but he kept her bent over where she was as he read it. She listened as her words, in his voice, echoed through both their heads.

Mom, I'm sorry I couldn't call or text, but I'm staying at a friend's. Don't worry. I'll do my homework. I've even got a tutor helping me with the hard stuff. And I'll stay out of trouble. I get away with even less here than I do at home. I love you lots. Tell Dad not to worry. XO –Torie

"You call this staying out of trouble?"

She braced herself for the blow and yelped when it landed, but more out of fear than pain. It smarted plenty, but had Sage wanted to hurt her, she knew she'd be feeling a lot worse.

"They'll be time for that, later. You still have to face Darian and Markus when we get home."

While she trembled at that threat, a new one arrived. Rocky looked ready to rip her head off. "Not now," he snarled. "There isn't time to deal with her antics. I'd like to be able to face Markus myself later tonight."

Sage handed him the letter. His scowl softened some as he read it.

"Your mom visits the witch?" Rocky asked.

Torie nodded. "Frequently since . . . " Charlie's face filled her thoughts, but she didn't fight it. Better Sage see it now in relation to this conversation. Then he wouldn't be worried when Charlie's name and image crossed her mind later on. She worried Sage heard this thought, too, as he turned to her.

"Is that—"

"The male Alex spoke to at the ball? Yes." She listened in as Sage turned to Rocky.

"The male from the wedding album."

Torie sucked in a sharp breath. She hadn't heard about the album before, but as the pieces of Sage's thoughts came together, she shook. Another reminder of why it was right to leave.

"He's alive?" Sage asked.

She nodded. "My mother helped nurse him back to health. He's as good as he'll get at this point, so I don't know that she'll get that." She pointed to the letter. "But if there was a chance, any chance, I had to try. I know I said I wouldn't, but this seemed safe. Abigail doesn't take sides, but she'd pass it on for me. I know she would."

"Abigail?" Rocky asked.

"The witch," Sage replied.

"She has a name. I doubt she likes being called 'the witch' any better than you like it when Darian calls you 'Knower.'"

"You think *Abigail* has a remedy for getting your ass whipped on the back roads of Bristol?"

Torie threw a Hail Mary and dove behind Rocky as Sage reached for her.

"Sage." Rocky shoved him back. "Priorities. Let's not stoop to the selfishness level of a twelve-year-old. Alex's life is at stake." His glare wasn't aimed at Sage, though. Torie shrunk back feeling as small as he made her out to be. She couldn't tell him he had it all wrong. But she'd prove it—if she could make it to Bristol before Sage plucked her plan from her head. Luckily, as she slid silently into the backseat, she had just enough else on her mind, most of it concerning her stinging rear end, to keep her secret.

When they pulled up in front of Moonstones, the eclectic little storefront a few streets from downtown Bristol, she sighed in relief.

"Salem Street? Seriously?" Rocky said getting out of the car. His right hand lingered near his concealed weapon as he scanned the street. "At least she has a sense of humor."

"Yeah, she's a real hoot. Go clear the shop." Sage then turned to her. "Put your hood up, and don't make eye contact with anyone. And keep your mouth shut about this until we have what we need." He shook the letter in his hand.

"You'll give it to her? I was careful enough, right?"

"For who? The ten-year-old warriors Ty has out on the streets after losing half his experienced ones at the ball? Maybe. For Leonce or Ty himself? Hell no. You willing to risk that?"

She picked at her nails unable to meet his eyes. "It proves she and my dad didn't know I was planning it, not that she'd be stupid enough to keep it once she read it. She'd want to know I'm alive."

"Your call. But this is it, kid. Got it? Good. Now get out."

"It's okay," she replied perhaps too quickly. "I don't want to mess anything up for Alex. I'll stay here as long as you promise to ask Abigail. Tell her it's for Jessica from Torie. She knows us."

Sage raised a brow. Whatever relationship he had with Abigail, it wasn't positive. And whatever they needed from her was important, for Alex's sake.

"No. I think you should come in," he said.

She nodded resignedly. She would do anything for Alex, but she wasn't sure this was the best way.

"Neither am I, but it's a start," Sage said in response to the thought. "You help us get what we need from the—from Abigail, and I might just hand you over to Markus rather than the Regan when we get home."

He made it sound like a favor. She didn't buy it. Even after only a week in her head, Sage knew her enough to realize even facing an enraged Regan was far preferable to her than further worrying and disappointing Markus. Unless she had good news to give him. She crossed her fingers and followed him into the shop.

"Sage Matthew, to what do I owe this displeasure?" Abigail sashayed out from behind the counter. Her honey colored waist length hair swinging just above the curve of her hips.

"Karma's a bitch, witch. I suspect a couple centuries of poisoning people with your magic mumbo jumbo could be coming home to roost. But I'm not here for a social visit," Sage said. He avoided eye contact by scanning the shop's modern merchandise with a look of distaste. He was disgusted there were enough humans who bought into this occult crap to legitimize the storefront that enabled her to sell potions, pills, and 'spells' to the few remaining witches and the far too many remaining vampires who hadn't embraced modern medicine and science.

"No, I don't suppose you are. Though I hadn't heard you and the tiny mill girl you manipulated into feeding you had gotten mated, never mind had young." She looked first at Torie then at Rocky. The young warrior became very interested in a candle on the shelf behind him, but Sage heard the tittering.

"They're not mine," he spat. "This one's technically not even Rectinatti. But you know that. You know exactly who she is."

Abigail had been eyeing Torie since the minute she'd entered on his heels. She'd never explained her methods, but had always been able to distinguish members of the two covens, something most humans could not. Then again, Abigail broke most rules of being human.

Torie pulled off her hood. "Hi, Abby."

"Hi, sweetie." Abigail went to her immediately, cupping Torie's face in her hands. "It's nice to see you resurrected." She winked and Torie smiled.

"I know. I shouldn't be here, but when I heard they were coming, I thought . . . " she turned to him.

He sighed and slapped the letter on the counter. *So much for waiting.*

Sorry.

Abigail caught the exchange and her eyes widened. "You've made a connection . . . with him? Is that why they took you? Oh, you poor thing."

"We didn't take her," Rocky said. He was losing patience. "She came to us, and we helped. But that's not why we're here." He glared at Torie again.

"He's right," she jumped in. "This is for my mom, to let her know I'm okay. But the female who helped me, the Rectinatti who got me away from Leonce, she's in trouble. She needs our help, your help, Abby. That's why we came."

"We?"

Sage kicked Rocky's boot, and he shut up. The kid was smoother than Sage had hoped. No sense interfering. Abigail nodded and led Torie back to the counter. Sage almost choked when he saw her hand the girl a tissue. Was she crying? Could all females fake that? He almost felt guilty about whacking her earlier. Almost.

Torie wrapped up her brief sob story about how Alex had rescued her from Leonce's clutches but was now being charged by the Rectinatti Elders as a traitor. It wasn't precisely accurate. That move wasn't even disclosed to the other Elders until after Antonio had formally charged the Seer, but it had the witch's attention.

"So how can I help? You know I don't meddle in coven affairs, Torie. I treat individuals—"

"Without taking sides. Yeah, put it on a pamphlet. We just need a handful of inhibitors and some instruction on how to dose them to a hundred pound Seer so that it'll knock out her gift for the night without the pills killing her or her gift killing us."

The witch stood with a hand on one hip of her skintight jeans. "I'm sorry. I must have misheard. You're looking for me to sell you some of the pills your Regan outlawed a few years back—after his mate suffered a miscarriage, a natural and common occurrence among vampires."

"Sarah took—?"

"No." Sage cut Rocky off. "An ignorant midwife gave them to Sarah without her knowing. She thought she was doing the coven a favor by preventing the Regan from being 'disgraced' by giving birth to a gifted young."

Torie's jaw dropped. Abigail rushed to explain. "I don't encourage females to use them, Torie. Although that's not because they're unsafe. I just don't agree with denying Creator given gifts. But those with gifts are often feared or shunned; I'm sure your parents explained that. So I provide inhibitors for those who ask. At least I did, until someone chose to use me as a scapegoat to sooth his mourning Regan. After I nearly had my throat ripped out, I promised never to sell another inhibitor to a member of your coven on the risk of being, quote: skinned, drained, and left to die in a ditch."

If she was going for the shock factor, she failed. All three of them had the same threat launched at them the previous night for talking too loudly at breakfast and waking Sarah.

"He was mourning then. His mate's expecting again now, his mate who's taken the Seer under her wing and who'd be crushed if anything were to happen to her. He'll make an exception. Trust me."

"Even if he would, the answer is still no. I sell to those who want a remedy. I'll not allow my recipes to be used as weapons against someone unwillingly."

"She is willing," Torie piped up with the half-truth. "She wants to fight the charges." True. "But she won't be allowed at the trial to defend herself if the Elders think she can influence them with her gift." Also true.

Sage was making a mental note not to underestimate the kid when the witch interrupted.

"And she knows the risks?" She glared at him.

"She will as soon as you tell me. I'm hoping in the century and a half since I last tried the crap, the recipe's improved?"

Abigail smiled. "It has, some." She pulled a jar from under the counter. "The essentials are the same: vervain, monkshood, and acacia to suppress your magic."

"Magic?" Torie's tone echoed Sage's disbelief; only he'd taken it and knew it worked, temporarily.

"Power, magic, gift, different words for the same things, Torie," she said, before turning back to Sage. "I have used modern methods and medicine to lessen the side-effects. The capsule releases it more slowly for longer lasting, more even results. And I've added some herbs to soothe the headaches and stomach pains that often follow. But I've never tested it on a Seer before, obviously. You'd probably want to have her try a dose beforehand to get a more accurate feel for the correct timing. But she should be closely monitored to watch for any unusual reactions, and I suppose to assure your Elders of its effectiveness." She said the last with as much distaste as Sage felt.

He had already considered this. Ardellus wouldn't approve of this type of compromise without proof it would work. That meant dosing Alex twice. Soothing herbs aside, he was pretty sure it would suck. But better miserable than dead.

"Hey, put those down. And don't get any ideas." He hadn't been paying close attention to Torie who was rolling a handful of the pills in her hand. She dropped them back onto the counter.

"You took them before. You just admitted it."

"After I matured and my gift matured. And even then, I wouldn't repeat or recommend the move. You'll be trained and prepared ahead of time, a luxury I didn't have. You won't need this crap."

Torie bore her blue eyes into his. "You're assuming they won't burn me alongside Alex." She spun on her heels and yanked the door open. A cacophony of chimes echoed behind her as she stomped to the Jeep. Sage waited until he heard the car door slam before rolling his eyes at Rocky.

"And others wonder why I don't want young?"

Rocky smiled briefly before getting back to business. They spent the next twenty minutes discussing doses, and promising immunity if the plan backfired and Alex accidentally set fire to the witness stand with her new too-hot-to-handle hands.

As they left the shop, Sage tucked the bottle into his jacket pocket, and pulled out the keys.

"So you two were an item at one point in your sordid history?" Rocky asked.

Sage swore. "That obvious?"

"Oh, yeah. Don't ever let Vivian see you two in the same room. If she smelled a tenth of the pheromones oozing off either of you, blood would spill." Rocky had already reached the passenger's door, too busy laughing to register what or who was missing.

"Son of bitch!" Sage pounded the side of the Jeep so hard he dented the door. "Someone's blood's gonna spill later tonight when I get my hands on that little—"

***

Shit. The pill wasn't working yet. Torie had to wait before swallowing it until she was out of the shop and could slip it from where she'd rolled it into one sleeve. With a lack of water and an abundance of nerves, it stuck in her throat. The bus was approaching her stop, but if Sage heard the station name in her head or saw a street sign or familiar business, they'd find her in no time. Of course, she knew that was a risk when she'd slipped into the back of the car at the farmhouse. She hadn't planned then to use an inhibitor to block Sage. She'd been to her desired destination so many times over the years that she hardly had to think about it. She was just hoping her repertoire of pop songs would get her where she needed before he figured it out. Of course, that was when she thought she could make it into the city undetected. Sage and Rocky discovering her in the car meant they'd notice if she wasn't there when they returned, and from the array of curses and threats popping into her head, it was clear Sage had definitely noticed.

With her hood pulled down as low over her eyes as it would stretch and the lyrics to the Pitch Perfect soundtrack running through her head, she dashed across the street from the bus stop. It was late, but the lights of the office building she entered still lit the lobby in soft yellow light. Ducking her head in case of security cameras, she bolted to the elevator and jabbed the up arrow. As soon as the metal doors slid apart, she barged in, crashing face-first into the gentleman leaving. One look at the brown tweed jacket and she threw her arms around him.

"Charlie!" She felt him stiffen and feared he'd react before recognizing her. With Alex's boots, Ellie's shirt, and a recent hug from Abigail mixing in with her own scent, she had to smell like a paranormal medley the likes of which no one ever had a whiff of before. "It's me, Victoria." She pushed back the hood and looked up at him with the bright blue eyes he'd known since she was born. His own widened with sudden recognition. He pulled her into the elevator and pushed the button for the fourth floor where his office was located.

"What the hell are you doing here?" he asked as the doors closed. "If you had an out, why would you come back?" His voice was seeped in despair rather than anger. She sighed in relief.

"I'm not coming back. I came to get you, because if I'm going to stay, then the Seer needs your help." She was purposely being a bit dramatic when she told Sage she worried about being burned with Alex, but that didn't mean there wasn't some truth to it. Without Alex's guidance and protection, she was one teenage mood swing away from making a fatal mistake.

Charlie was still making sense of her words when the doors opened.

"I'll explain everything, but in your office, please. I'm starting to feel queasy."

"From the elevator?" Charlie raised a brow. A lover of modern amusement rides, he had taken her on every rollercoaster in the state and a few in surrounding states.

"Um. Maybe?"

His eyes narrowed as he led her through the waiting room of the law firm with one hand on her neck. "Or maybe you've gotten yourself into a whole lot more than hair dye and make-up since you disappeared."

That was the understatement of the century.

"Start talking, and do it quickly. I have a feeling those two aren't the cleaning crew." He pointed out the window overlooking the street. She caught a glimpse of Rocky and Sage glancing up and down the sidewalk before she backed out of view with a gasp. There wasn't time to figure out how they found her or to worry about what would happen once they got her home, assuming they'd take her back. She launched into her story, starting all the way at her last period English class two weeks ago. She sped along without pausing for breath, let alone giving Charlie a chance to ask questions. Her speed dramatically increased as Charlie's head turned in the direction of the hallway. He no doubt heard the elevator. Sage and Rocky tracked her final destination.

"So Rocky, who's a warrior, but apparently trained a little to be a lawyer first, is the only one left to defend her. And though it's really nice and all, everyone in the house, from the Regan to his own girlfriend, thinks he's in way over his head."

"Thanks for confirming that."

Torie scrambled out of her chair and began backing toward where Charlie sat behind his desk. Rocky stood in the doorway, his pistol aimed at the breast pocket of Charlie's jacket. Sage, who stood behind him, had his eyes on Torie as he cracked his knuckles. Charlie, who hadn't reacted at all to their sudden appearance, did react to this. Not exactly how Torie hoped.

"Though I assure you I share the general sentiment, perhaps such punishments should wait until after we've sorted this out." He turned to her with a look as equally menacing as Sage's, "And even then, as her compater," he said, using the vampire term for godfather, "I think I've earned the right to dole them out."

Sage grunted. "We'll see." He motioned to Rocky to put the gun down and then turned to her. "Start talking, or all three of us might just jump you, you little twerp."

Torie couldn't remember her name, let alone what she'd been about to say. Charlie must have registered her panic stricken expression.

"I'm hoping you were about to get to tonight's events and exactly how and why you ended up here in my office," he prompted.

"Right." She looked at Rocky. "No offense, but Alex needs a real lawyer."

"No shit, but how's some Vengatti godfather supposed to help that?" Rocky waved his gun at Charlie.

Sage cleared his throat. He swiped his partner's weapon from him before Rocky killed one of them and pointed with his other hand to the name plate on Charlie's desk: Charles Anderson, J.D.

"You're a lawyer?" Rocky asked. He appraised the scruffy, middle-aged looking male with disbelief.

"A defense attorney mostly, these days at least," Charlie answered coolly.

"Days? You mean—" Rocky scanned the law books and framed newspaper clippings of prominent cases Charlie had successfully won. "For humans? Aren't you too—"

"Old?" Charlie laughed and tossed Torie a wink.

"Well, shit. That's how Leonce does so much during daylight hours," Sage said breaking his usually cool persona. "You're a soltator."

"A what?" Rocky asked.

"A sun dancer, a day walker," Sage said. "Guess that explains why her parents picked you for a guardian. You're the only thing more rare than a female Knower."

Charlie nodded. "I was uniquely situated to prepare her for life as a gifted member of our coven." He stood and rested a hand on her shoulder. "Her leaving us was a blow, especially given . . . the timing, but we hoped she'd found her way to the Seer."

"Alex," Torie reminded him. Her father couldn't stand being called male, warrior, or worse, when he was younger, boy. He said those were titles, and titles belonged to royalty or property. He was neither. Alex was neither. "People have names," she echoed his words.

Charlie smiled. He knew the reference. "He'd be proud, but not of tonight's actions." His expression darkened again. "Even if they'd let me help with her defense, there are a thousand considerations you never took into account. For Alex's sake, there's the fact I haven't tried a case with coven laws in nearly a century." He turned to Sage and Rocky. "There's little need for lawyers in a coven whose Regan serves as judge and jury, accepting only what evidence he can pull from members' minds."

"But you know the laws; you told me once our laws and theirs are almost identical. You practiced for centuries before Leonce took over," she argued.

"I do and I did, but what then? What about after the trial? I couldn't very well return any more than I could stay."

"They let me stay. And Alex herself invited you to switch sides."

"You don't need to feed yet. I do, and without a mate, that'd be a problem. Laws about feeding at least are very different." He glanced quickly at Sage who'd snorted. "Besides, I imagine Alex's invitation is largely to blame for her predicament."

He looked to Rocky who nodded in agreement.

"Your mate," Sage interrupted. "She didn't make it?"

Charlie raised a brow and glanced at Torie.

"I could have pulled it from her head. We've made a connection despite her age, but someone thought she'd have better luck escaping tonight if she stole and swallowed what could potentially be poison to someone whose gift has yet to mature," he spat.

"That explains the queasiness." Charlie shook his head. "But not how you knew about Rebecca."

Sage's expression softened. "We saw a picture. Leonce sent Alex a mating gift, a book of threats, past failures, and losses. She recognized you, but not easily. We assumed the female was your mate. I'm sorry."

Torie slipped her hand into Charlie's as he nodded. "She survived the beating, initially, but refused to feed to recover. She'd had enough of life in our coven and asked to return to the Creator. Granting her permission was the one act of mercy Leonce has ever been 'guilty' of, one he's already regretting. With Rebecca gone and Torie safe, I have far fewer reasons to partake in such projects."

Sage and Rocky both furrowed their brows.

Charlie sighed. "I think I took one of the most recent pictures in that album, the one of the girl's mother. I'm sorry, and I wish I could help to make amends for that and for everything else I've been a part of over these last few decades." He turned and placed both hands on Torie's shoulders. "I do, Toodles, I really do."

She wasn't sure if it was the use of her childhood nickname, the implications that came with his answer, the drug that suddenly turned off Alex and Sage's thoughts leaving her suddenly alone with her fears, or the accumulation of everything she'd been through in the last two weeks, but she found herself sobbing into Charlie's chest. Her body shook so hard, he sat with her on his knees, and squeezed her against him to try to quiet her.

"If we could find a way around all the other crap, would you really help me? Would you defend Alex?" Rocky spoke over her crying. After a very brief pause, she felt Charlie nod, and for a moment, at least, she could breath again.

"Call the Regan. Let's do this right this time. Ask permission. Beg if you need to," Rocky called as he sprinted to the stairs.

"Where the hell are you going?" Sage called after him.

He skidded to a halt at the door. "To the car. I've still got three hours before my responses to those motions need to be back to Ardellus. Before Darian and the elder Markus show up and decide it would be easier to murder the whole lot of us, I plan on getting Mr. Anderson, here, to help draft them." He disappeared down the dark stairwell.

Charlie brushed Torie's hair out of her face and whispered in her ear. "Just to be clear, I charge my top clients over four hundred dollars an hour. If we're both still alive at the end of this trial, I fully intend on collecting. And if you do one more foolish thing that jeopardizes your safety between now and the next century, I'll take it out of your hide. Understood?" He pushed her from his chest so she had to look him in the eye.

She tried to regain some dignity as she nodded, but her sniffling and Sage's sniggering hampered the effect. She reminded herself it was all worth it as she slinked into the armchair in the corner. Though as the first of the shooting pains stabbed her stomach, and Darian's cursing could be heard from Sage's phone, she wondered if

Alex would be thanking any of them for the work they did to 'help' tonight.

CHAPTER 18

A distant sound awoke her. She tucked her feet further under her thin coat. Her breath came in gasps. She knew there were rats in here. Nasty little vermin. She peered into the dark, half expecting beady red eyes to stare back. The sound came again. It was a door shutting in the house above her. Her heart slowed.

Great. Add paranoia to the growing list of mental disorders she had begun developing in the three, or was it four days since she'd been locked up like a prisoner?

You are a prisoner, she corrected herself.

Alex hadn't fought them when they brought her here, hadn't dragged her heels through the door or tugged on her restraints. She certainly hadn't given Antonio the satisfaction of begging Darian to leave on the light. She was innocent. She was right. Waiting two weeks to prove it, even two weeks in this hellhole, would be worth it. She could survive anything for two weeks, right? She was tough. At least she was when others were looking. Alone, with no one to be strong for, she was falling to pieces.

The dark got to her first. She hadn't even begun to get her bearings in the small cell before Darian closed the door blocking out all but a few pinholes of light that seeped in from the hallway. It was irrational, of course. What she really feared was the unknown, and a three-tiered chandelier wouldn't have helped ease that. Liam, who'd been guarding her by day as Ardellus slept, proved as much. As soon as the Elder Regan was asleep, he opened the slide on the door's hatch so he could more easily chat with her. She was grateful for both the light and the company, despite it throwing off her sleep cycle. The conversation helped pass the time, and the light was ample to see into the grimy corners, but even knowing what was there, and what wasn't, didn't ease the anxiety that arose each evening when the Elder Regan and his usual guard relieved Liam, left her her meal, and slammed shut the small opening, plunging her again into solitary darkness.

The claustrophobia came next, but that one she expected. She got stir crazy at the farmhouse which boasted three floors furnished with dozens of distractions and plenty of company to keep her mind occupied. She battled this by spending the daylight hours standing by the door, looking out into the hall. She hoped to fool her mind into believing she was out with Liam instead of locked inside a cell whose walls she could feel closing in on her every time she thought too much about them. The evening hours that she couldn't fill with sleep, she tried hard to think of things far more mundane. She mentally ran through her old karate katas and tried to remember the real term for fear of the dark, which she was sure she knew at one point.

Add amnesia to the list. What the hell, right? Just getting one step closer to the final stage that was sure to strike as she got further from her last feeding and closer to the trial: hysteria. She hoped it wouldn't come to that, at least not publically. She didn't want to show any of them as much as a tear. Besides she was a god awful ugly crier. What a way to be remembered.

She laughed before mentally slapping herself. "Christ, you're already losing it," she said reverting to her pre-vampire curses. Then again, who was she to be picky about her saviors these days?

"I hope you mean that."

"Sage?" She jumped to her feet and was nearly knocked over when the door swung in on her. "Rocky!" She flung herself at the stocky silhouette in the frame, all pretense of dignity vanished as she struggled to see around him. He turned her obvious attempt at escape into an awkward one-armed hug as he carried her back into the dark.

"He's not here, Alex. I'm sorry," he whispered as he dropped her on her feet.

"Yeah, right. I guess I knew that." She'd been so lost in her thoughts that she hadn't registered Rocky or Sage until they were right outside the door, but she wouldn't have missed Markus. Since the night she woke up with her gift matured, her sense of him had been like a lodestar. Even when she wasn't consciously thinking of him, she knew where he was if he was near. What she hadn't realized, until faced with the possibility of never sensing him again, was just how lost she felt without that sense.

"Uh, Alex, you okay?" Rocky patted her back. She was still holding onto him as if with a tight enough grip she could transform him into the male she longed for.

She stepped back. "Sorry. I'm kinda shitty, actually." Why hide it? "And then, well, Darian told me I wasn't allowed visitors, so I just thought . . . It was stupid."

Rocky shook his head. "No it wasn't. He misses you too, a lot. He, ah, sends his love," he said squirming just a little.

"Thanks, Rocky." She smiled. "I won't ask you to return the message. I think Torie might be better suited for it once she wakes up."

There was a half grunt, half growl outside the door. Her eyes widened as she realized the noises had come from two different vampires, Sage and . . .

"Who else is here?" she whispered to Rocky, though truth be known, whoever it was could still hear.

Sage poked his head in. "Can I turn on the light without blinding you yet?"

She nodded. The light from the hallway had helped her eyes adjust. She only blinked a few extra times as a single exposed light bulb flickered on above her. When her vision cleared she saw that Sage stood behind . . . a ghost. She stumbled backwards. Seeing things had to be the final stage of insanity. She looked at Rocky again, then Sage. They all looked equally solid.

"Get a grip, woman. You're no more nuts than you ever were," Sage said. "He's alive, and real, and just got tentative approval to head your defense, along with Rocky."

A dozen different questions ran through her head, but the only word she could form was, "Huh?"

The male hid his smile by scratching his short salt and pepper beard. "Let's hope she can be a bit more eloquent on the stand," he said to Rocky.

Sage scoffed. "You ought to be more concerned with how much she'll say and the foul language she'll use to say it."

Alex shot him the bird.

"I think it's time Alex got to talk with her lawyers privately," the male said.

Alex waved her hand aside. "It doesn't matter. He hears my thoughts wherever."

"Yes, but you needn't hear his replies. Thank you, Warrior." The Vengatti male, no bigger than Markus, waved Sage away like he was shooing a fly.

"You're welcome," Sage said to her and Rocky. He spun on his heels and headed to the door. Just before shutting it behind him, he spun around. "Achluophobia is fear of the dark. And you don't have paranoia; the rats are real."

She hugged herself to stop her shuddering before turning to Rocky. "I never said I wasn't grateful. I know he's been helping— Markus, Torie, probably even Darian. And from the sounds of it, you, too. And he's clearly been listening in on my thoughts, to check on me, I guess. I even appreciate that. He's a good friend; I know that."

Rocky raised a brow. "He purposely just skeeved you out, after insulting you. Don't get all sentimental and apologetic. It makes you sound like you're ready to return to the Creator." He was annoyed— with both of them. "Besides, he knows all that."

She crossed her arms. She'd earned the right to be a little emotional, not to mention the right to some answers. "I am not giving up, but I want to know my chances, and how this all works, and how you became my lawyer, and you—I don't even know your name."

Both Rocky and his new partner smiled.

"Let's start there then. I'm Charles Anderson; Charlie is fine though. As for how you got a warrior and a Vengatti as your legal team, that's a long story, and two weeks is a surprisingly short time, so it'll have to wait a bit. I need to hear your story first, with as much detail and as little editorializing as you can." He looked around the near empty room. Realizing the old camp roll she'd been given to sleep on was the best he'd get, he gestured her to take one end. "Please, sit."

"And then you'll answer my other two questions?" she asked, remaining on her feet.

Charlie looked up from where he was pulling a pencil and yellow legal pad from his briefcase. When he saw the defiance in her stance, he squared his shoulders to her.

"This works by you accepting that you know nothing about how this works. If you want to save yourself, your mate, and very likely my goddaughter and me, you'll answer what I ask, do what I say, and spend your remaining hours praying to whatever god or Creator you believe in. Because although your chances somewhat depend on what you're about to tell me, the truth is, in a treason trial, no one's chances are good. Now, again, please sit."

She should have been scared, terrified, instead she grinned. "I'd say nice choice," she said to Rocky, "but I'm guessing he was a last resort. I think even your father would feel compelled to sit after an answer like that."

"And yet you're still standing," Rocky said with a sigh.

"Oh, right." She sat and waited until Charlie settled next to her with his notebook on his lap. "So what's different about a treason trial?" she asked as soon as he looked ready.

He shared an exasperated look with Rocky. "Have you seen a coven trial? Or even been on a human jury?"

"No, neither. I read a lot of crime fiction. Does that count?"

"I've watched far too many commercials for feminine products in my overly long life. Does that make me remotely qualified to understand a woman's menstrual cycle?"

Alex laughed sincerely for the first time since Sage had burst into Darian's office prior to the Elder Council. "No, not at all," she finally managed.

"I didn't think so," Charlie said. He cracked a grin. "I stole that one from a colleague. It's crude, but gets the point across. Nearly everything is different, coarser, far less glamorous. It'd take days to familiarize you with everything, and if you follow my other rules, you won't need to know most of it anyway."

She nodded and hugged her knees. "The stuff I need to know?"

Rocky sat cross-legged in front of her and with a nod from Charlie took over for a bit. "The trial will start at sundown on the night of the full moon and end at sunrise."

"That's symbolic, isn't it?" she asked.

"Yes. Important trials are held on full moons so 'the truth can be illuminated,'" he said in his best James Earl Jones voice. "And also so the defendants can be weak from not being fed, and so defense attorneys have to wrap it up quickly. Whatever doesn't get said that night, doesn't get said. The Elders will have the daylight hours to come to a decision, which will be announced at sunset the next night."

"The Elders are the jurors, and Ardellus is the judge, right?" She had surmised this much from the discussion swirling around her after she came to while the charges were being discussed.

"Pretty much. But unlike in a human court, Ardellus also gets a vote."

"Does Antonio?"

"No, and neither does Darian, though he'll be present during deliberations. Treason is the only verdict a Regan can't overrule. He'd be the tie-breaker in most cases, but with my father prosecuting, there's already an odd number."

"Wait! It doesn't have to be unanimous?" Alex's hands slapped the cold dirt floor. The idea that a mere seven males were needed to decide her fate was tremendously more terrifying than thinking all thirteen had to come to an agreement.

"No, it's just a majority. And . . . " Rocky looked to Charlie.

"Tell her."

"There's something else that's going to sound shocking and scary, I imagine, as someone used to human law." Alex tucked her shaking hands under her knees and nodded for him to continue. "Well, being a coven and all, the belief is that no one would charge another member unless there was a lot of evidence against her. So the burden of proof is on the defense, which means—"

"I'm guilty," she gasped. "I'm guilty unless you can prove without a doubt that I'm not."

"Reasonable doubt," Charlie said gravely. "We share that with the humans."

"Fantastic." Alex put her head in her hands and tried to breathe. It felt as if someone were squeezing her lungs.

"It doesn't change anything, Alex," Rocky said. He rested a hand on her knee. She slapped it away.

"It changes everything! It changes the way they'll see me when I walk in there. Confidence in my innocence will look like arrogance. Every word out of my mouth will sound like a lie or a desperate attempt to change their minds. Every action I took will be assumed to have been planned with malice." Her voice had peaked with an obvious note of panic before Charlie broke in with such composure it was infuriating.

"Are you innocent?"

"Yes, of course, but I don't know how the hell I'm supposed to prove that!"

"Why?" he asked.

"Because I did what they're accusing me of. I did talk to Seamus and unknowingly tell him information he passed to Leonce. I did knock out all the males at the ball to let you and the other good Vengatti go. I did bring Torie, a Vengatti Knower, into the Regan's home. But I didn't do it for the reasons they're implying."

"Then why did you do it?"

She shrugged. "Because they were the right things to do. I reached out to Seamus, because I learned he had been Rocky's friend, and I thought both of them could use a friend again. I knocked everyone out to minimize bloodshed, and I let you all go because my sense allowed me to know you were good regardless of your coven, just like with Torie."

Charlie nodded. He looked to Rocky whose expression was grim. "You see the problem, don't you?"

"Yes," Rocky said. He struggled to meet her eyes. "By your own admission you acted regardless of coven ties to help members of the Vengatti. Legally, that is treason, Alex. Whether the law is right or wrong, as it's written now, you've broken it."

Alex had moved from panic to outrage. "So what? We quit? I plead guilty? Because I won't lie. I did nothing wrong." She pounded the floor with her fists.

Rocky started to respond, but Charlie held up a hand. "You're not being tried for right or wrong. You're being tried for treason. That definition can cut both ways. Without hearing the whole story, which I do intend to hear before the Knower and Regan return at nightfall, I think we've got two options for our defense. One is to argue she acted each time to help the coven or its members, foolishly, but loyally. You helped a friend. You prevented casualties. You upheld the coven's value of righteousness. And you converted an enemy whose gift would surely be used against you in the future. None of that would be a lie, right?"

"No," Alex answered, "but the burden of proof thing. It would just be my word that those were my intentions."

"Yes," Charlie answered. He watched as she and Rocky exchanged looks. "Is credibility a problem?"

"Maybe you ought to stick with the plan of hearing her whole story, Charlie, before we decide on a game plan," Rocky suggested. He returned to picking at the dirt floor to avoid looking at her. So it was Alex Charlie looked to for more details.

"I've had some slip-ups in the honesty department here and there. Most of them involved witnesses at some point or another." Alex felt her blush creeping up her neck, a slow burn bound to turn her cheeks crimson.

"Here and there. At some point or another." Charlie shook his head. "At least you keep it interesting, Ms. Crocker. I suppose, to be safe, you should start at the night you were first attacked by my former coven members."

"I'm Mrs. Markus now," she corrected. "Wait. How did you know I was attacked?"

"It's a small coven, for which I unfortunately did far too much daylight damage."

"Daylight?"

"Not now, Alex. Just tell him—everything."

She nodded and adjusted her position on the floor. Everything was going to take awhile. "Um, just to be clear, does coven law include an attorney-client privilege clause?"

"You've been charged with treason," Charlie answered. "Assume you have no privileges and few rights, but also assume your life depends on me not being surprised in court with something you edited out of your story, because it does."

She swallowed, closed her eyes, and fought against the cold to bring herself back to a hot June night.

Charlie was into his second legal pad by the time sunset rolled around. Alex had talked herself hoarse, but she'd just about told him every major event and plenty of minor ones that happened to her since the night before school ended almost eight months ago. She looked to Rocky on occasion to fill in any pieces he felt she'd missed or put a spin on. He didn't outright contradict her once, but at times shared another point of view, his or one of their housemates. He also filled Charlie in on conversations he'd overheard or been privy to that she had not. She was most grateful though for the times he jumped in because he knew she couldn't bear to relive certain events.

When all the mundane moments—dinnertime banter, tea with Sarah, Tuesday nights with Rocky, and just about every pleasant moment with Markus—were stripped away, what was left was a highlight reel of tension and terror.

"It really wasn't as bad as all that makes it sound," she said, unsure whom she was trying to convince.

Charlie looked up from the last notes he'd scribbled down. "Funny, isn't it, how both species have the same survival instinct to persist even when all the evidence tells us it's not worth the effort?"

"Maybe it's our hearts that tell us to persist for the sake of those we love, those who make it worth it." It was just another part of being interdependent. She thought back to her web of loved ones. She told Darian her feelings would get her killed, but they'd saved her more than a few times, too.

Charlie dropped his gaze back to his notebook. "Maybe, but as we both know, that list dwindles the longer you're a part of this life."

Sensing a grief only one kind of loss could evoke, her hand went to her mouth. She glanced at Rocky who nodded.

"Charlie, I'm so sorry. I only meant to help that night. I never thought—"

"Of course you didn't. No one apart from a few monsters in my coven could have predicted that. I didn't when I stepped forward."

Alex's jaw dropped. He had volunteered to take the beating that nearly killed him? "You meant to take the blame for all of them," she said. His mild manners and unassuming dress hid so much she never could have predicted, even after sensing him for the last ten hours.

He nodded. "But Leonce knew I was doing it for the very reason you said, to protect those I loved."

"So he took the one you loved the most. Sick bastard," Rocky spat as he paced the cell. Leonce had taken the one he loved most just months ago. Hearing Charlie made him appreciate even more what a miracle it was to get Ellie back alive.

"Sick, but predictable. I should have known better. Leonce never accepts a request outright. There's always a price to pay. I had expected something like the others being forced to witness it. But I never expected him to pull Rebecca from the crowd. No one did, or they would have stopped it. Stopped me. The only good that came from it was that it gave Torie the strength and urgency to approach you when she had the chance."

There was a thick silence in which Charlie wrestled with his grief and Alex with her guilt. Rocky was the first to pull free.

"That's what Torie meant when she said she'd seen worse. She was there. Creator, those poor kids." He shook his head in disgust.

Alex's maternal instincts were new but keen. "When would she have said that? What are you letting her watch?"

Rocky blanched. Whatever it was, it was far worse than a rated R movie.

Markus. Alex was on her feet tearing at him. "You said he sent his love. You said—" As little as possible. He never said Markus was fine. She had read into his words, because that was what she needed to hear. "What did they do to him? Tell me, Rocky!"

He tried to swipe her hands away, but she managed to grab one wrist.

"Ow! Damn it, Alex." He pulled his arm free just as she felt the sting on her palm. "Markus is fine. He was punished, but he's healing. And no one meant to have Torie see it; she saw it in Sage's thoughts. Not that it will matter, because if you do this in court," he waved his burned wrist in her face, "you'll never see either one of them again."

Her knees gave out beneath her. She slumped to the dirt floor. She didn't realize she was crying until Rocky kneeled in front of her and wiped her face with his sleeve.

"Hey, I'm sorry. I didn't mean that. You just caught me off guard with that thing." He motioned to the red swelling welt on her palm.

"That makes two of us." She shuddered. "I'm sorry, too. But is he really okay?"

Rocky grimaced. "Well, it wasn't a picnic. It made my beating after that first Elder Council meeting we went to last year look mild. But honestly, to see the look on my father's face when Markus's knife struck the table . . . I think even Markus would tell you it was worth it. Will tell you, soon. You'll see him again, okay?"

He didn't promise. She knew it was as much a hope and a prayer as a statement of conviction, but it still provided some comfort.

"Okay. Would it be all right if we wrap up for the night? I'm tired and clearly not in control. Besides, Sage is here with Darian and some others. I'm assuming the Regan has a few things to work out with Charlie." She'd bullied the story out of them during the day and still couldn't believe what Charlie, Rocky, and Torie had done to help her.

"He does," Charlie said standing. He rubbed his right knee as if it were arthritic. "Injuries and a bit of old age," he grunted catching her stare. "Unfortunately, I believe at least one of those other guests is for you."

As if summoned by the statement, a sharp knock struck the door before it swung in. Sage held it open for the Elder Abram. Rocky tugged on his sleeve. Alex took the cue too late. The healer saw her blistered hand before she shoved it into her pocket. He shook his head.

"Alex was just answering some questions for Charlie and me, and, ah, demonstrating some of what she can do."

Abram set down his medical bag and rummaged in it as he replied. "The Seer's gifts are fascinating, though I do recall telling you to be more careful with that one. There's more than a week before the trial. You need to save your strength." He stood up with a small tub of salve in his hands. Alex recognized it as the same soothing compound Rick had applied to her wounds just weeks before. "Give me your arm, Rocky."

"I'm—"

Charlie shot him a look.

"Grateful. Thanks, Elder." Rocky pushed up his sleeve appearing anything but.

She rolled her eyes. "You can hand him a law book and a briefcase, but he's still a warrior," she teased.

Abram looked up as he finished. "Be thankful he's capable of being both. Your unique group of friends has thought well outside the box to help you." He put the tub away. Apparently the privilege of medical treatment was one she no longer had. His words to Rocky more than made up for it, though. "You'll give your father a run for his money."

Rocky puffed out his chest, full of pride, and a bit of hidden trepidation. "It's not about money or power. It's about justice. And that's why he'll lose." He thanked Abram, then turned to her. She wasn't surprised when he pulled her into a hug. "I'll tell him all the sappy stuff, okay? And we'll be back sometime tomorrow or the next day to start trial prep. Until then, I'm sorry if this makes you sick, but do what Abram asks and try to rest, alright?"

She didn't have time to ask what he meant. She was shaking hands to say goodbye to Charlie and thanking him and Rocky. Before she knew it, she was alone with Abram and Sage.

"You'll be staying with her and keeping records for me and Ardellus?" Abram asked Sage.

"Since I'm the only one besides her who can say for sure how quickly they kick in and wear off, I don't have much choice. I suppose I'll be the one dosing her the night of the trial?"

"I'll be there, of course, should anything go wrong, but yes, you'll be mainly responsible for it."

Sage took a bottle that sounded like aspirin out of his coat and handed it to Abram. He shook a pill into his hand and studied it. Alex's anxiety peaked.

"Dose of what? What is that? Why do I have to take it?" She knew Rocky had glossed over parts of the story of the previous night, but had been too grateful to ask. Her gratitude was waning as she sensed Abram and Sage.

"Nice of them to leave us the dirty work," Sage said realizing his partner had left her in the dark. "These are inhibitors to temporarily kill your sense. You need to take them now so we know how many and how often to give you the night of the trial, which," Sage continued after hearing her question before it could be spoken, "is the only way you'll be allowed to attend your trial."

"What? Why? Is this—"

"You're not that dense, twerp. Figure it out. Elder Abram has better things to do than listen to your indignation." It was a warning to shut up, a reminder that Abram would soon be voting on her guilt or innocence.

"Of course. Sorry, Elder," she said to Abram. "It's just a bit of a surprise." She shot Sage a scathing look. Now was a fine time to learn there was a pill that would turn off her gift.

"It's quite alright. I imagine all of this is overwhelming. Sage and I will do what we can to minimize the physical side effects. This practice run will help with that and hopefully ease your anxiety about at least one aspect of the trial. The fewer surprises you face then, the more in control you'll be, yes?"

She dug her burning hand deeper in the pocket of the dress coat she'd been wearing when she was arrested. "Yes, Creator willing."

Abram handed her one of the pills and a bottle of water. "It's your will you'll be wrestling that night. Save your strength." He turned to

Sage, who'd stood silently witnessing. "She'll need to stay awake, but do your best to keep her calm."

He scoffed. "Like she will be that night?"

Abram narrowed his eyes. He had been patient with Alex, but he wasn't accustomed to the attitude Sage emanated.

"Tonight is simply to prove to Antonio and Ardellus that this will work. She doesn't need to live through the horror of that night twice."

"No," she said attempting a weak grin, "but once would be nice."

Abram looked torn. Alex sensed part of him wanted to comfort her, but she knew he couldn't. She didn't expect him to, didn't really even want him to. It was enough to know he was uncomfortable with the situation. He gave Sage a few last minute instructions and a number to call should an emergency arise before he returned. He left unable to meet her eyes again as he shut the door behind him.

Alex went and sat back on the mat where she had spent the day with Charlie. "Will you show me, before it kicks in?"

"Show you?" Sage asked before he followed her line of thought. "Hell no. You really are a twisted masochist, aren't you?"

"It's partially my fault he was beaten, and he's my mate. I know for a fact you showed him I was okay after he came to."

"Showing him you were okay to keep him from biting his wrists to shreds is a little different from showing you images you don't really want to see just so you'll have something to brood over other than your own situation."

Her mouth moved, but nothing came out. Her lungs were empty. She'd heard the stories about how he'd refused to feed after he lost his first mate. Sarah had insinuated he'd spent the better part of a century acting more like a zombie than a vampire, going through the motions with little purpose and less feeling. But he had gotten through, eventually. The thought that he'd actively take steps to end his life was more terrifying than the prospect of what would have to transpire first to lead to it.

"We didn't let him," Sage said. She knew he was also implying they wouldn't let him in the future, but they couldn't watch him forever.

"Make him promise me. Tell him it's the only thing I want. He needs to take care of my mother and Torie—and himself. He promised to love me for eternity; he needs to live that long to keep that promise. Make him say the words," she pleaded. "Make him pledge to me, Sage. Promise me."

"Alright. I get it. I'll try, if you promise me you'll calm the fuck down. Creator, kid, it's going to be a long ten nights if you can't remember to breath."

She breathed, and not just for show, but because she trusted he would do as she asked. And she trusted Markus to keep his word.

"Feeling better?" he asked after a few minutes of quiet had passed. He checked his watch.

"Much. I—" She stopped when she realized why he asked. She wasn't feeling anything other than her own emotions, and though those weren't light and fluffy, not having them compounded with everyone else's was a source of relief.

"You realize I can't hear your thoughts, right? I can't finish your sentences for you."

She smiled. "It's so much better than blocking. I don't have to do any of the work," she said. Her earlier annoyance resurfaced. She leaned over and punched him in the leg. "Why the hell didn't you tell me about these months ago? I nearly killed myself to get a moment's rest, and all that time I could have just popped a friggin' pill?"

Sage swiped her second punch aside. "Two reasons. One, you needed to get used to your sense. These pills are no different than draining your essence down a drain or getting drunk. Their effect is temporary. Your gift is not."

She sunk back against the wall. He was right, of course. "Fine. What's the second reason?"

Sage cringed. "The side effects are similar to the other two methods. If Torie's little experimentation is any indication, you're a few hours from a hangover that'll knock you on your ass and leave you begging to be fed."

She shot to her feet. "I'm not allowed as much as an aspirin, never mind essence. What were you all thinking?"

Sage stayed where he was on the floor, completely nonplussed. "We were thinking you need to be allowed at your own trial if you want to defend yourself."

"Little good that'll do if I'm curled in a ball half unconscious."

"Charlie and Rocky know that. Why do you think Abram was asked to come all the way here to hand you a pill? They need a coven doctor, or more importantly a coven Elder to say you'll need to be fed in order to make it to the trial date. So a word of advice, drop your habit of playing tough. There'll be no need to be a drama queen. That dose is likely twice what a human your size needs, so just embrace the misery, okay?"

She no longer had the luxury of her gift to sense whether or not he was exaggerating, but she feared he wasn't. Her face must have shown it.

"You still have a few good hours." He pulled a deck of cards from his coat pocket. "You up for some poker? It'll probably be the only opportunity either one of us ever has to play a fair game."

Alex grinned. "Fine, but only if I'm dealing. You vamps use your super speed to stack the deck when you shuffle."

"Maybe you just have crap luck," he said handing her the cards.

She looked around her at the cell they were currently locked in. "Gee, you think?"

CHAPTER 19

"We told you this was a possibility before, and you still agreed to it, insisted on it, actually. You can't change your mind now that the damage is done." Rocky pounded his fist onto Ardellus's dining room table.

"You said it was slight," Antonio said.

"I said it, and I believe the word I used was uncertain. Even the witch who made it didn't know how it would affect a human," Sage said.

"She's no more human than you or I," Antonio responded. "And you've no place in this discussion. You're not her lawyer or an Elder."

Sage mumbled something about small blessings but backed down after a look from Darian.

"The counselor's correct." Charlie spoke up from the corner where he'd been unobtrusively observing this round and round argument. Rocky gawked, but Charlie continued calmly. "If she were a vampire, she wouldn't require essence after just two doses, and if she were merely a human, she wouldn't require essence at all. But she does. At this point all sides, including the coven's most experienced healer, have shared their opinions. It's time we all stand down and let the Elder Regan decide whether to allow her to be fed, so we can proceed to trial, or to deny her and condemn her here and now without a trial or the say of the rest of the Elder Council."

Ardellus and Antonio were taken aback, but behind him Darian smiled. Vengatti or not, Charlie was growing on him.

When the Elder Regan regained his composure, he turned to Abram. "Does it need to be decided tonight?"

"She's gotten worse, not better in the last few hours. If she gets too weak to feed properly, it'll be much harder to get enough essence in her for it to work effectively. She's been granted permission to attend. I assume you don't want her carried in looking like a victim," Abram said to Antonio.

"They might," Darian said pointing at Rocky and Charlie. "There aren't too many males who can see a female in such a state of distress and not feel sympathy. That's assuming the females she's befriended, my mate included, don't see her in such a state first and rip our throats out before the trial begins."

Antonio obviously took the Regan's point. He'd be shooting himself in the foot to drag her in half dead. If he couldn't keep her out of the room entirely, better to have her healthy enough to fight back. She was known for losing her cool. There was a possibility she'd hang herself if she had the strength.

"Fine. I withdraw my objection. Have your ten minutes."

Markus had been watching and listening to all this from the sidewalk across from the brownstone. At Antonio's words, he bolted. Nicolo, who was acting as the Elder Regan's guard, but who'd been purposely sent outside to watch Markus as well, lunged at him. Markus ducked under his fellow warrior's reach and flashed to the door. Sage saved him crashing through it by swinging it open at the last second.

"I told you to wait outside, Warrior," Darian snapped as he tumbled into the house. He didn't fight Sage who picked him off the floor and held him tight by his upper arms.

"You had him ready and waiting?" Antonio asked. "A little cocky, aren't you, boy?"

"Confidence wins cases, or at least that's what some equally cocky old codger once told me," Rocky retorted.

"Enough," Darian called over the two of them. "Markus is here as my guard tonight. Is it convenient? Yes. You'll pardon me for the foresight, Elder. It's part of my job. Sage, take him to Alex. Markus, mind the time."

In keeping with this advice, Markus didn't stick around to say a word to the others. None of what he had to say couldn't wait, and all of it would likely land him back in the cell he'd been beaten in just nights ago.

Sage was quick with the keys, but Markus yanked the door open before the Knower. Alex fell right into his arms. She must have sensed him coming. He was so happy to be holding her it took a moment for him to realize she was shaking. It was more than just her sobbing; her body was violently reacting to whatever the hell they'd given her. He turned to Sage and snarled, fangs out.

"It was the only way—"

"Get out!"

When the door closed, he swept Alex into his arms and sat with her cradled in his lap along the wall. She hid her face in his chest.

"It's okay, Alex. I'm here to feed you. You'll feel better soon."

"It's not that," she said finally looking up at him. "It's just . . . you're here. You're real."

"I am. Now feed." He pushed his punctured wrist against her lips and sighed with relief when she began to draw his essence. It had been over twenty-four hours since she'd taken the first of the pills. It worked as planned and better. Sage was able to tell exactly when the first dose began to lose effectiveness and administer the second dose before any side effects kicked in. The trouble began when the experiment was complete. The doses had been too strong. Her essence had been too weak. Sage and Abram monitored her all day. The vomiting and the headaches were followed by shaking so violent it physically drained her, but her sleep was fractured with fevers and night terrors. It was during these, she called for him. Sage suspected she was hallucinating. He'd left the brownstone at sunset, and barged into the farmhouse shortly after searching for Rocky. All of them were awake, waiting for an update. There was no objection from the Regan this time when Markus insisted on coming. Darian had taken one look at his own mate and Markus's smoldering eyes and nodded. He was doing his best to keep his promise, to pay his debt.

After just a few mouthfuls, Alex began to stir. Her eyes opened. Her lucidity regained, she reached forward to cup his face in her free hand. Her other released its grip on his wrist.

"Make love to me," she said using what little strength she had to sit up and kiss him. The taste of his blood was still heavy in her mouth.

"We've only a few minutes. You need to feed more."

"We can do both." She was unbuttoning his jeans as she wrapped one leg around him. He felt himself straining against the fabric. He wanted so badly what she did.

"Sage is just outside, and the others—" Her lips silenced his.

"To hell with them," she whispered after the kiss. "If they can watch me burn, they can listen to me make love."

He hissed, not at her but at the truth to the statement. He flipped her on her back knocking her shallow breath from her.

"I can't be gentle," he said pulling a knife from his belt to pierce his neck.

"I don't want you to." She pulled his head down by his hair to bring his vein to her mouth. She bit hard enough to break the skin herself.

He dropped his weapon and tore at her fly while wriggling his own jeans down just enough. There wasn't time for foreplay or proper undressing. He needed to feel himself inside her, just as she needed to take him in, both body and blood. He filled her up and felt her teeth and nails dig deeper into his flesh. He was fast and fierce. He hated knowing he was likely hurting her, hated feeling satisfaction that she'd wake to bruises he caused, but that was the only thing he could leave her with, a lingering reminder of this moment, of his love.

There was a sharp rap on the door, a warning from Sage.

"No, finish it," she said tearing at him with her short nails. "Finish the exchange."

He knew what she wanted. He wanted it, too. He pulled them both upright, his hands holding her hips, their bodies still entwined. They fell into the door, her back slamming against the metal. He jammed his foot against it to keep it closed as they reached their climax together. Just as the second knock came, just as their joy began to shatter them, he bit into her soft flesh. He drew one long, sweet dram of her essence into his body to carry with him.

The pounding increased. "I said time's up, Warrior. Open the damn door." It was Darian this time.

He pulled out of her. Alex released her legs and slid down the door until her feet hit the floor. She leaned on him, utterly spent, as he helped her rearrange her clothes. When he had guided her out of the way of the door, renewed tears flowed down her face, nearly killing him.

"Thank you," she mouthed as he pulled his own hoodie back into place.

"It won't be the last time. I promise." He leaned in and kissed her, lapping the remains of blood from her face and neck.

"Markus!"

"Regan," he said with a slight bow after opening the door. The crowd that gathered behind it avoided eye contact, except for Darian who glared and Sage who gave him a lewd wink. *Prick*. He packed as much gratitude in the thought as such a remark could hold.

"Abram needs to reexamine Alex, to make sure she's recovering. Go wait outside," Darian ordered.

Markus nodded, but turned back to Alex who still clung to his hand. A sudden wave of love and longing stole his breath. He looked at their joined hands and smiled.

"She's recovered, Elder," he said over his shoulder to Abram, his eyes never leaving hers. "I know, Alex. I do too. From now until eternity." He kissed her hand then forced himself to release it. Flashing from the house before she could feel the fear, which for him always accompanied such love.

CHAPTER 20

Markus turned the throwing knife end to end, not being particularly careful of its precision sharpened tip. A little physical pain might be a comfort. The raw scratch marks left by Alex's nails and the cut and bruise from her teeth where she'd fed from him had healed too quickly in the last few nights. Instead of prodding his fingers into them for the small twisted comfort the pain provided, he sat in his office searching for little reminders of her. The doodles she drew on his desk pad when she was bored. The scent her sweaty palms left on the extra set of knives he kept in his desk. The holes she left on the back wall, as well as the floor, and even one on the ceiling, while trying to teach herself to use them.

He knew she'd been doing it during the days he and Darian had her working at the club. He'd seen the stray pocks, far from his own accurate marks, and knew she used the practice knives to kill time and work off her frustrations. He hadn't said anything. He hadn't asked her to stop. She wasn't supposed to carry weapons for fear one could be too easily turned against her, but he already knew about the knife Rocky snuck her. If she were going to carry a weapon, it was better she train with it. He hadn't offered to assist her, though. She lost so much of her independence becoming a part of this world. He had decided to let her learn on her own. If she got to the point she wanted his help, she'd ask. From the small cluster of marks in the center of his own target, marks too shallow to be his and too numerous to be 'lucky shots,' he wasn't holding his breath until the day she asked.

But he was holding his breath, holding in her scent from the handle of the blade. The faint knock made him bobble it. He jerked upright in the chair. The tip landed on the seat between his legs, the haft vibrating ominously like a steel hard-on. He yanked it out and slammed it back in his top drawer as his visitor stuttered and stammered from the doorway.

"It's fine. What do you want?" He wasn't usually such a dick to the young males, leaving that to Sage, Nicolo, or a few of the other older warriors who loved terrifying the trainees. He had too many more pressing matters on his mind tonight, though, to worry about manners.

"I have a note from the Regan, sir, but he asked me to give it to the lead warrior."

"I *am* the lead warrior." He cursed. Technically, his father had stepped in until he was 'fully healed' and had 'dealt with his other distractions,' Darian's diplomatic terms for telling him he was sidelined until he got his shit together. He shook his head. In his mate's absence, he'd adopted her bad habit of swearing. Thankfully he managed to keep most of it in his head so Sarah hadn't taken his tongue. He looked back at the boy still dancing from foot to foot biting his lip.

"My father's just helping out for a bit. Whatever it is, I can see it. I'll pass it along to him later. Okay?"

"I guess so, sir." He stepped forward and handed the folded note to Markus, but didn't leave.

"Is the Regan waiting a response?"

"Oh, um, I don't think so. He stopped by the training room looking for your father. When he wasn't there, he asked me to leave this for him on the desk."

"My desk?"

"The lead warrior's desk was all he said, sir. Does your father have another office in the club?"

"No," Markus said tapping the letter on his knee. "Go back to training. And close the door!" The young male had flashed out of sight before the final order. Markus stood to close it himself as he flipped open the folded paper with his other hand.

Just a reminder that I'd like you at tomorrow's final pretrial meeting of the Elder Council to discuss security measures. In addition to pulling patrols closer to the perimeter of the club, the Elder Regan reminded me this morning that a formal guard in full regalia is required for treason trials. You'll need to find a dozen warriors willing to serve as protection in the courtroom that night.'

It was signed D. Just D. It was a nickname Sage had christened Darian with in their youth when the foolish young Regan-to-be would leave notes for the two of them revealing his whereabouts or seeking help to cover up his ridiculous antics. He always signed them with just an initial, as if his father wouldn't figure out who had left them if he found one. Darian stopped the practice after one such incident. Sage and Markus had taken a beating on his behalf when out of a mixture of stupidity and loyalty they both refused to reveal the obvious answer of whether it was Darian who had written the note Ardellus found. He doubted any of them could recall what the note said, but Ardellus and the elder Markus made sure none of them would forget the outcome. Sage still occasionally called the Regan D to aggravate him, but Darian would never sign a note meant for the elder Markus that way. And his father would never need a written reminder of a request given to him by the Regan. This note was meant for Markus.

He reread it, searching for the message. *A dozen willing warriors.*

He picked up his phone and hit the group message alert used to call the warriors to an emergency meeting. "Let's see who's willing."

———◆———

There had been no opposition. A few chose to abstain, but Markus guessed that was more out of fear of losing jobs than questioning Alex's innocence. And he made it clear that was what this was about. He had trained nearly half the current warriors, and those he hadn't had trained alongside him. He didn't need a confirmation of their loyalty and trust. This was about their feelings for Alex, and he couldn't be as sure about those. They razzed her at meetings. They picked her up off the floor after knocking her on her ass the few times she, or rather he, had been brave enough to allow her to train with them. Both were signs they were beginning to accept her. Acceptance and trust, though, were two different things. The perfect example of this stood beside him.

"You sure you want to do this?"

Nicolo looked down at him. He was one of the most experienced warriors serving under Markus. He was old-school before the term even existed. He certainly hadn't accepted a female in their ranks, especially one who knocked him on his ass the first time they met, which was why Markus had been speechless the night before when he stepped forward.

"I sure as hell don't want to serve on some 'honor guard' for anyone who thinks there's any honor in this bloody circus."

Markus gave him a quick nod and a word of thanks. Then they waited. Finally the door to the closed meeting opened slightly, and Sage's hand motioned them in.

"I hate to contradict you, Markus," Sage could be heard interrupting the elder Markus. A chorus of gasps told Markus and Nicolo how the rest of the Elders felt about the audacity of a mere warrior, a guard, butting in. "But you might have more trouble than you think finding your dirty dozen."

The door swung the rest of the way, and Nicolo strode in without even a glance back at Markus. He walked directly to Darian, who stood to greet him. Markus thought the Regan could have faked his surprise a bit better, but no one else in the room was watching anyone but the large warrior in full formal regalia.

"Regan." He bowed deeply then stood. "I'd like your permission to speak on behalf of the warriors."

"You've no say in the matter, Warrior. This is a closed meeting to which you weren't invited," Antonio spoke up. A few of his fellow Elders nodded in agreement.

"Yet you ask us to play a part in it." Nicolo gestured to the nearly two-dozen other warriors who'd filed in silently behind him. Those Elders with their backs to the door craned their necks and dropped their jaws.

Darian crossed his arms and spoke grimly, but Markus caught the flicker of pride in his eyes. Though the Regan's years with the warriors were shorter than he would have liked, he still felt a part of their brotherhood. "Speak your piece, Nicolo."

Nicolo nodded. "Over three centuries ago I spoke the words of the warriors' oath, promising to serve and protect my coven, my Regan, and all the innocents from those who meant them harm. I'll admit, the night I said those words I thought innocents referred only to humans, not mouthy, gifted little girls. I also thought the harm would only ever come from the Vengatti. But that doesn't change the promise I made, the vow I gave. I will continue to serve as a warrior, but I will also honor that vow. So I will not be a part of this trial." He began unbuckling the sword from his belt, but Ardellus interrupted.

"I respect the sentiment, Warrior, but it's not your place to decide Alex's innocence or guilt. That's the job of the Elder Council."

Markus stepped forward. Nicolo had done more than anyone could have asked. As lead warrior, it was time he had his say. "With all due respect, Elder Regan, none of the council, with the exception of the current Regan, has ever served as warriors. Perhaps you forget we govern ourselves. The warriors judged Alex to be no more guilty than any of us were back when we too were that blissfully naïve, foolishly cocky, and dangerously independent. She was punished accordingly. I'm sorry that wasn't good enough for some of you, but as warriors, we have to make split second decisions every night as to who's guilty and who's in need of protection. Right or wrong, that's all Alex was doing. Now I'm doing it as well. I choose to honor my vow by relinquishing my sword." Markus didn't bother with the buckle. He yanked his belt carrying his ceremonial sword from his waist and dropped it at the Regan's feet. With his fist over his heart, he bowed to Darian, then stepped back.

Nicolo followed, repeating Markus's words and dropping his weapon. One by one the other warriors came forward adding their swords to the growing pile, and bowing to the Regan before retreating.

"Do you plan on doing anything about this, Darian?" Antonio asked.

"What would you like me to do, have them all beaten? Fire them all? That would leave a few rookies, the elder Markus, and Sage protecting the entire coven and all of Bristol."

"Like hell." Sage stepped forward from where he had been standing guard at the door. He hadn't been able to come in full uniform without giving the rest of them away, but he intended to say his piece. "I'll be there, as your Knower, to help with the pills, so that Alex can be present, but I won't be wearing this." He held up a hand and one of the warriors from the back tossed him his sword. He dropped it into the pile with a grin. Markus gave a final nod to Darian and started out.

"Wait." Rocky had remained silent from his seat at the table. He was at the meeting as Alex's lawyer and had tried to maintain the composure that position required as he watched all his fellow warriors declare their allegiance to his best friend and partner. Markus thought that in itself spoke volumes about his loyalty, but

Rocky apparently thought the others present needed further confirmation. He stood and pulled his gun, the only weapon he had on him, from his waistband. He secured it and placed it on the table. He waited to assure his father recognized it as the Berretta he'd given his son on his fifteenth birthday, back before their relationship had soured. "Just so there's no confusion, Regan." He slid the piece across the length of the glossy table. Darian caught it deftly at the far end.

"Understood, counselor," Darian said. With a sigh he sat and dismissed the rest of them with a wave of his hand. Markus caught Rocky's eye. He didn't have Sage or Alex's gift, but he knew Rocky understood the gratitude he tried to convey with just a nod. As Markus shut the door behind him, he heard Darian address the room with more amusement than seemed prudent for a Regan whose warriors had all just refused an order.

"So, where does this leave us, gentlemen?"

Rocky bound into Alex's cell glowing with good humor. As soon as her eyes adjusted to the light, she saw he wasn't even attempting to hide it. Somehow grinning down at your best friend who was two days from facing a capital trial didn't seem appropriate.

"Can you wipe the grin off, please?"

"Maybe I've got a good reason to smile." He kissed her on the top of the head before she could duck away. He was obviously high on something.

"If you tell me you snuck home between the meeting and here to have a quickie with Ellie, I will use this hand of death to sear your balls right off."

"Precisely the kind of comments you oughtn't be overheard making between now and the trial, Alex." Charlie had followed Rocky in, carrying his battered briefcase and looking acceptably grim. He had spent enough time with her and Rocky over the last week and a half not to be overly shocked by their crass bantering.

"Sorry," she said to him. There was no need to apologize to Rocky; he was laughing off the threat. She scowled. "Seriously, though, Rocky, your mood's a little tough to take tonight."

He cringed sympathetically. "You're getting hungry again."

She nodded. "And I don't know whether this is helping or hurting." She pulled Markus's thick parka tighter around her. In his haste to exit after their brief encounter the other night, he 'accidentally' grabbed her light dress coat, leaving behind his heavy, winter one. It was blissfully warm and smelled of his cologne, sweat, and the soap he used. It smelled of him, which was both a comfort and a constant reminder of his absence, and lately of her thirst.

"So how was the Elder Council meeting?" she asked to change the subject.

Rocky's grin returned. "Amazing."

Charlie, she noticed, remained far more reserved as Rocky launched into the tale of the warriors' surprise appearance.

"So what is Darian going to do?"

"The Regan," Charlie corrected. He'd been hitting her over the head for days with his various rules for testifying, one of which was that she was under no circumstance to refer to the Regan by his name, lest it be seen as disrespectful and precocious.

"Right," she said. "But if the Regan can't provide protection, there can't be a trial. Can there?" She heard the desperation in her voice.

"No," Rocky said. Only his defeated tone told her a 'but' was coming. "But Ardellus called in a favor to Jamison. He's sending a dozen warriors on an overnight flight tonight." Jamison was Ellie's father and the Regan of the West Coast coven. Alex had only met him once but had thought he had taken quite a liking to her.

Charlie read her expression and cut in. "He did you a favor. The alternative was to postpone the trial another month, which you wouldn't survive in these conditions, even if you were granted further essence."

With little sleep, one meager meal a day, and the cold, damp atmosphere of the basement, she supposed he was right. Even if Markus's oversized coat hid her weight loss, and the poor lighting masked her exhaustion, there was no hiding the racking chest cough she was developing.

"Then why so happy? It's not that I don't appreciate the show of support, but if nothing came of it, it really was just for show."

"If you haven't noticed, Alex, most of what goes on in the coven is just for show. And this was a show that very likely got the Elders thinking. The warriors are more trusted by most than the Elders themselves, who to the average coven member seem out of reach due to their wealth and out of touch due to their age. It won't look good that they're acting against those trusted to protect us. That worry will be on their minds when they make their decision," Rocky said.

She couldn't believe this was the same male who'd cowered in the corner of the Regan's office the night she first met him. He was starting to sound and think like the son of a first family lawyer. Sort of.

"I know you said before that many of our traditions seem old fashioned to you, but this is one time when ceremony and symbolism might help save your ass," he continued. Charlie glared at him. "Skin. I know. No swearing. Lawyers don't swear. I got it. We'll stick to the plan."

Charlie chuckled, "I swear plenty. More and more each day I'm with you two, in fact. Just keep it out of court."

"Are we going to go over that plan soon?" Alex chimed in. She'd asked the same question a dozen times in a dozen different ways since Charlie had first mentioned he had two possible strategies for her defense. The first, the good intentions plan, was ruled out as a primary defense when Charlie saw how easy it would be to question her credibility. The second was still a mystery, at least to her.

Charlie shook his head the same way he had every other time she'd asked. "The plan is for you to follow my rules and trust us. Repeat after me—"

"I'm not a Sunday school child learning her prayers, Charlie. You've said them enough for both of us."

He stood over her solemnly. "If you want to save your skin as badly as those cute little catechism girls hope to save their souls, you better pray you know them. They may be the best benediction you'll get."

"Yes, Father," she said mildly mocking her childhood religion. She made the sign of the cross as she parroted his rules back to him. "Answer only what's asked, keep it short, keep it clean, and keep calm."

"Amen," Rocky said with a wink.

Alex laughed setting off a coughing fit that had Rocky fretting. She waved it off and settled herself back in the position she had spent the previous nights preparing. "So we're back to practicing?" she finally wheezed.

"Yes," Charlie said. "Only this time Rocky will be asking our questions. I'll be asking those Antonio and the Elders are likely to ask."

She nodded. "Will they be allowed to interrupt, though, during your examinations?"

"In coven law we call it clarifying. Ardellus will keep anyone from hijacking our line of questioning, but any questions directly related to one we ask will likely be allowed. But wait until he gives the order to answer it and—"

"Keep it short?"

Charlie glared at her. "Yes." His voice was prickly. She sensed he was one wise remark from losing it on her.

"I'm sorry, Charlie. I am. I just don't think I can do this without a little humor. I know that sounds crazy. Like the first time I went to a wake for some great aunt and people sat around laughing and telling stories the dead person definitely wouldn't have shared herself. I thought that was crazy, too. Then my brothers died, and I did the same thing. Only I was old enough then to realize why people did it. If you can't distract yourself with laughing, then you have to face reality. And I can't. Not now. So please don't fault me for laughing at my own wake."

Charlie stood and picked up his briefcase.

"Where are you going? She said she was sorry. She just explained," Rocky attempted to stop him from reaching the door. Charlie turned back to where she, too, had stood.

"Yes, she did. And in doing so proved no advice I can give her or practice you can provide will help."

"Why? Because I'm guilty? Do you think I deserve to die for it?" She was shouting, but his response was as even as ever.

"I don't. But you obviously do. And if you walk in there with the defeatist attitude that nothing you can say or do will make a difference in the outcome, then you might as well strike the match yourself and save the rest of us the trouble."

Rocky released a low growl, but Charlie just shrugged. Alex tried to collect herself.

"I haven't given up. I'm just scared, all right? You need to hear me say it, Charlie? Fine. I'm terrified of leaving behind my mother, and Markus, and Torie, and my friends." She locked eyes with Rocky momentarily before plowing on. "And I don't want Darian to have to kill me, not just because I'm afraid to die, but also because, despite all our bickering and head butting, I know he'd never forgive himself, and you can't lead a coven or be a good mate or father if you hate yourself. And I'm sad I might never get to meet the babies. I'm even sad I might never get to have one myself, which is pretty messed up if this is the world I'd be bringing it into. And I'm pissed I wasted time worrying about some stupid prophecy only to be stabbed in the back by members of my own coven, a coven I was dragged into against my will and stayed in only after I was promised protection and a chance to help people. I'm the one being betrayed, and that just sucks, because I still can't stop myself from loving them and loving my new life among them. And I'm willing to fight for it, for them."

She leaned against the wall and allowed her body to crumple to the floor, the weight of her emotions and those of her loved ones pushing her knees to the dirt. Charlie's briefcase landed by her side. Slowly he lowered himself down onto his bad right leg.

"So then we persist with the plan," he said with one hand on her shaking shoulder, echoing her words from the morning they met, "for the sake of those we love. Including yourself. Okay?"

She sniffed and started to wipe her running nose on the sleeve of Markus's coat. Charlie caught her hand. He reached into his jacket and pulled out a handkerchief like the ones her father had carried. She accepted it and wiped away the last of her tears. She forced a smile.

"I still don't know the plan."

"Yes, you do, Alex," Rocky said sitting by her other side and also resting a hand on her shoulder. "You just said it." He looked at Charlie, who nodded, finally allowing him to explain.

CHAPTER 21

When they wrapped up a grueling but successful day of preparing, she struggled to say goodbye. The fears she had finally vocalized loomed so close. Both Rocky and Charlie left her with quick embraces. Rocky promised they'd return a little before sunset the night of the full moon to bring her to the club for the trial. Having two lawyers and a guard, Liam, all able to be out in the sunlight allowed her to remain at Ardellus's until the last minute. From what Rocky hinted about the state of the cell at the club, she ought to have been thankful she could stay somewhere familiar. As zero hour approached, though, she felt any change of scenery might be a welcome distraction. The one blessing was that whatever illness had settled into her chest exhausted her completely, allowing her to sleep through some of the remaining time.

With twenty-fours hours remaining, Liam woke her at the end of his shift by sliding in her tray. "Last meal until you're out of here, Alex," he said cheerfully. She sensed his real emotions, but focused on those he tried to fake.

"Is it better than any other night?" she asked pulling herself to her feet. "Filet mignon, perhaps? Pizza and a beer?" If she never saw another mug of chicken broth and another egg on toast again it would be too soon. Even the orange, which had been one of her favorite fruits, didn't appeal to her anymore. She pulled the tray in anyway.

Liam leaned down to see through the hatch and smile at her as he did every night before he left. Tonight he winked. "You never know," he whispered before heading down the hall. "I'll see you tomorrow," he called before ascending the stairs.

Alex sat with the tray in the small window of light that fell from the open hatch. Despite Liam's tease it was the same meal she'd been given night after night. She held the hot broth in her hands warming them until it was cool enough to drink. She didn't wait long, wanting the warm liquid to ease her sore throat. She debated about the rest. On previous nights she'd forced herself to eat every last crumb knowing she needed the strength and nourishment. It didn't seem so important tonight. Either she'd be home in a little over forty-eight hours gorging herself on Sarah and Diane's cooking, or she wouldn't be. Deciding not to decide, to wrap it for later, she pulled the cloth napkin from beside the plate. Something slid out of it and hit the tray with a thunk. She snatched it up and smiled. Even without being able to read the label clearly in the poor light, she knew what it was: the way to a woman's heart, chocolate. She tore the wrapper and inhaled as deeply as she could without setting off a coughing fit. Ardellus was awake. She knew she'd only have a few minutes before he came to retrieve the tray and check on her before leaving with his guard for the club. She hated to scarf down such a treat, but after one slow, savoring bite couldn't restrain herself. The king-sized candy bar didn't stand a chance.

Warm from the hot broth, and full and content from Liam's contraband, she slipped easily back to sleep. She hoped not to wake and not to dream until Rocky, Charlie, and Liam returned to retrieve her. When the gentle touch pushed her hair back from her face, she figured one out of two wasn't bad, especially if the dreams were going to be pleasant.

"Those won't be necessary."

"But—"

"You're dismissed, Dalton. Wait outside the door if you must, but you won't stay in here, and you won't leave her cuffed so I can't help her dress."

"Yes, Madame Regan."

Alex's eyes popped open and blinked against the light. It wasn't a dream. Sarah kneeled in front of her, smiling down at her. Though it had only been two weeks since Alex last saw her, she couldn't get over the size of Sarah's baby bump.

"Wow," she said sitting up.

Sarah merely chuckled. "I didn't want to wake you, but thought you might like a little company and some assistance as you cleaned up."

She looked behind Sarah. There was a small tub of water, steaming water. Next to it was a laundry basket with what appeared to be a couple towels and some of Alex's clothes, clean clothes.

"You're an angel. How did you manage that?" she asked pointing, trying not to cry. Warriors, even woman warriors, did not cry at the mere sight of clean clothes and soap.

Sarah pulled her into an embrace, and they helped each other to their feet.

"I'm in charge of looking after the females in the coven, even the female prisoners." She held Alex's face in her hands. "Though I feel I've done a poor job in your case. No one told me you were sick. And why aren't you eating?" She pointed to the tray on the floor, which still held her untouched egg and orange.

"It's just a cold. And I was tired when that arrived. I'll eat it later. I promise. Is that water as hot as it looks?"

Sarah let her go and laughed. "Yes. Come on. I'll help you wash your hair and give yourself a sponge bath. It's the best I could do."

"It's amazing. Thank you." She unabashedly stripped and knelt next to the tub. Plunging her hands into the scalding water, she sighed before splashing her face, then finally dunking her whole head. Sarah couldn't bend over easily, but she did her best to help Alex shampoo. When that was done, Alex stood shivering as her naked skin rippled with goosebumps.

"Let me," Sarah said taking the warm wet cloth from the sudsy tub. Alex let her tears mingle with the water dripping from her hair as Sarah gently washed her as she had just months ago before her and Markus's mating ceremony. With the ablutions completed, Sarah wrapped her in an oversized bath sheet. It was still warm. Alex knew she must have heated it in the dryer just before packing it. Growing up, her mother used the same trick when she or her brothers came home from cold rainy sports' practices.

"Sarah, how's my mother?"

Sarah looked up surprised.

"I know they didn't tell her," she clarified. "Rocky told me Darian made, uh, asked Markus to tell her he was finally taking me on our honeymoon. But I just wondered if she bought it, if she was worrying." Markus was as good at lying without getting caught as she was, which was to say he sucked.

"Get dressed. Then I'll fill you in on everyone, okay?" Sarah motioned her away from the mud puddle they'd made. Alex followed her to the dry mat along the wall, but didn't drop the towel.

"I'm sick and a little light on essence, but my sense works just fine. What happened?"

Sarah sighed. "She's fine, Alex, but you're right, she did worry after a week went by and you hadn't called. Markus tried again, calling to say you were having a great time, but didn't have good cell reception. That only made matters worse. He really is a terrible liar."

She didn't laugh as Sarah might have hoped. Pulling the towel tighter, she attempted to control her temper. "So Sage messed with her memory," she said through a clenched jaw.

Sarah nodded. "Darian ordered him to. He had to, Alex, for everyone's safety. He and Sage both felt awful."

She wanted to rage, but she believed Sarah. Sage and Darian weren't the ones to blame.

"What will happen to Antonio if—when I'm found innocent? Sage and Darian made it sound like it was risky to accuse someone, but I never had time to ask why?"

Sarah emptied the last of the water from the tub and carried it over to sit on. "If you're hoping for some grand revenge, I'm sorry to have to disappoint you. There's no criminal punishment for accusing someone of a crime unless it can be proved that it was done falsely and maliciously, which is nearly impossible. After all, if someone really were a traitor, we'd want others to step forward without fear. The difference is, had a regular coven member stepped forward, there would have been an investigation and a pretrial hearing. As an Elder and coven lawyer, Antonio's accusation held more weight. He had the power to bring the case directly to court, but by doing so he's claiming to have the evidence to back it up. If he doesn't, it'll be a blow to his credibility. His influence and his business will suffer."

"That's it? A blow to his wallet and his ego?"

Sarah shrugged. "If that's all you value, losing it can be devastating."

"If that's all he values, I pity the bastard."

"Shh," Sarah hushed. There was still a guard outside the door. "Remember that tomorrow night. Use it. Deep down he'll be as afraid of losing as you are."

Alex nodded. Sarah saw her teeth chatter as the last of the warmth from the water and towel dissipated.

"Your stubbornness really will kill you one of these nights, but not on my watch. Get dressed." Sarah began handing her layers.

"My fashion godmother strikes yet again?" Alex asked dropping the towel once her underwear and bra were on.

"Not exactly. I had help." Sarah handed her the pair of thermal long underwear she had bought Alex when she first agreed to be a warrior. "Charlie didn't want you dressed to look like one of us. He wanted you to just be you. So we each picked something that we thought fit you best. The warm under layer was my choice. I know how you hate to be cold, and I also remember how brave I felt you were the night you accepted them, accepted a role you were still unsure of, in order to help your best friend."

Sarah had bought them for Alex the previous fall when Alex first agreed to work with the warriors to help Rocky find and rescue Ellie. Alex hadn't felt at all confident in her ability but would have tried anything to ease Rocky's fears. Just as he was doing now.

"Thank you," she said thickly. She popped her wet head through the collar and reached for the next item. "My lucky white tube socks?" she asked examining the never worn socks briefly before pulling them on her frozen feet.

"Charlie. He asked that you keep them clean, though I don't think he was just referring to the socks."

Alex laughed and promised to stifle her swearing as best she could. Then she slipped on a pair of the new jeans Ellie had bought her, the ones that fit just perfectly on Creator's Day and were only slightly loose tonight. The next item, though, Alex didn't recognize as hers. She unfolded a t-shirt with the name and most recent album cover of her favorite band.

"That's from Torie and Sage. Torie's taken over your iPod in your absence and wanted to thank you for introducing her to some new music," Sarah said.

"And Sage?" she asked slipping it on over her head.

"Drove her over an hour each way to go to a music store in Boston to buy it after making her promise she'd erase the entire 'chick rock' playlist when you come back home."

"She better not. I'll ground her for the century following the one she's currently grounded to and burn his beloved book collection in a bonfire. And, yes, they are both awake and likely listening."

Sarah smiled. "I imagine they are. I wish Torie, at least, wouldn't."

"So don't I, and I'm sorry if what she's heard hasn't always been positive, never mind polite. But I'm too tired to block her. Will someone keep her distracted tomorrow?" By someone she meant Sarah and Ellie.

"Your mother will have her tomorrow. I'll be at the trial with Cormelia, Vivian, and Ellie."

"Why? I mean, thank you, but don't you think . . . the stress?" She tried to dance around it, but her eyes were on Sarah's bulge.

"It'll be more stressful not knowing, and I think a female presence in the courtroom is important. Besides, as you may have heard, the warriors are stretched a little thin tomorrow night. We can't have guards at the farmhouse and your mother's cottage and still have enough around the club. It's rare that the Regan, Elder Regan, and Elder Council are all together at an announced and public place. The last time was the ball."

And they all remembered how that turned out.

"Well, thanks again. It'll be nice to have some familiar, friendly faces in the crowd."

"I wish you weren't being forced to take those pills again, Alex. I think you'd be surprised to sense how many of us are on your side." Sarah handed her a worn grey hoodie three sizes too big for her. It was Alex's favorite nonetheless.

"It was Dave's," she said unfolding it to see the East Bristol baseball logo on the front. "I wore it the night I took the warrior's pledge, because he never got to, but would have."

"I know that. So does Darian. There's a note for you in the pocket, I think."

Alex slipped the sweatshirt on before digging into the pouch and pulling out a slip of paper, the same slip of paper she had given him with the full prophecy written out. Only Darian had made some edits. On the line 'The last of three will yield more power than them all,' he crossed out 'will yield' and wrote 'already has' in his neat cursive. Where he had written in the final line after prying it from her, he crossed it out again. On the bottom of the page he penned a few lines to her.

It's good in tough times to remember where you're from, but it's more important not to forget where you're headed. We've still got work to do, kid. And when it comes down to it, you decide how and when it ends.

Alex leaned over and wrapped her arms around Sarah, squeezing tightly. "You'll pass that along?"

Sarah nodded and pulled the final items from the bottom of the basket. She handed Alex her running shoes, not the newest ones she'd been wearing, but the ones she'd worn the night she was first attacked and brought to the Regan's. There was still a stain on the inside of the right shoe where blood from her stab wound had dripped into it.

"I figured these got thrown out ages ago."

"It did take some digging, but Rocky finally scrounged them up from the bottom of your closet."

"Rocky? I thought—" She stopped herself. "Well, I guess Markus already left his coat," she said swallowing the lump. "So why these? Why not one of my bugged boots he's so fond of?"

"You've already got a pair of those," Sarah motioned to the pair on the floor. "And they're probably warmer than cloth sneakers, but Rocky insisted on these."

"He didn't say why?" She checked the inside for a note of some sort.

Sarah shook her head. "I assumed it was because you were wearing them the day he and Sage brought you to us. You've been a pretty important person in his life since then. You're lucky to have each other."

"You mean we're lucky our mates haven't killed one of us yet." She laughed and Sarah joined in.

"Ellie belongs to your generation where male-female friendships are more commonplace. And Markus, well, he'd adapt to just about anything to keep you, Alex, just as you've done for him."

Alex nodded, unable to say more without her voice breaking.

Sarah stood and called for the guard. "I've go to go, unfortunately, but I'll see you soon."

They embraced a final time as Dalton carried the tub and basket into the hall. Alex repeated her thanks continuously until Sarah reached the door and paused. Alex had been struck with another phlegm-filled coughing spasm.

"You can show your gratitude by not arguing with me when I order you to bed and a visit from Rick or Briant when this whole thing is over."

Alex smirked. Bed was exactly where she wanted to be when she was freed.

"Not with Markus!" Sarah ordered reading her expression. "And put your hood up; your hair is still wet, and it's freezing in there."

"You're going to be a natural mom, Sarah," she let slip. Her hand went to her mouth.

"It's okay," Sarah said.

"Can I—" She was being positive, heeding Charlie's advice, but she also really wanted Sarah to know, just in case.

"Go ahead," Sarah said after checking the hall was empty. Dalton hadn't returned.

"I just want you to know they're happy. I don't sense them like adults or even human kids, but I can sense them, and everything about them just oozes contentment and love."

Sarah closed her eyes and rested her hands on the top and bottom of her stomach as if cradling them. "I'm not a Seer, but I sense that too," she whispered just before closing the door behind her.

Maybe it was the clean clothes, or her friends' accompanying messages, or the after-effect of the chocolate, or maybe it was that thing Darian called faith, which she was never sure she had or wanted, but she didn't flinch this time when the door closed and the darkness engulfed her. She felt . . . if not calm, then at least hopeful.

Or maybe euphoria was just the final stage before hysteria.

When the door creaked open waking her, her stomach lurched. It couldn't be time. Not yet. She was certain she had just fallen asleep. The light clicked on, and the door shut, and her sense caught up with her.

"Markus!" She flung herself at him just as he had knelt beside her, knocking them both on the ground. With her flushed face against his hard heaving chest, she allowed herself to melt into him for the moment. He wrapped his arms around her and breathed in the scent of her shampoo.

"Did Sarah just leave?" he asked playing with her damp hair.

"I guess. What time is it?"

"A little before sunrise."

She propped herself up, her elbows on his chest. "You need to go then. Ardellus will be home any minute. If you're caught—"

He pulled her back into him, smothering her warning with a kiss. "Calm down. Ardellus is already at the club with the Regan and the rest of the Elders. They'll be staying the day so they're ready come sunset."

"But then Liam will be here. We can't ask him to cover for us, it's not fair."

Markus growled. "None of this is fair. But you're right, I wouldn't ask that of him. I'm here in his place, as your guard. A small token of apology from my father for not telling us what he knew about yours."

She sat up again, straddling him. This time he didn't fight her. "Seriously? He assigned you? He gave you the key?" Liam never had the key to the cell. It always remained upstairs with the Elder Regan.

Markus grinned. "He assigned me. As for the key," he pulled out the heavy ring containing a key to nearly every important building and house in the coven. "It may have been overlooked that as lead warrior I have my own. Liam might be a little surprised when he arrives to unlock you later today with the Elder Regan's copy. But we've got hours before we need to worry about that."

She collapsed back onto his solid body. "Hours." It was both a gift and a deadline.

"Even eternity is made up of hours, Alex. Let's not waste these by worrying, okay?" He kissed the top of her head.

"You have better plans to keep us distracted?" Her hand trailed down his torso, following the line of muscle that arched around his hips and down below his belt.

He inhaled sharply. "Sarah texted to say you should rest." His hands gripped her arms hard as she traced her hand over the fly of his jeans and down the inside of his leg.

"Yeah? Well text her back, and tell her not to worry. I'll let you be on top, at least the first time." She rolled onto her back. He allowed her to take him with her, so he was straddling her.

"Your clean clothes will get dirty," he breathed between sucking her earlobes.

"Then you better take them off." She lifted her hands over her head and arched her back as he stripped off all three layers at once. He grabbed his coat from behind him where she had been using it as a blanket before he arrived. He lifted her off the ground with one arm and spread the fabric beneath her back with the other. Gently laying her back down, she was cocooned in his scent, covered by his warmth, and completely, one hundred percent distracted by their synchronous desires.

"Take it slow. Make it last," she said when they were both undressed, shivering from anticipation more than the cold.

"I can draw it out all day, Babe," Markus said kneeling by her feet, nipping at her toes, and caressing her ankles. He worked up her calf at a torturously slow pace before looking up. "Can you?" He caught her biting her lip to keep still and quiet.

Time was a double-edged sword bound to slice her to pieces one way or another today. Better the cuts come from Markus, who knew his way around her body as well as he knew his precious knives.

"Probably not," she gasped. "But make me try."

Markus started in on the bottom of her other foot, holding her firmly by the thighs when she began to squirm. "My pleasure," he answered before tracing the muscles of her lower leg with his tongue and the tips of his fangs.

Her body's desires battled admirably against its needs, but eventually the latter won out. She had fallen asleep blanketed by Markus whose usually cool skin was pleasantly flushed after intercourse. They were as content as any couple could be under the circumstances.

"When did the wheezing start?" he asked at the first flutter of her eyelids, all pleasantness a memory. He had obviously lain and listened to her labored breathing as she slept. He teemed with worry, but there was enough fury mixed in that she didn't dare try to fake a smile and appease him with a white lie.

"A few nights ago. Sarah knows. She'll have Briant or Rick at the house to take care of it as soon as I'm home." From his glare, she gathered optimism was one notch away from dishonesty in his book.

"No. I'm taking care of it. Here. Now." He bit into his wrist and brought it to her mouth. She pursed her lips and pulled away. She wanted it, needed it, but wouldn't risk his safety to satisfy her body.

"Essence doesn't cure colds," she said turning away.

"No, but it'll give your body the strength it needs to fight it." He grabbed her face with his free hand. "I'm not giving you a choice, Alex. Please don't make me force you. It'll only hurt us both." Every aspect of his sense, tone, and expression confirmed he meant it. His fingers were already biting hard into her cheeks. She wouldn't win, so why not lose gracefully.

She grabbed his wrist and drew hard on the two small wounds. She never before struggled to extract essence from Markus's blood. His goodness, honor, and dignity were always right at the surface. Tonight, though, his blood was a muddled mix of resentment, fury, and fear. She tried not to think about his goodness being diluted by the dark sides of loving someone so much. She couldn't cry anymore.

"You need to help me." She tried influencing him with a soothing wave of love, the only positive emotion readily available. She reached out to run her hands through his thick auburn hair.

"I'm sorry," he said. She could sense him fighting back his feelings.

"Remember our first time," she suggested, pausing to swallow. "On the beach, coming home to face the Regan with sand, well, everywhere."

He smiled. Remembering that night would be easy. She was sure that memory was as clear in his mind as it was in hers. Remembering the emotions that accompanied it would be harder. "I'll try."

And he did, enough for her to feed sufficiently. With both of them more at ease and sunset nearing, they dressed, ready to wait out the remaining time together. He settled himself along the wall and beckoned to her. With his coat back around her shoulders, she crawled onto his lap.

"Wait," he said before she curled up in his arms. He reached into the back pocket of his jeans and pulled something out. "I didn't forget you tonight when Sarah asked each of us to pick something out. I just wanted to put this on you myself." He opened his hand to show her the necklace he had first tied on her neck on Creator's Day. He had explained the meaning the coven assigned to its intricate charm that night. Tonight its ring of flowers and tiny dagger were just symbols of the two of them. A young woman who fell foolishly and completely for a creature whom she found far more beautiful than terrifying. And the warrior who fell for her because of, rather than despite of, all that made her perfectly flawed.

He finished tying the velvet ribbon and wrapped his arms around hers. It was how Liam, Charlie, and Rocky found them shortly after.

Charlie said little, other than that it was time, before heading back up the stairs. Liam fiddled with the handcuffs he would eventually have to put on her before bailing in Charlie's footsteps. Rocky was far less embarrassed and not at all intimidated by his boss.

"You fed her?" he shouted after one violent sniff. "Are you nuts? Both of you?"

"I forced her," Markus said. "She's got the bruises to prove it." He turned Alex's cheek to him. Without a mirror she had no idea whether anyone would be able to see what he claimed was there. Rocky didn't bother to look closely. He didn't buy it either way.

"You better hope they think her scent is from that coat, or bruises will be the least of your worries, Markus. And you," he said to Alex, "better use whatever strength you just gained to keep quiet and in control. We need you to be flawless, Alex, and this isn't a great start."

Markus's fangs snapped, but she pushed against him to keep him from pursuing Rocky, who had spun on his heels and flashed from the cell.

"He needs to be in command tonight, Markus. He needs to be seen and respected as his father's equal, not the Regan's former ward or your rookie warrior. His head, and his confidence, are exactly where we need them to be."

Markus let out a long breath, then nodded. When he pulled her up off the floor and straightened her hood, he met her eyes. "And yours?"

"Well, don't tell my defense attorney, but your essence is helping, and the love making didn't exactly hurt." She winked.

"Damn it, Alex. I love you so much it hurts." He pulled her into what she knew was a final embrace. He couldn't go farther than the top of the stairs; the setting sun would spill across the living room when they opened the doors to leave.

"I know. I feel it. But don't let that part consume you, Markus. Love heals more than it hurts." It wasn't goodbye, but like with Sarah, it was something he had to hear.

"Then why are you crying?" He leaned over and kissed her tears.

"Women can't always explain why we cry. Haven't you learned anything after three centuries of sharing the planet with us?" she tried to tease.

"You re-taught me just about everything important in life, in far, far less time."

"Let's hope we've both been good students then, because I hear there's a test later." She kissed him on the lips, tasting him, feeling him a final time. "Liam's in the hall. I've got to go. See you soon?"

"A second after sunset," he said with a thick voice.

She nodded and headed to the stairs. She didn't look back. If she turned to him for even a split second, she'd never have the strength to part.

CHAPTER 22

It honestly hadn't occurred to Alex that she wouldn't be the only one testifying. It seemed stupid now, but they'd spent so much time preparing her for the questions she'd face and not a second on how to sit through the rest of it. Antonio hadn't made it halfway through explaining the charges before Charlie slid his notebook against her elbow. 'Calm' was written in all caps in the margin of his notes. He tapped his pen on it until she forced her face into a neutral expression, took a breath, and nodded. It wasn't long before she was trying to convey the same message to Rocky who sat on her other side shaking with suppressed anger. With the witch's pills silencing her gift, though, influencing him was impossible. He needn't work himself up anyway; Ellie could handle Antonio.

It was clear the Elder intended to lay the full blame for her abduction on Alex. Alex had never been sure how much Ellie believed that herself, but one way or another she wouldn't make it easy for Antonio. Rocky had apparently spoken enough about his estranged father to make Ellie hate him as much as Alex did.

After a few niceties, Antonio got to the meat of his questioning. He asked Ellie to describe her time held captive.

"No."

"Excuse me?" Antonio asked in disbelief.

"I understand that, like me, you probably don't hear the word often, Elder, but I'm quite sure you know its meaning. I will not relive the worst weeks of my life, recalling for the council horrific details that they either already know or can easily surmise, so that you can utilize their pity. If my captors had so much as implied Alex had anything to do with my abduction aside from my being bait to lure her in, my father and my coven would have strung her up long ago." As if to prove her point, she looked to the warriors at the doors, her coven's warriors. They all nodded in agreement.

Alex wasn't exactly expecting Ellie to be making her friendship bracelets after a comment like that, but it was as much as she could ask for. Antonio, however, wanted more and wouldn't give up so easily.

"You said your captors didn't say it was the Seer who gave them your location and connection to our coven."

"They weren't particularly chatty," Ellie replied curtly.

"Of course. But at this point, who in the coven aside from your partner," Antonio merely gestured in Rocky's direction, "and the Regan knew of your location?"

Ellie shrugged. "I guess the members of the Regan's household. His lead warrior, the Knower, his mate—"

"And the Seer."

It wasn't a question, but Ellie nodded. Alex had begun scribbling frantically on her notebook, but Rocky was a step ahead.

"Could we clarify the use of location?" he asked standing up. Charlie had made the opening remarks, so it was the first time Rocky had addressed the council. Ardellus nodded. Rocky paused for just a beat to collect himself before posing his question.

"You just implied to the court that all the members of the Regan's household knew your location—"

"I didn't imply anything. I simply answered his question," Ellie snapped at her partner.

Rocky held his ground. "Ellie, you need to let me ask the question."

She nodded, though no one in the large, packed courtroom missed the 'we'll-talk-about-this-later' look.

"Do you know for sure who knew your actual location, the address of the apartment you were abducted from?"

"No, other than you and Sage."

"So when you say the others knew your location, you just mean they knew you were in Bristol?"

"Yes."

"Thanks, Ba—ah, Miss Jamison." He flashed her a quick grin.

"And you, Elder, for allowing the interruption."

Ardellus, who never had great love for Rocky, simply nodded. Alex so wished her sense was working, because she was sure he was just a little impressed. She was, but tried not to look it as Rocky sat beside her.

Antonio plowed on like Rocky never spoke. He asked a few more questions trying to lead Ellie to say she thought Alex was the one who led the Vengatti's Regan right to her doorstep. Ellie didn't bite, informing the Elder Council and the courtroom that Rocky had been visiting her for nearly a year prior to being taken captive. The first six months he'd used the Regan's truck, the other five months, Sage had driven him in the Jeep. There were a few whispers at this, but the Regan had dealt with Rocky's indiscretion long ago.

"The Vengatti watch the club, I'm sure. They know the vehicles of the VIPs and most certainly seek them out hoping to find them in more isolated parts of the city. That could just as easily have led them to me," she argued.

Antonio smiled the minute she said it. "Just as easily as Alex telling them, you mean? Yes, I suppose either is possible." He didn't wait for her answer. He had no burden of proof, just that of possibility. "No further questions."

Ardellus turned to Charlie and Rocky. "Anything else before we dismiss Elizabeth?"

Charlie looked at Rocky who nodded. "Yes," Charlie said standing and approaching Ellie where she sat between Ardellus and the rest of the Elder Council. He smiled at her with his hands in the pockets of his warm brown tweed coat. "It's a pleasure to finally meet the female I've heard so much about in the last week and a half."

Ellie looked over his shoulder at Rocky and smiled.

"I imagine this is more difficult than most of us can fathom. I'm sorry for that. I'll keep it short."

"Thank you," Ellie said sweeping her long red hair over her shoulder and sitting up straighter.

"The day you were rescued, who was it who came with your partner, Rocky, to help bring you to safety?"

"Alex."

"Pardon me for noticing, but you don't say that with the gratitude one might expect to hear. Why?"

"Because she used her 'gift' to trick me into leaving behind someone I cared deeply about, someone who ought to have been rescued with me."

"Why would she do that?" Charlie asked looking back at Alex. She wasn't sure Ellie's answer would necessarily be the same she'd give.

Ellie shrugged. Her hands curled into balls. "I suppose she had to. Mallory was unconscious, which Alex had done, but only after we attacked her, thinking she was one of our captors. Rocky was outnumbered outside, so he couldn't help. I was weak, and she was injured, and she isn't exactly large even for her own species. Saving Mallory meant risking the rest of us not making it."

"Yet you're still angry with her for not trying hard enough, despite the risks?"

"Yes," Ellie said. "And I won't apologize for that."

"I wouldn't dare ask you to," Charlie said. "Because you loved her, this Mallory, didn't you?"

Ellie nodded. "She saved me, and not just by feeding me. She kept me sane and strong. So, yes, I loved her, like a best friend, a sister."

Alex felt the tears run down her own cheeks as Ellie brushed hers angrily away.

"And just to clarify, Miss Elizabeth, who was Mallory, the female who saved you, whom you loved?"

Ellie glared at Charlie, then at Rocky. "You're as bad as he is." She gestured to Antonio, a comparison that had to hurt her lover. "This has nothing to do with the charges against Alex."

"Agreed," Antonio said objecting to the question.

Ardellus looked to Charlie. "Does it?"

"It establishes motive, other than treason, for the accused's actions. It has everything to do with the charges."

Ardellus leaned back in his chair. "I think we need to hear the answer before deciding whether it'll have any relevance to our final judgment. Please answer, Elizabeth."

"She was a Vengatti female being held with me. Her family locked her up for refusing to feed their Regan."

"So, despite having been raised as a Rectinatti, the daughter of a Regan, you believe, as Alex does, that some Vengatti are worth saving, that some of us are worthy of a second chance."

"Yes, I believe that."

"And if Alex hadn't influenced you, you would have risked Rectinatti lives to help her?"

"Yes. I would have."

"Thank you," Charlie said and returned to the table. Ardellus dismissed her. Alex watched as she walked with her chin up back to the row where Vivian and Cormelia, both past victims of the Vengatti themselves, welcomed her back with gentle smiles and warm touches. Alex turned in the other direction to the row directly behind her, seeking her own comfort. Markus sat between Sarah and his mother, his hands digging into his knees. Instinctively, she reached for him. The metal digging into her arm and Rocky's nudge reminded her that it was neither possible nor prudent. She settled for seeing him mouth 'I love you' before she was forced to face forward.

The other witness's testimonies were similar to Ellie's. No one said anything too damning, but no one helped disprove she was guilty. The hardest to sit through was Jonathan's, who still believed his mate Monica would have recovered if Alex hadn't convinced the Regan otherwise. It wasn't the guilt that rattled Alex. She didn't feel guilty, just sad; she knew she was right about Monica's inability to recover. What tore at her heart was having to listen to Sage, Liam, and even the Regan be smeared in front of the council and the coven, all just to prove there were others at fault, all just to save her from being executed for something that was solely the fault of the Vengatti.

As Sage walked back from the stand, she tried to tell him through her thoughts that she was sorry, but, of course, he couldn't hear. He seemed to see it in her face, though. He shrugged and seemed to hide a smirk.

Next up was Briant, called to the stand by Antonio to talk about what happened at the hospital the night of the ball. He told how Alex influenced Rocky and projected on him to sneak off unattended. She had good reasons for both, reasons she hoped she'd get to explain when it was her turn.

Rocky, who chose to question Briant after his father, didn't seem concerned about these events, glossing over them without so much as a clarifying question. He wanted Briant to talk about two other nights. The first was the night she saved the Regan. The Elders were already familiar with those events, but Rocky and Charlie wanted to make sure the rest of the coven knew exactly who they'd be condemning if the council found her guilty.

Then Rocky asked about the night Alex nearly killed herself trying to drain her essence down the sink. A night Briant only knew about because of Sage. The smirk made a little more sense now. It was her turn to squirm.

"The Regan had Sage call me the next night to let me know what happened and ask if there was anything else they could do to help her recover," Briant explained.

"Did he tell you why she did it? He hears her every thought; he had to know," Rocky said.

Briant looked at her, and she dropped her eyes in embarrassment. "She thought she'd killed Leonce. She remembered feeling pleasure while doing it. Having such power terrified her. She was scared of hurting one of them."

"So just a couple months before she supposedly turned traitor, she tried to kill herself to keep the Regan, and his mate, and her other housemates safe?"

Alex clenched her fists under the table. Charlie squeezed her hands until she stopped.

"She claimed, still claims, that wasn't her intent, but the outcome would have been the same, either way, if Sage hadn't figured it out and found her before she bled out."

Rocky wrapped up and Briant was dismissed. Alex tried to ignore the burn in her cheeks while it was decided what the next order of events would be.

"Alexandra." Ardellus's tone had the sharpness of someone who wasn't used to having to repeat himself. She clearly hadn't heard his first address.

"Sorry," she said. "What was the question?"

A few members of the gallery chuckled, but even over their tittering she heard Charlie and Rocky's teeth being ground into nubs.

"Do you need a break before you begin your testifying?"

She glanced at the table. Charlie turned his pen vertically. "Yes, please," she said following his signal, a system they had devised during their days preparing.

"Fine. Ten minutes. Sage," he nodded to the Knower, passing along some message he didn't want the whole courtroom to hear. Apparently it was a secret she was being drugged to keep from exerting her power on the untouchable Council of Elders.

"Just take the pill," Sage said over the rustle of talking that had erupted. He'd been sitting behind her acting as a guard all evening.

"You heard that?"

"I didn't hear anything," he whispered. "Let's keep it down so no one else does either. I was referring to your scowl. You wonder why I kicked your ass at cards the other night." He handed her a pill. As promised, Rick and Abram had lowered the dose to something more appropriate for someone her size. So far the side effects had been minimized.

"Would it be possible to undo this?" She pulled on the chain that had been attached to her handcuffs. The other end was bolted into the marble floor. It was long enough for her to put her hands on the table to write notes to her lawyers, but wouldn't reach her mouth to take the pill.

Sage nodded. It would need to be undone for her to take the stand anyway.

Alex stood and cracked her back. She popped the pill and Rocky slipped her his glass of water with which to swallow it. Rocky anticipated her next move and grabbed her arm. Markus was already at the banister.

"One quick hug," Rocky hissed in her ear. He nodded his head in the direction of the Elders to remind her they'd be watching. "Make it look like you both know we're winning."

"Are we?" she whispered back.

Charlie heard her and shrugged. "That was just a warm-up. It's all going to hinge on how you do."

"Nothing like piling on the pressure right before she steps up there," Markus growled.

"She knows the stakes and the rules. I have confidence in her. Having a little yourself would be helpful, Warrior." Charlie gave him one final glance before pulling Rocky aside for some last minute strategizing.

"I do have confidence in you, Alex. You know that. I've seen you face the Regan's interrogations on more than one occasion."

Alex turned to glance at Darian. Despite having no official role in the trial, as Regan he sat next to his father in a chair she could only describe as a throne. He hadn't once spoken. He'd hardly moved. He simply sat overseeing his subjects with a stony expression. Pills or no pills though, she knew this was one of those nights he'd trade places with just about anyone in the room.

"How many of those interactions did the two of us leave

unscathed?" she replied turning back to Markus and taking his hands in hers.

"The bruises to our bodies and our egos built up a thick skin—thicker, I should say. You arrived with a pretty thick skin to begin with. You're ready for this." He kissed her forehead just as Ardellus cracked the gavel one authoritative time.

———◆———

She'd pictured this a thousand times over the last two weeks, strolling to the stand, laying out her case, the very picture of defiance and dignity. As the toe of her old stretched out running shoe caught the leg of Rocky's chair and her wobbly knees nearly gave out under her, that image washed away. Rocky caught her elbow to steady her, then gave it a reassuring squeeze. She didn't meet his eyes, didn't dare look back at the crowd behind her whose stoic faces she couldn't read and whose senses she couldn't feel. She set her eyes on the chair next to Ardellus and didn't look up until she was seated in it.

The Elder Regan waited until she settled before addressing the lawyers. "It's after midnight. Since the burden lies with the defense, they'll get to start. But don't dawdle, gentlemen, and be prepared, since Antonio's time will be short, I plan to be lenient with allowing him to clarify along the way."

Charlie agreed and stood. As planned, he would be handling most of Alex's questioning. It wasn't just that he had centuries more experience than Rocky. Alex and Rocky both agreed that their history could cause problems, affecting their emotions, the Elder Council's, and certainly Antonio's. They wanted to win, to beat him, but antagonizing an already anxious opponent wasn't wise.

"The Elder Regan called you to the stand by your full name, Alexandra, but you prefer Alex, correct?"

"Yes." These were the easy questions, a few soft balls to work out her jitters.

"Why's that?"

"Alexandra always sounded too formal." She looked down at Dave's worn sweatshirt and her blue jeans. "It never seemed to fit."

"Yet it is fitting. It's another name for Cassandra, the famous Seer from mythology."

"I suppose, but I didn't learn that, I mean who I was, until last summer."

"Your parents never told you?"

"My mother never knew. Still doesn't," she added quickly. She wanted her mother out of this. "My father planned to, but after Dave's death and Levi's disappearance, he lost it. He was only lucid for moments at a time. And then when my gift didn't mature at the same age as my brothers, I suppose he hoped it never would, that there wasn't a reason to try to tell me."

"When did your gift mature, Alex?"

"Late July."

"This July? Less than a year ago?" Charlie shook his head and looked out at the crowd. "I was still flashing myself into walls a year after my fangs came in, and you're already out on patrols as a warrior?" Regardless of their feelings about a Vengatti lawyer addressing them, more than a few coven members tittered.

Alex just shrugged. "Yeah, but it feels like a lifetime since then."

Charlie smiled. "A lifetime, huh?" He turned his back to her to look at the Elder Council this time. Whatever expression he wore, she knew it was at her expense. "And how long does that feel to someone who's twenty-five?"

"Twenty-six," she corrected, not answering his mocking question.

"Of course. We don't mean to begrudge you that whole year." He was once again looking at the Elders. A few of them returned his smile before catching themselves and wiping it away. They had accepted his presence because Darian and Ardellus hadn't given them a choice. His unoffending scent, from centuries of feeding exclusively from his mate bought him tolerance. But it would be Charlie's own unassuming manner and easy humor that would allow them to overlook who he was and listen to what he had to say. If he were allowed to say it.

"Are we going to work our way through the Seer's complete family history and her own fascinating two and a half decades on earth?" Antonio cut in. He was clearly unhappy with the bonds Charlie was building with the exclusive club to which the Vengatti male certainly didn't belong.

"Only those parts that are pertinent," Charlie answered.

Ardellus looked over the tops of his bridged fingertips at Charlie. "I did warn you not to stall. Get to the point, or I'll pass it over to the prosecution."

"Yes, Elder." Charlie bowed before turning back to Alex. "Were you born into this coven, Alex?"

"No."

"Was your father?"

"Yes, though I didn't know that until very recently. He ran away to escape having to serve them."

"So if he never told you about Seers, are we to assume he also never told you about vampires, about the covens?"

"That's right. From what Levi told me last summer, though, my father had made it clear to my brothers that he didn't want us to be a part of either coven."

Antonio was on his feet again. "Hearsay. Neither her brother nor her father are able to testify to confirm that."

"No, because the Vengatti killed them both," she snapped.

"Alex." It was Charlie who reprimanded her. He then turned to Ardellus. "As Miss Elizabeth Jamison eluded to earlier, all we have here tonight is speculation and hearsay. If there was hard evidence, you wouldn't have held a trial."

"But there were witnesses to Levi's statements." Back at the defense table Rocky had stood. "The Regan was there when we first discovered Alex's brother. He can testify to what was said."

The courtroom collectively drew a breath.

"You're calling the Regan to testify?" Antonio asked. "Are you arrogant or just stupid, boy?"

"It's counselor tonight. And I'm a realist," Rocky said. "If I were to testify, you'd discount it because, to you, I'm just a thug and her friend and lawyer. Markus you'd claim would say anything to save his mate. And half the coven holds the same prejudice against Sage as they do against Alex simply for possessing a gift they fear, because they won't take the time to understand it. I assume you'll concede that the Regan doesn't have such credibility problems?"

Antonio sputtered. "The Regan can't be asked to testify."

"But he can volunteer information when it's pertinent," Darian spoke up. The room's attention shifted immediately. "I was there when Levi made it clear he didn't trust vampires, regardless of coven. He called us monsters, if I recall correctly, and wanted his sister to stay far away from us all. Whether that came from his father, his years of captivity, or most likely, a combination, we never found out. As Alex said, his throat was slit shortly after as she was forced to watch."

"Thank you, Regan," Rocky said. Proving her family had a less than loyal history might have seemed counterproductive, but it was all part of the plan.

As soon as everyone settled, Charlie continued summarizing quickly that until last June Alex had no knowledge of covens or even vampires.

"Then how did you come to be with the Rectinatti?"

"I was brought to the Regan's home after I'd been attacked by the Vengatti. Sage and Rocky saw me dragged into an alley and came to rescue me."

"You were very lucky. You must have been quite grateful. Is that why you agreed to allow two strange men to take you to an unknown location rather than to the police or hospital?"

Alex scoffed. "I was lucky. And I am grateful now, but I wasn't that night. I didn't know what I'd been rescued from and who was doing the rescuing, which at the time felt more like abducting."

"So you didn't go willingly?"

"Well, Sage knocked me unconscious with a punch to the head. I don't suppose I argued much after that." She looked across the courtroom at where the Knower sat.

He gave a one-shoulder shrug. "She screams like a banshee and kicks like a mule. Besides, the human cops were coming."

Charlie shook his head and moved on. "When you awoke, were you allowed to leave then?"

"No, but I tried to anyway. I waited until it was daylight when I thought they'd all be . . ."

"Locked in a coffin?" Charlie chuckled.

She blushed. "Something like that. Only they'd taken my shoes," she glanced down at the running shoes Rocky had chosen for her to wear. "I only made it half way up the stone driveway before Rocky dragged me back."

"And after that?"

"I was guarded, watched."

Charlie nodded. "So at what point did you go from being the coven's prisoner to a member?"

Alex glanced at Markus wondering briefly if she ever would have made that decision had it not been for him. Yes, she would have, but not as easily.

"I don't know, exactly. I suppose when I agreed to stay after a couple days. The Regan had explained to me about the two covens.

He had figured out what I was, and Sage was attempting to teach me about my gift. They learned the Vengatti had been hunting me, and Dar—the Regan offered me the Rectinatti's protection. He even showed me the prophecy that foretold me ending the feud between the covens. I wanted to help with that."

"So at that point all the rules and responsibilities of being a coven member were explained to you, and you were allowed to go about your life with the same freedoms and restrictions as other coven members?"

"Not exactly," Alex answered. "I learned most of the rules the hard way, by breaking them, much to the Regan's chagrin, I imagine." She glanced at Darian who didn't look particularly amused with Charlie's line of questioning. She couldn't worry about that; everything she had said so far was true.

"And the freedoms?" Charlie urged her. "Were you allowed to come and go as you pleased? Visit family? Call friends?"

"No," Alex answered. She should have stopped there, but Markus's pained face in the front row made her break the first of Charlie's rules. "But some of that was for my own protection. Staying at the Regan's was safer than going back to the city where the Vengatti knew I worked and lived. And some was done for the coven's protection. I was still an unknown. I understood it would take time for them to trust me. By the fall I was able to call my mom regularly and check my email."

Charlie didn't react to her info dump, staying the course. "And return to teaching?"

"No. I had resigned my full-time job. I struggled a lot with my sense after it first matured." Briant's testimony meant she wouldn't have to elaborate.

"And later when you were ready to return to work? Did you?"

"I did. Without anyone's knowledge or permission. I snuck out a couple nights a week to teach a class for a few weeks in the fall." She raised her cuffed hands to brush her bangs from her face in an attempt not to catch the Regan's glare.

Charlie saw it. "I take it that didn't go over well. What happened when you were caught?"

She hesitated.

"Answer the question, Alex."

"The Regan's first reaction was to lock me in the cell in his basement."

Charlie strolled closer. "This is one outsider asking another, I know, but to your knowledge, Alex, is it common for the Regan to lock up coven members who seek work outside the coven?"

"Not that I know of. No."

Antonio stood. "May I?" he asked Ardellus who granted permission with a wave of his hand. "The Regan's location isn't known by most of the coven, but for safety reasons it certainly isn't in walking distance of downtown Bristol. So how were you getting to this job, Seer?"

She sighed. She and Rocky had warned Charlie this question might come up. They had no knowledge of anyone other than Seamus and her housemates knowing about it, though, so he'd passed it off as a minor risk.

"I was taking the Regan's truck most nights. The keys were always left by the door."

Antonio nodded. "As an outsider to the human world, enlighten me. Is it common for car thieves to be locked up by the authorities?"

"I wasn't exactly stealing it."

"You just admitted the Regan had no knowledge of your actions and you had no permission to take them. Our laws are black and white, Seer." Antonio slapped his hand on the stack of coven law books he'd brought. "The only grey you'll find is the smoke rising from the ashes of those who failed to obey them."

The room erupted. Markus was out of his seat before his mother or Sarah could stop him. Other hands reached out, but it was Sage who caught him before he cleared the bar separating the gallery from the court participants. A few of the warriors from Jamison's coven stepped in to help drag him from the room. Luckily the other shouts from Rocky, Ardellus, and Antonio, as well as those from the benches, where Alex saw Vivian on her feet, tiny fists balled, drown out whatever threats her mate had thrown at the Elder.

Finally, Darian stood. "Silence." He was imposing to begin with. Put him on a raised throne, and piss him off, and people listened—immediately.

"Alex, calm down."

Every silent face turned to her. She didn't understand at first. She was one of the few who hadn't moved or spoken. Then she felt the heat and looked down. Her hands, cupped like talons shook in her lap. The energy burning just beneath the inflamed red surface subsided as the chaos passed, but not before alarming Darian. She quickly hid them in the pocket of her hoodie, hoping the half wall in front of her had kept the rest of the court from noticing. If Antonio realized the pills didn't affect this part of her power, she'd be locked in a cell for the remainder of the trial.

"Yes, Regan," she answered a little delayed. She caught Sage's eye just in case. He shook his head at Ardellus who must have asked what she wondered. The rest of her gift was still suppressed. This was a power stronger than the witch's magic. It drew strength from her own emotions, and no pill could contain those.

"Wrap it up, Charlie. It's clear where you're headed. Make your point and move on." Darian had been restoring order while she collected herself. Antonio was back at his table, as was Rocky. She even caught Markus slip back in, though now flanked by two warriors twice his size. Charlie nodded to the Regan and began again.

"He's right. I've made my point, Alex. You may have pledged your help to the Regan, even taken the warriors' vow, but feeling that you belong to a coven doesn't make it so. You weren't treated like a coven member because you weren't one. They went so far as to place tracking devices in all your shoes so your location would always be known. Hard to have secret meetings with the Vengatti when you're wearing a GPS, I imagine." She grinned, but he plowed on. "I'm not saying the Regan deceived you or thought of you as property, like both covens have been guilty of in the past. From the few conversations I've had with him concerning you, I'd say he certainly wanted you in the coven and believed you to be one of his subjects, just as you believed yourself."

"Then why wasn't I?" It wasn't an act. She'd gotten as caught up in his statement as the rest of the courtroom.

He chuckled. "I'm supposed to be asking the questions, but since you just answered mine, which was going to be whether you knew the only two legal ways of being a member of a particular coven, I'll explain. You are a coven member now. You mated Markus on New Year's, yes?"

"Yes." She found his face in the crowd and smiled.

"Congratulations. You joined the coven the only way an outsider not born into it can, by mating a member with the Regan's permission. Aside from birth and mating, anyone else who comes to the coven is simply a visitor."

"But even visitors are still bound by our laws," Antonio broke in.

Charlie grinned. "Yes, they are." He walked back to the table and worked his way gingerly onto one knee to reach into the box underneath it. He stood holding a book with one hand, rubbing his knee with the other. "Copied from your own set, I believe," he said indicating the leather-bound volume Alex knew to be one of Rocky's law books. Charlie let the tome fall open with a soft thud as he thumbed to the bookmarked page. "If the council will forgive me for reminding them how Rectinatti law defines treason." He read from the page, "Any act which may be judged as a betrayal of one's coven." He looked up as he shut the book. "Well, there's a slight problem with applying that law to visitors, isn't there? At the time of these charges, Alex was unbound to either coven, and therefore cannot be charged with, never mind guilty of treason. You said yourself, counselor, it's black and white."

Unless you count the grey from Antonio's case going up in smoke, Alex thought as Charlie headed back to his seat.

She couldn't hear it, but she knew Sage chuckled. He stood up just as the buzz of emotions began seeping inside.

Ardellus nodded. "A quick break before the defense finishes."

Charlie looked up from his notes. "We're done. In a human trial this is where the charges would be dropped entirely, since the law doesn't apply, but if you must go on, then by all means." He gestured his indifference to the shock of the council and most of the courtroom.

Alex had paused with the pill halfway to her mouth. Sage nudged her to swallow it before returning to his own seat with the glass of water. He eyed Charlie and Rocky warily.

"You don't wish to address the actual charges?" Ardellus asked, though it sounded more like urging. Sage had slipped on the timing of the third pill, caught up in her testimony. She tried to use her weak returning sense before it vanished. If Ardellus wanted more of a defense, perhaps he wanted to find her innocent.

"The charges which legally don't apply to her, you mean?" Rocky asked. Charlie elbowed him. Confidence was one thing, but cockiness wouldn't win them any friends, or votes.

"I don't deny most of the charges," Alex interrupted. The courtroom once again buzzed. Darian leaned forward, settling most of the room quickly. "I don't," she repeated. She was breaking Charlie's rules again, but he sat back and let her. "My intentions weren't nearly as nefarious as the Elder Antonio implied when he gave his opening statement this evening, but I admit to my actions. I did use my gift against the Regan when he denied me the opportunity to see my father who was dying. I used it again on Rocky and Briant in the hospital so I could try to get to the ball to warn everyone, to help everyone. And, yes, I even used it against all the males who stayed to fight, so that I could let Charlie and the other Vengatti males who were being forced to fight go free. I realized later, with a little help from more experienced warriors," she glanced at Sage, Darian, and Markus, "that I took a greater risk than I realized and than perhaps I should have. I was confident in my gift, but I understand now that had I missed just one Vengatti male who wasn't good like those I let go, a lot of people I love could have been hurt.

"But that was a spur of the moment decision made to help people, and no one was hurt by it. And frankly, even in hindsight, I don't see another way I could have spared them. Either way, it wasn't a betrayal of anyone, it was an acceptance of a hard truth: things aren't black and white, red or blue. The Vengatti tortured and killed my brothers. They had killed my father that very night. But go back not all that far in Seer's histories, in your histories, and the Rectinatti knocked off a few of my relatives as well. And, yes, the Rectinatti I know have protected me, befriended me, even loved me," she looked to Markus who nodded emphatically. "But Mallory protected Ellie, and Charlie helped Rocky to defend me, and Torie, the young Vengatti knower who came to us for help, has become as smitten with my mate as he has with her."

Alex turned to the council. "You and Charlie mocked my measly twenty-six years, but even I know enough history to know what becomes of societies or groups within them that twist loyalty and pride into intolerance and prejudice. You're not Seers, so you need another way to judge others, I get that, but judge me as you'd judge your allies and as you should judge your potential enemies, by actions and intentions."

When she finished, the room was eerily quiet. No one so much as shifted in his chair, except her. She wanted madly to fidget with her cuffs or brush aside her bangs, anything to not have to stare at them all. Abram finally relieved her by speaking.

"It'll be sunset soon enough, Alex, and we will have to judge you. By your own standards then, how do you judge yourself?" The pill had kicked in, but she didn't need it. She knew Abram asked with a fair and open mind.

"By my actions and intentions?" she asked. He nodded. "Well, on a good day I'd say brave and righteous."

"And on the night of the ball?"

She thought for a moment. "I guess brash, but still righteous. When Darian first explained to me about the covens, it seemed cut and dry. The Rectinatti were named such because they helped the weaker species fight against an enemy they couldn't hope to beat. They do the right thing even if they get no recognition, even if they risk their own safety. Legally, I might not have been a coven member, but I felt as though I was acting as a true Rectinatti would."

"Thank you, Alex," Abram said. "That helps."

"We're getting short on time. Are there any more questions for Alex or any of the other witnesses?"

"Yes," Antonio said. He remained sitting, leaning back in his chair as if he were about to offer her a drink. She knew there'd be poison in the cup. "Assuming things go your way tonight, Alex, do you wish to remain a member of this coven?"

It was a trap, a poisoned cup indeed, but she saw no way around drinking it. "I'm mated to Markus. I chose him knowing I was also choosing this coven. So, yes, I do."

"But by your own admission, had you legally been a coven member, your actions at the ball would see you burning at midnight tomorrow."

"Was that a question or just another attempt to scare me?"

Antonio leaned forward. "The Elder Council may or may not find you innocent of treason, but they, like all of us, need to consider the future of this coven and the safety of its members. You said yourself you still don't see another way of helping those Vengatti who you claim were all 'good.' You said yourself you still believe your actions, which if made by a coven member would be treason, were righteous. So if a similar situation were to arise, now that you are legally a coven member, would you do it again?"

Alex closed her eyes. She didn't need to see Markus shaking his head or Charlie and Rocky turning their pens horizontally, signaling no. She didn't need to sense Sage or Darian's advice. If she were going to survive, it needed to be because they trusted her, not because she lied.

"I trust my sense. I trust that when I sense someone's fear, anguish, regret, their need for my help, that it's genuine. My gift makes it painful to walk away from someone in need, someone worthy of help. So, yes, Elders, if you let me live, you need to understand that I will continue to help others regardless of their coven or species. I don't retract the vow I gave as a warrior. I will protect the members of this coven, its Regan, and its secrets with my life, so long as they remain worthy of protecting. But I'll do the same for anyone else worthy, as well. And if that's not good enough, then maybe you're not all as righteous as I truly believed you to be, and for that I would be sorry."

Antonio grinned. Alex was dismissed and walked back to her seat between Charlie and Rocky without meeting anyone's eye.

"Sorry," she whispered as she sat.

"For what?" Rocky asked. She looked up into his eyes, but he tapped his notebook. Returning her gaze to the table she saw his and Charlie's pens planted firmly in the middle of their pads, vertically for yes. She'd answered just as they wanted her to, with a hint of defiance, dignity, and unabashed honesty.

CHAPTER 23

The last half hour was the worst, not because Antonio once again painted her as a villain and ran through a list of coven members whose deaths could be linked to her and her mistakes, pointing out their widows in the watching crowd. His own insistence her sense be numbed actually made all that bearable. What ate at her was time. Time left surrounded by those she loved was waning, while the time she'd have to spend waiting alone in the dark would undoubtedly seem endless. Finally, Charlie and Rocky stood, urging her to do the same as the Regan, Elder Regan, and the eleven members of the Elder Council who would decide her fate filed past. In an odd twist, she wanted nothing more in that moment than to remain chained to the floor, but Sage released the lock and he and Rocky began to guide her to the exit.

With the Elders gone, the remaining members of the courtroom let down their guards, their previously stoic faces now a myriad of emotions. Walking past as they stared and whispered felt like walking the receiving line at a wake, her wake—but no one was laughing or telling funny stories. They had heard her story and were still deciding what to make of it.

When she made it to the back of the room, she rushed forward. Sage grabbed her hood just as two of Jamison's on-loan warriors each clamped one of Markus's arms.

"Give them a minute." A large hand fell on her shoulder, but it wasn't Sage's. She looked up at the elder Markus whose green eyes were as dark with worry as his son's. The two warriors exchanged a look but released Markus. It was clear who they were taking orders from tonight. "Be quick, then meet me in the hall."

Markus nodded at his father before wrapping her in an awkward embrace, her hands still cuffed in front of her. "You were great, just great," he said. He held on tight.

"We gotta go," Sage said gently tugging her hood.

"Wait," Markus said. "I never got to tell you. Your shoes—" He pointed to her old running shoes. "No one hid them from you that first night. I had taken them outside to rinse the blood off while I was washing your vomit from my boots." He smiled. "They were drying right outside on the porch next to mine. You ran right past them when you were trying to escape."

She searched his face. "Why are you telling me this now?"

He ran his hands over her shoulders and down her arms. "Because you spent the last two months since reading the prophecy fearing fate. But fate brought us together. No Elder Council can take that away."

"So I'm Cinderella now? One shoe changed my whole life?" *For the better?* she wondered before shaking her doubt. *Yes, for the better.* No matter how this ended, she had met Markus, and that had made her life so much more than 'better.'

He squeezed her arms. "Fairy-tale princesses live happily ever after." Leaning down to kiss her cheek, he whispered in her ear, "And so will we—no matter what." He stood up and nodded to Sage, who began pushing her down the hall leading away from the courtroom, away from Markus.

Her hands felt numb. Her breath was short by the time they reached a hall empty enough for her to ask him.

"The promise I asked him to make—"

"He made it," Sage assured her.

"But then . . . " If he hadn't been referring to being together in death, there was only one other way for them to be together if she wasn't exonerated. She glanced at her shoes, the only sturdy pair she owned that didn't have tracers. "But Sarah said these were from Rocky."

Sage nodded. They were all involved.

"He'll get us all killed, Sage. You can't let him try anything stupid."

Sage laughed sardonically. "You aren't the only one who wants to save someone, twerp. Other promises have been made, and they'll be kept."

"At what cost?"

Sage stopped so he could face her. "No greater cost than you'd pay to save him. So if it comes to it, you damn well better be ready to help."

"They won't have me drugged again tomorrow?"

Sage grinned and pulled the bottle from his pocket. "Oh, they will. In fact, I'm to hand these to the guards who'll be watching you today to be sure you're given one every three or four hours lest you influence them to set you free."

"Then how—?"

He pulled out another bottle, a small bottle of generic aspirin he carried around for when his sense, or hers, gave him a headache. He dumped the witch's prescription into his hand and refilled it with the aspirin, pouring the inhibitors back into the aspirin bottle. "Now, if you can just try to vomit quietly when the pills already in your system wear off, we just might get away with it."

"You mean like I coughed quietly all through Antonio's closing statements?" she smirked.

"Exactly not like that. Your hacking did little for your defense. Abram was the only one distracted, and he was already on your side."

"And the others?"

Sage shrugged and stuffed the aspirin bottle in an inside pocket. "Better safe than sorry," he said putting the real aspirin in its new container.

When they finally reached the far corner of the basement where the club's jail cell she was located, the awaiting warriors were accompanied by the elder Markus. Sage swore under his breath.

"What the hell took you so long?" the acting lead warrior barked as they approached.

"Got lost," Sage replied wryly.

"You're about to lose your position as a warrior as well as the skin off your back, Knower."

Alex hoped at least part of this was an act put on for the West Coast warriors, but she wasn't so sure. "I had to use the bathroom," she piped in. "Things take a little longer with your hands cuffed." She glared at Sage who played along.

"Hey, your other option was to pop a squat in that cell. You ought to be thanking me."

"All right. Enough." The elder Markus clearly didn't want to discuss his daughter-in-law's bowel movements at the moment. "Do you have the pills?"

Sage handed them over. "She'll be good for about another hour."

The elder Markus opened the cap and shook the bottle to assure there were enough remaining pills, but something stopped him from recapping them. He brought the bottle to his nose and sniffed. He hesitated, but by then the other warriors were curious.

"Empty your pockets, Sage."

Sage shrugged. "Whatever." He pulled out a flask, an extra set of cuffs, and a set of keys. He spread it all out on the seat of one of the chairs outside the cell door.

"And the one inside."

Sage didn't react. He reached in and pulled out the aspirin bottle and a worn picture, which he placed face down. The elder Markus went right for the aspirin bottle. He held out both open containers.

"Remarkably similar. You just happen to have these on you?"

Sage looked him right in the eyes. "No. I brought them tonight for a reason—your son. Unlike Alex, I wasn't given a break from listening to his thoughts all night. I'd rather have used that," he pointed to the flask, "but thought the Regan and the Elders might have frowned on me getting plastered in court."

Markus's eyes narrowed. He knew a guilt trip when he saw one and a lie when he heard one. "Well, then by all means, you've earned these." He grabbed Sage's hand and shook three of the inhibitors into his palm. It was a challenge or perhaps just a reminder that rash actions would have unpleasant consequences.

Sage didn't flinch, but she wasn't sure she didn't as he popped all three pills at once. Even the weaker formula in that quantity was likely to make him sick as a dog in a few hours.

"Don't suppose I can have that whiskey to wash it down?"

"I'll be keeping that," the elder Markus said. "You're on patrols upstairs with Markus. I'm telling you what I already told him. I find you more than ten yards from your assigned post, and I'll have you flogged and fired without even asking to hear your sorry-ass excuse. Is that clear?"

Sage put the rest of his things back in his coat without answering. He stopped to glance at the picture. He flipped it so she and the elder Markus could see. It was black and white, taken sometime in the forties or fifties she guessed by the clothes. It pictured Sage and Vivian, Darian and Sarah, and Markus. The Regan looked dapper with one arm draped over Sarah's shoulder, his coat hung over his other. Sage wore a smirk as he held Vivian in his arms like an infant. Even in the still shot it was clear she was fighting him tooth and nail to be put down. Markus stood between the two couples with a haunting emptiness to his gaze. He was staring past the camera, into a long ago past he couldn't reclaim.

"I'll keep him safe," Sage said tucking the picture back in his pocket. He didn't stick around to answer how he planned on doing that.

Alex avoided the elder's gaze as he handed the bottle to the older of the guards with instructions.

"Should we wake her if she's sleeping?" the younger one asked.

She met her father-in-law's eyes. They both knew the chances of her sleeping.

"No. If she's blessed with a few short hours of rest, let her be."

She nodded her thanks and was about to turn to the door the guard held open when the elder Markus startled her. He leaned over and kissed her forehead. "Dia dhuit, Child. May the Creator be with you—and my son."

She could only nod as the two visiting warriors took her by the arms and led her into yet another dark, dank cell.

CHAPTER 24

Even the short bout of sleep had been a blessing, though she paid the cost for it up front. Her sense returned fully but not before fully kicking her ass. The vomiting had inflamed her cough, which in turn made her retch more. After nearly an hour of it, she managed to pull herself far enough from the pool of sick to collapse onto the ice-cold dirt. At the time, the temperature cooled her feverish sweaty cheeks, but she woke shivering. She sat up and wiped the muddy smears from her face the best she could with her sleeve. The guards had removed the handcuffs, so she was able to brush herself off and run her hands through her nest of short tangled hair without alerting them she was awake. She needed a moment to collect herself before having to face anyone.

She had never gone so long without her sense. Having it back was a relief, a sentiment that surprised her. It was comforting, though, alone, in the dark, to feel others around her. The first sense she expected was Sage's, but of course his own gift was being muted. She hoped it wore off in time for the evening, when their silent form of communication might be necessary. She sensed the two guards outside her door most strongly, though one of them was fighting sleep. There were a couple other senses close enough for her to sort out, but none she recognized. Then there was just the faint buzz of emotion that came anytime she was in the club, or anywhere in Bristol for that matter. She'd always been a city girl, but after everything, she kind of hoped Markus had a nice deserted island in mind for their eternity on the run.

Markus. She tried to find his sense within the din, but he was too far away with too many others awake. All she felt was the empty spot he should have filled. She could almost feel it with her in the cell.

She could feel it. It wasn't a longing for Markus, though, it was an emptiness of a whole different sort. Her spine straightened and her muscles tensed. There was someone with her, someone whose emotions she couldn't feel, someone who simply left a void in her sense. She stumbled to her feet and lunged at the door. Before she could call out, a blast shook the basement. She crashed to her knees.

"What the hell was that?" one of the guards called.

"Explosion. Far hallway. Bomb?"

"No, they swept the building top to bottom before letting anyone in last night. Boiler maybe? It's an old building."

"I'll check. Stay with her."

Alex was thrashing, screaming despite the hand over her mouth and the cool metal of a blade against her throat.

"Hush. It'll only be a minute now," Leonce whispered in her ear. His cool sweet breath made her shudder, but not nearly as much as the remaining guard's surprised yelp followed by a crunch. It was the sound of his neck being snapped. Her sense of him extinguished like flipping a switch. "There now. See?" Leonce's hand left her mouth but wrapped tightly around her ribs to stop her clawing at his face.

"You killed him," she screamed.

"Actually, I did that." The door had swung open. She blinked against the light, but instantly recognized the male in front of her, and just as quickly reacted. Ty hit the floor with a thud. She redoubled her efforts to escape Leonce.

"Tsk. Tsk. You'll pay for that, I'm sure. Now let him up." The blade turned so the edge rested just under her jaw.

"I can't. He'll come to on his own," she lied.

"Bullshit. You did it at the ball." He slid the blade a quarter inch, slicing the top layer of her skin.

"Fine." She hated herself for giving in, but getting killed before she could warn anyone would be a waste. Even using her new power to take Leonce with her was too risky. Assuming she'd regained enough physical strength to kill him with it, she'd still be leaving Ty and anyone else with him alive and easily able to find whomever else they came to kill.

Releasing the twisted bastard who killed her brother hurt almost as badly as the blow to the gut Ty dealt the minute he stood. She gasped for air, convinced she'd suffocate before her lungs worked properly again.

"That's enough, Ty, for now," Leonce told him as he drew back for a second blow. "The only ones you'll be knocking out from here on in are the Rectinatti warriors, understood?"

"Like hell. Do your own dirty work," she gasped as she attempted to stomp back into his knee. Leonce was too fast. He avoided the kick and clamped her leg between his own.

"Do that again and Ty starts removing appendages. Like you, he has an affinity for knees since last July." Leonce nodded to his warrior. Ty stepped forward swiping at Alex's pinned leg. The tip of his blade sliced through the denim and enough of her skin to make her yelp.

Ty sneered. "Just wait until I get to the tendons in the back. I'll take it slow."

She tried not to react. She had sliced a knife across the back of Ty's knee after he'd slit her brother's throat. It seemed a fair turnabout to her, but Ty had had a bounty on her head ever since. She knew it was only with great restraint that he hadn't killed her already.

"As I was saying," Leonce said dragging her out into the hallway, stopping before the smoldering body of the dead West Coast warrior, "you'll knock out the warriors as soon as you sense them, or I'll kill you and give Ty free reign to kill whomever he comes across."

"The two of you against all of them. Crap odds if you ask me." There had to be more Vengatti, but where? If she could just get information, then maybe she could think, plan, do something more than panic.

"Ah, but I didn't ask you. In fact I don't want you to speak unless asked from now on." He ran a finger roughly over her ribs, stopping on one just below her bra. "Let's hope you're more easily trained than your brother." Like pushing a button he snapped the bone. She screamed, her eyes squeezed shut against the searing pain in her side. It stabbed deeper with each gasping breath.

"You're pretty stupid for a smart-ass. You don't think our males can get in the same way we did?" Ty said.

"How?" she gasped. Leonce pushed on another rib. "He asked," she cried.

"A rhetorical question, but since you won't live long enough to share the information, I'll answer you." Leonce gestured back in the direction of the cell. "Did you know this building was originally built by the city? I didn't either until this fall. Recovering from a stab wound and severe burns provided me plenty of time to read." He pushed on her side again and she released an unbidden moan. "Apparently as a last ditch effort to keep the mills from going south, city leaders had the brilliant idea to build a subway system. They went broke just after the first tunnel was started and were forced to sell the building to a group of old, eccentric buyers, the Rectinatti Elders, to recoup some losses." Leonce continued with the unwanted history lesson as they made their way slowly up a side stairwell. "Conveniently, when the middle of the tunnel collapsed a few decades ago, the city went in and shored up what was left of it. Their end was a ready-made place for some underground electrical boxes for the nearby streetlights. The Rectinatti end apparently became the perfect prison cell—at least until we discovered a back door."

"The fucking manhole." She had tripped on it less than a month ago, catching her toe on a raised side that hadn't been put back properly. Markus teased her and made an off-hand remark about it being the sewer rats' entrance to the club. Clearly the Vengatti had shifted enough of the rock and debris from the collapsed stretch of the former tunnel to squeeze in more than a couple over-sized vermin.

Leonce chuckled deeply. "Yes, I suppose I can no longer say the humans never helped me."

"We're here," Ty interrupted as they reached the door to the top floor. "How many?" he whispered.

She only realized he was asking her when Leonce poked her broken rib. She cried out even with his hand on her mouth again.

"Quietly," he said lowering it.

"One outside the door. Two more down the hall to the left."

"That's it?" Ty asked. "Bullshit. She's lying"

"I'm not. Those are all the guards I sense. There could be more on the other side of the floor, but they're not close enough for me to feel accurately." If they were, she'd be doing her damnedest to try to alert them.

"Fine," Leonce said. "Take out the three, but stay alert. If any others get close enough that Ty and I need to call in back up, you won't be the only one burning come sunset."

He knew. Well, of course. Why else would he have picked today to try to infiltrate the club? But how? Who told him? Was there another traitor? Or was it possible that some innocent coven member happened to unknowingly mention it in the vicinity of a Vengatti?

"Today, Seer," Ty snapped.

"I already did it," she said. "You're the one just standing there."

Ty growled, his fangs in her face, but Leonce urged him through the door. Ty immediately headed for the unconscious guard across the hall.

"No!" She hit him with a wave of anger, not enough to knock him out, but enough to shock him. "I did what you asked. They're out and will stay out until I release them. There's no need to kill them."

"I've got twenty-seven reasons, one for each male I've lost in the eight months since you showed up." His knife tip pointed directly at her chest.

"These warriors aren't responsible. They're not even from our coven."

"What?" Leonce asked.

"Our warriors refused to help at the trial. They believed me."

"Morons," Ty spat.

"But loyal ones, at least loyal to her," Leonce said. "So where exactly are these Rectinatti from?"

She hesitated. Was there any danger in telling him? She couldn't think of any, but she hadn't thought there was danger in talking to Seamus last November either. A finger in the ribs decided for her. "The West Coast coven," she blurted. "You've no vendetta against them. Please," she pleaded.

Ty sheathed his knife. He stood directly in front of her cracking his knuckles. "What's it worth? A jaw? Your nose? A kneecap perhaps?"

She waited, hoping in vain Leonce would stop him. She couldn't see his expression behind her, but Ty didn't back down. She closed her eyes.

"Do it. But they stay untouched."

Leonce laughed. "I love a good martyr. But do keep in mind she's human, Ty. I need her conscious and preferably able to walk."

"Fine." The backhand blow would have knocked her on the ground, but Leonce held her tight. Blood from her split lip filled her mouth. She spit it out at Ty's feet. He grinned. "And for that, any I recognize are dead. No questions asked. Better hope your mate isn't near by."

Alex's heart raced. She wanted help more than anything, but she silently prayed none she knew would come too close. Leonce was dragging her down the hall. She dug her heels in the floor.

"Where are we going?" They were headed to a set of double doors she recognized immediately despite only having seen them one other night.

"Shopping. Next on the list is the Regan. We were rudely interrupted during our last family reunion, and I don't like leaving things unfinished, which, of course, is why I started with you. Ty might as well complete his collection of Crocker children tonight. It's clear you'd be too much trouble to train." He snapped a second rib. "That's for asking questions and dragging your feet."

Her vision blurred. Her legs seemed to disappear beneath her. To her ringing ears, her scream sounded like it came from underwater. To the four females in the room, however, it was loud enough, and familiar.

"Alex!"

"Sarah, no! Go back inside!"

Markus's mother, Diane, had the longest experience as a warrior's mate. Seeing Ty and Leonce, she didn't hesitate to pull Sarah back in and lock the door, even though it meant leaving Alex at the mercy of her captors. Alex felt her anguish; it was apology enough. Diane had made the right decision. Sarah was not just the Regan's mate, she and the babies inside her were the coven's future.

A heavy metal gate dropped from the top of the door and crashed into place before Ty could stop it.

"Turn it off," he called out. "The silent alarm you just activated, disarm it now, or I disarm her."

Leonce tossed Alex toward him. She was in too much pain to fight him as he twisted her right arm.

"She's gifted, Ty. Do the left. Its loss will mean more to her."

Ty grinned. He glanced at the corner of the doorway finding the small camera in the corner. He tossed her to the floor and put a heavy boot on her chest while holding her left arm straight up by her index finger. "Three." He dislocated it at the bottom joint. She shrieked as the tendons strained. She tried to silence herself. She didn't want her cries to cause Vivian, Cormelia, Diane, or Creator forbid, Sarah to come to her aid. "Two." Her middle finger popped out of joint. She didn't make it to one without passing out.

She came to at the sound of the gate lifting. Her face was soaked in sweat and tears. "No," she moaned.

"Very good, ladies. Now send out the Regan, and we'll be on our way."

"He's not here," Diane's voice called through the doors.

"And we wouldn't turn him over if he was, you bloody bastards," Vivian shouted. Alex wanted to smile.

"Let me guess, a friend of yours?" Leonce asked looking down at her. "Perhaps we ought to teach her the rules. Ty."

"No!" Vivian shouted. They were obviously watching the security screen and saw him reach for her ring finger. "I'll take you to him. I know where he is, but you'll leave Alex behind."

"If you haven't noticed, my dear, we've got all the leverage right now. You send out the Regan's glowing mate," he said confirming he hadn't missed Sarah was pregnant, "and I'll refrain from blowing up the entire building." Leonce reached a hand into the pocket of his black dress pants and pulled out a cell phone. "Ty and I can be out of range before you and your mates even know what hit you."

"Not before sunset," Vivian said. Alex heard triumph in her voice. So did Leonce.

"Maybe. Maybe not," he said. He checked his watch. "But staying until then would give Ty over an hour to torture your Seer. And if she doesn't last that long, he could always break down the door and start on her mouthy friend." Leonce glanced down at Alex. "Aw, we've reached your engagement ring. Blue for Rectinatti. I do love symbolism. Break that finger, Ty."

"No!"

Alex could hear the protestations behind the door, but Sarah's strong voice carried over all of them.

"That's an order from your Madame Regan. Let me go to her." The chaos settled, and Sarah emerged from the door. She was armed with only a small dirk, but from the comfortable way she carried it, she appeared acquainted with how to use it.

"I will go with you. I'll take you and Alex safely to my mate. But in exchange you will not touch me," she waved the knife at Ty who had stepped closer. "And you'll stop torturing her. You need her to knock out the warriors along the way, otherwise she'd be dead already. But she can't wield her gift if she's delirious with pain."

Leonce had been appraising her the whole time. He was a mixture of impressed, amused, and jealous. She was another example of what Darian had that he could only grasp at.

"So long as you both remain silent and obedient."

"Fine, but if you want her quiet, let me fix her fingers first. You, step away," she ordered Ty. He snarled but backed off at Leonce's command.

Alex hadn't even realized she'd been whimpering aloud until Sarah made reference to it. She was too miserable to be embarrassed. Sarah pulled a clean handkerchief from a pocket of her cardigan and twisted it into a rope.

"Bite on this." She placed it between Alex's teeth. Closing her eyes she took Alex's hand and felt tenderly around the joint of her first and second fingers. Alex saw her nod and bit down as Sarah popped first one then the other back in place. To say they felt better back in joint assumed one could define better as swollen, stiff, and excruciating to move. But it was better. Sarah's gentle touch as she removed the cloth from between Alex's teeth and used it to wipe away some of the blood, snot, and tears did more, though, for her strength and spirit than anything else could have.

"I'm sorry," she said, helping Alex to her feet.

"Me too," Alex said looking at her belly and feeling a renewed wash of tears trickle down her cheeks. "I'm doing what I can," she breathed. Sarah acknowledged it only with her eyes, before stepping back as Leonce grabbed for Alex.

"Lead the way—silently," he ordered Sarah. "And you," he said pushing Alex down the hall in the wake of Sarah's stride, "better be on your toes, or I'll be breaking those next."

She said nothing, as commanded, though she hoped Sarah was taking the longest route to whatever room Darian was in. She needed time to think. More importantly she needed to give Sage time to relay all he'd just overheard in her head to Markus and the other warriors. Because sometime after passing out, but well in time for him to hear Vivian's life threatened, the Knower's gift had kicked back in. Even as the only sound in the empty hallways was their four sets of footsteps echoing off the wood, she could feel the warriors closing in.

"Hold up. Call in the others," Ty told Leonce. "This is the third hallway we came down without encountering a warrior."

"I didn't think you wanted to encounter them. And I'm quite positive I was told to remain silent," Alex said. "I knocked two out at the top of that stairwell the minute we rounded the corner." She hoped to hell Sage could get a message to the two warriors she sensed in time for them to fake it. Her other options were to actually knock them out or lose a leg for lying.

Ty and Leonce both glanced in the direction of the door she pointed to. "No matter. I called in the others the minute the females triggered the alarm. I like to delegate, Warrior, but I'm not inept at this."

Alex sensed Ty didn't completely agree, but Sarah drew their attention in another direction. She had strolled on a few paces, pausing in front of a door halfway down the hall.

"Darian is in the room on the end. Alex can confirm."

Alex nodded. "He's in there with—" She cut herself off and gasped for good measure.

"With whom?" Leonce dug the knife he held to her throat a little deeper when she didn't reply.

"With the Elders. There are two warriors just inside the door, too. If you just want Darian, I can—"

"Oh, no. When I instruct you, take out the warriors, but leave the Elders. Might as well kill two birds with one stone, as the saying goes."

"They're old, but I'll warn you, they're plucky." Sarah's hand was on the knob of the door she stood in front of. Alex had been urging her to escape at every door they'd passed, but she'd strode on until she reached this particular one. "Good luck," she said to Alex before disappearing. Ty flashed to her spot and tugged open the wooden door only to be faced with a steel wall. A safe room. Alex had heard Rocky suggest adding these in various spots throughout the club. She'd never realized his advice had been utilized.

"Damn it. We just lost our leverage, Leonce!"

"Nonsense. We have the Seer."

Ty scoffed. "Who they're planning to burn at the stake in an hour anyway. Not the best bargaining chip."

"I don't need chips. I've got the right tool. You will remain out of sight. Call in our location just in case. She will convince them Sarah didn't quite make it to the safe room and is with you. Won't you?" Leonce jabbed her ribs. She hesitated out of show, but caved quickly when he reached for her hand.

"Yes. I'll try. It's not easy with so many. I'll have to influence all of them. It's hard to do that and keep all the warriors out."

"You worry about the Regan and the Elders. My males will take care of any stray warriors, though from the sounds of it, they're a bit preoccupied at the moment." Leonce pushed her toward the end of the hall. They were on the second floor now, nearing the section of hallway that overlooked the lobby. She heard the shouts and grunts, the clink of metal on metal, and knew that the room, which just two months ago held her mating ceremony, was now the scene of another union, a clash of covens. Thanks to Sage's warning, Leonce's warriors had been discovered.

When Leonce and Alex reached the door Sarah had pointed to, they were directly over the fighting. Alex turned her back. She couldn't look to see who was in danger below her. Her only comfort was that Markus wasn't down there. He was where she expected to find him, in the room with the Regan, posing with half a dozen other warriors as one of the Elders. The Elders themselves were in the safe room with Sarah. If she could manage to give the Regan a few seconds head start, he could join them. Then she could help Markus and the warriors take care of Leonce and the rest.

Leonce waited until Ty was hidden behind the nearest corner before knocking.

"That must be one of the warriors with the update on the blast they heard. It's about time," Darian said from the other side. She hoped it was only her sense and that Leonce couldn't hear the tension in it.

"Now," Leonce hissed as the door opened.

Now indeed. She flung her hands over her head aiming for his eyes as she released every ounce of fear, pain, anger, and loss she could summon. He cried out and stumbled backwards as the heat seared through the palm of her hand. She could smell the vile scent of burnt flesh, his and hers. He dropped the knife and dug viciously at her hands. Despite his far greater strength, she managed to maintain contact. It was as if the current that coursed through her hands bound him to her so long as she willed it. She'd meant to use it as a distraction, but she knew now she couldn't stop until he was dead or she had no will left. This gift was fueled by her own emotions. With all he had done to her, he had created it, stoked it, and would suffer at its wielding.

He knew it. He felt what she did. As her energy waned, it took with it his strength. He was dying. She was killing them both. Unlike last time they met, there was no sickening sense of pleasure. She'd pay a terrible cost to take his life. To ensure the safety of her loved ones, of her coven, of the humans, and even of the Vengatti Leonce would destroy if allowed to live, she would have to risk her happily-ever-after. This world required balance. His demise and hers would be just.

Still cursing and tearing at the flesh on the tops of her hands, Leonce crashed them both against the banister. He was blinded but seemed to know just what he hit. His curses became a cackle. His hands stopped clawing and instead clasped her wrists. She tried to pull back a second too late. He leaned back and let his weight pull them both over the edge. The last thing she saw was Markus at the balcony holding what looked like her sneaker as Ty loomed behind him.

CHAPTER 25

There was only one good thing about being smaller and lighter than a vampire intent on killing you: he has a stronger gravitational pull.

Leonce's body hit the marble floor with a sickening thud. Hers bounced off his with enough force to steal her breath and leave her entire back bruised. Bruised, but not broken. The fact she could feel pain meant she was alive. She opened an eye and raised her right hand enough to see her palm. It was burned, but not much worse than her neck the night she zapped Darian. Little of her power rebounded on her because there was no good in Leonce, and therefore no guilt. She rolled on her side to look at him and retched, thankful there was nothing left in her stomach to purge. His eyelids were burned off, exposing the melted mess beneath. A halo of blood was spreading around his cracked skull.

"It's over," she whispered as she sat up, though the battle around her still raged.

"Not quite." Leonce lunged at the sound of her voice with one final burst of life. His fangs scraped her face before her hands hit his heart. The bolt of energy hit his chest and reverberated back up her arms. Their bodies careened across the floor in opposite directions. The pain vanishing as she closed her eyes.

Darian had tried first, diving out of the door to pull her off. Ty had torn around the corner and nearly taken the Regan's head off before Markus and Sage toppled him. By then the hallway was flooding with warriors. Vengatti came from both directions. Markus's own males spilled out from the room behind him. He fought his way toward her, but every time he made some headway, another opponent materialized to hinder him. Fighting with half his attention elsewhere was proving dangerous. He was covered in cuts and had taken two blows to the kidneys. Sage's job was to get Darian to the safe room, but twice he'd had to step in to knock a second fighter away from Markus.

"Do your job," Markus reprimanded glancing over his shoulder to see Darian in a hand-to-hand match up behind him.

"Then do yours. And have some faith she can do hers." Sage tossed a Vengatti into the wall and fought his way back to the Regan.

Markus caught his newest opponent under the ribs with his blade. He twisted his wrist and bolted before the dying body hit the floor. Alex and Leonce were at the end of the hall pinned against the banister. He saw her face change from concentration to fear. Leonce had her wrists.

"No!" He flashed to their location one second too late. He lurched desperately to grab her sneaker, but her foot simply slid out. She fell for what seemed like an eternity before slamming onto the marble floor. Leonce's body beneath her was all that broke her fall. Markus's right foot was on the banister, ready to jump to her aid, when his left leg collapsed beneath him sending him sprawling onto his back.

"Lead warrior and the Seer's mate," Ty said standing over him. Markus realized it was his blood dripping from the Vengatti's blade. He couldn't move his right knee. The ligaments and tendons had all been severed. Ty glanced over the edge. "You'll have to do since your mate is already dead." He started to lean over with a sickening grin. It was his death grin. He never even heard the shot that hit him in the center of the forehead.

"I guess you are a good shot," Rocky said kicking Ty's corpse aside.

"Thanks." Charlie handed him back his gun and knelt beside Markus. "Sorry. I know you and your mate would have liked that kill, but that was for Rebecca."

Markus winced. "I'm willing to share." As he pushed himself onto his elbows, both Charlie and Rocky looked back and saw the knife Markus had jammed into Ty's ribs just as the shot hit. Charlie started to speak, but Markus cut him off. "Alex?" he asked Rocky pointing to the banister.

Rocky's eyes grew wide at Markus's urgency. He obviously hadn't seen it. "Oh, shit, no." He and Charlie were on the far end of the building when the fighting broke out. Sage had asked him to gather whatever warriors or males he could to block off the tunnel. "I can't tell, Markus." He already had both hands and a foot on the railing.

"I'll meet you down there. Get her someplace safe. Go," Markus ordered.

Rocky nodded once before dropping himself over the edge. Markus tried to stand. Charlie stopped him.

"Let me wrap it first," he motioned to the badly bleeding knee.

"Could you . . . stem the bleeding some? I'll need to feed Alex."

"Of course. Roll over."

They were far enough from the nearest pair of fighters to be safe, and warriors often used their venom to close another comrade's wound, but it was an act of intimacy, of trust and brotherhood. For a Vengatti to offer such aid to a Rectinatti was a sign of just how far their worlds had shifted recently.

When Charlie had stopped as much bleeding as possible, he ripped off the sleeve of his white dress shirt, the one he wore in court the night before, and tied it tightly over the remaining wound.

Between Charlie's bad knee and Markus's useless one, the progression down the side stairwell seemed to take an eternity. As they limped onto the final stair they heard a noise behind them.

"Markus?" Rocky's head peaked out from under the stairs. The instant Markus heard his voice, he knew. If Charlie hadn't already been bearing the brunt of Markus's weight, he would have collapsed under the weight of Rocky's agonized expression.

"No. No." Markus kept repeating it as Charlie led him to what lay hidden under the stairs.

"Just as I got down, Leonce made a final lunge for her. She hit him with something. Her new power. He's dead. I checked. But . . . I can't find a pulse on her either. I've been doing CPR for," he checked his watch, "nearly two minutes now." Rocky hadn't stopped as he spoke. When he leaned over to give her another breath, Markus grabbed his shoulder.

"Let me."

Rocky helped him down in an awkward position, but one that allowed him to lean over her. He could see the hint of blue around her lips even through his haze of tears. He blew two breaths into her body before Rocky started again with compressions. After another minute he felt Charlie's hand on his shoulder.

"Markus, let her go."

"No!" Charlie flinched at Markus's fangs. "I can't. I won't. You know how many times I've thought I've lost her?" This couldn't be it. Every other time she'd come back to him, sometimes on her own, sometimes with a little help. Markus spun on Rocky.

"Stop."

Rocky looked up, his own eyes red. "You sure?"

"Yes." He pushed the kid's hand away and replaced it with his own, right over her heart. She wasn't the only one capable of shocking someone into or out of life with emotion. They'd done it before. The night her gift matured, it was their love and concern that brought her back. It had taken six of them that night, but Markus knew he didn't need help this time. If his love wasn't enough, nothing would be. With one hand on her heart and the other on the side of her face, he focused as hard as he could on his love for her and on his need for her love. He pushed harder, feeling her limp body press into the floor. She didn't rouse.

"Markus, stop. Enough." Rocky pulled him back as if he were hurting her.

When his hand broke the connection, he felt the current under it. Her chest heaved. She gasped.

"Alex!" Markus and Rocky both cried out.

"Blessed Creator," Charlie said behind them.

Markus brought his wrist to his mouth. Rocky grabbed it.

"Let me. You've lost too much already."

"No," Markus said. "You can feed me, or her, or both later, but I need to do this now."

Rocky nodded. "At least let me hold her up so you don't need to lean on that." He pointed to Markus's knee.

Markus agreed. He brought his wrist to her lips, which were slowly regaining their color. "Drink, Alex. Just swallow." He clenched and unclenched his fist to keep the blood flowing. Any essence she absorbed at this point would be beneficial.

"She's not swallowing. You'll choke her," Rocky said.

"Rub her throat," Charlie suggested.

Markus nodded. He remembered Cormelia rubbing his own

throat right below his Adam's apple causing him to swallow involuntarily when he refused drink from her willingly after Alia died. He found the spot and put light pressure on it, then a little more. The muscles moved.

"It worked," Rocky smiled up at him and Charlie.

"Come on, Babe. You need to help me," Markus said recalling what she told him just twenty-four hours ago. He felt the pull. She was sucking. It was weak, but it was her.

"You did it," Rocky said. "She came back to you."

"For you." It was a squeak, but he understood it fine.

He ran his hands through her short soft hair and found he could breath again as her heartbeat strengthened. "For eternity."

The door crashed open. Rocky leapt to his feet, his gun aimed at Sage's chest. He caught himself in time and lowered it, swearing up a storm.

"Hate to interrupt the resurrection, but eternity might end in less than twenty minutes if we can't find a way out of here without frying half the coven."

"Remalt couldn't disarm them?" Rocky asked alarmed.

"He could and did, but he only found one bomb next to the small one that already went off in the basement. There's no way that would take down the building."

"Maybe it was a bluff?" Markus said pulling Alex's head up onto his good knee. He felt dizzy. He should have stopped feeding her by now but couldn't, wouldn't pull his wrist away.

"Alex, you're killing your mate. Feed from Rocky for a minute while we figure this out."

"I liked you better on the drugs," Markus snapped when she stopped drinking and turned her head away.

"It's okay. I got it," Rocky said kneeling beside her. Markus allowed it only after she opened her eyes, sat up with some help, and leaned over to kiss him.

"I'm okay. Help Sage help the others." She didn't notice his leg, so he wasn't about to point out he was little help to anyone. Sage pulled him to his feet, then turned to Charlie.

"Was Leonce the type to bluff?"

"If it got him what he wanted. But he's also the type to blow up an entire city block if he didn't get what he wanted. Though with all the males he lost at the ball, I'd have thought Ty would have demanded an escape plan for his remaining warriors."

"He did. Liam saw from an upstairs window that they had a truck parked above the manhole they used to get in. He and a group of Jamison's warriors cornered a bunch of them when they found the tunnel blocked."

"Are the safe rooms full?" Rocky asked. He had lifted Alex to her feet and was helping her toward the door where Markus, Charlie, and Sage stood talking.

"There's room for you and Alex. Take her and go," Markus ordered.

"We don't need it. The three of us can evacuate," she said. Her voice was getting stronger. It was music to his ears. "You two go."

"I know you don't want to leave her, Markus, but she's right," Sage said.

"It could be a trap," he argued.

"This whole trial was a trap. A way to get us all in a known place at a known time. I'd bet a fang Antonio got an anonymous tip telling him about the ball. Between what he heard from Charlie and Seamus's thoughts, Leonce had all the information he needed to incite a power-hungry Elder. So, yes, if there are really bombs in here, then there will likely be warriors waiting to ambush anyone leaving as soon as it's dark enough. They've still got a few minutes. Let them go while there's time." Sage knew how hard that would be, but he didn't back down. Markus cursed.

"Wouldn't the bombs be outside?" Alex croaked clinging to Rocky's arm. "Ty snuck the two bombs into the basement, but he couldn't have planted them throughout the building. His scent would have been noticed if nothing else. But one young warrior could have rigged the outside of the building while we were fighting in here. It's probably why Leonce didn't just blow it up to begin with. Maybe the bombs weren't even set until after sunrise. His coming in to torture me and kill Darian was a distraction—and for his own sick pleasure. He probably always planned to blow the building just before sunset."

They all looked at her. It wasn't her newfound strength that startled them. It was that everything she said made sense.

"Well, we all know you didn't mate her for her looks," Sage said. Markus would have swung at him but knew he'd only knock himself over.

Rocky was already on the phone. He hung up, handed Alex off to

Sage, and then spat orders at Markus. "Get all the young warriors and males who'll volunteer. Remalt will walk us through disarming them."

"I'll help," Charlie said following Rocky into the hall.

"And get yourselves to a safe room," he called behind him.

"I'd watch your back around that one," Sage said to Markus. "He's after your job."

Markus looked down at his ruined leg. "He might get it."

Alex noticed for the first time and gasped. "What happened?"

"Ty." He could see her starting to shake with anger. "He's dead, too. Charlie and I killed him. Mostly Charlie. He saved me from him. After I couldn't save you." He lifted her swollen left hand to his lips. Creator, he felt so useless.

She glared at Sage.

"There wasn't time to be delicate. He had to know what was happening."

She nodded, then turned back to him. "You did save me, Markus. I felt it. Your love, it pulled me back."

He tugged her into him, nearly knocking them both over as they kissed.

"Okay, lovers. T-minus ten minutes. Can you hold on if I help you on my back?" Sage asked Alex, knowing she was still too weak to move with any great speed.

"For a little while."

"Good. And I'll carry you, too," he said to Markus.

"Like hell you will."

"Fine, I'll knock you out like I did with Darian." He held out some badly bruised knuckles.

"You—? Never mind. He can kill you later. Do what you got to do." Markus grit his teeth as Sage picked him up like a child and carried both him and Alex to safety. He'd try to remember later never to do the same to Alex again without her permission. Or at least he'd try to remember not to smirk like Sage.

CHAPTER 26

"Charlie and Liam disarmed the last one with seconds left on the timer," Sage told Darian as he hung up the phone. "The sun has set." Everyone in the room seemed to exhale as one.

She and Markus were being triaged by Abram and Rick. Briant, the warriors' medic, had opted to be part of the party who'd just successfully completed disarming what they hoped were all of the bombs set around the building's foundation.

"Give it ten minutes just to be safe. Then we'll evacuate and sweep it fully," Markus said as Rick finished bandaging his knee.

"You won't be doing anything," Darian said. "Rick's right. Boston has the best surgeons. He'll take you. And Sage should go, too, in case there's any suspicion about your rate of healing." He glared at the Knower briefly but didn't mention the lump on the side of his skull.

"Then Alex comes with me."

The room grew quiet. Sage had picked the closest safe room. It was also the one that held the entire Elder Council, which prior to the ambush had been deciding Alex's fate. Nothing had been said when Sage carried her into the room, released and uncuffed. Sarah had clearly filled them in on as much as she knew. They'd overheard the rest as Abram and Rick asked about her injuries and Sage and Markus explained about her brush with death. They'd been as shocked as she was to hear how long she'd been gone before Markus brought her back, but they'd said nothing, pretending they hadn't been listening. They couldn't ignore her now.

"You all watched her save the Regan, again," Markus said, his voice rising as he pointed to the security screen which showed the feed from the cameras in the nearby hall. "You can't seriously still be considering the charges of treason. She killed Leonce, for Creator's sake. She literally died to save us, to fulfill the prophecy."

"They know, Markus," Darian said. "But they'd already decided."

The blood pressure monitor began beeping. Rick rested a soothing hand on her shoulder.

"Decided what?" Markus demanded. He lurched forward wanting so badly to stand, to face them on his feet. Alex leaned over and tugged his sleeve to keep him still.

Darian looked to Ardellus who nodded. "You can wait, Alex, until your lawyers are present."

She shook her head. "No. It won't change your decision. I've waited long enough." She reached for Markus's hand. "We've waited long enough." He squeezed tightly.

"The council found that by our laws you are innocent of treason."

Markus beamed at her, but she felt there was more to it.

"But?" she asked as calmly as possible.

Ardellus raised a brow, not as accustomed as Darian to her sensing such things. It appeared Darian had hoped to wait to tell her the rest later, but Ardellus wouldn't tolerate being questioned in front of the others without responding. "But you admitted in a very crowded courtroom that you'd do it again," he said.

Darian glanced at his father and sighed. He had no choice but to have the conversation now. He turned to her. "We don't want to repeat this six months from now."

"So change the laws. Make it legal to help a Vengatti who wants our help. You bent them already for Torie and Charlie. Rewrite them altogether."

"That process takes time, Alex," Darian said. "But I can change one tradition at least without the council, although for the most part they agree." The other males nodded. They had already discussed whatever he was about to do.

"What are you talking about?" Markus asked.

"I didn't like hearing it, especially in public," Darian said with a smothered scowl, "but Charlie was right. When you were brought to us and agreed to help, I took you in, but I didn't treat you like a normal coven member. I guess on some level I'm as bad as my predecessors," he glanced at his father, "for wanting to keep you, at least the Seer part of you, more like a possession than a person. Your species, or kind, whatever you call it, ought to be free to decide who they help and how. As a . . . well, weaker doesn't seem quite right considering all you can do, but as a more vulnerable species, let's say, your protection should be a given. As you reminded us, that's how we became the Rectinatti. It shouldn't have been bartered for your obedience."

She was shaking her head. She knew where he was headed. "Stop, please. I don't want what you're offering. I'm mated to Markus. You gave us your blessing."

"And I can't take that back if I wanted to, and I don't. All I'm doing is offering you and your kind back your freedom. Your union to Markus, not to mention your unique feeding habits, bind you to him and through him to us, but the rest of your life—who you choose to work for, where you choose to live, even your choices about who to help and not help—should be yours to make."

"So aside from the legal distinction, if I wanted everything else to stay just the same?"

"You're agreeing to the micro-chipped shoes and archaic coven punishments?" Sage asked. A few of the others chuckled.

"Okay, minus those, although Rocky will argue the shoes are for my protection."

Darian smiled. "I could argue the 'archaic coven punishments' are for our protection. This offer doesn't come without responsibility. If you endanger any of us through your decisions, I'll still need to act as their Regan and your employer. But, yes, even if you choose to no longer be a member of the coven, the rest can stay the same."

"What about our young?" Markus asked quietly. Her breath caught in her chest. "I know you haven't decided," he said to her, "but you should be able to make an informed decision if the time comes when you're ready to think about it."

She nodded. He was right to ask.

Darian seemed to have thought about it already. "Any vampire young will automatically be part of the coven, as they would with any other coven couple. The Seers will receive the same protection and opportunities you're getting, Alex, but also the same independence. If they also need essence and choose to mate within the coven, great. If they don't and choose to live, and work, and marry as humans, though, that'll be their choice."

She looked to Markus.

"It's not my decision," he said. "So long as it doesn't change us, you should choose."

"Do I really even have a choice?" she asked Darian.

"Yes, but if you chose to remain a full member of the coven, then you're agreeing to our laws, all of them, as they are written until they are rewritten, and not just for you, but for other Seers who follow you. If something were to happen to me, I can't promise another Regan will make you or your descendents the same offer. I can promise that if you choose freedom, I will write it into the histories, so that it's precedent, which is as good as law."

Her first thoughts were of Markus, of how she wanted every possible link to him. But this wouldn't change what really bound them. She thought of her father, who wanted his freedom so badly he risked everything for it, and her brothers who never got the choice. What if they had lived or had children?

"I can't make that choice for them. I'll take your offer of independence for me and any Seers who follow. But just to be clear, I'm keeping Markus—and my job as Seer and warrior." She smiled at her mate. It turned into a scowl as he bit his lip.

"How 'bout Seer and warriors' aide? Warriors are Rectinatti males, Babe, or Rectinatti Seers, which no longer exist, apparently."

She looked over her shoulder at Darian. "Fine, so long as this new role involves me being back on patrols, why not. I've never been big on titles anyway, right boss?"

"Unless you want the Seer's new job description to include cleaning toilets, you better get big on proper titles," Darian grumbled.

"Not very creative, but not archaic," Sage said to Alex. "He's getting there."

Darian rubbed the egg on his head. "Speaking of punishments—"

He was interrupted by a pounding at the door.

"Saved by—" Sage stopped. His color drained. He flew to the door and yanked it open.

Rocky and Briant each stood somberly at the threshold holding a body in his arms. The choking smell and smoldering forms confirmed Alex's initial fear. The bodies were not brought for medical attention. They were not bodies at all anymore. They were corpses. Alex couldn't see over the rush of the others as they lay the dead on the floor, but she could hear Rocky's broken voice and feel Sage's anguish.

"They were attacked on their way back into the building by the last few Vengatti. He can't run at full speed any more, and Liam wouldn't leave him. There were too many. We followed at least four, but they got away. Had a car around the corner."

"I'm sorry, Rocky," Sarah said. "I know you'd gotten close to him."

At that point Alex had pushed her way to the front. She saw the tweed jacket before she recognized the swollen blackening face with its scruffy salt and pepper beard.

"Charlie!" She fell to her knees by his side. All the words she should have said to him sooner lodged in her throat. She reached out and rested a hand over his heart projecting her gratitude. Too little, too late. There was nothing left to sense in return. Nothing but the others' pain. She looked up at Rocky whose grief cut even deeper than hers. Charlie was everything Rocky's father was not. Because of that and because of his faith in him, Charlie had given Rocky back everything Antonio had stripped away.

"We couldn't leave them out there. I was afraid they'd try to take the body or desecrate his ashes somehow. He doesn't belong to them, Darian. Not anymore."

Darian stepped forward and pulled Rocky into him to smother his sobs. "I know, son. And he'll be returned as such, with full honors." He patted Rocky's back a final time and turned to Sage who stood staring down at the second body in shock. "And so will he, Sage. You have my word."

Looking at the corpse, which rapid decomposition was rendering ageless, Alex gasped. She could have been looking at Sage. But it was Liam. Liam, who talked her through the toughest two weeks of her life, telling her stories of his little girls to make her laugh, and sneaking her chocolate to provide what little comfort he could offer in the final hours before her trial. The memories increased the grief, hers and Sage's, so she stopped and stood, looking askance of Sarah.

"His nephew," she whispered. "The son of the baby sister who was born after his father threw him out. He's supported her and Liam since she left Ireland, pregnant and unmated. Their father had no tolerance for gifts of any kind, it seemed." Sarah put her hands on her belly feeling the swell of her own two gifts growing inside her.

For a brief moment Alex's jealousy was greater than her grief.

Sage eventually looked up and met Alex's eyes. "You go with Markus to Boston. You can handle the doctors . . . better than I can according to that wise-ass," he said gesturing to the smoky ashes that now lay at his feet. "I've got to go see my—his mother." He strode off down the hall only pausing to put his fist through a nearby door.

Darian drew a deep breath before beginning the daunting task of putting his coven back together. Everyone was assigned a job or a place to go for safety. The elder Markus was called from the second safe room, and Darian ran through the lists of tasks that needed to be seen to before escorting Sarah and some of the Elders to an evacuation location. With his father off doing his job, Markus was left leaning on the doorframe.

"I can't do this. I can't sit and watch," he said finally letting it out.

Alex embraced him. "No, you can't. So you need to have it fixed properly. You'll be back on patrols in a matter of months."

"Months?" His voice sounded as panicked as if she'd said decades.

"A couple months is a drop in the bucket of your lifespan, Warrior. Suck it up," she said. "Now you'll know how I feel when you and Darian keep me home. Kept, I should say. You can't do that anymore." She smiled devilishly at him, but he wasn't amused.

"I'm your mate. I can and will if I think it's unsafe."

She raised a brow. "Oh? How fast you think you can hop?"

He squeezed her rear end. "I had to lay down the law with Torie when you were gone. Don't think I'm afraid to do the same to you."

"Oh, god, Markus" All their playfulness evaporated. "Charlie was Toric's godfather."

"I know," he said. His heart felt as heavy as hers. "Do you think . . . ? Should we go home and tell her ourselves?"

"Not if you want to walk correctly again," Briant said coming down the hall following a conversation with Rick who was headed in the opposite direction to tend to other injuries. "He filled me in. We gotta go before that starts healing incorrectly. Whoever you need to see will have to wait." He grabbed Markus under the arm and began marching him slowly to the elevator.

"I'll text Rocky. He and Ellie can bring her to us if we're there past sunrise."

"I'm not spending a day trapped in a hospital in a strange city," Markus argued. Pain and fear were turning him into a stubborn mule.

"Briant?" she asked sweetly.

"On it, Alex." His free hand jabbed Markus in the thigh with some form of heavy duty sedative. He swept Markus up into his arms just as his good leg gave way. Markus mumbled something about retribution before completely drifting off.

CHAPTER 27

"Hey, sorry I'm late," Markus called over the din at McNally's. All the warriors and quite a few of their mates had taken over the small pub in celebration of the birth of the coven's new heir, Alaric, and his baby sister by six minutes, Analise.

"It's fine."

Markus pulled Alex into an embrace misreading her terse answer as annoyance rather than anxiety. She felt his brace beneath his cargo pants as he leaned over to kiss her. He whispered further apologies as he nipped her earlobe. His appetite for her since the trial had been insatiable. Not that she minded much most nights, but tonight wasn't the time, and this wasn't the place.

She pushed him away, sensing more than a few pairs of eyes on them. "I said it's fine, and it is, I swear. I'm not about to get mad at anyone for being late at the moment. Were you just at PT?"

When the surgeon in Boston promised Markus a full recovery if he was careful about both rest and physical therapy, he had no idea what Markus was, but he had a good read on who he was. He used just the right words on the injured warrior after he woke from surgery, telling him, "Most people aren't patient enough to rest properly or disciplined enough to continue the right amount of exercise for a sustained recovery."

Markus simply responded, "I'm not most people."

He'd been a vamp on a mission ever since, following Briant's accelerated version of the doctor and therapist's plan to a tee. He was recovering well, extremely well by the smile on his face.

"The brace comes off tomorrow. A week, two tops, of combat training with the guys, and I'll be able to jump back in. You sick of Sage yet?"

Alex glanced over the heads of the crowd where Sage's blond crown could be seen even over Darian's. He was slowly returning to his usual self after weeks of battling grief and the layers of guilt that accompanied it.

"He's doing okay."

Markus had filled her in one morning after Sage fell asleep. Apparently, even though Sage had supported Liam and his mom, he hadn't exactly been uncle or big brother of the century. He refused to associate himself with them when they arrived in Bristol. He likely convinced himself keeping his distance would save the single mother and her son the further stigma of being the Knower's family. His good intentions weren't enough to assuage his guilt, though. Since Liam's death, he'd doing his best to rectify past mistakes. For the past three Sundays he'd gone with Vivian to have dinner with his sister Cecilia, Liam's widow Alison, and their two young daughters Maggie and Lizzy. He was a bear in the hours before leaving, but returned home with a lighter heart, though he grumbled loudly about the many flaws of little girls, so no one but Alex knew they were growing on him.

His head snapped around seeking her out as he caught at least part of her thoughts. She spun Markus so he blocked Sage's view of her.

"You hardly have the time for regular patrols anyway, do you?" she asked, changing the subject before Sage showed up and changed it for her. "Rocky told me you and Jason were vetting another family tonight."

Markus smiled. She knew he was mirroring her own beaming face. This was the fourth Vengatti family to come forward and ask for asylum after Torie's. Her parents had turned up at Charlie's returning ceremony. Ellie and Rocky had brought Torie to the hospital so she could hear the news of Charlie's murder from Alex and Markus, but she had known the instant Alex and Sage recognized who the bodies belonged to. Neither adult had thought fast enough to block her from the painful image. The minute Torie entered the hospital room Alex knew she and Markus couldn't provide the comfort Torie needed. So she exercised her newly granted freedom by giving Torie the exact location of the returning ceremony and access to her cell phone. No one was angry; Darian welcomed them to the seaside ceremony as if nothing were amiss. The details of their staying had been dealt with later.

Following that, Jason, Torie's father, had been given permission to quietly reach out to a few other families and offer them a probationary place in the Rectinatti coven. So far, all had accepted. It was happening, slower perhaps than Alex envisioned, and far too fast for most of the Elders, but brick by brick the walls dividing the covens were crumbling. It was possible to picture a future in which what coven you were born into might not matter, where the descriptor of righteous might be one anyone could earn and no one was born with. That possibility had become far more important to Alex a few hours earlier.

"Markus—"

"The parents seemed nice, honest, but my pal Torie was a little too pleased with their oldest son, and he looked at her like . . . " Markus shook his head.

"Like teenage boys tend to look at a beautiful teenage girl?" she laughed. "It'll take the rest of the coven a while to let their young hang out with the 'new kids.' She'll need a friend or two her own age, and so won't he. Besides, you're not her guardian anymore, Markus. Leave threatening of suitors to Jason. You'll have your own hands full soon enough."

"I saw the look he was giving the two of them. He won't mind a little help. Trust me. As for Analise, she's got a big brother and a father who's the Regan. I doubt too many young males will be daring enough to cross them, but if they do, and I see it without stopping it, I assure you, you'll be mopping my blood off the floor."

Darian was still making the rounds, having his back slapped. Alex wondered how a vampire with his vision and sense of smell hadn't noticed the sour spit up on the back shoulder of his black t-shirt. The fact no one else dared inform him was a sign of the respect they had for his position, both as a Regan and a dad. Apparently not too many past Regans burped their own young. He was being progressive beyond just the relationships between covens, if you didn't count tonight.

Alex tried for the third time. "This is kind of a crappy tradition, isn't it? The father gets toasted, pun intended, by all his buddies, while the mom gets left at home with a week-old newborn, or in this case, two colicky week-old newborns? I'll take the traditional shower with cake and punch, thank you."

Markus laughed. Creator, he was dense. "You can have your human traditions, Babe, but I'm still a coven member. When the time comes, if I've survived nine months of a Seer's hormonal mood swings on top of my own anxiety, I'll deserve a drink, or twenty," he said cringing as Darian downed yet another shot. Sarah was going to kill him.

"Seven months, and that's assuming I go full term. Being the first female Seer, it's hard to say."

Bells were slowly starting to ring in her mate's head. "But human pregnancies are nine months, aren't they?" His building emotions slowed his speech to a crawl.

She smiled. "Yes, but I'm already over eight weeks along."

The beer bottle in his hand crashed to the floor shattering the glass and splashing the contents on those around them. Half the room had turned to look.

"You mean . . ." He couldn't or wouldn't say it.

She could and would. "Yes, I'm pregnant. Yes, it likely happened at Ardellus's." She blushed knowing at least a few people in hearing range would figure that one out. "And yes, I'm sure. Want to see the little gummy bear?"

"Yes. No. I—" He glanced around frantically. She reached up and grabbed his face.

"It's our baby, not theirs. What's your heart telling you?" But she already knew. His emotions were practically suffocating her own. "That's what I thought," she said reaching into her back pocket and handing him the small ultrasound image Briant's friend at the hospital had printed for her.

A dozen heads craned to see. Few females in the coven delivered babies in hospitals, partly because it would be hard to hide vampires' physical differences and partly because of their beliefs surrounding pregnancies. She doubted any who had an ultrasound ever dared to bring home an image, never mind pass it around the pub.

"He's perfect, just beautiful. And healthy?" Markus asked.

She'd been sick, drugged, starved, and tortured surrounding the time of its conception, all the reasons she'd ignored her first missed period. Yet the doctor assured her everything was just as it should be.

"Very," she said. "A blessing."

"For sure," Markus said kissing her forehead.

Darian, Rocky, and Sage had made their way over. The news spread at vampire speed, of course. Rocky was squinting at the photo as he turned it around. Darian didn't glance at it, but he didn't criticize either, quite the contrary.

"One you two deserve after what you went through," he said shaking Markus's hand and slapping him on the arm. He patted Alex on the head, making her scowl.

"Don't worry, twerp, there's a chance he'll get his father's height," Sage said. "Oh, wait," he patted Markus on the head, "that won't help much, will it?" The closing crowd kept him from dodging Markus's blow to his ribs. She sent Sage a silent thank you as he rubbed his new injury. He'd kept quiet over the last few days as she panicked over what the hell to do, and then dropped her off at the hospital when she was supposed to be on patrols after she finally did decide. He shrugged and passed another round of booze to Darian and Markus. She wasn't the only one who was going to be sick come morning.

"What's the matter, Rocky?" she asked sensing his worry. "If it's about me keeping you home, I promise I won't. I'll stay at the club or with Sarah and her guards so you can go out on patrols without neglecting your duty. Right?" she said to Markus with an urging nudge of her sense.

He was already looking at her like she could shatter at any moment. It was going to be a long few months. She hit him harder with her request.

"Okay. All right. So long as someone's with you."

Darian chuckled. "So glad I granted you your freedom."

She rolled her eyes.

Rocky handed her back the picture. "That's not it," he whispered. "It's the baby. You're sure it's okay? The pills didn't hurt it?"

"No," she assured him. She'd had every possible test and put in a phone call to Abigail to assure herself. Aside from a stronger likelihood the baby would be a vampire rather than a Seer, the pills had done no damage.

Sage reached over and slapped Rocky in the back of the head. "You idiot. It's supposed to look that way at this stage." He turned to Alex and to Markus, who had grown concerned himself at Rocky's question. "He's worried because he does closer resemble a gummy bear than a baby at the moment."

She laughed, although the males around Rocky seemed more forgiving. Apparently male vampires didn't commonly study the stages of prenatal development.

"Before you all get too comfortable referring to it as a he, keep in mind it might very well be a she," Alex corrected before anyone got too excited. She glanced at Markus to see his reaction to this. He didn't flinch. His happiness was unwavering. He was also shocked, anxious, and completely overwhelmed, but completely, undeniably happy. So was she.

They each got swept on separate tides of congratulations. Markus and Darian were dragged away by the warriors who were already fathers, likely to be plied with plenty of liquor while hearing horror stories of hormonal mates, nasty messes, and all the means of escaping both. Alex was surrounded by curious females who shyly asked to see the ultrasound. Some she knew had young already, but had never had the opportunity to speak about, let alone see, the miracle that was happening inside them.

Miracle. How long ago was it that she thought she didn't want young? Not long. Before her father's gift somewhat eased her fear of raising a Seer, before Darian granted her and her young the freedom to live as they choose, before Leonce and Ty's deaths ended her hidden terror of losing her own life and allowed the possibility of a brighter future for everyone, she wouldn't have wanted this.

Now it was all she wanted.

Finally able to slip away from the main crowd, she stood near the open door drinking in the brisk early May breeze. She didn't realize her hand was resting over what would soon be a growing baby bump until Markus's hands reached around and covered hers.

"I love feeling you this happy," she said leaning back into him. She wasn't ignoring his worry or her own. It had been a hard fall and winter. No, it had been an awful fall and winter. Having each other had made it both bearable and simultaneously more difficult. Expanding their family would be the same. There would be one more member to worry about, fear for, and protect. But that was the price you paid for love, and it was all worth it.

"I love you, too," Markus said feeling her soft projection. "Both of you. Can I say that already?"

She looked up into his bright green eyes. "You might as well. It's obvious you feel it."

"It's obvious to you," he smiled down at her.

She shook her head. "I don't need any gift to sense your love. Throughout the whole trial I saw it in your eyes and I felt it, gift or no gift."

"Maybe the pills just weren't strong enough," he said.

"They blocked everything else."

"Of course they did." He turned her around and pulled her in close. "Because nothing else ever really mattered."

GLOSSARY

Council of Elders/Elder Council – The male heads of the first families who form a governing/advisory council. While final decisions are left to the Regan, they still hold sway both with him and the rest of the coven due to their wealth and status.

Creator – The deity worshipped by the vampires, depicted as a virginal female who created both humans and vampires. It is believed the Creator wanted there to be a balance to everything. Gifts are balanced with dangers, like a Seer's maturity. Strength is balanced with vulnerabilities, like the vampires losing their ability to be out in daylight beyond the lifespan of a human (around eighty to hundred years).

Creator's Day – A day of the year set aside to give thanks to the Creator, celebrated on the winter solstice, the longest night of the year and therefore the night vampires have the most freedom for which to thank the Creator. The celebration begins at midnight and lasts through noon. Traditionally Rectinatti vampires wear white and silver on the holiday. Silver symbolizes the coven; white represents the purity of the Creator. Decorations include a wreath of moonflower with a silver dagger placed in the center. The flower, a white, night blooming flower which, although beautiful, is poisonous, represents the females or protectors. The dagger symbolizes the males or warriors.

Dia dhuit/Dia is Muire dhuit – Irish greetings translated to "may God bless you" and "may God and Mary bless you." The Rectinatti adopted them shortly after moving to Ireland to blend in with the locals, but also because the Irish revered and depicted the Virgin Mary in ways similar to how the vampires viewed their Creator. The greeting and response is still used formally, especially on Creator's Day, to show respect and reverence to the one being addressed, as well as to the Creator.

Elder Regan – A living male who served as Regan, but has since stepped aside for his son.

essence – The substance carried in one's blood that holds his or her spirit or life energy. Essence encapsulates all that is good about a vampire or person. Without a certain amount of essence one is left conscienceless. Vampires need to draw essence from another to maintain their enhanced strength and speed. The Rectinatti exchange essence with their mates or family members. The Vengatti drain essence from humans. An average vampire can't live more than four or five weeks without another's essence.

First Families – Families who can claim a pure bloodline, with no members having ever fed from humans. There are about a dozen first families (each with multiple generations) in the Bristol coven. Most first families have both status and wealth. Since mating outside a first family would taint the bloodline, it is frowned upon for all and absolutely forbidden of first-born sons.

Knower – A vampire who can hear others' thoughts and manipulate their memories. Most of the time this requires eye-contact or physical touch, but the thoughts of those with whom a Knower becomes close can often be heard anywhere within a relatively short distance (up to a half mile). Knowing is considered a gift granted by the Creator because of the importance of this power to a coven. Knowers are usually males and are marked with two scar-like lines in their brows. The gift, which develops shortly after they mature into adult vampires, is not necessarily hereditary, but can be.

mate – The vampire equivalent of husband or wife. Mating ceremonies are much like marriage ceremonies, except for the essence exchange and the cleansing ritual, which takes place the night before. Matings are for eternity. Only if one loses a mate prior to having young can he/she mate again by first undergoing a renewal ritual.

Rectinatti – The coven of vampires who believe in a balance of power between humans and vampires. They feed exclusively from other vampires and work to protect humans from becoming the prey of the Vengatti.

> **History:** Originally there was one Rectinatti coven residing in Italy. Most then moved to Ireland in the late 1500s to escape the Vengatti, who learned the locations of the Regan and first families through a traitor. When the Vengatti were forced to leave Ireland in the 1840s due to the famine killing off their food source (humans), the Rectinatti followed them to assure the safety of the humans in their new home, America. The majority of both covens settled in Bristol, MA, although smaller groups formed their own covens in other areas of the US and Canada, currently Portland and Vancouver.

> **Facts:** The coven is led by a Regan, a position passed on through bloodlines to the first-born male. The Regan is advised by the Council of Elders, a group consisting of the male head of each of the coven's first families. The Regan and males of first families wear a ring of sapphire and silver to symbolize their status and their pure heritage.

Regan – The leader of a coven. Both Vengatti and Rectinatti covens have Regans. The position is passed on through a family to the oldest male. A Regan ascends when his father steps aside or dies.

returning (ceremony) – When one has served his/her coven, raised young, and lived a full life, one can choose to return to the Creator. In the vampire world, this is not suicide. Such ceremonies honor the life of the one returning; they're dignified and accepted, just as the passing of elders ought to be. The ceremony is also given to vampires or Seers who are killed prior to choosing death.

Seer – A human with the gift of being able to sense and sometimes manipulate others' emotions. Seers have traditionally always been males; Alex is the exception to this. Their gift is hereditary and matures to full strength sometime around twenty, a process many don't survive due to the physical toll it takes on one's body. Over history, different Seers have developed different powers to varying degrees, all related to affecting others' emotions. Seers age slower, develop stronger essence, and heal quicker than average humans, possibly allowing them to live as long as vampires. No one knows for sure, because no Seer has ever died a natural death.

Vengatti (sometimes referred to as the Others by the Rectinatti) – The opposing coven of vampires who split from the Rectinatti centuries ago back in Italy. The Vengatti believed that humans were growing too quickly in numbers and strength and resented having to live in secrecy from them. Feeling they were the superior race, the Vengatti began to feed from humans rather than each other. Because humans have less essence and it is not an exchange, feeding from them often leaves them unable to recover, rendering them conscienceless.

ABOUT THE AUTHOR

Lauren Grimley lives in central Massachusetts where she grew up, but her heart is on the beaches of Cape Cod where she spends as much of her time as possible. After graduating from Boston University, she became a middle school English teacher. She now balances writing, reading, and correcting, all with a cat on her lap and a glass of red wine close by.

To learn more about her or her writing or to connect with her online visit her website at www.laurengrimley.com.

www.ingramcontent.com/pod-product-compliance
Lightning Source LLC
Chambersburg PA
CBHW071243170626
46809CB00001B/72